The Billionaire's Club

Meet the world's most eligible bachelors...
by
Rebecca Winters

For tycoons Vincenzo Gagliardi,
Takis Manolis and Cesare Donati,
transforming the Castello di Lombardi into
one of Europe's most highly sought-after hotels
will be more than just a business venture—
it's a challenge to be relished!

But these three men,
bound by a friendship as strong as blood,
are about to discover that the chase is only half
the fun as three women conquer their hearts
and change their lives for ever...

Available now!

Return of Her Italian Duke
Bound to Her Greek Billionaire

And look out for Cesare's story coming soon!

D0320380

BOUND TO HER GREEK BILLIONAIRE

BY
REBECCA WINTERS

First Published in Great Britain 2017
By Mills & Boon, an imprint of HarperCollins*Publishers*
1 London Bridge Street, London, SE1 9GF

© 2017 Rebecca Winters

ISBN: 978-0-263-92311-7

23-0717

Our policy is to use papers that are natural, renewable and recyclable products and made from wood grown in sustainable forests. The logging and manufacturing processes conform to the legal environmental regulations of the country of origin.

Printed and bound in Spain
by CPI, Barcelona

Rebecca Winters lives in Salt Lake City, Utah. With canyons and high alpine meadows full of wildflowers, she never runs out of places to explore. They, plus her favourite holiday spots in Europe, often end up as backgrounds for her romance novels—because writing is her passion, along with her family and church. Rebecca loves to hear from readers. If you wish to email her, please visit her website at www.cleanromances.com.

To my first editor and friend, Paula Eykelhof,
who believed in my writing and helped me find
a happy home at Mills & Boon Romance.
I've been there ever since.
How blessed could an author be?

CHAPTER ONE

Lys Theron arrived ahead of time for her appointment with the detective at the prefecture in Heraklion, Crete. The officer at the desk looked her over in a way she found insulting and hurtful.

From her early teens she'd had to get used to men young and old staring at her. But his scrutiny was different because the unexpected and unexplained death a month ago of Nassos Rodino, the Greek multimillionaire hotelier on Crete, continued to be under police investigation and she was one of several people still being questioned.

The well-known, forty-nine-year-old owner of the Rodino Luxury Hotel and Resort in Heraklion had died too young. Nassos had always been an object of fascination in the news. But since the divorce from his wife, Danae, four months ago, there'd been rumors that he'd been having an affair with twenty-six-year-old Lys, his former ward who'd lived in their household since the age of seventeen.

While Lys struggled with her grief over his death, and many people lamented his demise, the media had done their best to sensationalize it, developing a story that had played every night in the television news cycle. Had Lys conducted a secret affair with the famous hotelier for several years? Questions had been raised as to what had actually caused the divorce and his ultimate death.

Without answers, speculation grew that foul play might have been involved. Rumor that Lys might have caused his death to gain access to part of his money had caught hold. Though the detective conducting the investigation hadn't put the blame on anyone, the reason for Nassos's death still hadn't been declared and a cloud hung over her. Lys's heart shuddered over the cruel gossip. Nassos was the man she'd loved like a father since childhood.

At seventeen, her millionaire Greek father, Kristos Theron, owner of a successful hotel in New York City, had been killed in a small plane accident. He'd left a will with a legal stipulation. If he died before she was of age, his best friend and former business partner, Nassos Rodino, would become her legal guardian.

Nassos had come to New York often throughout her early childhood and she had seen him as part of her extended family. When her father died, it was no hardship to travel to Greece with him.

But the moment Nassos had brought her to his home, she'd discovered that he and his wife had been living in a troublesome marriage.

Lys had never known the reason for their struggles, but it grieved her because she'd sensed that deep down they loved each other. It was all very complicated and she'd tried not to add to their problems. But in that regard she felt she'd failed when she'd started dating men neither of them approved of.

Nassos called them rich men's playboy sons.

Danae saw them as opportunists with no substance, adding to Lys's insecurity that somehow she didn't have the ability to attract the right kind of man. None of her relationships developed into anything serious because she sensed her adoptive parents' disapproval.

Since coming to live with them, the paparazzi had followed her around, never missing a chance to exploit her private life by filming her accompanied by any rich man she may have been seen with in public. Unfortunately in her work at Nassos's exclusive hotel chain, wealthy people made up her world. She'd never known anything else.

If she'd met and fallen in love with a poor fisherman, would they have approved of her choice? She didn't have an answer to that question, nor to the many others that she often thought of as Lys suffered from a lack of confidence. Having lost her mother at the age of nine hadn't helped.

Their disapproval hurt her terribly because she'd loved Nassos and his wife so much and wanted their acceptance. Lys's father had entrusted her to Nassos. Right now she felt like she'd let down three of the most important people in her life, but not on purpose.

Though he and Danae had suffered marital difficulties, they'd been wonderful to Lys and had made life beautiful at their villa on Kasos Island while she'd dealt with her sorrow. They'd helped her through those difficult years and had made it possible for her to go to college on the mainland.

Nassos was the kindest, dearest man Lys had ever known in her life next to her own father. The two men had been born on Kasos and had always been best friends. Early in their lives they'd gone into the fishing business together and had slowly amassed their fortunes. Kristos had ended up in New York, while Nassos stayed on Heraklion and had eventually married.

For Lys, the underlying strife during their divorce had been devastating. Since then she and Danae had been estranged. It tore her heart out. At this point Lys didn't know how to overcome her pain except to pour herself into work at the hotel, and avoid the press as much as possible.

Deep in tortured thoughts, she heard a voice. "Kyria Theron?" She lifted her head to see another officer in the doorway. "Thank you for coming. Detective Vlassis will see you now."

Hopefully this meeting would provide the answer that let her out of proverbial jail and allowed the funeral to take place. She walked inside.

"Sit down, Kyria Theron."

Lys found a chair opposite his desk.

"Coffee? Tea?"

"Neither, thank you."

The somber detective sat back in his chair tapping the tips of his long fingers together. "I have good news for you. The medical examiner has turned over his findings to my office. We know the truth and foul play has been ruled out."

"You're serious?" Her voice shook. The rumor that she might have poisoned Nassos with some invisible drug in his penthouse apartment in order for her to get a portion of his money had been devastating for her.

"It's been determined he died of a subarachnoid hemorrhage probably caused from an earlier head injury."

"Why did it take so long?" she cried.

"Unfortunately the bleeding went undetected. The reason it was difficult to find the first time was because it's not unusual for SAH to be initially misdiagnosed as a migraine."

"So the doctor didn't catch it."

"Not at first. A human mistake. It caused a delay in obtaining a CT scan."

A small gasp escaped her lips. "After he'd hit his head on the kitchen cupboard several months ago, I thought he must have suffered a concussion. I told him I wanted to talk to his doctor about it, but Nassos told me to stop fussing because the pain went away. That must be why he had a stroke." Tears rolled down her cheeks. "Thank heaven he can now be laid to rest."

"This has been a very stressful time for you, but it's over. The press has been informed. I'm sorry for your loss and wish you well in the future."

Another miracle. "Thank you. Have you told his ex-wife?"

"Yes."

"Good." Now Danae could make the funeral arrangements. "You'll never know what this means to me."

Lys jumped up from the chair. "Thank you." She couldn't leave the police station fast enough and rushed past the officer posted at the front desk without glancing at him. She couldn't endure one more smirk.

Once outside, Lys hurried to her car, running past the usual news people stalking her movements to take pictures. She got into her car and drove back to the

Rodino Luxury Hotel where she had her own suite. She'd been living there and working in the accounts department for Nassos since graduating from business college in Heraklion four years ago.

The moment she reached her room on the third floor, she flung herself across the bed and sobbed. It was over at last. But with Nassos's death and Lys's unwanted estrangement with his ex-wife, there was no one to pick up the emotional pieces.

The couple's tragic divorce had fragmented Lys. If they'd been going to end their marriage, why hadn't it happened years before now? She simply didn't understand. And then had come the shocking news of his death… The loss was almost more than she could bear.

They'd worked together at the hotel. He'd taught her everything about the business. He'd been her friend, confidant, mentor. How was she going to be able to go on without him?

For Nassos not to be there anymore was killing her and she missed Danae terribly. Until the police had closed the case, Lys had been in limbo, trying to do her usual job, but her mind and heart hadn't been there. When she did have to leave the hotel for any reason, she'd felt accusatory stares coming in all directions and avoided any publicity if she could help it.

Thankfully this was over and there'd be an end to the malicious talk that he'd been murdered. Hopefully everything would die down, but where did she go from here? Lys felt like she'd been driving her car when the steering wheel had suddenly disappeared, leaving her to plunge over a cliff. She was so heartbroken she could hardly think.

While in this state, the phone rang. Lys turned over to look at the caller ID. It was Xander Pappas, Nassos's attorney. She picked up and learned that he'd be in Nassos's private office at the hotel in a half hour to talk to her. The detective had already been in touch with him.

"I have something important to give you."

She sat up in surprise. "Will Danae be meeting with us?" Lys longed to talk to her.

"No. We've already spoken and I've read her the will. She'll be calling you about the funeral."

"I see."

Stabbed with fresh pain, Lys thanked him and hung up. If there hadn't been a divorce, she and Danae would have planned his funeral together. Now everything had changed. More tears gushed down her cheeks before she got off the bed to freshen up.

Of course she hadn't expected to be present at the reading of the will and hadn't wanted to be. Danae had been married to Nassos for twenty-four years. That business was between the two of them.

A few minutes later she left for the corporate office downstairs. On the way, she couldn't help but wonder what Xander wanted to give her. Nassos couldn't have known when he would die, so she couldn't imagine what it was.

After nodding to Giorgos, the annoying general manager of the hotel, she walked in to Nassos's private office. The attorney greeted her and told her to sit down.

"I have two items to give you. Both envelopes are sealed. You'll know what to do after you open the envelope marked Letter first. Nassos wrote to you at the time he divorced Danae." He put both envelopes on the desk.

She swallowed hard. Nassos had written something that recently? "Have you read it?"

"No. He gave me instructions to give them both to you upon his death, whenever that would be. Who would have imagined he'd die this early in his life? I'll miss him too and am so sorry since I know how close you two were. I'll leave now. If you have any questions, call me at my office."

After he left the room, Lys reached for the envelope and pulled out the letter with a trembling hand. She knew Nassos's handwriting. He wrote with a certain panache that was unmistakable.

My dearest little Lysette,

Immediately her eyes filled with more tears.

I'll always think of you that way, no matter how old you are when you read this letter. You're the daughter I never had. Danae and I couldn't have children. The problem was mine. I found out early in our marriage that I was infertile. It came as a great shock, but I'd dreamed of having children, so I wanted to adopt. She didn't, and I could never talk her into it. I decided she didn't love me enough or she would have agreed to try because I wanted children more than anything.

Six months ago, Xander let me know that he knew of a baby we could adopt. I went to Danae and begged her. It could be our last chance, but she still said no. In my anger I divorced the woman I loved and always will. Now I'm paying for it dearly because I don't believe she'll forgive me.

You need to know that you were never the reason for our marital troubles. I ruined things at the beginning of our marriage by making an issue that she stay at home. I insisted she quit her job because I was raised with old-fashioned ideas. I was wrong to impose them on Danae. She's very much a modern woman and a part of me resented the fact that she couldn't be happy at home.

Please realize that your coming to us helped keep our marriage together and deep down she knows it. I'm afraid it was because of my damnable pride—my greatest flaw—nothing more, that made me divorce her, so never ever blame yourself. If I was hard on you because of the men you dated, it was only because of my desperate fear you might end up in a bad marriage with a man who didn't value you enough. Danae felt the same way.

Forgive us if we hurt you in any way.

"Oh, Nassos—" Lys cried out in relief and anguish.

You have a massive inheritance from your father that will be given to you on your twenty-seventh birthday. He dictated that specific time in his will to make sure you'd be mature enough when you came into your money.

Lys was incredulous. She'd thought it had all been incorporated into the Rodino empire. Nassos would have deserved every euro of it.

Again, I have no idea how old you are now that I'm dead. I suspect you're a very wealthy woman, hopefully married with children, maybe even grandchildren. And happy!

As you will have found out from Danae, she inherited everything with one exception…the hotel is your inheritance from me to own and run as you will.

Lys reeled physically and clung to the arms of the chair.

No. It wasn't possible. The hotel should have been given to Danae, who understood the hotel business very well. It was Nassos who'd hired her away from another hotelier to come and work for him twenty-four years ago. How sad that even after his death, Nassos couldn't allow her to continue in a career she'd enjoyed.

Lys's eyes closed tightly for a moment.

Danae hadn't contacted Lys yet. There hadn't been time. How could Nassos have done this to the woman he'd loved? Wiping her eyes, she went on reading.

But you're not the sole owner, Lys.

What? The shocks just kept coming.

Before you take possession, you must give the sealed envelope to Takis Manolis. You've heard me and Danae talk about him often enough. When he came to Crete periodically, we'd discuss business on my yacht where we could be private. I never did believe in mixing my business matters with my personal life. The two don't go together.

You'll know where to find him when the time comes. The two of you will share ownership for six months. After that time period, you'll both be free to make any decisions you want.

By the time you read this, he's probably married with children and grandchildren too. I've thought of him as the son I never had.

It was my thrill and privilege to be your guardian, friend and adoptive father for the child of my best friend Kristos.

Love always,
Nassos.

You can't go home again.

Whoever coined the phrase was wrong. Yes, you could go home again.

In the last eleven years, Takis Manolis had made four trips a year to Crete and nothing had changed… Not the pain, not the landscape, not his family.

Naturally they were all a little older each time he flew here from New York and later from Italy, but everything had stayed the same if you looked at the inner vessel.

The village of Tylissos where he'd been born was still situated on the northeastern mountainside of Psiloritis near the sea. Time hadn't altered it a whit.

Nor had it altered the views of Takis's father or his elder brother, Lukios, who helped their father run the old ten-room hotel.

His family followed the philotimo creed for all Cretans to maintain their unflappable dignity even if their existence bordered on poverty when the hotel didn't fill. They respected the rich and didn't try to become something greater than they were. Takis was baffled that they didn't mind being poor and accepted it as their lot in life.

Until recent years there'd been very little inherited wealth in Greece. Most of the Greek millionaires were self-made, but envy wasn't part of his brother's or his father's makeup.

Takis's older sister, Kori, married to a cook at one of the village restaurants where she worked, didn't have to tell him that she and her husband, Deimos, struggled to make a decent living.

They had a little girl, Cassia, now three years old, who'd been in and out of the hospital after her birth because of chronic asthma and needed a lot of medical care. He was thankful that at least Kori kept the cash he'd given her for a belated birthday present, knowing she'd use it for bills.

Though the family accepted the gifts he brought whenever he came, pride prevented his father from taking any monetary help. Lukios was the same. Being a married man with a wife and two children, who were now four and five, he would never look to Takis for assistance to make life a little easier for his family and in-laws.

This centuries-old pride thwarted Takis's heartfelt need and desire to shower his family with all the things of which they'd been deprived and caused him deep grief.

Early in life he'd known he was different from the rest of them, never going along with their family's status quo. Though he'd never openly fought with his father or brother, he'd struggled to conform.

His mother knew how he felt, but all she could do was urge Takis to keep the peace. When he'd told her of his dreams to go to college to better himself, she'd said it was impossible. They didn't have the money. None of the Manolis family had ever gone for a higher education.

Takis just couldn't understand why neither his father nor brother didn't want to expand and grow the small hotel that had been handed down from an earlier generation. He could see nothing wrong with trying to build it into something bigger and better. To be ambitious didn't make you dishonorable, but his father and brother weren't risk takers and refused to change their ways.

There were times when he wondered if he really was his parents' birth child. Except that his physical features and build proclaimed him a Manolis through and through.

By his midteens, Takis had feared that if he stayed on Crete, he would turn into his brother, who was a clone of the Manolis men before him, each having so little to show for all their hard work. More and more his ideas clashed with his father's over how to bring in more clients and build another couple of floors on the hotel.

Takis had worked out all his ideas in detail. One day he'd approached his father in all seriousness, wanting to talk to him man-to-man. But when he made his proposals, his father said something that stopped him cold.

Your ideas do you credit, my son, but they don't reflect my vision for our family business. One day you'll be a man and you'll understand.

Understand what?

Pierced by his father's comment, Takis took it to mean his ideas weren't good enough and never would be, even when he became a man.

At that moment something snapped inside Takis. He determined to go to college despite what his mother had said.

So he bought a secondhand bike and after helping his father during the week on a regular basis, he rode the few kilometers to his second job at the famous Rodino hotel and resort in Heraklion on weekends to earn extra money. The manager was soon impressed with Takis's drive. In time he introduced him to the owner of the hotel, Nassos Rodino, who had several talks with Takis about his financial situation.

One day the unimaginable had happened. Kyrie Rodino called him to his office and helped him apply for a work visa and permit to travel to New York. His best friend, Kristos Theron, the owner of a successful hotel in New York City, would let Takis work for him. He could make a lot more money there and go to the kind of college that would help him get ahead in the business world. He'd improve his English too.

Takis couldn't believe anyone would do something so fantastic for him and returned home to tell his parents about the opportunity.

His mother kept quiet. As for his father, he listened

and nodded. *If this is what you want to do, then you must do it.*

But how do you feel about it, Baba? Takis had still wanted his father's approval.

His father shrugged his shoulders. *Does it matter? You're eighteen years old now and are in charge of your own destiny. At eighteen a man can leave his father and make his own way.*

That isn't the answer I was hoping for. His father hadn't given him his blessing and probably resented Nassos Rodino for making any of this possible.

If you're a man, then you don't need an answer.

Takis had felt rebuked. His mother remained silent as he left the room with a hurt too deep to express. After the talk with his father, he'd had the feeling his parent had already felt abandoned before he'd even approached him.

Combined with the pain of having recently lost his girlfriend, who'd been killed in a bus accident, he finally made the decision to leave home. She'd been the one he could confide in about his dreams.

After all their talks, she'd known he'd been afraid to leave his family in case they thought he was letting them down. But she'd encouraged him and told him to spread his wings. They'd talked about her joining him in New York at a later date.

With her gone, he'd had no one who understood everything going on inside him. Her compassion had made her such an exceptional person, and he'd never found that incredible quality in the women he'd met since leaving Crete.

In the end, he'd made the decision to go after the opportunity that would enrich his life and he vowed, one day, that he would return and help his family in every capacity possible.

That was a long time ago.

On this cool March day, he held in the tears as he embraced his mother one more time. On this trip he noticed she'd aged and hadn't exhibited her usual energy. That troubled him. "I promise I'll be back soon."

"Why don't you come home to live? You can afford it. We miss you so much." Her tears tugged at his heart.

His father didn't weep, but Takis detected a new sorrow in his eyes. Why was it there? Why didn't his parent speak the words of love and acceptance he longed to hear?

"Do what you have to do." Those were similar to the words he'd said to Takis before he'd left for New York eleven years ago. "Be safe, my son."

But his father still hadn't been the one to ask him to come home or tell him he'd like him to work at the hotel with the family again. Had Takis done irreparable damage to their relationship?

"You too, *Baba*." His throat had swollen with emotion. "Stay well."

He turned to his mother once more. Was the sorrow he'd seen in his father's eyes over concern for his wife? Was there something wrong with her? With his father? Something no one in the family was telling him?

This visit had troubled him with thoughts he didn't want to entertain. He hugged everyone and kissed his nieces and nephews. Then he climbed into the taxi in front of the family-owned hotel that needed refurbishing. Heaven knew it needed everything. *They* needed everything.

His eyes clung to his mother's once more. *Had she been trying to tell him something?* He blew her a kiss.

The flight to Athens would be leaving from Heraklion airport in four hours. First he would attend the funeral services for Nassos Rodino at the Greek Orthodox church in the heart of Heraklion. The recently divorced hotel owner, rumored to have a mistress, had suffered a stroke in the prime of his life—a stroke that had preceded his death. This had shocked Takis, who'd met with the man, who had given him so much, on his yacht to talk business when Takis had last come to Crete.

Most important to Takis was that he owed the hotelier a debt that bordered on love. His gratitude to the older man knew no bounds.

In truth he couldn't think of another successful man who would have gone to such lengths to give Takis the chance to better himself, even to go as far as sponsoring him in the United States.

Once the funeral was over, he'd fly to Athens. From there he'd take another flight to Milan, Italy, where he was part owner, and manager of the five-star Castello Supremo Hotel and Ristorante di Lombardi.

But all the way to the church his mother's words rang in his ears. *Why don't you come home to live. You can afford it.* His mother had never been so outspoken in her thoughts before.

Yes, he could afford it. In the eleven years he'd been away, he'd made millions while his family continued to eke out their existence.

Was she telling him something without coming

right out and saying it? Was she ill? Or his father?
Death with dignity? Never saying a word? *Damn that
pride of theirs if it was true!*

Neither Kori nor Lukios had said anything, but
maybe his siblings had been kept in the dark. Then
again maybe nothing was wrong and his mother, who
was getting older, was simply letting him know how
much they'd missed him.

He missed them too. Of course he'd come back
in an instant if they needed him. But to come home
for good? Even if his two business partners were in
agreement and bought him out—even if he sold his
hotel chain in New York, would his father allow him
to work alongside him? What if he refused Takis's
help? What would Takis do for the rest of his life?
Build a new hotel conglomerate on Crete?

His eyes closed tightly. He could never do that to
his father and use the Manolis name. A son honored
his father and showed him respect by never taking
anything away from him.

Two years ago Takis had built a children's hospital in his hometown village of Tylissos on Crete
in order that his niece Cassia would get the kind of
skilled medical help she needed. The hospital gave
free medical care with no child turned away.

He'd kept his dealings anonymous, using local
people who had no idea Takis had funded everything
including the doctors' salaries. It helped him to know
he was doing something for his family, even if they
weren't aware of it.

Long ago Takis had lost hope that one day his father might be proud of him for trying to make something of his life in order to help them. His parent had

never been anything but kind to him, but deep in his heart lived the fear that his family had always compared him to their ever faithful Lukios and would never see Takis in the same light.

In his pain he needed to get back to Italy and ask advice from his partners, who were as close to him as brothers.

"Kyrie?" The taxi driver broke in on his tormented thoughts by telling him they'd arrived at the corner of the square.

Takis had been in a daze. "If you'll wait here, I'll be back in an hour." He handed him some bills and got out to join a crowd of people entering the church, where the covered coffin faced east.

Once he found a seat, he listened to the white-robed priest who conducted the service. After leading them in hymns and scriptures, the priest asked God to give Nassos rest and forgive all his sins. As far as Takis was concerned, the man had no sins. Because of him, Takis had been given a precious gift that had changed his life completely. But at what price?

Soon the bereaved, dressed in black, started down the aisle to go to the cemetery. One dark-haired woman in a black veil appeared particularly overcome with sorrow. Nassos's ex-wife? Takis had never met her. Nassos had kept their few meetings totally private.

Because he'd arrived late, he'd taken a seat on the aisle at the back. While he waited for everyone to pass, his gaze happened to fasten on probably the most gorgeous young dark-blonde woman he'd ever seen in his life.

Her two-piece black suit provided the perfect foil

for her stunning classic features only rivaled by violet eyes. Their color reminded him of the Chaste plant belonging to the verbena family that grew all over Crete. They peered out of dark lashes that took his breath. But he could see she was grief stricken. Who *was* she?

He turned his head to watch her walk out the rear of the church. If he weren't going to be late to catch his flight, he'd drive to the cemetery and find out her name. Hers was a face and figure he would never forget, not in a lifetime.

CHAPTER TWO

FIVE DAYS AFTER the funeral, Lys left Giorgos, the manager of the Rodino Hotel, in charge. The paparazzi took pictures as she climbed in the limo taking her to the airport for her flight to Athens. It connected to another flight to Milan, Italy. Her destination was the Castello Supremo Hotel and Ristorante di Lombardi.

In the year before her father's death, she'd heard her father and Nassos talking about a new employee at her father's hotel named Takis Manolis. Nassos had made it possible for the younger man from Crete to get a work visa and go to college in the United States while working at her father's hotel in New York. Lys's understanding was that he was exceptional and showed real promise in the hotel industry.

Their interest had piqued *her* interest, but she'd never met him since she and her father had lived in their own home in the city. She'd rarely gone to the hotel for any reason.

After her father's death, and the move to Crete to Nassos and Danae's villa on Kasos, the name of Takis came up again. Nassos spoke fondly of him and she learned more about him. The Manolis teen had come from Tylissos and had needed help to escape a life that was close to the poverty line.

When Lys asked Nassos why he cared so much, he'd told her the young man had reminded him of himself at that age. Nassos, who'd gotten little help from his ailing grandfather, had to fish from a row boat and sell his catch at the market to support them. Lys's father, Kristos, also dirt-poor, started fishing with him.

Both men had wanted more out of life and had gone after it. In time they built businesses that grew until Kristos decided to travel to New York and take over a hotel there.

Nassos was able to buy property in Heraklion and build a hotel on Crete. He'd made it into a huge success story. Nassos had seen that same hunger in Takis, who he said was brilliant and had vision in a way that separated him from the masses. Both men wanted Takis to realize his dream. That's why Nassos had made it possible for Takis to travel to New York and work at the hotel Lys's father had owned. Their hunch had paid off in a huge way.

Later on, through Nassos, Lys learned more about the enterprising Takis. His chain of hotels and stock market investments had turned him into a billionaire. She found herself fantasizing about him, and loved Nassos for his goodness. He was a saint who'd become the father she'd lost. Imagine making such a thing possible for the younger man, who was a home-grown Cretan like himself!

Though she couldn't imagine how Takis Manolis would feel when he heard the news that he was the new half owner of the Rodino Hotel, she was excited to be able to carry out Nassos's final wish. In truth she couldn't wait to meet this twenty-nine-year-old man she'd heard talked about for so long.

She'd endowed him with her idea of what the perfect Cretan man looked like. It was very silly of her, but she couldn't help it. Both her father and Nassos had made him out to be someone so unique and fascinating, she'd wouldn't be human if her imagination hadn't taken over.

As for her being the other half owner, she didn't know how she felt about it yet. Everything depended on today's meeting.

It was midmorning as Lys left her hotel in Milan dressed in a heavy black Ralph Lauren shirt dress she could wear without a coat. After setting out on her mission, she gave the limo driver directions to the *castello* outside the city. Then she sat back to take in the fabulous scenery of farms and villas lined with the tall narrow cypress trees indigenous to the region.

Mid-March felt like Heraklion, a cool fifty-eight degrees under cloudy skies. The only difference was that Milan wasn't by the sea. According to Nassos, this refurbished Italian monument built on top of a hill in the thirteen hundreds—originally the home of the first Duc di Lombardi—was a triumph that Takis shared with two business partners. It had become the showplace of Europe.

Lys had come to Italy without letting anyone know where she was going, or why, only that she'd be out of the country for an indefinite period. It was heaven to escape Crete for a little while where few people would recognize her. If anyone knew her reason for coming here, it would make more headlines she didn't want and would do anything to avoid.

Hopefully the press would leave her alone from now on. Though sorrow weighed her down, she intended to ignore any further publicity and carry on as Nassos had expected her to do.

The driver let her out at the base of steps leading to the front entrance. During her climb, she marveled at the trees and flowers surrounding the building. This was a magnificent edifice, high up where she could see the landscape in the far distance. No wonder the Duc di Lombardi found this the perfect place to rule his kingdom.

Inside the entry she was struck by the palatial grandeur with its sweeping corridor of glass doors and chandeliers. The exquisite furniture and paintings of a former time created a matchless tapestry of beauty in the Italian tradition.

A few hotel guests came out of the dining room area. Others walked down the hallway toward the front desk. A lovely woman at the counter, maybe thirty, smiled at her. "May I help you?" she asked in Italian.

Lys answered in English because she could only speak a few words in Italian. "I'm here to see Mr. Manolis, if that's possible."

"Do you have an appointment?" Her switch to excellent English was impressive.

"No. I just flew in to Milan. If he's not available, I'll make an appointment and come back because this is vitally important to me."

"Are you a tour guide?"

"No."

The woman studied her briefly before she said, "What's your name?"

"Ms. Theron."

"If you'll take a seat, I'll see if I can locate him."

Wonderful. He was here somewhere. She'd been prepared to fly to New York to see him if necessary. By coming here first, she'd saved herself a long overseas flight.

This close now to meeting the man her father and Nassos had cared so much about, she felt an attachment to him difficult to explain. Apparently if she'd met this Takis in Heraklion and had started dating him, Nassos would have given his wholehearted approval.

Lys was dying to know what he looked like. As Nassos had explained in his letter to her, he never liked mixing business with his personal life, so she could only guess. Neither he nor Danae had ever mentioned that aspect of him. With a heightened sense of excitement, she turned and sat on one of the beautiful upholstered chairs with the distinctive Duc di Lombardi logo. Her heart pounded hard while she waited to meet Takis.

Midmorning Takis sat with his partners in the private dining room on the second floor of the *castello*. This was the first time he'd had a chance to speak to them after returning from Crete. So far he was no closer to knowing what to do about his worry over his parents and he wanted their opinions. Vincenzo had asked that breakfast be brought up from the kitchen, but Takis had lost his appetite and only wanted coffee.

"You don't have to make any kind of a rash decision right now," his friend counseled. "Rather than just a weekend visit, why don't you simply go back to Tylissos for a couple of weeks? We'll be fine without you. Stay with your family, see what you can do to help out. Surely if there's something wrong with either of your parents, you'll pick up on it and go from there."

As usual, Vincenzo, the present-day Duc di Lombardi, made sense.

Cesare Donati, whose oversight of the restaurant had turned the hotel into *the* place to dine in all of Europe, eyed him over his cup of coffee. "What would be wrong by going home and asking them outright if there's a problem they don't want you to know about? Do it in front of the whole family so if anyone squirms, you'll see it."

That was good advice too. Cesare wasn't one to hold back. He acted on instincts, thus the reason he was the best restaurateur on five continents.

"I'm listening, guys, and am taking both ideas under consideration." Two weeks with his family would give him enough time to get the truth out of them. While he was there he could also track down the woman he'd seen at the funeral whose image wouldn't leave his mind.

While he was deep in thought, his phone rang. Takis checked the caller ID. It was the front desk. He clicked on. "Yes, Sofia?" The woman was Swiss-born and spoke six languages.

"Sorry to bother you when I know you're in a meeting, but a woman I don't recognize has flown to Milan and come to the *castello* to see you. She's not a tour guide and says it's of vital importance, but she didn't explain the nature of her business. She had no card. Her last name is something like Tierrun."

"What's her nationality?"

"She sounds American to me." Maybe she'd been sent from his headquarters in New York for a special reason, but Takis found it strange that his assistant hadn't said anything. "Do you wish to meet with her, or shall I make an appointment?"

Takis had no idea what this was all about, but he might as well take care of it now. "I'll be right there. Take her back to my office." He rang off and glanced at his friends. "I've got to meet someone downstairs. Thanks for the much needed advice. I'll talk to you later."

Lys followed the concierge down a hall lined with several doors. She opened the one on the right. "Mr. Takis will be with you in a minute. Make yourself comfortable. Would you care for coffee or tea while you wait?"

"Nothing, thank you."

After the woman left, Lys sat down near the desk. On the top of it were several little framed snapshots of what she assumed were family photos. Some she surmised were of his parents, some were his siblings and small children. Along with those pictures was a small statue of King Minos, the mythological leader of the great Minoan civilization on Crete, who was clothed in mythology.

As she continued to look around the uncluttered room, a cry escaped her lips. Hanging on the wall across from her was a large framed picture of a younger Nassos with a lot of black hair, standing on the deck of his yacht in a sport shirt and trousers. Takis must have taken it with a camera and had sent the photo to be enlarged. There were no other pictures.

With pounding heart she jumped up from the chair and walked over to get a closer look. Nassos's signature was in the bottom right hand corner. He'd personalized it. *Bravo, Takis.* He signed everything with a flourish.

Seeing him so alive and vital in the picture brought tears to her eyes. He would be thrilled if he knew his autographed photo hung in the office of his unofficial protégé in the most prominent spot. The fact that this man had honored Nassos this way told her a lot about his character and she knew he was deserving of the gift he was about to receive.

Lys heard a little rap on the open door and whirled around.

She hadn't known what she'd expected to see. Only her imagination could have provided that. But it wasn't the tall, hard-muscled male so striking in a rugged way who'd just walked in his office…an olive-complexioned man come to life from ancient Crete though he was dressed in a stone-colored business suit and tie.

"Oh—" she cried softly because the sight of him caused her thoughts to reel.

Those penetrating hazel eyes of his put her in mind of one of those heroic dark-blond warriors depicted in frescos on the walls of temples and museums. She studied his arresting features, remembering one prince who could have been his double. The five o'clock shadow on his firm jaw gave him a sensual appeal she hadn't been prepared for.

While she continued to stare at him, she realized he'd been examining her the way someone did who couldn't believe what he was seeing. He gave her a slight nod. "The woman at the desk thought you were American, but didn't quite get your name." The man spoke English with a heavy accent she found exciting.

"I'm Lys Theron," she said in Greek.

A look of astonishment crossed over his face. "Wait," he said, as if sorting out a puzzle. "Theron… Kristos Theron. He was *your* father?"

"Yes."

Clearly her answer shocked him.

"He was a wonderful man. It came as a terrible blow when I heard about the plane crash. He'd been very kind to me. I'm so sorry you lost him."

"So am I."

The second she'd spoken, silence enveloped the room's interior. His eyes seemed to go dark from some unnamed emotion. A hand went to the back of his neck, as if he were questioning what he'd just heard. "I saw you at Nassos's funeral last weekend," he murmured in Greek.

His admission shook her to the core. "You were there?"

"That's right. I wouldn't have missed it. Aside from my father, Nassos Rodino was the finest man I ever knew. His death came as a great shock to me."

He'd been at the church! No wonder he'd stared so hard at her, but she hadn't seen him. Her pain had been too great.

She took a deep breath. "To know you flew to

Heraklion to honor him, and that you have his photograph hanging in this office, would have meant the world to him."

A strange sound came out of him. "You're a relation of his?"

"I was seventeen when my father died. Nassos was his best friend and became my guardian. He took me back to Crete where I lived with him and his wife."

He shook his head. "I can't credit it. You and I never met, yet your father and Nassos are the reason I have a life here."

"I've heard about you for years and have been wanting to meet you. You're the brilliant son of Nikanor Manolis from Tylissos. Nassos's belief in you was clearly deserved."

His chest rose and fell visibly. "His support was nothing short of a miracle," he whispered.

"A miracle couldn't work if the seeds of greatness weren't already there."

Another unearthly quiet emanated from him, prompting her to speak. "I was sixteen when I first learned about you. Nassos came to visit often and asked my father if he'd give you a job at the hotel in New York. I thought it was so wonderful that they wanted to help you so you could go to college. They really believed in you!"

He moved closer. "Your father's close friendship with Nassos made it possible for me to work and go to school. He was very good to me."

"To me too." She smiled. "It was hard to lose him when I did."

She felt his compassionate gaze. "I can only imagine your feelings right now. I'm sorry you've suffered so many losses."

"Death comes to us all at some point." She sucked in her breath, still dazed by his striking looks, in fact by the whole situation. "To be honest, I've always wanted to meet the famous Takis Manolis. The last time Nassos spoke of you, he said you were already a living legend before you were thirty."

His dark brows furrowed as if in utter disbelief over those words, revealing a humility she found admirable.

"Please. Sit down." While she did his bidding, he paced the floor looking shaken, then he stopped. "Can I get you anything? Have you had breakfast?"

"Thank you, but I ate before I left the hotel in Milan several hours ago. I should have contacted you for an appointment ahead of time, but decided to take my chances and fly here first. I haven't taken a real trip in a long time. I love getting away from everything for a little while."

"I don't blame you. I saw what was written about you in the paper while I was in Crete. The press manages to find a way if they're looking for a story." By the tone of disgust in his voice, she imagined he'd had to deal with his share of unwanted invasions. She could relate to his feelings, making it easier to confide in him.

"Nassos's unexplained, unexpected death wasn't solved until a week ago when the medical examiner said he'd died from a subarachnoid hemorrhage. Over the last month while everything was up in the air, the press labeled me everything from a murderer who'd poisoned him, to an opportunistic floozy. You could add adulteress, narcissistic liar and evil spawn of Satan in some of the more sordid tabloids. The list goes on and on."

Their eyes met. "Is that all?" he teased unexpectedly, catching her off guard. His bone-melting charm, not to mention his refreshing humor was so welcome, she felt a great release and laughter bubbled out of her.

She could easily understand why Nassos had found him an extraordinary human being in ways other than his business acumen. After reading Nassos's letter, she knew Nassos hadn't talked to him about her or Danae. Nassos had always been a very private person.

"I came to see you for a very specific reason, but if this isn't a good time to talk, please say so. I can return to Milan and wait until I hear from you. Or I'll fly back to Crete and come another time when it's more convenient."

His eyes narrowed on her features. "The daughter whom Nassos helped raise for his best friend has my full, undivided attention. Tell me what's on your mind. Obviously it's very important to you, otherwise you wouldn't have flown all this distance during your bereavement. I'd do anything for him, so that translates I'd do anything for you. Just name it."

Lys felt his sincerity sink deep into her psyche. "Thank you for saying that. I guess I don't have to tell you what this means to me."

Takis sat on the corner of his desk. "How can I help you?" he asked in a quiet tone, drawing her attention to his powerful legs beneath his trousers. She couldn't stop noticing every exciting male trait about him.

"It concerns the hotel in Heraklion."

One of his brows lifted in query. "Go on."

She got up from the chair, struggling with how to approach him. "In his will, every possession and asset of his *except* the hotel was left to his ex-wife, Danae."

The man listening to her didn't move a muscle, but she saw a quickening in his eyes, not knowing what it meant.

"That was as it should be," she continued. "Danae was his devoted wife for twenty-four years. When they divorced, he left her with everything she would need. Now that she has received the full inheritance he left her, I know she'll be well provided for all of her life."

"So I'm presuming the hotel is now yours."

Lys shook her head. "I only have half ownership and didn't want the half he left me."

Lines marred his features before he got to his feet. "That's very strange, but what does any of it have to do with me?" Confusion was written all over his handsome face.

Lys had tried to present this the right way, but she wasn't getting through to him. Taking a deep breath, she said, "Nassos hoped to leave a lasting legacy. Since none of us knows when we're going to die, he took precautions early to preserve that legacy when the time came, whenever that was."

"I still can't believe he's gone." His mournful comment touched her heart.

"Neither can I. Because he didn't have children, it meant putting the hotel in the hands of someone who understands and shares his vision."

Takis was listening. "That was you."

She took a deep breath. "I worked for him, yes. But I think this decision was made because he'd been my guardian and was always protective of me. He probably felt I needed someone to share the responsibility so I wouldn't make a serious mistake."

His brows dipped. "Mistake?"

"Yes. He loved the myth of King Minos, who forgot to rule wisely. Because of his mistake, he was killed by the daughters of King Cocalus, who poured boiling water over him while he was taking a bath. I notice you have a little statue of him."

"The story of King Minos intrigued me as a youth too."

Lys smiled sadly. "It proves you and Nassos had minds that thought alike. More than ever I'm convinced there was only one other person he could think of who would honor what he'd built."

She opened her handbag and pulled out the sealed envelope she handed to him. "That person is you, Kyrie Manolis. His attorney instructed me to give this to you. Any explanations are inside. I don't know the contents."

If Nassos had another flaw besides his pride, it was his secrecy, which had left Lys at a loss.

After clearing her throat she said, "In case you're not aware, it made Nassos happier than you could ever imagine to know that the little help he gave you in the beginning was the only thing you needed to go all the way. It means a lot to me to have met you after all this time. Not everyone could accomplish what you've done in so short a time. I'm truly impressed."

She moved to the door while he stood there in a trancelike state. "I have to get back to Crete. Please don't take long to let me know your plans. I wrote my private cell phone number on the back of that envelope. I live at the hotel and will meet with you at your convenience. Now I must get going. My limo is waiting in the front courtyard. *Kalimera.*"

She hurried down the hall. To stay in that room with him any longer wasn't a good idea. They'd only just met, yet she'd felt a strong, immediate attraction to Takis that had rocked her world. It had gotten its start in the long-ago conversations between her father and Nassos, and the impression she'd created of the younger man who'd been hungry to better his life.

She knew she had to get away from him and leave the *castello* before she didn't want to leave. Lys had never felt these kinds of initial feelings about any man in her life.

Those playboys who'd passed in and out of her life couldn't touch this extraordinary man, who'd earned the highest praise from her father and Nassos. The intense way he was looking at her, the emotions he'd aroused, had caused her bones to melt.

CHAPTER THREE

TAKIS KNEW HE HADN'T dreamed up this meeting with the woman Nassos had helped raise. When she left his office, her flowery fragrance lingered, providing proof she'd been in here.

He'd seen tears in her eyes when she'd heard him enter the room. She'd just been looking at Nassos's picture. The exquisite woman who'd walked down the aisle at the funeral had been his ward at one time. Shame on Takis for wondering if she could have been the mistress talked about in the news.

How old was Lys Theron? Twenty-five, twenty-six? And now she was half owner of the hotel, with Takis owning the other half.

Several emotions bombarded him, not the least of which was the attraction to her he'd felt at the funeral. He looked at the envelope his hand had squeezed without his being aware of it. According to her, this was Nassos's gift to him.

Utterly incredulous, he opened it and pulled out a letter and a deed. To his shock it was official all right, signed with Nassos's distinctive signature, stamped and dated. There it was in bold letters.

Takis Manolis, half owner of the Rodino Hotel
in Heraklion.

The letter indicated he should get in touch with the
attorney Xander as soon as possible. Once Takis returned to Heraklion, he could sign the deed in front
of witnesses so it could be recorded and filed for the
court.

He read more. Neither owner would be free to do
what they wanted with the hotel until six months had
passed.

Aghast, he shook his head. What on earth had possessed Nassos to do such a thing?

Once Takis's hotels in New York had started making money, he'd paid the older hotelier for the help
he'd given him. No amount could really be enough.
How did you assign goodness a monetary value? He'd
tried, but to his chagrin Nassos was now gone and
there'd be no last time to thank him for everything.

This unimaginable development had thrown him.

For Nassos to turn around and simply give him
half the hotel in Heraklion made no sense whatso-
ever. Takis didn't want the hotel! He'd paid him back
generously.

What in the hell was Nassos thinking? Now that
he'd passed away, there was no way to confront him
about this. The inconceivable gesture made him feel
as if he'd always be the boy who'd come from near
poverty. The thought hurt him in a way that went
soul deep.

To add to the hurt, this deed had been delivered
by special messenger in the form of Nassos's beauti-

ful former ward. Why would he force Takis's hand by making him a co-owner with her?

She was *too* damn beautiful. The kind of woman he never imagined to meet. Didn't want to meet. Only one other woman had touched his heart and she'd died. He didn't want to experience those kinds of feelings again. Yet a few minutes with this woman and a fire had been lit.

How did *she* feel about being half owner with a stranger, even if she knew a lot about him from Nassos and her father?

His thoughts centered on what she'd told him about the way the press had labeled her in the cruelest of ways. With her kind of unforgettable looks, she was an easy target. Was Nassos's divorce the result of his taking on Kristos's lovely teenage daughter to raise?

What business is it of yours to care, Manolis?

Unfortunately it *was* his business until he could fly to Crete and clear up this whole mess with the attorney of record.

Adrenaline surged through his veins. He wished to hell none of this had happened. He still couldn't believe Nassos was gone. Worse, he didn't want to know anything about *her*. Takis wished he'd never laid eyes on her. He didn't want this kind of a complication in his life. Loving a woman made you vulnerable.

A violent epithet flew from his lips. In his rage he tossed the deed across the room. It hit Cesare in the chest as he walked inside Takis's office.

With great calm his friend picked it up and put it on the desk. He shot Takis a questioning glance. "I take it this had something to do with the drop-dead-gorgeous woman I saw leaving the hotel a minute ago. Where on earth did *she* come from?"

Takis had trouble getting his emotions under control. "You don't want to know."

"Yes I do. You've been with several women over the years, but I've never seen you turned inside out by one before."

"It's not just the woman. It's everything!" His voice shook. "I feel like my world has been blown to smithereens and I don't know where I am anymore."

Takis should never have left his parents' home. He should have stayed on Crete and worked alongside his brother. He'd been so certain he'd had all the answers to help his family. But in the end he'd accepted the help of a wealthy man.

The thought of the deeded gift sickened him. That kind of gift might be given to a son, but Takis hadn't been Nassos's son. He was the son of Nikanor, who after all these years still didn't want his money. Neither did his brother. Worse, one of his parents was probably ill and Takis didn't have a clue because he'd been living out of the country for years. He was the ingrate of all time.

"What's the point of anything, Cesare?"

Worry lines darkened the features of his Italian friend. "Hold on, Takis. Come with me. We're going for a ride. My car is parked in the rear lot of the *castello*."

"You don't want to be with me."

"Well, I refuse to leave you here alone. It wouldn't do for Sofia to find you in this condition." Cesare was right about that. He didn't want his assistant privy to his personal life. "Whatever trouble you're in, we're going to talk about it. Let's go."

Takis grabbed the papers and stuffed them inside his suit jacket. They walked swiftly through the corridors past some of the guests to the outside. Cesare started up his sports car. He followed the road around from the back of the *castello* and they drove down the hill to the little village of Sopri. Before long he parked in front of a sports bar on the outskirts that didn't look crowded this time of day.

They went inside and found a quiet spot in a corner. Cesare ordered appetizers and their favorite Peroni, a pale lager from the brewery that had been founded in Lombardi. Once they'd been served rolls along with a hot plate of *grigliata mista di carne,* he eyed Takis.

"You didn't eat breakfast, which might explain the state you were in. You need lunch, *amico*, and you've got me for an audience. Now start talking and don't stop."

Cesare knew Takis's weakness for their grilled sausage, lamb and steak mix. Combined with the lager, it did taste good and he could feel his strength returning.

He pulled the deed out of his pocket and pushed it toward Cesare. "As you know, I attended Nassos Rodino's funeral while I was in Crete. Would you believe in his will he gave half the Hotel Rodino in Heraklion to me as a gift? The other half was given to that woman you saw. She was the courier who delivered it."

His friend studied it. "Who is she?"

"Lys Theron, the daughter of Kristos Theron, the

hotel owner in New York who gave me my first job after I reached the States. You remember me talking about him. When he died, his best friend, Nassos, Rodino became her guardian and brought her back to Crete to raise."

A low whistle came out of Cesare. But Takis didn't want to talk about the beautiful woman who'd robbed him of breath the moment he'd laid eyes on her. She was another problem altogether.

"I thought the money I sent to Nassos for his help had changed his image of me as the poverty-stricken teen from Tylissos." He swallowed part of his lager. "But I was wrong. In his mind's eye I would always be the poor son of poor Nikanor Manolis, humbly scraping out a living day after day.

"I never wanted anything from Nassos. His kindness gave me a new life, but I paid him back. To be handed a deed to part ownership of a property that isn't mine, that I never earned, is worse than a stiletto to the gut."

Cesare shot forward in his seat. "You couldn't be more wrong. It's his tribute to your raving success."

"You think?"

"Of course."

Takis shook his head. "Maybe the problem lies inside me. Maybe I've been too proud wanting to make a success of my life. Nassos's gift of the hotel takes me back to the time when I was eighteen. He approached me about furthering my education, not the other way around, Cesare.

"The hotel manager I worked for arranged for me to meet Nassos. I never asked for his help. When I finally accepted it and left for New York, I started paying him back as soon as I could. But being given half ownership of his hotel now doesn't feel right and has made me feel…guilty all over again."

"What's gotten into you, Takis? Guilty for what? Help me understand."

"That I've failed my family."

"In what way?"

"I left them to do something purely selfish. I accepted a rich man's help. My father couldn't give me that kind of help or encourage me. If I'd been any kind of a man, I would have stayed home and helped him."

"That's crazy talk, Takis. I left home too in order to pursue a dream and accepted a lot of help along the way."

"This is different, Cesare. You're not a Cretan."

"So what? I'm a Sicilian. What's the difference? My pride is no less fierce than yours."

Takis had no answer for that. "You don't understand. My brother stayed behind to work with my father. He never failed him. But that wasn't the case with his second-born son. What did I do? I took off. When I think about it now, I cringe to realize how deeply I must have disgraced him."

"Disgraced?" Cesare sounded angry. "You don't know any such thing. He must be bursting with pride over you. When was the last time you had a real heart-to-heart talk with him?"

"Before I left for New York, we talked. I went to him with ideas for what we could do with the hotel. He looked me in the eye and told me my plans for the family hotel didn't fit his vision, and that one day when I was a man, I'd understand. That was it! End of conversation. It shut me down. After eleven years I'm afraid I still don't understand."

"Then you need to force another conversation with him and find out what he meant."

"My father isn't easy to talk to."

"Then it's time you faced him so you won't stay in that hellhole you're digging for yourself. Let me ask you a question. Do you think *me* selfish? Or Vincenzo?"

Takis didn't have to voice the easy *no* that came to his mind.

"Come on and finish your food. Then we're going back to the *castello* to talk to Vincenzo before he leaves for Lake Como with Gemma. You're not the only one who has known the pain of separation from family. Don't forget that he *ran* from his father as fast as he could and hid out in New York under a different name for over ten years."

Takis had forgotten nothing. The three of them would never have met if they hadn't left their homes and their countries and gone to New York. He couldn't imagine what his life would have been like if he hadn't met Cesare and Vincenzo. The friendship they'd forged in college had changed his entire world.

All because Nassos made it possible for you, Manolis, said a voice in his head, sending him into worse turmoil.

Cesare paid the bill and got to his feet. "Are you ready?"

Once Lys had received the return phone call from Danae at noon, she walked out the door of the penthouse foyer to the elevator off the small hallway to await her arrival. The penthouse in Crete had been Nassos's domain, and a decision had to be made about the furnishings.

After being back a week from Milan, Lys still hadn't heard a word from Takis Manolis. But she'd daydreamed about him and what it would be like to go out with him. Since meeting him, she couldn't imagine ever being attracted to another man. She'd hoped to know his plans before telling Danae the latest state of affairs, but no such luck.

The doors of the elevator opened. Lys greeted the dark-haired beauty and walked back in the penthouse with her. Dressed in mourning clothes, she looked particularly elegant in a Kasper color-blocked black Jacquard jacket and skirt. Danae had always been a fashion plate and was the true love of Nassos's life.

No matter what he'd told Lys in his letter to her, she feared Danae might still blame her for their divorce. The pain of that would never leave her. No olive branch offered could ever change the past.

If Lys had known what would happen after Nassos had insisted she leave New York and come to live with him and Danae, she would have run away rather than have stepped foot on Crete. Hindsight was a wonderful thing, but it came far too late.

"Thank you for coming, Danae. I'm sure you hoped we'd seen the last of each other at the funeral, but I'm carrying out one last thing Nassos would have wanted done, even if it wasn't in the will. Come in the living room and sit down—I'd like to explain a few things."

The older woman followed her and found a seat on one of the upholstered chairs. Danae's natural olive complexion had paled. "I can't imagine what would have been so important you had to see me in person."

"Maybe you'll think it isn't important when I tell you, but I have to do it. As you know, Nassos left me half the hotel and nothing else. That means everything in this penthouse is yours. He lived up here after he left the villa. I happen to know you are the one who designed it and put it all together years ago. You're a real artist in many ways. All this furniture you picked out, the paintings… You know he would have wanted you to have everything."

She jumped to her feet, visibly disturbed. "I don't want anything," she bit out too fast, revealing her pain.

Lys could understand that and her heart went out to her. "If you don't want any of it, then you need to make arrangements for it to be sold or given away, or whatever you think is best. Otherwise I'll ask the co-owner of the hotel to do with it as he or she wishes."

"Who is it?"

"Would it surprise you to know its Takis Manolis?"

Danae's head reared. "Actually it doesn't. Nassos liked him very much."

Lys was glad she'd told her the truth. "I don't know if he wants it. But until he signs and files the official document with the court, it's still up in the air. On Xander's instructions I flew to Italy, handed him the documents and left."

"So you met him."

"Yes."

"What's he like?"

She took a deep breath. "Very attractive, but I haven't heard from him. Maybe he's trying to find a way to get out of it and possibly designate a person from his New York chain. That could be the reason there's been no word yet.

"Xander will have to be the one to keep us informed. I just thought you might like to have the movers come before anything else happens."

No sound came out of Danae. Lys could tell she was in a bad way and she wanted to comfort her.

"Nassos's death came as a painful shock to both of us." The anguished look on Danae's face prompted Lys to reveal something she'd held back since the divorce. "I'd like to talk frankly with you. When my father died, I was afraid to come to Crete, where I didn't know anyone. But I was underage and as you know, Nassos made a promise to my father to take care of me in case he died. I realize that my arrival was probably your worst nightmare, but it was something I had no control over."

Danae lowered her eyes.

"You were so wonderful to me, I got over a lot of my pain and started to be happy with you. In time I learned to adore you. But you must know that *you* were the great passion of Nassos's life."

The other woman started to tremble.

"I have something to show you." Lys pulled the letter from Nassos out of her purse and handed it to her. Nassos hadn't meant anyone else to read it, but Lys couldn't keep it from Danae, who deserved to know the truth.

"So you won't think I'm holding anything back, I want you to read this. Xander gave it to me after reading the contents of the will to you."

She watched as the older woman took in the contents. Soon her shoulders shook.

"As you've read, Nassos wanted children and I happened to fill a hole in his heart for a while as the daughter you two never had."

Danae looked crushed and put a hand to her throat. "I—I was afraid I wouldn't be able to love a child that wasn't mine. That's why I didn't want to adopt."

"I can understand that. I'm sure a lot of childless parents worry about the same thing when they adopt. But you showed me so much love, perhaps it was just that Nassos had more faith in your parenting abilities than you did. When he moved to the penthouse after your divorce, he was a ruined man."

"Why didn't he tell me all these things?" she cried in agony.

"His pride. What about yours? Would you have listened?"

She shook her dark head. "I don't know. I don't know. I harbored a lot of resentment over the years because he didn't want me to work. When he begged me to consider adoption, I felt anger because of the many times I'd begged him to let me try even part-time work. We were both so hardheaded."

"I'm so sorry, Danae." As they stared at each other, Lys reached for the letter she put back in her purse. "I hope you'll listen to me now because there's something else I've wanted to tell you since your separation from him." Her throat swelled with emotion.

"I love you. You were kind and loving and helped me so much. The two of you had a beautiful marriage in so many ways. For what it's worth, you would have made a wonderful mother. Maybe there's a man out there who could fulfill that dream for you. Many women have babies at your age. It's not too late if you decide to get married again. You're a very beautiful woman."

A long silence ensued before Danae jumped up from the chair and hugged her hard. "Thank you for saying that to me. I love you too, Lys. You have no idea how much I've missed you."

With those words, Lys's pain was lifted. "I feel the same." She finally let go of Danae, and wiped her eyes. "Tell me something else. Would you have liked to inherit the hotel and run it?"

Danae shook her head. "It doesn't matter what I would have liked. He wanted a stay-at-home wife and didn't want me working at the hotel after we were married. Now I'm not interested."

"But you could read between the lines in his letter to me. He admitted he was wrong about divorcing you, and he was wrong not to have let you work alongside him after you were married."

She grasped Lys's hands. "You're very sweet, but it's too late for that."

"Are you sure? You could talk to Xander and fight for it. I'd step aside in an instant if I knew it was what you wanted."

"It isn't. Truly. But I'll take your advice and get movers in here to ship everything back to the villa."

"I'm glad about that!" Lys hugged her again, then headed for the foyer.

Danae followed. "Where are you going?"

"Back to my room. I need to return Anita's call. You remember my mother's friend? She came to Nassos's funeral."

"Of course. It was wonderful of her to come."

"I know. I couldn't believe she'd fly all this way from New York." Lys pressed the button that opened the elevator doors, then turned to Danae. "If you need anything, just phone me."

"I want you to come to the villa as soon as you can. It's so empty now."

"I promise to visit you all the time."

"You mean it?"

"Of course I do. I love you, Danae. *Yassou*."

Lys rode the private elevator six floors to the lobby, then took the main elevator back to the third floor. She needed to make a phone call to Anita on Long Island. They'd stayed in close touch over the years.

Anita had invited Lys to stay with her and her husband, Bob, for a time. Maybe a little vacation would be a good thing. Maybe not. She just didn't know.

The limo pulled up to the Rodino Hotel in Heraklion. For the moment he had business to take care of here. Lys Theron had no idea he'd flown to Heraklion two days ago to stay with his family. Now he was ready to talk to her, but he wanted the element of surprise on his side.

Before he'd left for New York, Takis had done every job there was to do there at the hotel for that year. He'd often escorted VIPs to the penthouse Nassos used for business. No doubt Lys Theron lived there now.

There was a private elevator down the right hall that went straight to the top. If Nassos hadn't changed his six-digit birthday code on the keypad, Takis would be able to go on up. Otherwise he'd have to phone her from downstairs. His pulse raced at the thought of seeing her again.

The code hadn't changed. After the doors opened, he stepped inside for the short ride and entered the outer hallway when it stopped. But he needed to alert her he was here. Even if it was presumptuous, when he explained how he'd gained access to the elevator, he hoped she'd understand.

Takis had just pressed the digits of the phone number written on the envelope she'd given him when the door to the penthouse opened. He received a surprise because instead of Lys Theron standing there, the stylish black-haired woman he'd seen at the older man's funeral emerged without her veil.

She glared at him. "No one is permitted up here. Who are you?"

"I'm sorry to have alarmed you," he murmured. "I was just calling Kyria Theron to let her know I was out here."

The attractive woman scrutinized him. "This isn't her apartment."

What?

"How did you get up here?"

Takis would have to proceed carefully. "I'm the new co-owner of the hotel." After many talks with his partners in the last week, that's what he was saying right now, but it was subject to change depending on many things.

"What's your name?" she murmured.

"Takis Manolis."

Her eyes widened. "Lys told me."

He nodded. "I saw you at the church on the day of

Nassos's funeral." This had to be the widow. "You must be Kyria Rodino."

"Yes. I was married to Nassos for twenty-four years and heard your name mentioned with fondness for the last twelve of them."

The revelation stunned him. "He was instrumental in changing my life. I'll never forget him."

Her eyes glistened over. "Neither will I."

Takis had a hard time taking it all in. "I'm very sorry for your loss. Please forgive me. I thought Kyria Theron lived here. Do you know where I can find her?"

"She has her own suite at the hotel. I have to leave and will ride down in the elevator with you."

Takis had made a big mistake coming up here.

Once they reached the hotel foyer, he thanked her for her help and the two of them parted company. He walked into the main lounge where he could be private and rang her number.

Before long he heard, "Kyrie Manolis?" She sounded surprised. "I wondered when I might hear from you."

"I just arrived at the hotel and am in the lounge. We have to talk." Before any more time passed he needed to explain that he'd trespassed earlier and had alarmed Nassos's former wife. "When will it be convenient for you?"

"I'll be right down."

"Efharisto."

Within two minutes the dark-blonde woman he'd come to see walked toward him dressed in a storm-gray crewneck sweater with long sleeves and a matching skirt. Some Cretan women in mourning wore darker clothes, if not black, for a long time.

Yet even garbed in somber colors, the feminine curves of her figure and the long legs he admired couldn't be hidden. She not only ignited his senses, but those of every male within her radius.

Takis had the additional advantage of being able to stare into those violet eyes at close range. When he'd been inside the church, he'd thought no eyes could be that color. At the time he'd assumed the sun shining through the stained glass had to have been responsible.

But the hotel lounge was no church. If anything, their color bordered on purple and mesmerized him almost as much as the enticing curve of her mouth. He wondered how many men had known its taste and had run their hands through hair as luscious as swirling caramel cream.

"It's nice to see you again, Kyrie Manolis."

"I've been looking forward to talking to you too. Since we're co-owners, I'd rather you called me Takis."

"So you've decided."

"Yes. Do you mind if I call you Lys?"

"I'd prefer it. If you'll come with me, we'll go to my suite to talk. Until the situation is settled and made official, I'd prefer us to meet in private rather than Nassos's office so we don't have to make explanations to anyone."

"You took the words out of my mouth."

They walked to the bank of elevators and took the next empty one that carried them to the third floor. He followed her to the end of the hall where she opened the door to a small foyer. It led into a typical hotel suite sitting room. Nothing special here, nothing that told him about her personality.

"There's a guest bathroom down that hall. If you'd like to freshen up, I'll call the kitchen and ask for lunch to be served. Anything special you would like?"

"Why don't you surprise me?" He watched her disappear before he left the room. When he returned, he found her seated in one of the chairs around the coffee table with the phone in her hand.

Her gaze wandered over him as he sat down. He enjoyed the sensation far too much and castigated himself. "Danae just called to tell me she met you outside the penthouse door looking for me. I'm curious. How *did* you gain access to the private elevator?"

He leaned forward with his hands clasped between this legs. "When I worked here for a year, I was given the code to take VIPs to the penthouse for Nassos."

A genuine smile broke out on her beautiful face. "You knew his birthday code."

"I'm afraid I couldn't resist finding out if it still worked, but I caught Kyria Rodino off guard. For that, I'm sorry."

"That's my fault. When I told you I lived at the hotel, I failed to be more specific. It wasn't until Nassos separated from Danae that he moved to the penthouse."

"I had no right to do what I did."

"I'm sure Danae was more amused than offended once you introduced yourself. It's something Nassos might have pulled if he'd been in your shoes. He had an impish side and indicated you were clever."

"If you translate that, it means I went where angels feared to tread far too often." The gentle chuckle that came out of her coincided with the rap on the door to the suite. Takis got up first. "I'll get it."

After tipping the employee, he carried their tray of food into the sitting room and put it on the coffee table. He removed the covers on *horiatiki* salad and Greek club sandwiches filled with lamb while she poured the coffee for them.

They both sat back to eat. She appeared hungry too. He swallowed his second half in no time. "This is an excellent lunch. Kudos to the chef."

"You can tell Eduardo yourself."

Takis glanced at her over his coffee cup. "My attorney examined the legal work and it is quite clear that Nassos didn't give either of us a choice. We're stuck for six months. How do you feel about that?"

She averted her eyes. "I don't have a right to feel much of anything. As I told you earlier, it's possible he didn't want me to be the sole owner for fear I might make bad decisions. The one man he felt he could trust was you, so I can understand why he made certain you would be there to help me if I got into trouble."

Nice as that compliment sounded, he didn't buy it. "*Have* you gotten into trouble in the past?"

His question seemed to unsettle her. She put her coffee cup on the table. "Not in business, but he didn't always approve of the men I've dated."

That had been the one thing on his mind since he'd

seen her in the church. If she was in a relationship now, he should be happy about it.

No doubt Nassos hadn't liked any male who tried to get too close to her. He'd probably had a man in mind for her, but only when the time was right. By becoming her guardian, he'd taken his responsibility seriously.

"Though I can't imagine it, is it possible he didn't want you to fall for someone who wanted more than your love?" A man would have to be blind not to want a relationship with her if he could. The fact that she was the owner of one of the most famous hotels in Greece would make a man heady if he could have both.

She sat back in the chair. "He couldn't have known that he would die this early in his life."

"No," he muttered. "No man knows that."

"But I wouldn't put it past him to have worried that I might make a bad emotional decision because of some man, even at the age of sixty or seventy."

"If Nassos had a fear that you could put the welfare of the hotel at risk no matter your age, he would never have willed half of it to you. I'm convinced your personal happiness was all that concerned him."

"Coming from you, that means a lot."

What Takis still hadn't worked out yet was why Nassos had made *him* co-owner. His partners had tried to disabuse him of the notion that when Nassos had made out his will, he'd seen Takis as the needy boy from Crete.

He still didn't want his father to know he'd inherited it from Nassos. He feared his parent wouldn't understand and would wonder what Takis had done to deserve such a gift.

Her features grew animated and she got to her feet to pour herself another cup of coffee. "Now that you're here, I have a proposition for you."

The course of their conversation intrigued him. "Go ahead."

"When six months have passed, Nassos said we could do whatever we wanted with the hotel. I'll be honest and tell you up front that I'd like to buy your half. I'll be twenty-seven by then and will have come into the inheritance from my father. Whatever price you set, I'll be able to meet it."

Takis hadn't been expecting a proposition like that. Her own father's inheritance would make her independently wealthy. There was no question she'd be able to buy him out. In half a year's time this unwanted situation could be turned around and he'd be done with it.

"On the face of it I like the idea. Since you worked with Nassos, then he would have taught you how to invest your money wisely."

Her eyes lit up, reaching his insides. "I'd like to think that's true. Takis...if it suits you, I'll continue to run the hotel, leaving you free to go back to your other businesses." If she was eager to see the last of him, he had news for her. "But if you want to be here full-time in a hands-on capacity to honor Nassos's wishes, then we'll work things out any way you'd like."

Hands-on?

Not only was she gorgeous, she was too good to be true. He hadn't known what to expect, but it wasn't this amenable woman whose only agenda he could see was to eventually own the hotel outright. If she had an ulterior motive somewhere, he hadn't detected it yet.

When she'd told him at the *castello* they were co-owners, hadn't Takis wanted to be free of Nassos's gift?

He got to his feet, troubled because she was seducing him without even trying. Not since losing his girlfriend had he felt such emotion. But this was much stronger because he was no longer an eighteen-year-old boy.

"You've made this insanely easy for me in every way. Why don't we meet tomorrow morning at the Villa Kerasia outside the city? The quiet, small back room of the dining area will help us to keep a low profile while we talk business and discuss where we go from here."

"That sounds good to me," she answered without taking a breath. "Before you leave, I wanted you to know that within the week the penthouse will be empty. You can use it, decorate it, do whatever you want."

"Thank you. But when I'm in Crete, I stay with my family."

Her eyes went suspiciously bright. "Of course. Tylissos isn't that far from here. How lucky you are to have family to come home to. I envy you."

"I *am* fortunate," he admitted, but his thoughts were on her. She'd just lost Nassos and would be vulnerable for a long time. Takis didn't want to feel any emotions where she was concerned, but to his chagrin she'd aroused much more in him than the urge to comfort her. "Thank you for lunch. I'll let myself out and see you in the morning. How does eight thirty sound to you?"

"Perfect."

So was she. Tomorrow he'd be with her again. It was the only reason he could leave the hotel at all.

CHAPTER FOUR

Lys awakened early the next morning. She'd been
restless during the night, otherwise her comforter
wouldn't be on the floor at the side of her bed. The
unexpected advent of Takis Manolis in her life had
shaken her world.

The fact that he would be co-owner of the hotel
with her for the next six months wasn't nearly as
disconcerting as the man himself. He was a Cretan
Adonis who'd gotten under her skin and had turned
her insides to mush the first time she'd laid eyes on
him. She wished to heaven she weren't excited to be
meeting him for breakfast, but she couldn't turn off
those hormones working madly inside her body.

There was nothing professional about her feelings
for him. She had no idea how she was going to be
able to work with him and not reveal how suscepti-
ble she was to his male charisma. No woman alive
could be indifferent to him. Somehow she needed to
be the exception. But she feared that it would be an
impossible task.

Once she'd showered and washed her hair, Lys
changed her mind five times about what to wear,
something she never did, which proved he was in

her head. She eventually settled on pleated navy pants with a navy blouse edged in navy lace and matching sweater.

Not only would she continue to wear dark colors to honor Nassos's memory, but she refused to dress in order to attract Takis's attention. Other women probably did it on a regular basis. But his appeal had affected her so greatly, it was embarrassing. She had no idea how long Danae would wear black before returning to her normal wardrobe. Lys would follow her example.

Once she'd brushed her hair and put on a soft pink lipstick, she left the hotel driving one of their service vans so she wouldn't be recognized by the paparazzi. She headed out of town under an overcast sky to the little settlement of Vlahiana southwest of Heraklion. She took in the beauty of the hills and vineyards rolling in the distance. Several villages clung to the hillsides, beckoning her toward them.

Takis had lived on Crete until he was eighteen and probably knew every inch of it. She was pleased he'd wanted them to meet at the small country inn hidden away where there wouldn't be any press around.

Nassos had once brought her and Danae here, explaining about the building that had been completely restored with ancient stones, a perfect blend with the near-white bleached wood. The artist in him had liked what had been done to it. She didn't wonder that Takis had chosen this same place to talk.

To her surprise, she saw his tall, well-honed physique walking toward her as she pulled up in the small parking area. He could have no way of knowing what she'd worn, but he'd dressed in charcoal-colored trousers and a navy sport shirt open at the neck, looking marvelous.

"We match," he said after opening the van door for her. As she got out, the scent of the soap he'd used in the shower assailed her senses. Her arm brushed against his chest by accident. The slight contact sent a thrill of excitement through her body. "I've already ordered our breakfast. It's waiting out on the back patio for us."

It turned out they had the area to themselves. The trellis roof above them dripped with shocking red bougainvillea. He helped her to sit at the small round table before he took a seat opposite her. The sight of so many delicious-looking items told her he was a typical Cretan who loved his food. There were sausages, smoked pork, eggs with *staka*, cream cheese pie and coffee.

She bit into a piece of pie. "If I ate this way every morning, pretty soon I wouldn't be able to get through the doors to the office."

"That will never be your problem, and I happen to think it's much nicer to eat while we talk business."

"I won't argue with you there." Her awareness of him made it difficult to keep her eyes off him while he devoured his food.

As he drank his coffee, he asked, "Were you running the hotel singlehandedly before Nassos died?"

"Pretty much, along with the general manager. Nassos spent most of his time watching over his other investments, which are now Danae's. But there's no question Nassos kept his eagle eye on everything. Since he's been gone, I've continued to do things the same way, but I'll admit I worry that I'm missing something."

"Do the staff know you're the new owner?"

"No. I'm sure they think that Nassos gave the hotel to Danae even though he divorced her. I know the manager assumes as much."

His piercing gaze stared directly into hers. "How do you feel about having to share the business with me?"

She sat back in the chair. "To be honest, when the attorney gave me Nassos's letter and I read what was inside, I almost went into shock. But by the time I flew to Italy, I'd managed to calm down."

"Your anger didn't show."

"I never felt anger. Not at all. If anything I felt hurt for Danae, who should have inherited the hotel. They met years ago while she'd been working at another hotel. She would be a natural to run everything, but he was too blind to see what he was doing."

He lowered his coffee cup. "You didn't expect to inherit?"

She frowned. "I didn't expect him to die, but I know what you meant to say. I had no expectations. I imagined that in time I'd meet a man, get married and years from now lose Nassos. Instead, he's gone and he has made you co-owner. That's all I know. But to answer your question, no, I'm not angry."

"What did you mean he was too blind?"

Lys shouldn't have said what she did. Now he'd dig until he got the answer he wanted. At this point it didn't matter if he knew the truth. In fact it would be better if it did.

"Tell you what. If you've finished eating, why don't we go to the hotel?" She was enjoying this time with him far too much. "If I show you the letter Nassos instructed the attorney to give to me, then you'll understand and won't have so many questions. I wish I had brought it with me. Did you bring a car?"

"No. I came in a taxi from home."

"Then I'll drive us back to town and we can talk in my sitting room at the hotel. Would it bother you if I'm behind the wheel?"

His half smile gave her a fluttery feeling in her chest. "I'm looking forward to it." He put some bills on the table before helping her up. It had been a long time since she'd been with a man, let alone have one to help her into the van.

The thrill of being with him was like nothing she'd ever experienced. She wished they were going off and not coming back. A silly thought, but one that told her she was in serious trouble where Takis was concerned.

Before long she pulled into the private parking space in the hotel garage and they rode the elevator to her floor. They'd done this before when she'd welcomed him inside her room. After telling him he was welcome to freshen up, she went into the bedroom to get the letter out of the side table drawer.

Once she'd made a detour to her own bathroom, she entered the sitting room and handed it to him before subsiding in one of the upholstered chairs around the coffee table. She'd never invited a man into her hotel room before. But with Takis, everything was feeling so natural.

Takis felt her eyes on him as he opened it to read. Within seconds he couldn't believe what Nassos had written to her. Near the end of it came the part where Takis's name was mentioned.

> Before you take possession, you must give the sealed envelope to Takis Manolis. You've heard me and Danae talk about him often enough. When he came to Crete periodically, we'd discuss business on my yacht, where we could be private.
>
> You'll know where to find him when the time comes. The two of you will share ownership for six months. After that time period, you'll both be free to make any decisions you want.
>
> By the time you read this, he's probably married with children and grandchildren too. I've thought of him as the son I never had.

The son Nassos never had?

"What's wrong, Takis? You've gone pale."

He must have read the whole letter half a dozen times before he realized he wasn't alone in the room. His head swung around. Takis had gotten it all wrong. He could throw the idea of pity out the window. Nassos *had* looked at him as a son. More than that, he'd looked on Lysette, his French nickname for her, as his daughter.

This letter explaining the reason for the Rodino divorce helped him understand why Lys had been hurt for Danae's sake. It showed his love for Lys and hinted of the affection and regard Nassos had felt for him.

Takis sucked in his breath. Nothing about the hotelier's actions where Takis was concerned had been the way he'd thought!

His friends had tried to convince him that the gift of the hotel had been Nassos's way of honoring him for making a success of his life. They'd been right. But without this letter, he'd have gone on threshing around for reasons that had no basis in truth.

He handed it back to her. "Thank you for letting me read it." His voice throbbed. "It's a gift I didn't expect. Because of your generosity I was allowed to see into Nassos's mind. Bless you for that, or I might have gone through the rest of my life being…unsettled."

Those heavenly purple eyes played over his face in confusion. "Why?"

"It's a long story."

"I'd like to hear it. Won't you sit down?"

He couldn't. Takis was too wired. If anyone deserved to know what had been going on inside him, she did. Her honesty and willingness to share something so private humbled him.

"Let me just say I thought Nassos pitied me because of my poor background."

She got to her feet. "I'm sure he did. The grandfather who raised him was ill and so poor, Nassos had to sell the fish he caught from a rowboat so they could live."

Takis's head reared. "I didn't know that."

"I'm not surprised. It pained him to talk about it. My own father's parents died in a ferry accident and a near-destitute aunt took him in, but sadly she too died early. My father and Nassos joined forces and started catching fish to sell so they wouldn't starve."

What she'd just told Takis blew his mind.

"No doubt when he discovered you were working at the hotel and showed such amazing promise after coming from a similar background as himself, he was glad to help you. He was always kind to people.

"If he'd known he was going to die this soon, I have no doubt that he would have given the hotel to you outright. He knew I'd be coming into my inheritance soon and would be able to make my way in the world just fine."

The more she talked, the more ashamed Takis felt for being so far off the mark. These revelations changed everything for him. He cleared his throat. "Do you like running the hotel?"

"Yes, but I haven't known anything else. When I flew to Italy to find you, I thought I might have to track you all the way to New York. My mother's best friend still lives on Long Island. When she came to the funeral, she invited me to stay with her for a while. I've toyed with the idea that if you wanted to work here and be by your family, I'd find a different kind of job in New York."

The thought of her not being here in Crete disturbed him more than a little bit. "You think I need breathing room?"

She cocked her head. "I don't know. *Do* you?"

What Takis needed was to put his priorities in order. His family took precedence over every consideration. Nassos's gift had opened up a way for him to have a legitimate reason to be on Crete for the next six months. But it was vital that as co-owner, she be the visible owner on duty while he was the invisible co-owner who helped behind the scenes.

"I'm going to share something I've never shared

with anyone but my two best friends and business partners. Except for visits to my family, I've been gone from Crete for eleven years. On my last visit here when I attended Nassos's funeral, my mother begged me to come home for good."

"That sounds like a loving mother," Lys said softly. Her genuineness made him believe she was truly happy for him.

"But they've never asked me for anything, or wanted anything from me, whether it be financial or something else. Now I'm worried about them and their health. Maybe I'm wrong about that. Nevertheless I'm planning to sell my hotels in New York and move here permanently to be near them all the time."

"I suspect they've been hoping for that for years."

"If that's true, I'm the last to know." Lys was easy to talk to. She made it comfortable for him, but the warning bells were going off that he was getting in over his head.

"Then you should move here and find out. It would be perfect for you and me. While you run the hotel and live around your parents, I can leave. If I find a new career in New York, then I might not want to buy out your half. In that case, when the six months are up, I'd rather you invested my half of the money from the hotel. Nassos's trust in you is good enough for me."

"I'm flattered that you have more faith in me than I do." But he shook his head, not liking that idea for any reason. Takis didn't want her to leave. It stunned him how strongly attracted he was to her. She was in his blood and he hadn't even kissed her yet. But that day was coming.

"In truth I don't want or need another hotel. The last thing I want is for anyone to know I'm co- owner. Yet for another half year that's the way it has to be and I plan to live out the rest of my life here. So unless your heart is set on going to New York, I'd prefer it if you would call the staff together and tell them you're the new owner of the hotel."

She got to her feet. "But that isn't the truth."

How strange that a few weeks ago he hadn't wanted this gift. Yet in just a short period of time everything had changed. Takis knew himself well and wondered if he could fallen in love with her in such a short space of time. He was overjoyed that for the next six months they'd be forced to remain joined at the hip so to speak.

"No one else needs to know that. I'll explain to Kyrie Pappas why I don't want any mention of me as the co-owner."

Her arched brows knit together. "I don't understand. You're being so mysterious."

"My family must never know my name is tied to the hotel."

She moved closer. "Why?"

"Because I'm a Manolis and there's only room for one Manolis hotel owner on Crete."

A long silence ensued. "You mean your father." She'd read his mind.

"If he knew the kind of gift Nassos had deeded to me—the kind only a father would give to his son—it would hurt him in a way you couldn't comprehend."

"Are you so sure about that?"

"Not entirely, but I love my father."

Tears filled her eyes. "I loved mine too. It's the

only reason I went to Crete with Nassos at the age of seventeen when I didn't want to."

"That had to have been very hard."

"It was in the beginning. I had to leave my friends and school, everything I knew. What I didn't know at the time was that in honoring Baba's wishes, I would learn to love Nassos. He gave me a new life and protected me because he understood a father's love and wanted to honor his best friend's wishes. I get the honor aspect, Takis."

Lys Theron was amazing. "Do you have any idea how grateful I am that you told no one about the will and came all the way to Italy to talk to me in person? Because of you, the secret is still safe."

She studied him for a long time. "I'll keep it. You're worried that if your father knew the truth, he would believe you had a much greater friendship with Nassos than he'd been led to believe. I can see why you think it could ruin your relationship for life."

How did someone so young get to be so wise? "I'm afraid it could," Takis whispered.

"I think you're wrong about it, but no one will ever know from me. I'll talk to Danae so she understands how serious this is to keep absolutely quiet."

No matter his feelings for her, he felt he could trust Lys with his life. "Thank you. But this brings us to our immediate problem. We'll have to conduct business without anyone suspecting the real reason we're together at all."

"What are you suggesting?"

"I've been giving it a lot of thought. When I leave you in a minute, I'm headed straight to the airport. I need to fly back to Milan and talk to my partners.

Among other things I'll have to make preparations to sell my hotel chain in New York and will probably be gone at least a week. When I come back, I'll have a proposition for you."

"Proposition?" she questioned.

"What goes around, comes around," he teased, reminding her of their conversation yesterday when she'd made one to him.

"Aren't you going to give me a hint?" The corner of her sensual mouth lifted, sending a burst of desire through him.

"Not yet. Certain things have to fit into place first."

"You're talking about the hotel in Milan. Do you plan to remain part owner?"

"Possibly." But that wasn't what he had on his mind while she filled his vision to the exclusion of all else. He had plans for them and knew in his gut that she wasn't involved with another man. Otherwise he would have to come up with another idea, but nothing had the appeal of the one he had his heart set on.

"Would you like a ride to the airport? I have an errand to run anyway."

Nothing she'd said could have made him happier. He still wanted to talk to her. "I'd appreciate it."

"I'll just ring Giorgos to let him know my agenda."

"That name isn't familiar to me. What happened to the other manager Nassos relied on in the past?"

"Yannis? He had to retire because his knee operations didn't work out well. He was hard to replace."

"I'm sorry to hear that. Is Giorgos a good manager?"

"Six months ago Nassos hired him as a favor for a close friend, but he had one reservation."

"What was that?"

"He was recently divorced, but he decided to give him a chance."

"Why would that matter?"

"I asked Nassos the same thing. He said it was just a feeling he had that Giorgos might not be able to concentrate on the job, but only time would tell. After the letter Nassos left for me revealing his torment over divorcing Danae, I suppose his concerns about Giorgos made sense. The man moved here from Athens, where he'd been a hotel manager with an excellent reference."

Interesting. "How do you like him so far?"

"I think he's very good at what he does."

"But?"

"I can tell he's lonely."

"Why do you say that?"

"Whenever I start to leave the office, he wants to talk for a while."

Takis struggled not to smile. "Is he attractive?"

"So-so."

"Does he have children?"

"No."

"How old is he?"

"Thirtyish I believe."

A dangerous age. Giorgos must have thought he'd died and arrived in the elysian fields when he discovered Lys on the premises.

While she made the phone call, the proposition he intended to put to her had grown legs.

CHAPTER FIVE

When her phone rang, Lys had been out on the patio of Danae's villa talking with her about Takis and his fragile relationship with his father. She checked the caller ID before clicking on. "Yes, Giorgos?"

"I don't mean to intrude on your day off, but there was a man at the front desk asking for you a few minutes ago. He didn't leave his name. I told him I'd schedule an appointment, but I needed information first. All he said was that you would know who he was and he'd be back later."

Lys shot to her feet out of breath. *Takis?* But surely he would have phoned her if he'd flown to Crete! He'd been gone a week, but it had felt like a month. Seven days away from him had proven to her how much he had come to mean to her, feelings that went soul deep.

"Did you hear what I said? Do you want security when you return?"

She'd forgotten Giorgos was on the phone. "Was this man threatening in some way?"

"No. But he had an attitude that sounded too familiar and possessive for my liking."

If anyone sounded possessive it was Giorgos, whose observation surprised her. "Thank you for the warning, but I'm not worried. I'll be back at the hotel later."

After hanging up she told Danae what happened. The older woman cocked her head. "Who else could it be but Takis? Aside from Nassos, he's the most exciting man I've *almost* ever bumped into."

Lys chuckled.

"The man's charm is lethal. I have no doubt it rattled Giorgos, who, according to Nassos, was interested in you from the moment he came to work."

"You're kidding—"

This time it was Danae who laughed. "When Nassos realized Giorgos was invisible to you, he stopped worrying that he'd hired him."

"I had no idea I was that transparent."

"There were two or three men you dated that gave us concern because you seemed so swayed by them. We felt you were too young and we ran interference for your sake. But it was when you started seeing Kasmos Loukos, whose father owns the Loukos Shipping lines in Macedonia, we grew very nervous.

"That spoiled young man had already been seen with too many wealthy celebrities. Nassos knew Kasmos was shopping around for the best female prospect to build on his father's fortune. When we saw the way he went about seducing you, we were fearful you might really be in love with him. The problem was, you were an adult. We couldn't do anything about it, and only hoped you could see through him before it was too late."

"Which I did. One night he started talking to me about Nassos, asking questions that were none of his business. That's when a light went on and I remembered all the lessons you'd tried to teach me. I was no longer blinded and told him I didn't want to see him anymore. You should have seen his face—"

"Thank goodness that relationship didn't last! I'm afraid neither Nassos nor I ever thought you'd met your match. Speaking of which, I think you'd better take the helicopter back to the hotel so you can meet up with this mystery man before you die of curiosity."

Heat crept into her cheeks. "I'm not dying," Lys muttered.

"You could have fooled me." She reached for her phone. "I'll alert the pilot."

Lys checked her watch. Ten after one. She'd been here a long time. The two of them were closer than ever. They were family and needed each other while they mourned their loss. No longer did Lys want to go to New York except for a visit to the Farrells'. Her life was here. Takis was here and not going anywhere. *Joy.*

She walked over to hug her. "Have a lovely evening with Stella. Don't get up. I'll see myself out."

"Let me know how this ends."

"You know I will. Love you."

After leaving the villa, she walked out to the pad and climbed on board the helicopter. Within fifteen minutes the pilot landed on top of the Rodino Hotel. She took the elevator to the third floor and freshened up in her suite. With the blood pounding in her ears, she went down to the lobby.

If Takis was here and waiting in the lounge, he'd see her. But since he still hadn't phoned her, she began to think it must have been some other man. Lys couldn't think who that would be unless it was a high-tech salesperson not wanting to go through Giorgos to reach her.

Magda, one of the personnel on duty at the desk, waved her over. "Giorgos told me to watch for you. I'll get him." The woman hurried off before Lys could tell her not to bother.

A second later he came out of his office and walked toward the counter where she was standing. At the same time, she felt two hands slide around her waist from behind.

"Forgive me," Takis whispered. "I have my reason for doing this."

The intimacy brought a small gasp to her lips. She whirled around, meeting those intense hazel eyes that were devouring her.

"Don't look now, but Giorgos is having a meltdown," he murmured. She wouldn't have understood what he meant if she hadn't just had a certain conversation with Danae about the manager. Their mouths were mere centimeters apart. His warm breath on her lips excited her so much, she forgot that she was clinging to his arms. "I'll answer your questions later. Come with me first. We're going for a ride."

Her heart nearly ran away with her as he kept an arm around her shoulders and they left the hotel. Instead of walking her to a taxi, he helped her into a black, middle-of-the-line Acura parked in the registration check-in line. Leon, one of the staff members outside, stared at the two of them in surprise.

Takis started up the engine and darted into the heavy main street traffic in front of the resort. When she could find her voice she said, "This smells brand new."

He flashed her a smile. "I just drove it off the lot. I'm here for the next six months and need transportation." His choice of car made total sense considering the modest income of his family.

"My driving must have frightened you more than I realized."

"Are you saying you would have agreed to be my chauffeur day and night? If so, we'll drive back to the car dealership and turn it in."

Lys laughed gently while he drove them along the harbor road to the Venetian Fortress of Koules. He pulled into a parking space where they could watch the boats.

After shutting off the engine, he turned to her, stretching his arm along the back of the seat. "I owe you an explanation. Thank you for going along with me back there."

"I take it you wanted to make a statement. So why did you do it?"

"In order for us to be together so no one knows the underpinnings of our relationship, I'm proposing we do something shocking. How would you feel about getting engaged to me?"

Engaged?

Lys looked away, literally stunned by what he'd just said.

"Hear me out before you tell me how outrageous I'm being. It could be the one thing that will make it easier to help us achieve our main goal."

"What do you mean?"

"Don't you agree the most important one is for us to get through the next six months honoring Nassos's wishes?"

Her pulse had started to race. "That goes without saying."

"An engagement will give us the perfect cover. While you run the hotel, I'll spend real time with my family. When I whisk you away for a little personal time together, or spend time in your hotel room, no one will know I'm helping you behind the scenes."

Lys struggled to sit still. Nassos had told her Takis was a genius with vision, but this proposition went beyond the boundaries of her imagination. The thought of being engaged to him robbed her of breath.

"The only way the manager will understand why you and I are spending time together and not become suspicious is *if* he thinks we're romantically involved. I was simply setting the scene."

A thrill of alarm passed through her body. "There's no doubt you accomplished your objective a few minutes ago," she said in a tremulous voice.

"It had to be convincing. Tell me something. When you flew to Italy, did the staff know you were leaving the country?"

"Only Giorgos, but I didn't tell him where and let him assume what he wanted."

"That's perfect. Just now it didn't hurt for him and other members of the staff to see us meet in the lobby and assume we have a history away from Crete. When we walked out of the hotel with my arm around you, it no doubt created a new wave of gossip."

"You *know* it did." Being that close to him practically gave her a heart attack.

"If we're engaged, it'll be about you and me for a change. I'm aware the old gossip came close to crucifying you. An engagement would put an end to it."

"I can't imagine anything more wonderful than changing that particular conversation." She took an extra breath. "I'll admit it was awful for Danae too."

He studied her for a moment. "Neither of you deserved this. It pains me for both of you. The new gossip you and I create will cause people to see you in a new light. With a ring on your finger from me, the old news will be forgotten."

She closed her eyes tightly. He was making it sound possible and that increased her nervousness. If this proposal had come from his heart, she'd be in heaven. But it hadn't, and she needed to remember that.

"Lys?" he prodded.

"Can you tell me what you've decided to do about your other businesses?"

"I'm already in negotiations to sell my chain of hotels in New York and invest the money. After talking it over with my partners, I'm going to stay committed to them. The *castello* hotel-restaurant will be the only asset I own and I'll fly to Milan when necessary."

"I'm sure they'll be happy about that." Her voice shook from emotions sweeping through her. "Do your parents know what you've done?"

He nodded. "I've told them I've come home for good and want to help out at the family hotel. My father hasn't said anything about that yet. Lukios has indicated I'm not needed. He explained they would have to let someone else go who must keep their job. I understood that and told him I'd be happy to do some advertising around Crete to bring in more clients."

"What did he say?"

"He shook his head and left the living room with

the excuse that he was needed at the front desk and we'd talk later."

"I'm sorry, but these are early days. Your mother must be ecstatic!"

"I think she's still in shock that I haven't gone back to Italy yet."

"You'll have to give your family time before everyone accepts the fact that you're home permanently. But you have to know she's thrilled, and she's the one to work on. After all, your mother was the one who begged you to come home permanently. In the meantime, you can offer to do little things for her."

Takis studied her intently. "You're a very intuitive woman, so I'm going to take your advice. A few more days and they might be more receptive to the idea of my helping around the hotel. Maybe I'll be able to break my parents down enough so they'll start confiding in me."

Lys moistened her lips nervously. "I'm sure things will get better for you, but I'm afraid you haven't thought out your proposition carefully enough where I'm concerned."

"What do you mean?"

"If you were to tell them we're engaged, it could make things a lot worse for you. I've been in the news recently. Have you thought they might not approve of me?"

His brows furrowed. "If you're the woman I've chosen, they won't say anything no matter their personal feelings. I know that if my mother heard your whole story, she'd be thrilled. Besides, deep down she's had a fear I'd end up with some foreigner and as you're half Cretan, she'll be overjoyed."

"I *am* part foreigner," Lys murmured. "How would you explain our meeting?"

"That's simple. We met at the *castello* hotel in Italy while you were on vacation a while ago. It was love at first sight and we've been together ever since."

His words sank deep in her psyche. It might not have been love at first sight, but a powerful emotion had shaken her to the core when he'd walked in his office to find her there. That emotion continued to grow stronger until she knew he was the man she'd been waiting for all her adult life.

Lys looked away from him. "How will you explain it when we break up in six months and call off the engagement?"

"I don't know. Right now I'm trying to navigate through new waters because of what Nassos has done to us. This situation could have happened forty years from now, but it didn't. You and I are both vulnerable for a variety of reasons and we need to think this through carefully if we're going to do it right."

"I agree."

"Isn't it interesting to realize Nassos had no way of knowing that he'd done me a favor when he deeded me half the hotel. It has forced me to come home and try to make a difference for my family, something I should have done a long time ago."

Lys could feel his pain. "I'm sorry you have the worry of their health on your mind."

"I've been living with it for a while. Maybe I've been wrong and misread what I thought about mother. Just because she has aged a little doesn't mean she's ill."

"That's probably all it is."

"Cesare has accused me of leaping to conclusions. Still, if one of them is ill, I need to find that out. But they're so closed up, it'll take time to pry them open if they're keeping a secret from me. Nothing else is as important to me right now."

"I can relate," her voice trembled. "After Nassos hit his head, he pretended that everything was fine, but I could tell he wasn't himself and it gnawed at me. So I can understand how disturbed you are by your mother's plea that you move back here."

He flicked her an all-encompassing glance. "No matter what, it's my worry. The decision of our getting engaged is up to you. If I see one problem, it's how Danae would feel about it. If neither of you is comfortable with the idea, then we'll figure out another way to proceed."

After Lys's conversation at the villa with Danae earlier in the day, she had no clue how the other woman would react over such an unorthodox idea. But you couldn't compare Takis in the same breath with any other man. Even Danae had admitted as much.

"I—I don't know what Danae will say…" Her voice faltered.

"I realize you love and respect her, and you are uncertain with good reason. Even if Danae could see some value in it, she would probably tell you no. Six months of being engaged to me will prevent you from meeting a man you might want to marry. It will rob you of an important chunk of time out of your life."

"And yours!"

"Let's not worry about that. What matters most to me is to be back with my family where I'm able to make a contribution any way I can and still be a sounding board for you without anyone knowing."

Lys was so confused she couldn't think straight. He'd brought up some valid points that went straight to the heart of their individual dilemmas. But she needed to sort out her thoughts and would have to talk to Danae.

He sat back and turned on the engine. "I need to get home, so I'm going to drive you back to the hotel. I'm in no hurry for a decision. There's no deadline. I'll leave it up to you to contact me when you want to discuss hotel business."

Before long he pulled up in front of the hotel. Lys could tell he was anxious to leave. "We'll talk soon, Takis. Take care."

"Just a minute." He leaned across and kissed her briefly on the mouth. She couldn't believe what had just happened. "I needed that," he whispered before she opened the door and got out.

Her heart thudding, she rushed past Leon without acknowledging him. Her only desire was to get to her room where she could react to his kiss in private. After what he'd just done, the thought of a fake engagement to Takis had caused her heart to pound to a feverish pitch. She feared she was already running a temperature. When she could gather her wits, Lys would phone Danae. They needed to talk.

Takis drove to Tylissos, still savoring the taste of Lys, whose succulent mouth was a revelation. He'd never be the same again.

Before long he stopped by the children's hospital. After phoning his mother to find out if she needed him to do any errands for her, he discovered that Kori had taken Cassia to the doctor because of another asthma attack. It meant she'd been forced to leave her part-time work at the restaurant. Takis told his mother he'd look in on them.

He found his older sister holding his niece in her arms while she recovered after the medication they'd given her.

"Tak-Tak," his little niece cried when she saw him enter the room and held out her arms. Takis gathered her to him and gave her a gentle hug, kissing her neck.

"Do you feel better now?"

"Nay. Go home."

Takis looked at his sister, who had the same dark auburn hair as her daughter, the color of cassia cinnamon. "Did the doctor say she could leave?"

"Yes, but I have to wait until Deimos goes off shift to pick us up."

"But that won't be until nine thirty tonight. Tell you what. I'm going to slip out and buy an infant seat for my car. Then I'll drive you to work."

"You have a car?"

"I bought one this morning. I need transportation now that I'm back for good."

She stared hard at him. "You're really going to live here again?"

He nodded. "I never planned to be gone this long. Now that I'm home, I'm staying put." Just being here to help his sister let him know he'd done the right thing to come back to Greece for good.

Takis handed a protesting Cassia to her mother. "This won't take me long. When I get back, I'll run you by the restaurant and take her to the hotel with me." His mother tended Cassia when Kori had to go to work.

Her face looked tired but her light gray eyes lit up. "Are you sure?"

"There's nothing I'd love more." He leaned over to give them both a kiss on the cheek. "See you in a few minutes."

Takis hurried out of the hospital and drove to a local store, where he bought a rear-facing and two forward-facing car seats. That way he could take all his nieces and nephews to the park at once.

Within a half hour he was back and had fastened Cassia in her new seat. He would put in the other seats when he had the time. Kori sat next to him while he drove her to the Vrakas restaurant, where Deimos cooked traditional Cretan cuisine.

"Don't worry about anything. I'll take good care of her."

"I know that. She loves you. So do I." Her eyes filled with tears. "Thank you. I'm so glad you've come home." Her love meant everything to Takis.

After she hurried inside, he chatted with Cassia during the short ride to the old Manolis Hotel. He pulled around the back next to his father's truck. Lukios's car wasn't here, which meant he'd gone to his house a block away. Both his brother and sister lived nearby.

"Come on, sweetheart." He lifted her out of the seat and entered the private back door where his parents had lived in their own apartment since their marriage. "Mama? Look who I've got with me!" His mother came running from the kitchen into the living room. "She's breathing just fine now."

"Ah!" She pulled Cassia into her arms. "Come with me and I'll give you some grape juice." Grapes grew in profusion on this part of Crete.

"Tak-Tak!" his niece called to him, not wanting to be parted from him. He smiled because she couldn't say the *is* part yet. He grinned at his mother, who laughed.

"I'm right behind you, Cassia."

While his father was busy with hotel business, he had his mother to himself in the kitchen. She put a plate of his favorite homemade *dakos* on the table, a combination of rusk, feta cheese, olives and tomatoes. Cassia sat in the high chair drinking her juice while he devoured six of them without taking a breath and finished off the moussaka.

Afterward he held Cassia and read to her from a bundle of children's books he'd brought her on his last trip home. She had a favorite called *Am I Small?* He had to read it to her over and over again.

The little Greek girl in the story asked every animal she met if she was small. It had a surprise ending. Cassia couldn't wait for it. Neither could Takis, who was totally entertained by her responses.

At quarter to ten, Kori ran into the apartment and found her daughter asleep in his arms. She thanked him with a hug and hurried out to the car where Deimos was waiting for them.

Takis turned out lights and went to bed in the guest room he used whenever he came home for a visit. However, now that he was back for good, he needed to figure out where to live. Tomorrow he'd look around the neighborhood and find a house like his brother's and Kori's, close to the hotel.

Takis took a long time to get to sleep, knowing the nub of his restlessness had to do with a certain female who'd come to live in his heart. They weren't engaged yet, but the way he was feeling, he didn't know how he was going to keep his desire for her to himself much longer. Earlier in the car he'd kissed her, but it hadn't lasted long enough and he'd been forced to restrain himself.

The next morning, he installed the other two car seats before visiting a Realtor in the village. By late afternoon he'd finally been shown a small Cretan stone house he liked with a beautiful flowering almond tree. It had been up for sale close to a year and was two blocks away from the hotel. The place suited him with two bedrooms upstairs and a little terrace over the lower main rooms covered in vines.

Takis stood in the kitchen while they talked about the need to paint the interior and upgrade the plumbing. The house would do for him and not stand out. While he and the Realtor finished up the negotiations, his cell phone rang. One check of the caller ID caused his adrenaline to kick in. He swiped to accept the call.

"Lys?"

"I'm glad you answered." She sounded a little out of breath. "Can you talk?"

"In a few minutes I'll be free for the rest of the evening."

"I just flew back from Kasos." She'd been with Danae. "How soon can you meet me at my suite?" The fact that she wanted to see him right away might not be good news, but he refused to think that way.

"I have a better idea. I'll pick you up in front of

the hotel in a half hour. There's something I want to show you. We'll talk then."

"All right. I'll be ready."

He hung up and thanked the Realtor, who drove them back to his office. The older man handed him the keys to the house. Takis walked outside to his car with a sense of satisfaction that he was now a homeowner on Crete, the land of his ancestors.

En route to Heraklion, he stopped for some takeout of his favorite foods; rosemary-flavored fried snails, *Sfaki* pies and a Greek raki liqueur made from grapes. He liked the idea of sharing his first meal in his own home with Lys where they could be alone.

Before long he reached the hotel. Lys stood out from everyone when he pulled up in front. Her black blouse and dark gray skirt made the perfect foil for the tawny gold hair he was dying to run his hands through. He leaned across and opened the door for her.

"Hi!" Lys climbed in the front, bringing her flowery fragrance with her. "Umm. Something smells good," she remarked as he drove away and headed out of town.

"I'm hungry and thought we could eat after we reach our destination."

"Where are we going?"

"To Tylissos. I bought a house today and thought you might like to see it."

She made a strange sound in her throat. "Already?"

"My parents' apartment is small. They don't need another person underfoot while they tend my niece during the day. She naps on the bed I use while I'm here."

"How old is she?"

"Cassia is three. I'm crazy about her. The cute little thing has chronic asthma. Yesterday my sister had to take her to the hospital so the doctor could help her, but she's back home now."

"Oh, the poor darling."

"She handles it like there's nothing wrong. Now tell me about you. I take it you've had a talk with Danae."

"Yes."

The short one-syllable answer could mean anything. "Is it a good or bad sign that you can't look at me? Don't you know I'm fine with whatever you have to say?" At least that's what he was telling himself right this minute.

"After discussing everything with Danae, she surprised me so much I'm not sure what I am supposed to say."

He left that answer alone and drove into Tylissos and it wasn't long before he pulled up next to a house on the corner. "We've arrived."

While she got out, he reached for the bag of food on the backseat. After they walked to the front door, he put the key in the lock and opened it. "Welcome to my humble abode. I'm afraid we'll have to eat in the kitchen standing up."

Her chuckle reminded him not everyone had such a pleasant nature. So far there wasn't anything about her he didn't love. While she wandered around, he put their cartons of food on the counter next to the utensils.

After a minute, she came back and they started to eat. "Your house is charming, especially the terrace."

"Best seen at twilight." The house needed work from the main floor up.

"Takis—"

They both smiled in understanding. It felt right to be here with her like this. He'd never known such a moment of contentment and wanted to freeze it.

Once he'd poured the *raki* into plastic cups, he handed one to her. *"To our health,"* he said in Greek. They drank some before he asked her what Danae had said. She kept drinking. "Why are you so reticent to tell me?"

Her frown spoke volumes. "I wish I hadn't talked to her at all."

"Why?"

"Because she thinks an engagement could be a good idea for the reasons you suggested, but she says it doesn't go far enough."

"What does she mean?"

"Her blessing is contingent on us taking the engagement a step further, which makes this whole discussion ridiculous."

"How much further?"

She shook her head. "None of it matters."

"It does to me. Go on."

"I told Danae about everything you confided in me concerning your relationship with your family, especially your father. She was very sympathetic, but she's convinced they won't believe you're serious about living here for good unless we put a formal announcement of our engagement in the paper."

Elated with that response, he said, "I tend to agree with her."

Lys looked surprised. "That's not all," she murmured, not meeting his eyes.

"What's wrong?"

"She says we'll have to put a wedding date in the announcement, but the paper won't publish it if the date is longer than three months away. That's so soon!"

A strange sensation shot through Takis. If he believed in such things, he had the feeling Nassos had spoken through Danae. No one could sew up a deal like Nassos, covering all the bases. "What reason did she give?"

"I was raised in the Greek Orthodox church and so were you. She knows your parents are traditionalists. Because of the scandal that surrounded me after Nassos died, a promise of marriage to me in the writeup will show their friends and neighbors that you never believed the gossip about me.

"Danae said that in honoring me that way, they'll see you intend to be a good, loyal husband and they'll be happy you've come home for good. Every parent wants to see his or her child making plans to settle down and have a family. Anything less than a newspaper announcement with a wedding date won't carry the necessary weight."

The woman was brilliant. "Danae's right. Did she say anything else?"

After pacing the floor, she came to a halt. "Yes. After knowing your history, she says she likes you and approves of you for my husband. She knows Nassos would approve of you too."

That sounded exactly like something Nassos would have said in order to protect Lys. "I'm humbled by her opinion. She's a true Cretan. The more I think about it, the more I know she's right about everything she said. How do you feel about it?" The blood hammered in his ears while he waited for her answer.

"I—I didn't expect her to be so direct," she stammered.

"You still haven't answered my question. Does it upset you that I'm the first man Danae has ever approved of for you?"

Her knuckles turned white while her hands clenched the edge of the counter. "I'm not upset."

"Then why are you so tense?"

"We're not in love! We don't intend to actually get married—" Lys protested. "It would hurt your family too much to pretend something that won't happen. I told Danae as much, so we'll forget the whole idea of an engagement."

His eyes narrowed on her features. "I don't want to forget any of it. The idea of marrying you appeals to me more and more."

A quiet gasp escaped her lips. "Please be serious, Takis."

"I've never been more serious in my life. When I first suggested the idea of getting engaged, my main concern was to fit in with my family again and it seemed the perfect way to do it. But now I find that I want to be married, and Danae is right. Three months will be a perfect amount of time to grow close before we get married."

Color filled her cheeks. "We'd probably end up not being able to stand each other!"

Someone was on his side. Lys hadn't said no to the whole idea because she loved Danae and listened to her. "That's the whole point of an engagement, isn't it? To find out how we really feel? I know how I really feel at this moment."

In the next breath, he pulled her into his arms. After kissing her long and hard, he relinquished her mouth. "Do you think you could see yourself living in this house as my wife? I'd give you free reign to furnish it any way you like."

"Don't say any more," she cried softly and eased away from him. "You told me you want acceptance from your family. I can promise you that won't happen when they find out I'm the daughter of the man who gave you your first job in New York. I represent everything that took you away from them in the first place."

When he'd confided in her at his lowest ebb, she'd taken his pain to heart. Unfortunately, he'd done too good a job and needed to turn this around.

"Besides the fact that I left Crete of my own free will, keep in mind we didn't meet until a few weeks ago. When I tell them I've found the woman I want to marry, you have nothing to worry about."

CHAPTER SIX

THE WOMAN HE wanted to marry?

After the intensity of that kiss, Lys was dying to believe him. Deep in her heart she wanted marriage to Takis with every atom in her body, but she was too confused to think.

Astounded by the strength of her feelings, she said, "It's getting dark… I need to get back to the hotel."

Ignoring him, she put everything in the bag except the bottle of liqueur, which she left on the counter. They walked out of the house and Lys hurried to his car. As she put the bag in the backseat, Takis caught up with her and slid behind the wheel.

"On the way home I'll drive you past the Manolis Hotel. It looks like something Cassia would build with her blocks. Two for the bottom floor and one for the top."

Several turns brought them to the main street where the buildings sprang from the cement and had grown side by side. Because of his description, she picked it out immediately, painted in yellow with dark-brown-framed windows and matching tiles on the roof. A sign hung over the bottom right entrance.

He stopped in front, not pressing her to talk about

anything. During the last eleven years, she assumed nothing here had changed in all that time. She thought about the eighteen-year-old boy who'd wanted to help expand his father's hotel business. Instead, he'd ended up in New York thanks to Nassos and her father. Now he'd come full circle and was back for good.

"What are you thinking?"

She took a deep breath. "That you've accomplished miracles in your life."

His features took on a grim cast. "I'll take the one that hasn't happened yet."

She presumed he was talking about his relationship with his father. Her heart ached for what he was going through.

He started driving again and they headed for Heraklion. "Since you know where I'll be living and how I'm spending my time, I'll leave it up to you to decide when you want to get together to talk business."

Nassos couldn't have known his will would put them in such a difficult position. In Italy Takis had told Cesare he didn't want the hotel, let alone the complication of it being tied to Lys.

"Takis? Are you worried that if we don't get engaged, somehow word will reach your father that there's another reason you're tied to the hotel when we're seen together?"

"Anything's possible, but I'll deal with it by Skyping with you on the computer when you feel the need for a meeting."

"I still wouldn't do that in the office where Giorgos or one of the staff could walk in."

"Then we'll do it from your hotel room."

By the time he'd driven up in front of the hotel,

she was in torment. He got out and came around to open her door. "I'll be working on my house for the next week. If anything comes up, give me a call. *Kalinikta,* Lys."

"Good night," she whispered. "Thank you for the delicious food."

"You're welcome," he whispered against her lips before kissing her. Lys's attraction to him was overpowering. Obeying a blind need, she kissed him back again and again, relishing the slight rasp that sent tingles of desire through her body. After that, she found the strength to dash inside the hotel entrance to the elevators.

With pounding heart she reached her room, filled with unassuaged longings. After a minute when she had caught her breath, she called the front desk to find out if there were any messages for her. Thankful when she learned there was nothing pressing, she hung up and took a shower.

Lys had hoped to fall asleep watching TV, but she couldn't concentrate. Throughout the night she tossed and turned. Her fear that Takis's father would learn about Nassos's willed gift wouldn't leave her alone. Her mind relived what Danae had told her, that she approved of Takis and felt he'd make the right husband for her. Lys was so in love, she wanted him for her husband.

Takis hadn't asked for Nassos's gift. Who would have dreamed he would pass away this early in life? Nassos hadn't known the degree of fragility between Takis and his father, otherwise he wouldn't have put Takis in this situation. Nassos would have found another way to show his admiration.

When morning came, she felt like she hadn't slept at all and knew she had to see Takis again. He'd become her whole life! After eating breakfast in her room, she dressed in dark brown pleated pants with a matching-colored long-sleeved sweater.

Once she'd run a brush through her hair and had applied an apricot frost lipstick, she went down to the office to return phone calls and talk to some vendors. She texted Danae that she'd call her later in the day. Lys wasn't prepared to talk to her yet.

Around noon she told Giorgos she was leaving without giving him a reason and headed for the parking garage before he could detain her. Giorgos couldn't hide his frustration that she'd been avoiding him. Takis had planted a seed. Clearly it had taken root.

Once out on the road, she made several stops to buy souvlaki, fruit and soda. All the way to Takis's house she hoped she'd see his car parked outside. To her relief she did find the car there and parked behind it. Anxious to talk to him, she grabbed the sack of food and hurried to the front door. After knocking twice with no response, she tried the handle. To her surprise it opened.

"Takis?" she called out. "Are you here?" No answer. She crossed through to the kitchen and saw a couple of old wooden chairs and a card table. On the counter he'd left a coffee thermos. He must have gone somewhere. Maybe he'd gotten hungry and had walked to the hotel that was only a few blocks away.

She put the food on the table knowing he'd be back or he wouldn't have left the door unlocked. While she waited for him, she went up the small staircase to the second floor. Both tiny bedrooms were separated by a bathroom that needed work. And before she could prevent the thought from forming, she decided that one of the bedrooms would make a perfect nursery.

Each had a door that opened onto the terrace. You would need a railing if you brought children over here. In her mind's eye she could picture a lovely table with a colorful umbrella surrounded by chairs and pots of flowers.

Beyond the village the view looked out on the ancient Minoan site with its archaeological ruins, reminding her of the statue of King Minos on Takis's desk in Italy.

While she stood there near the edge, deep in thought, she saw a pickup truck turn the corner and pull up behind her car. All kinds of equipment filled the bed. Her pulse raced as she saw two men get out. The taller of the two, an Adonis dressed in jeans and a white T-shirt, looked up and waved to her.

"*Yassou*, Lys! I'll be in as soon as I unload the truck!"

"Let me help!"

Excited he'd come, she hurried downstairs and opened the front door. His brother—it couldn't be anyone else with those features—had red tinges in his dark blond hair. He brought in a ladder and some paint cans. Takis followed, carrying other paint equipment and drop cloths.

His eyes, that marvelous hazel green, played over her. "I'm glad you're here." His deep velvety voice wound its way through her body, igniting her senses. He put everything down in the living room. "Lukios?

I'd like you to meet Lys Theron. Lys? This is Lukios Manolis."

Takis had told her that Lukios hadn't been friendly the other day. Lys had hoped for his sake that his brother would warm up. It appeared they were getting along better now and that knowledge made her happy.

"You're the wonderful brother he's told me about. It's so nice to meet you. I've been anxious to meet Takis's family." She smiled and put out her hand.

The other man shook it. "How do you do," he said in a subdued voice. His eyes swerved back and forth at the two of them, trying to figure things out. She had no doubt he'd seen her in the news.

"I thought Takis might be hungry while he worked, so I brought lunch. It's in the kitchen. He has such a big appetite, I bought enough for half a dozen people. Please feel welcome to eat with us if you'd like."

He looked taken back. "Thank you. Have you known each other long?"

Without giving Takis a chance to answer, she said, "Quite a while. We met in Italy while I was on vacation. Those were your children in the photos I saw on his desk at work? Both yours and your sister, Kori's. They are adorable. Your parents must be crazy about their grandchildren."

"They are," he murmured.

"In case you didn't know yet, Takis asked me to marry him yesterday and brought me here to see where we're going to live."

Lukios blinked. "I had no idea."

"He surprised me too." She smiled at him. "Since he told me I could decorate it any way I want, I decided to start with a housewarming present by offering my services to help with the painting."

"How come *I'm* so lucky?" Takis interjected, as if they had no audience. His eyes gleamed.

She knew what her response had meant to him and heat swept through her body. By throwing herself into his suggestion for an engagement, she had no choice but to be a hundred percent committed and go all the way.

"This is such a cozy house, I'm anxious to see how we can bring it to life."

Takis moved closer. "All I brought with me today is the primer for the walls. After we've put it on, we'll go to the paint store and decide on the best color for the rooms."

Lys had really done it now! She'd taken him by complete surprise, but it hadn't thrown him. Nothing did. Takis was always several steps ahead no matter the situation. His responses since coming in the house had to have convinced his brother that their relationship was all but sealed.

"Come in the kitchen, Lukios. Let me serve you while you tell me about your family. What is your wife's name? I'm sure Takis told me, but I can't remember."

"It's Doris."

"That's it. I had a friend in school named Doris too! I understand your two children are older than Cassia."

He blinked, as if he were surprised she knew so much. "Paulos and Ava. They're four and five."

"What a blessing. I always wanted siblings, but

my mother died when I was little. My father never remarried, so it was just me."

"That must have been hard."

"Yes, but I had a father I adored."

While she served him on a paper plate, Takis helped himself and stayed in the background of the conversation. She took it that he didn't mind that she'd more or less taken over and was chatting away.

"Is Doris a stay-at-home mother?"

"No. She works with me at the hotel."

"How terrific for both of you." She handed him some tangerines.

He peeled one and ate the whole thing at once, reminding her of Takis's eating habits. "You think that's a good idea?"

Ah. He was coming to life. "If I loved my husband, I'd want to be with him as much as possible. She's a lucky woman." Poor Danae would have loved to work with Nassos like that…

Lukios darted Takis a glance, but she pretended not to notice. "Do you want a Pepsi? It's the only soda I could find."

"Thank you."

She turned to Takis. "What about you?"

"I'll drink one later. Why don't you sit and I'll wait on you?"

Their gazes met. "I'd love it."

After she finished eating, Lukios got up from his chair and put his empty plate on the table. "Thank you for the lunch. It was very nice to meet you, Kyria Theron."

"I'm thrilled I got to be introduced to you at last."

"It was my pleasure. Now I'm afraid I have to get *Baba*'s truck back to the hotel. Work is waiting."

Takis put down his soda. "I'll see you out, Lukios." He leaned over and kissed her cheek. "Don't go away," he whispered. "I'll be right back."

He walked out of the kitchen, leaving her trembling. She was a fool to be this happy when it wasn't a real engagement, but she couldn't help it. There was no one like Takis.

A few minutes later Takis came back in the kitchen and found Lys cleaning up. "You're a sight I never expected to see in here after leaving you in front of the hotel last evening."

She looked up at him. "I'm sure you didn't. But I couldn't sleep during the night because of worry over your secret getting out. I remembered back to that day in your office in Italy. When you saw the deed, the shock on your face stunned me."

He stared at her. *It wasn't just the deed, Lys Theron.*

"Later, after your return to Heraklion, we talked about what Nassos had done by giving you co-ownership of the hotel. That's when I realized why you worried it could be damaging to your relationship with your father if he knew."

"I shouldn't have said anything to you about that."

"I'm glad you did. I—I want you to be able to preserve that precious bond with your father," she stammered from emotion. "I loved mine so much."

He leaned against the doorjamb with his strong arms folded. "So you've decided to be the sacrificial lamb."

"I don't think of my decision that way and hope you don't either."

"Be honest. You'd do anything for Nassos and Danae."

She threw her head back. "I guess I would."

And now she was willing to help preserve his father's love by entering into an engagement of convenience. If Lys knew the depth of Takis's feelings for her, would she admit she couldn't live without him either and toss the pretense away? He cocked his head. "You realize my brother swallowed your act so completely, he gave me a hug for luck before getting in the truck."

Luck? Her heart leaped. "He isn't the hugging type?" she teased.

"After what I told you about him, you know he isn't. The last time it happened, my girlfriend had just died."

"Oh, Takis—how awful that must have been. Is it still too hard to talk about?"

"No. I remember there was pain, but I don't feel it anymore."

"What happened to her?"

"I was working at the hotel in Heraklion the day Gaia took a bus trip with her friends. It was the high school's year-end retreat. They went to the Samaria Gorge."

"I've heard of it but have never been there," Lys murmured.

"It's a place in the White Mountains where it's possible to hike down along the gorge floor past streams, wild goats, deserted settlements and steep cliffs. The plan was for them to reach the village of Agia Roumeli and take a boat back to the bus for the return trip to Tylissos.

"The tragedy occurred when a tourist drifted across the road and hit the bus, causing it to roll over and down the side of the gorge. There were thirty students on the bus. Three of them died. One of them was Gaia."

She buried her face in her hands. "I'm so sorry."

"Her death prompted me to accept Nassos's offer to leave for the States and go to work for the man whom I now know was your father. After her funeral, the move to New York helped me get over it."

Lys nodded and wiped her eyes. "Had you been close for a long time?"

"From the age of fifteen."

"How terrible." She shook her head. "Does her family still live here?"

"Yes."

"Do you visit them?"

"Only once, the first time I came back to be with my parents. They didn't need to see me as a reminder. One look at the framed picture of her on the end table was enough to prevent me from dropping in on them again."

"What about the latest woman in your life now? Will news of your engagement hurt her?"

He strolled toward her. "I've had several short-lived relationships, none of them earthshaking, as the Americans have a way of saying. For the last three years I've been consumed with earning a living and haven't allowed any serious entanglements to get in the way."

Her purple gaze fused with his. "And there you

were, minding your own business at the *castello* when destiny dropped in to change your life yet again."

Obeying a strong impulse, he put his hands on her shoulders. Takis could feel her heartbeat through her soft cashmere sweater.

"I watched you walk out of the church at the funeral and thought you were the most beautiful woman I'd ever seen in my life. If I hadn't had to catch a plane for Athens right then, I would have gone to the cemetery in order to meet you and learn your name."

"I had no idea," she murmured.

"You'll never know my wonder when I entered my office and discovered the daughter of Kristos Theron standing in front of Nassos's photograph with tears in her eyes. That was my first shock, followed by another one in the form of the deed that bound you and me together in an almost mystical way. Today I received a third shock to find you here waiting for me."

"I shouldn't have come in, but you left the door unlocked. I hope you didn't mind."

"Mind?" His hands slid to her upper arms and squeezed them. "To convince Lukios is half the battle. You did something for me in front of my brother I couldn't have done for myself. After my years abroad, he's in shock I've found my soul mate in Crete, when he didn't think it was possible."

Takis hadn't thought it could ever happen either.

"Had you mentioned me to him before today?"

"Never."

"What about your sister?"

"She's always on my side. Just so you know, when I walked him out to the truck, he brought up nothing about you. If he recognized you from the newspaper, he didn't mention it. That should tell you a lot."

Her eyes glistened with moisture. "Then I'm glad."

"Glad enough to come with me and get your engagement ring? When I introduce you to my parents, I want it on your finger."

He could see her throat working. "I thought you were going to paint today."

"I'm getting things ready, but will have to wait until tomorrow morning. The water and electricity won't be turned on until then. Since we've eaten, let's drive into Heraklion."

Without her saying anything, she walked with him to his car. After they headed for the city she turned to him. "You mustn't buy me anything that stands out."

"I've already bought it."

A slight gasp escaped her throat.

He smiled. "The ring *does* have unique significance, but don't worry. It's not a ten-carat blue-white diamond from Tiffany's worth three million dollars."

"When did you get it?"

"The day I suggested the engagement. Once I visualize an idea, I act on it. I'm afraid it's the way I'm made."

"You're one amazing man."

"Amazing as in crazy, insane, exasperating? What?"

"All three and more."

He chuckled. "I don't want to hear the rest. Admit you like me a little."

She looked away.

"Why don't you pull out your phone and we'll compose an engagement announcement for the newspaper. The sooner it gets in, the better."

"Danae will want to check it over first." She pressed the note app. He watched her get started. "I think it should begin with something like Kyria Danae Rodino is pleased to announce the engagement of Lys Theron to Takis Manolis, son of Nikanor and—" She paused and turned to him. "What's your mother's name?"

"Hestia."

"Goddess of the hearth. What a lovely name." She typed it in and finished with, "Son of Nikanor and Hestia Manolis of Tylissos, Crete."

His hands gripped the steering wheel a little tighter. "You need to add Lys Theron, daughter of Kristos and Anna Theron."

A small cry escaped. "I didn't know you knew my mother's name."

"Someone at the hotel told me after I started working there. As for the rest of the announcement, we can figure out the June date after you talk to Danae. Then end it with saying that the wedding will take place in the Greek Orthodox church in Heraklion."

"Which one were your parents married in?"

"Agios Titos. That's where we'll take our vows."

He was living for it.

CHAPTER SEVEN

TAKIS DROVE TO a specialty shop called Basil. It was located next to the Archaeological Museum of Heraklion that sold Minoan replicas the tourists could afford. He parked the car and walked her inside.

"I love this place! When I first came to Crete, Danae brought me in here every time we took visiting friends of theirs through the museum. We'd always buy a few trinkets."

He guided her past clusters of people to the counter where he asked one of the clerks to get the owner. "Basil is holding a ring for me." Takis couldn't wait to slide it on her finger. He wanted her in his arms and his life forever.

"A moment, please."

"Look at this, Takis!" Lys walked over to a fresco hanging on the wall representing a Minoan prince. He stood in his horse-drawn chariot holding the reins. A warrior on the road handed him a drink from a golden cup. "I've seen this in the museum. It's a splendid replica. Can't you see it hanging over your fireplace?"

"Don't you mean ours?"

"Yes. This is all still new to me."

He hugged her around the waist. Her interest intrigued him. "Why do you like it so much?"

"The plain with those trees where he's riding reminds me of the view from your terrace. Danae once took me out to the Tylissos archaeological site not far from your village. You have Cretan blood in your veins and live in a Cretan historical spot that's over seven thousand years old."

He smiled. "You were born in New York, which dates back ten thousand years."

"Except that I'm half-Cretan and I don't have part Native American blood. My mother was American through and through. Somehow it doesn't seem the same."

A chuckle escaped his lips, enjoying their conversation more than she would ever know. *"Touché."* He gave her a brief kiss on the mouth, unable to resist tasting her whenever he could.

"Kyrie Manolis!" He turned around to see the owner come up to him.

"Kalispera, Basil."

The older man stared in wonder at Lys like most men did, unable to help it. "You've brought your beautiful fiancée. Now I understand your choice of stone. Come with me."

Takis guided her over to another counter. Basil went around behind. On the glass he set a small gold box with a *B* on it and took off the lid. Takis heard her sharp intake of breath when the owner handed the ring to Lys.

"This is incredible." Her voice shook.

Takis had hoped for that reaction.

"It's a replica of old Minoan jewelry," Basil explained.

"I know. I've seen one like it in the museum."

"Look closely. The three-quarter-inch band is intricately linked by twelve layers of tiny gold ropes, some braided, some mesh. The middle one represents the snake of the snake goddess, known for being gracious, sophisticated and intelligent.

"This ring would be identical to the one you saw in the museum, but your fiancé wanted a cut glass purple stone instead of the red garnet in the center. Put it on and we'll see if it fits."

After she slid it on to her ring finger, her eyes flew to Takis. He'd never seen them glow before. "This is too much. Thank you." She kissed him on the side of his jaw.

Basil laughed. "If the ring was authentic, he would be paying over five million euros at auction. But the beauty of shopping with Basil is that it didn't cost that much."

"It looks like the real thing."

"My artisans are highly qualified. Does it mean you are pleased?"

"How could I not be?" she told him.

Takis kissed her, uncaring that they had an audience. Color suffused her cheeks.

"Wear it in joy, *despinis.*"

Takis pocketed the box. "Before we leave, I'll buy the fresco on the wall over there." He pulled out some bills and left them on the counter.

"Put your money away. I have more of those in the back room. This will be my early wedding present for you. You two are so much in love, I think you must get married soon. One of my clerks will wrap it."

After Basil walked away, Lys looked up at Takis. "Will your family believe you didn't spend a lot of money on this?"

"They'll *know* I didn't when I tell Kori it came from Basil's. She shops here every so often because it isn't expensive. If anything, she'll tell me a snake ring isn't at all romantic. She'll pity you for getting engaged to a man whose mind is steeped in Cretan history."

"Then she'll be surprised when I tell her my Cretan father immersed me in the culture too."

As Takis marveled over his feelings for her, Basil hurried over to them with the wrapped fresco. "Here you are."

Takis thanked him and they all shook hands. Then he walked her out to the parking lot and put it in the backseat.

"I think we need to celebrate our engagement. Where would you like to go before we drive back to the house?"

"I need to phone Danae before we do anything else. Do you mind?"

"Why would I? We're not in any hurry."

He listened while she made the call. After a short conversation, she hung up. "She'd like us to fly to the villa for dinner. How do you feel about that?"

"It's perfect. We can go over the final draft of our announcement with her."

"She'll alert the pilot that we're on our way."

"Good." Full of adrenaline, he drove them to the hotel.

"You can park in my spot. I'll show you."

Leon had seen them together enough to wave him on through. Takis helped her out of the car and locked it. After putting his arm around her shoulders, they walked to the bank of elevators. The feel of her body brushing against his side lit him on fire.

When they passed Giorgos in the main hallway, the other man said, "Lys—you've a dozen messages on your desk."

"Any emergencies?"

"No."

"Then I'll get to them later. Thanks."

Before long they climbed in the helicopter and headed for the island. Lys kept examining the ring. All of a sudden she flashed him a glance. "You were right when you said this would have unique significance."

His brows lifted. "You think Danae will approve?"

"She'll probably tell you she can see why Nassos found you such an amazing young man."

Within a half hour they'd arrived at the fabulous villa, a place that reflected the personality of the famous hotelier. Danae had a feast prepared with some of Lys's favorite fish dishes. As they walked through to the dining room the housekeeper was pouring them snifters of Metaxa, a smooth Greek brandy Takis loved.

Danae stood at the head of the table. "Before we eat, I'd like to make a toast to the two of you. May this engagement smooth the path with your family and take away some of the sadness in Lys's heart."

Amen.

"Wait! I have a surprise." She went over to the

sideboard and brought Lys a gift wrapped in plain paper.

"What's this?"

"I found it in the bottom drawer of Nassos's dresser while I was cleaning out the penthouse. When I opened it, I remembered. After Kristos's funeral, Nassos brought this back to give you one day for a special occasion. It was a small painting of Kasos Island that he once gave your mom." Danae smiled at Lys. "I think this is the perfect occasion now that you're wearing Takis's ring."

Takis could tell Lys's hands were trembling as she undid the paper. "Oh, Danae." Tears spilled down her cheeks. "This is so wonderful. I'll always cherish it."

Danae had just given Takis another reason to like the woman Nassos had married.

Lys quickly wrapped it up and put it on the empty chair next to her. "Thank you, Danae."

"Consider that it came from Nassos, who was born here too."

"I'm so touched he kept it all this time."

"He loved you." Her gaze flicked to Takis, after glancing at Lys's hand. "In my opinion you couldn't have chosen a more perfect ring for Lys, who was fascinated with Minoan culture from the time she first came to live with us."

"I could tell that," Takis said after taking another drink of brandy. "She was so taken with one of the frescoes at Basil's, I bought it for her."

Danae's glance fell on Lys. "I bet it was the prince in the chariot."

"Danae—"

The older woman kept right on talking. "Lys

wasn't so different from little girls everywhere, but she was never one to buy posters of the latest rock stars to hang on her bedroom wall. A Cretan warrior was her idea of perfection."

Two hours later they flew back to the hotel. To her relief, Danae hadn't expounded anymore on the fresco. She could have told Takis that Lys had taken one look at the prince years ago when they'd seen the real fresco in the museum, and had fallen in love on sight. The fact that he bore a strong resemblance to Takis was something she knew Danae would tease her about quite mercilessly the next time they were alone.

Only now did Lys remember Takis saying he'd tell his parents it was love at first sight after meeting her. But there was one difference.

Lys *had* fallen in love with him. For real.

She knew it to the very core of her being. From here on out she had to be careful he didn't find out how she really felt about him.

This engagement was on slippery ground because he was acting like a man in love who wanted to marry her. During dinner he'd shown excitement over the June 4 wedding date Danae had suggested. Lys would be the greatest fool alive if she started to believe that she might be able to have what she desired most in the secret recess of her heart.

At ten thirty they got out of the helicopter and headed for the elevator. Takis held the door so it wouldn't close. "Why don't I come by for you in the morning? We'll stop to eat somewhere on the way to my house. Your car will be safe parked outside tonight."

"I'm not worried about that." He noticed her clutching the gift in her arm. "What time were you thinking?"

"Since you're running the hotel, you need to take care of those phone calls Giorgos told you about. So why don't you call me when you're ready and I'll come for you."

"All right."

He allowed the doors to close and they rode to the third floor, where he walked her to her room. Lys was so afraid that he might want to come in and she would let him, she was totally thrown when he told her he needed to get going. After giving her a quick kiss on the cheek, he turned away and strode down the hall to the elevator.

She felt totally bereft. *You idiot, Lys!*

After entering her suite, she put the gift on the coffee table and left to go downstairs. Lys was too wound up to go to bed yet. When she entered the office she found Giorgos still at the front desk talking with Chloe, who helped run the counter. The second he saw Lys, he followed to her office. That habit of his was getting on her nerves.

She sat down in her swivel chair. "I'm surprised you're still here. Where's Magda?" She and another staff member served as assistant managers on alternating nights.

"I got a phone call that she's sick, so I stayed."

Lys was afraid she knew why. "That was good of you, but I'm here now so you can leave."

"Sometimes I don't feel like going back to an empty flat."

How well she knew that. "Tell me the truth. Do you wish you were home in Athens?"

"No," he answered almost angrily and moved closer to her desk.

"I hope you're telling me the truth. Now that I've taken ownership of the hotel, it's important to me that everyone is happy."

His eyes widened. "This hotel is *your* inheritance?"

"That's right."

She could see her revelation had completely thrown him.

"But you're so young—" *Whoa*. "I thought—"

"You thought Kyrie Rodino would have willed it to his ex-wife," she interjected. "That would have been a natural assumption. What else is troubling you?"

He hunched his shoulders. "Who's the mystery man?"

Lys decided it was time to set him straight and douse his hopes there could be anything between the two of them. She held out her left hand. He eyed it as if in disbelief.

"You can be the first on the staff to learn Takis Manolis asked me to marry him." What she would give if she could believe he truly did love her...

Giorgos's head jerked up. "How soon?"

"Aren't you going to congratulate me?"

"Of course," he muttered, then darted her a speculative glance. "I take it he knows you're the owner."

What was Giorgos thinking? Instead of answering him she said, "Thank you for going the extra mile to cover tonight, but you look tired. After putting in a full day's work already, you need to go home. I've let work pile up here and need to dig in. Good night, Giorgos."

Instead of indulging him further, Lys started scrolling through her messages until he left her office. After a half hour, she had cleared most of her work and after telling Chloe to call her if there was a problem, she went back to her suite to get some sleep. Not that it was possible with this incredible ring on her finger.

Takis phoned her Wednesday morning while she was drinking coffee in her room. "*Kalimera*, Lys."

Her heart thumped just to hear his deep voice. "How are you?"

"I'll be better when I see you later. At breakfast I told my parents I'd like them to meet you. They want us to come over to the hotel at two when business is slow."

Startled, she slid off the bed. "You mean today?"

"It surprised me too. My brother must have said favorable things about you. More than ever I'm convinced Danae was right about the engagement. My parents truly are anxious to see me settled." But they didn't know why Takis had asked her to marry him. "I'm leaving it up to you when you want me to come for you."

She glanced at her watch. "Where are you right now?"

"In my car on the way to the house. The water and electricity are supposed to have been turned on. I want to get over there and check things out."

"Then you have enough on your mind. I'm going to get ready and I'll take a taxi to your house."

"Lys—"

"No argument. I'll bring sandwiches and salad from the hotel kitchen." She rang off before he could try to reason with her.

Without wasting time, she called the front desk to let them know she was leaving the hotel. After hanging up, she showered, then washed and blow-dried her hair.

She didn't have to worry over what to wear and reached for her simple black gown she could dress up or down. It had sleeves to the elbow and a round neck. She wore tiny gold earrings and sensible black high heels.

When she was ready, she called the kitchen and gave them instructions. One of the waiters was to meet her at the hotel utility van in the garage with the food. Next she phoned the hotel florist. After telling them what she wanted, she asked that one of the employees bring the vase of flowers to the van and set it on the floor. After retrieving the flowers, she drove out to Tylissos.

It wasn't until she pulled up behind the two cars parked at the side of Takis's house that she realized there'd been a car behind her. She'd noticed it on the highway after leaving Heraklion, but it passed her by as she turned off the engine.

But seeing a hard-muscled Takis walk toward her drove every thought out of her mind and she trembled with excitement. Dressed in a casual cream-colored polo shirt and tan trousers, he was so striking, her breath caught.

"I've brought flowers," she said after he came

around to open the door. "I hope your mother will like them."

"It's a perfect gift."

"A woman can't resist flowers."

"I'll remember that." The way he eyed her made her pulse leap.

"They're on the floor in back."

He retrieved them while she brought the food and followed him into the house. But halfway through the living room she stopped because her eyes had caught sight of the fresco he'd rested on the mantel of the fireplace. The colors stood out, emphasizing the drabness of the room that needed a complete makeover.

He could see where she was looking. "I've been studying the fresco and think we need to pick one of the background colors that would look good on the walls."

She darted him a glance. "Do you have a favorite?"

"Yes, but I'd be interested to hear what you like."

"Well, I've loved this fresco for a long time and already know the one I'd use."

"In that case let's take it to the store and match the paint we want. I'll put these things in the kitchen and we'll eat later."

As she watched him disappear, Lys imagined that deep down he was anxious about introducing her to his parents and needed to keep busy. That was fine with her because her angst about being favorably received was shooting through the roof.

They went out to his car with the fresco and drove into the village. The thirtyish female clerk inside the store had them sit at a table. She couldn't seem to take her eyes off Takis even though she could see Lys wore an engagement ring.

After admiring the artwork, the woman set it on a chair before bringing in a dozen color strips for them to look through, but she addressed her remarks to Takis.

Though Lys knew Takis wouldn't be marrying her if Nassos hadn't given him half the hotel, she planned to help him redo his house. She adored him and wanted to help make it as beautiful as possible. This was where he planned to live until he died, so it had to be right.

His gaze fused with hers. "Let's pick our favorite color and see how close we come."

Being with Takis like this made every moment an exhilarating one. Among the various colors, her eye went to the pastel green shades until she found the perfect match in the fresco.

She would have reached for it, but Takis's hand was quicker. He lifted a certain strip off the table and glanced at her. "I knew exactly what I was looking for. Now it's your turn. Choose the one you prefer."

Lys couldn't believe it. "You're holding it. Soft sage is my choice too."

"You're teasing me."

"No."

The smile left his eyes. "I'm beginning to think we're dealing with something here beyond our control."

A little shiver raced through her. "I admit this is amazing."

"That was so easy, I'm afraid to ask what other colors you're thinking of for the rest of the house."

"How about these for the walls in the kitchen?" She picked up the Minoan red and canary yellow strips.

He looked astonished. "You've been reading my mind."

"The borders on the fresco influenced me."

Takis kissed her neck before getting up to talk to the clerk. He couldn't have done anything to please Lys more just then. She made a silent choice of pale blue for one of the bedrooms upstairs, but didn't say anything. Perhaps they'd make that decision later.

"I'll be happy to help you with anything else you need." The woman smiled into Takis's eyes and couldn't have been more obvious. Lys was glad to leave.

Again she thought she saw the same car she'd noticed earlier, but it disappeared around the next corner. After what she'd been through while the police were investigating the reason for Nassos's death, she was probably being paranoid.

CHAPTER EIGHT

SOON THEY DROVE back to the house with the paint.
While Lys carried the bags into the living room, Takis
brought in the fresco and set it back on the mantel.
"Shall we eat? I'm starving."

Lys chuckled. "Aren't you always?"

They walked into the kitchen, where he'd put the
wrapped vase of flowers in the sink earlier. She set
the food on the table and they sat down to eat.

Halfway through a second sandwich he smiled at
her. "We'll set up our computers to the hotel's main-
frame. Giorgos won't be the wiser when we use this
house to discuss business while we transform this
place. Have you told him we're engaged?"

"Last night I showed him my ring."

Takis's eyes glittered with amusement. "It's the
best thing that could have happened to him. He took
one look at you and fell hard. I feel sorry for him because there's only one of you."

"Speaking of problems, maybe I should go alone
to the paint store next time."

"Why?"

She laughed. "You do that so well."

"What?" He stared at her.

"Pretend you don't know that woman can't wait to see you again."

His mouth curved sensuously. "You noticed."

"Even blind, I would have been able to tell."

"Now you know what I put up with whenever you're with me. We both know Giorgos is already a lost cause. As for Basil, I've done business with him from time to time and have never known him to give anything away. But he was so besotted with my fiancée and her violet eyes, he lost his head."

She scoffed. "I thought he did it because he cares for you. More and more I'm convinced that's the way Nassos felt about you upon a first meeting, not to mention the manager, who was so impressed, he introduced you to Nassos twelve years ago."

He sucked in his breath. "Why do I feel I'm being set up for something?"

"Why don't you believe you're a wonderful son worth loving?"

They finished eating in silence before he started to clean up. "Thank you for bringing lunch." She felt his eyes on her. "We should leave for my parents' in a few minutes. If you need to freshen up, the water is on now. Don't worry. I cleaned the downstairs bathroom. This house has stood vacant for a long time."

"I thought as much."

She got up and discovered it next to the area for a washer and dryer down the little hall off the kitchen. There was a lot of work to be done, but Lys found she couldn't wait to help.

When she came out, he stood in the kitchen waiting for her. The realization of what they were about to do frightened her. "Takis? What if they can't accept me?"

"We've been over this before—they will adore you. Are you saying you want to back out?" His voice sounded too quiet.

"No, but I'm nervous."

His hands reached out and he drew her against him. "Perhaps now would be the best time to put the seal on our relationship." When his compelling mouth closed over hers, she'd been halfway out of breath in anticipation. The shocking hunger in his kiss robbed her of the rest and she clung to him in a wine-dark rapture.

There was no thought of holding back on her part. Her desire for him was so great, she had no idea how long they stood there clinging to each other, trying without success to satisfy wants and needs that had been kept in check until now.

"I've wanted you from the moment I saw you," he murmured, kissing every inch of her face and throat. "The desire we feel for each other is real. Don't tell me it isn't."

"I won't," she whispered, incapable of saying anything else.

Again he swept her away in another kiss that went on and on. His mouth was doing miraculous things to her. She couldn't bear the thought of this moment ending, but Takis had more control than she did and finally lifted his mouth from hers. His breathing had grown shallow too. "Much as I'm enjoying this, we're going to be late if we don't leave now."

She couldn't think, let alone talk, and was embarrassed for him to witness the state of her intoxication.

Needing to do something concrete, she pulled out of his arms and reached for the vase of flowers. After grabbing her purse, she headed for the living room.

He opened the front door and helped her out to his car. She hid her flushed face from him as much as she could for the short drive to the Manolis hotel. To her surprise he drove down an alley behind the buildings, parked by his parents' truck and came around to help her out.

"Are you ready?" he murmured.

She clung to the vase. What a question when her legs were wobbling! His kiss had changed her concept of what went on between a man and a woman now that she was so deeply in love with this fantastic man.

Of course she'd been kissed before and had enjoyed it, but she'd never gone to bed with the men she'd dated. During Nassos's talks with her about men and marriage, she'd learned that he expected her to wait until her wedding night. Maybe if she'd fallen in love with one of those men, she might not have been able to resist. But it hadn't happened and now she knew why after Takis had aroused her passion.

Suddenly the back door opened. Lys recognized his mother, who'd passed on her reddish dark-blond hair to Lukios. She cried Takis's name and reached out to hug him. But it was his same startling hazel eyes that fastened on Lys.

"Mama? This is my fiancée, Lys Theron. She's the light of my life." The words came out smooth as silk and sounded so truthful, it shook her to the foundations.

Lys looked for signs that she was upset or disappointed, but instead she let go of Takis to hug her, flowers and all. They were both the same medium height. "This is a great day. Welcome to the family."

The unexpected warmth brought tears to Lys's eyes. "Thank you, Hestia. Takis has talked about his angel *mama* so much, I feel I know you already." In that moment Lys shared an unexpected glance with Takis. From the intense look in his eyes, she'd said the right thing to his mother.

"She's brought you flowers. Shall we go inside and unwrap them?"

Hestia wiped her eyes. "Come on. Your father is in the living room waiting for you."

Nikanor Manolis. The man for whom this charade was all about.

Takis grasped her hand and took her through the kitchen to the living room.

Lys saw immediately that he took after his father in height and features. The older man with salt-and-pepper hair stood in front of the fireplace dressed in dark pants and a white shirt.

"*Baba?* I would like you to meet the woman I'm going to marry." Hearing those words almost gave her a heart attack. "Lys Theron, this is my father, Nikanor."

She shook his hand. "How do you do, Kyrie Manolis. It's an honor."

He gave her a speculative glance. "Lukios tells us you two met in Italy."

"Yes. I was on a short vacation."

"You love my son?"

After everything Takis had told her about his father, she guessed she wasn't surprised he would ask a blunt question like that. But Lys could hardly think for the blood pounding in her ears. "From the first moment I met him, I couldn't help it." She didn't dare look at Takis right then. To her surprise his father kissed her on both cheeks, putting his stamp of approval on the news.

"Look what she brought us!" Hestia came in the room carrying the vase of pink roses and lavender daisies, breaking the tension. "They are so beautiful!" She set them on the coffee table.

"I'm glad you like them. Those colors are perfect together."

"I think so too. Sit down. I've made tea."

Takis led her over to the couch and squeezed her hand, revealing his emotions. In a minute his mother came back with a tray of tea and *kourambiedes* to serve everyone.

"What are your plans?" his father asked.

"We've set the date for June fourth, provided that's a convenient time for you and Mama. It's not a holiday. The engagement announcement is ready to be given to the newspaper."

His father looked at Lys. His brows lifted the same way Takis's sometimes did. "Tell us about your family."

She'd been ready for that question. "My mother was an American, born on Long Island, who died when I was little. My father was working in New York, but he was from Kasos Island here in Crete. In his will he specified that he wanted his best friend to be my guardian should he die before I turned eighteen. That best friend was Nassos Rodino, who died very recently.

"He and his wife, Danae, raised me from the age

of seventeen after my father was killed in a plane accident. She's the only person I have left and still lives on Kasos. Contrary to what the media reported after his death, we love each other as mother and daughter and will always mourn Nassos's passing. He was like a father to me."

"We're sorry for your loss."

"Thank you. Danae met Takis for the first time the other night. When she learned he planned to live here for good and work at his family's hotel, she gave us her blessing. To be truthful, she never liked the men I dated. I'm pretty sure it's because they weren't from Crete."

Takis shot her a look of surprise.

"All along both she and Nassos insisted that one day I marry a Cretan who honors his family," Lys added on a burst of inspiration. It was only the truth.

The older man's gray eyes lit up before he turned to Takis. "That's what you want to do, my son? Work here at the hotel now that you're home for good?"

Lys's eyes closed tightly, waiting for the answer that would change Takis's world.

"It's what I want, *Baba*."

"Then so be it."

She knew those words had to be the sweetest Takis had ever heard.

"Hestia? They want to be married June fourth."

"I heard."

"In the Agios Titos church," Takis supplied.

"Ah. That's where we were married." Her face beamed. "How soon will it go in the paper?"

"We'll submit it tomorrow. It will probably show up the next day. We plan to see the priest next week."

His father nodded in what seemed like total satisfaction.

"When I'm not busy working for you, *Baba*, I'll be busy fixing up the old Andropolis house. You know the one that has stood vacant for close to a year. Besides paint, it needs new flooring and plumbing."

"You're good at those jobs."

A compliment from his father must be doing wonders for him, but Lys didn't dare look at him and instead munched on one of his mother's fantastic walnut cookies.

"We will have everyone for dinner Friday night to celebrate. Our whole family together."

If his mother had a serious illness, Lys couldn't tell. Nothing seemed wrong with Takis's father either. All she knew was that this get-together had to have left their son overjoyed.

Hestia moved over by Lys to examine the ring. "It doesn't surprise me he gave you the snake ring. My Takis was always immersed in our Minoan culture."

"I'm fascinated by it too. When he picked it up at Basil's, he also bought a replica of a fresco from the museum I admired. We're going to hang it over the fireplace and use those colors to decorate. You'll have to come and see it."

"I'll bring Kori and Doris with me."

"I'm looking forward to meeting them and the children."

"Everyone will be excited to get to know you. They love Takis and won't be able to wait to see his house."

"Takis will have to put up a railing on the upstairs terrace first so they won't fall."

"I'll take care of it before they come!" he spoke up,

as if they were an old married couple. She shouldn't have been surprised that he was listening.

Lys was getting in deeper and deeper. She loved him so much, but if he didn't love her just as intensely... While he kissed his father, Lys stood up, taking one more cookie from the plate. "These are so good, Hestia, I want the recipe."

"I'll give it to you."

In a moment Takis reached her side. "Mama, Lys and I need to leave so you two can get back to work. I'll be over for breakfast tomorrow and we'll talk hotel business."

She walked them out of the room and through the kitchen to the back of the hotel where the cars were parked. "Where do you live, Lys?"

"Since I started working in the accounts department of the Rodino Hotel four years ago, I've lived in a room there, but I've gone home to the island on weekends."

"Will you continue to work there when you're married?"

"I—I don't know." She hesitated. "Takis and I still have many things to talk about."

"Amen to that." He'd come up behind them. "We'll see you on Friday, Mama." He kissed her before helping Lys get in his car.

Hestia stood there smiling and waved as they drove down the alley to the next street.

"Your parents are wonderful," Lys murmured when they'd turned the corner.

He didn't respond. She turned her head toward him, waiting for him to say something. But he just kept driving until they arrived back at his house. Worried that something was wrong, she got out of the car and hurried toward the front door. In seconds, he'd unlocked it so they could go inside.

When it closed behind them, she felt his hands on her shoulders. He whirled her around. She couldn't understand the white ring outlining his mouth.

"Takis—" Her heart was thudding. "What did I do to make you this upset?"

"I'm not upset." He gave her a little shake. "Don't you know what you did back there was so miraculous, I'm afraid I'm dreaming."

Relief filled her system. "What do you mean?"

"You really don't get it, do you? You've charmed my parents so completely, you've made it possible for me to get in their good graces again."

She shook her head. "I didn't do anything. Can't you see how much they adore you?"

"That's your doing. You make me look good."

"What a ridiculous thing to say!"

"Ridiculous or not, you have my undying gratitude." His hands ran up and down her arms, bringing her against his hard male body. "Damn—we don't have a couch, let alone a bed, so I can't kiss you the way I want."

"It's probably a good thing there's no furniture."

"You don't really mean that." His deep grating voice sent waves of desire through her body. "I could eat you alive standing right here and know you feel the same way."

She took a deep breath. "I admit I've been strongly attracted to you from the beginning, Takis."

His gaze poured over her features relentlessly. "Have you ever been to bed with a man?"

"Would it matter to you if I had?"

"Yes," he bit out.

"Why? You've had intimate relations with other women."

A pained look crossed over his face. "I'm jealous of any man who has ever made love to you. I'd rather be the only one who knew that kind of joy."

"That works for women too."

"Are you admitting you're jealous of my past relationships?"

"Not jealous. But I do want to know about the one you had with your girlfriend in high school."

"We didn't sleep together, Lys. I was trying to honor her until we could be married."

Tears clogged her throat. "She was a very lucky woman to be loved by you. If the accident hadn't happened, you would never have left Crete and would probably be married with children by now."

"But destiny had something else in mind for me, and I'm in the battle of my life to regain what I lost."

She struggled to understand. "Tell me exactly what it is you think you lost. Your parents are thrilled you've come home and your father wants you working with him again."

His chest rose and fell visibly. "Because you're going to be at my side."

"You honestly believe it took *me* to make this happen today? If that's true, then I feel sorry for you."

Lines marred his striking features. "How else to explain why they want to tell the whole family Friday night?"

"How about accepting the fact that you're their son and they love you? Do you need more than that?

For so long you've been telling yourself that you're an unworthy son, you couldn't see what was in their eyes today. Why don't you just sit down with your father and tell him all the feelings in your heart?"

"My friend Cesare has asked me the same question."

"Then listen to him! Your fear has brought you to a standstill. For a man as outstanding and remarkable as you are, I find it inconceivable you're in such terrible pain. A simple conversation with your father could change the way you look at life." She lowered her head. "In a way, you remind me of Nassos."

Takis's head reared back. "What do you mean?"

"Remember the letter he wrote to me? Just think what might have happened if he'd gone to Danae and had admitted he'd been wrong to divorce her and wanted her back. But his fear that he might not be forgiven wouldn't let him do that and he died unexpectedly, never knowing how much she loved him and wanted to get back with him."

His brows furrowed. "How does that have anything to do with me?"

"It has everything to do with you. You're afraid to talk to your father for fear you'll hear him say he can never forgive you for leaving Crete. But the point is, he might say something else quite different to you.

"Just think, Takis. After my talk with Danae, I realized she would have told Nassos she wanted him back, but he never gave her a chance. It's so sad that it's too late for them. Please don't let it be too late for you and your father."

She kissed his firm jaw. "Now I'm going to leave and get back to the hotel. I've let work go too long.

When you're ready to start applying the primer, I'll come and help."

As she started out the door he said, "You still haven't told me if you've been to bed with a man."

She paused and turned to him. "Shall we make a deal? When you decide to have that talk with your father, then I'll tell you all the secret details of my intimate life with men."

"Was it true what you said about your boyfriends not being from Crete?"

"Yes."

"How many were there?"

"I only had three serious ones. All of them were born in other parts of Greece, the sons of wealthy parents who came to Crete for vacations and stayed at the hotel. I knew Nassos and Danae weren't impressed with any of them."

Her words brought a smile of satisfaction to his arresting features.

"By the way, I love your parents."

The next morning Takis made arrangements for a Skype conference call with his partners. He'd set up his computer in the kitchen while the guys sat at the computer in Cesare's office at the *castello*.

"You're looking good, amico." This from Cesare.

"It's great seeing you guys again."

"Before we hear your news, we have some of our own," Vincenzo exclaimed.

"Good or bad?"

"Definitely good. My cousin Dimi is going to marry Filippa in June at her church in Florence. They made the decision last evening, but want to keep it low-key with only family and close friends. You're invited, of course, if you can make it. We'll text you the time and address of the church."

Takis's mind leaped ahead. He would take Lys with him so his friends could meet her. Cesare had seen her, but it wasn't the same thing as talking to her. "I'm very happy for him. Dimi deserves it."

"Being that Filippa is Gemma's best friend, my wife is beyond thrilled. But now we want to know what's going on with you."

"Quite a lot actually. The sale of my hotels in New York has gone through. Furthermore I've bought myself a house two blocks from my parents' hotel in Tylissos and now have internet."

"You sound good."

"I am. Two days ago Lys Theron and I got officially engaged. Our announcement went in the newspaper today. I'm emailing you a copy of it as we speak."

After total silence, Cesare let out an ear-piercing whistle. "You're actually getting married?"

"We decided it was the best way to keep news about Nassos's will a secret. By implying that Lys and I are in a romantic relationship ending in marriage, no one will know or suspect I'm co-owner of the Rodino Hotel. She has informed the staff that she's the new owner."

Vincenzo leaned forward. "So what will you do? Get divorced after the six months' stipulation concerning hotel ownership has passed?"

"There'll be no divorce."

"Is she on board with all this?"

Takis had been waiting for Vincenzo's astute question, which meant his friend had been thinking hard about the things Takis hadn't explained. "I intend our marriage to last forever."

Cesare cocked his head. "The Takis I know wouldn't publicly announce his engagement to be married unless he wanted it more than anything else in this world."

"In the beginning I suggested the engagement in order to protect the relationship with my father. But I've fallen in love and yes, a life with her is what I want more than anything else in this world."

After a silence, "I take it you didn't have that conversation with him after all."

First Cesare, then Lys, now Cesare again. "I'm handling all I can for the moment. Any problems I need to know about business on your end?"

"Sofia, your assistant, might be getting married soon and will have to move back to Geneva," Vincenzo interjected. "That means we'll be needing to find a new person to replace her. Got anyone in mind?"

"Let me talk to her first. In the meantime I'll send Dimi a text to congratulate him."

"He'll like that."

"I know you guys are busy so I'll let you go."

"What's the hurry?"

"I'm waiting for a man to come and help me install a railing for the upstairs terrace on my house. You can't believe what a disaster this place is."

"Then we won't keep you. Ciao, Takis."

"Ciao, guys. It's always good to talk to you."

He ended the session and got back to work, purposely keeping their conference short. He knew they were worried about him and the rushed engagement. But he didn't want to let them delve into his psyche too deeply until Lys admitted that she was crazy in love with him too.

Once the wrought iron railing had been installed, he swept the stone tiles. Before long a truck from the local furniture store delivered a full-size swing with a canopy he'd ordered online.

The workers carried it upstairs to the terrace. They also brought up a round glass-topped table set in wrought iron with an umbrella and six matching chairs. There was also a matching side table he put next to the swing. Until the interior of the house was done, the terrace would be his hideaway with Lys. In the evening, the neighbors wouldn't be able to see them entwined.

After the men left, he phoned Lys. "How soon can the owner of the hotel come to my house this evening? I would pick you up, but I want to finish getting the primer paint on the walls by tonight. There's a surprise waiting."

"That sounds exciting. I'll be there as soon as I can with dinner." Click.

She did that a lot, cut him off so he wouldn't argue, but he found he liked everything she did. He was in love. The kind that went soul deep. One day soon he would get her to admit she couldn't live without him either.

CHAPTER NINE

As Lys pulled the van behind Takis's car at seven, she saw the surprise he'd mentioned. An attractive wrought iron railing with a motif of grapes and leaves had been installed on the terrace. He got things done so fast it was scary.

When she went inside, she was astounded to see Takis had put the primer on everywhere. It looked like a new house already!

She heard him call to her. "Come on up and bring the food!"

Lys needed no urging to dash upstairs. "Oh, Takis—this is fabulous!" she cried when she walked out on the terrace. It was even better than what she had imagined earlier.

He relieved her of the bags and put them on the table. She ran over to the swing and sat in the middle. "I love it!"

Takis followed her down so he was half lying on top of her. "So do I." He devoured her mouth until she was breathless. "I've been waiting for this since the moment I bought the house."

With his rock-hard legs tangled around hers and their bodies trying to merge, Lys had never known such euphoria. He was male perfection and she couldn't get enough of him. They lost track of time in their need to communicate.

"What if someone sees us?" she asked after coming up for breath.

"They won't. It's dark now, so I can do what I want." He bit her lobe gently.

"*Takis*—not here—"

"Are you afraid for us to make love?" He teased, kissing her throat.

"I thought that was what we were doing."

His deep laugh rumbled through her. "You say you had three boyfriends?"

She hid her face in his neck. "I did, but—"

"But it wasn't like this?"

Lys trembled. "We should eat. The food will be cold."

"Not until you tell me the truth. You've never been to bed with a man. Admit it."

"You're right. I haven't."

He kissed her with such tenderness, she couldn't believe it. "You have no idea how that changes my whole world."

"Why?"

"Nassos did the perfect job of protecting you so you could wear white to your wedding. Until we're married, I promise to honor his wishes for you."

She couldn't wait to lie in bed with him all night while they loved each other into oblivion. But what if he didn't love her the same way?

He kissed her lips once more. "You're so quiet. What's wrong?"

"Nothing," she muttered. Lys should never have admitted the truth.

"I think my fiancée is hungry."

"I think it's the other way around."

He gave her another deep kiss before standing up. "Come on." He reached for her hands. "Let's sit at our new table to eat."

After he'd set everything up he said, "I had a conference call with my partners this morning and there's news. We've been invited to Dimi Gagliardi's wedding in June. I don't know the exact date yet. He's Vincenzo's only cousin and one of my favorite people.

"He's marrying the best friend of Vincenzo's wife, Gemma, Filippa. We'll be flying to Florence for the ceremony."

"That sounds exciting."

He darted her a searching glance. "Now we have more important things to talk about. Next Tuesday evening the priest would like to meet us at the church."

Would he talk to the priest if he didn't love her? If he didn't want to marry her? She had to believe he meant what he said, but it was hard. "I think I'd better go. When I left the office, I still had some work to do."

He wiped his mouth. "In that case I'll follow you back to Heraklion and help you."

"I thought you didn't want to be seen."

"That was before our wedding announcement went in the newspaper. No one will think anything except that I'm so crazy about you, I can't stay away from you. For personal reasons, I want to make sure you get home safely. You're the most important person in my life."

No, she wasn't! Takis's father took priority, which was the reason they were in this situation now. Lys got up from the table and helped clean it off before going inside and down the stairs. Only a few minutes later, she had left the house and climbed into the van.

"Drive safely." He leaned in to kiss her hungrily. His touch caused her to melt before she turned on the engine and headed for Heraklion. Takis drove right behind her. At the hotel she parked the van and Takis parked in the empty space next to hers that Nassos had once used.

With his arm around her shoulders they took the elevator to the main floor and walked to her office. Along the way he kept her so close, anyone seeing them would assume they were lovers. By now the staff already knew.

Magda smiled her greeting before they disappeared down the hall to Lys's office. Takis walked her inside and pulled her into his arms. "I've got to have this before we do anything else."

She saw the blaze of desire in his eyes before he covered her mouth with his own, giving her a kiss that couldn't disguise his need. The slightest contact with him set her on fire and she found herself responding, helpless to do otherwise.

"We need a swing in here too," he whispered, kissing her eyes, nose, virtually every feature until he captured her mouth once more. "I'll arrange to have one sent from the store."

"*Takis*—" Lys finally found the strength to ease away from him. "I thought you wanted to help me work."

"I lied. Now that we're engaged, I don't want to be apart from you. I want you with me day and night."

"Please don't say that."

He caught her face in his hands. "Why? Because you know you want the same thing?"

"This is all happening so fast!"

His eyes gleamed like lasers. "That's not true. I saw you at the funeral and was determined to meet you the next time I came to Crete no matter what I had to do. Can you deny you felt something for me in my office in Italy?" he demanded before devouring her again.

Something in his tone convinced her he wasn't lying about his feelings. They'd both felt the chemistry between them when she'd flown to Milan. But a strong physical attraction didn't mean he loved her the way she loved him. Once they were married and he'd been reconciled with his father in his own mind, how would he feel then?

But for Lys, she'd never be able to love another man again. There was no one who came close to Takis. If their marriage didn't work out, she'd be like Danae and live a single life. With the money from her father, she could buy a place on Kasos near Danae. They could travel together, work on philanthropic projects together. But at this point the thought of Takis not being in her life was impossible to imagine.

"Lys?"

Startled, she tore her lips from Takis and turned her head to see Magda in the doorway.

"Sorry to intrude, but we have a problem."

"What is it? You can speak in front of my fiancé. Let me introduce you to Takis Manolis."

"It's very nice to meet you, Kyrie Manolis. Congratulations on your engagement."

"Thank you, Magda. I'm afraid you'll be seeing me around here a lot. I have a hard time staying away from Lys."

The other woman smiled before looking at Lys. "The finance minister Elias Simon from Athens has just checked in and was led to believe he could have the penthouse suite for the rest of the week."

Lys shook her head. "I can't imagine how that happened since we've never let guests sleep there. When Kyrie Rodino was alive, he used it for VIP meetings, nothing else. Tell the minister we'll put him in the Persephone suite."

"Will you tell him?" Her eyes pleaded with Lys, who understood her nervousness. Kyrie Simon had a forbidding presence.

"I'll take care of it."

"Thank you."

After she hurried away, Lys turned to Takis. "I'll be right back."

"I'll come with you."

The minute the two of them walked out to the front desk, the finance minister took one look and burst out, "Takis—"

"Elias—" The men shook hands.

"What are you doing here instead of New York? On business again?"

"I've moved back to Crete for good and got engaged." Takis grabbed Lys around the waist. "I'd like you to meet my gorgeous fiancée, Lys Theron, the former ward of Nassos Rodino. Now that he has passed away, she owns the hotel."

The other man's dark eyes fastened on her in male admiration and they shook hands.

"I envy you, Takis. If I were thirty years younger…"

"I'm a very lucky man."

"That certainly goes without saying," he said, smiling at her.

"Kyrie Simon? I'm sorry that there was a misunderstanding about the penthouse. It's not a guest room, but we'd love you to stay in the Persephone suite."

"No problem."

"Magda will check you in. Now if you will excuse me, I have some work to attend to back in my office."

"Of course. That gives me time to chat with Takis. You realize you're going to marry one of the most important men in the country. Has he shown you the hospital he built and funds in Tylissos? It provides such invaluable free medical care for the patients. There's another one being built in Athens as we speak. He's a remarkable man."

What?

"I'll tell you later," Takis said in an aside and kissed her cheek.

She went down the hall and sat down at her desk, but she couldn't concentrate on a thing. He'd built a hospital here? Another one was going up in Athens? How long had that been going on?

While she was alone, she phoned Danae, who was still awake. After catching her up on the latest news, she asked the older woman what she knew about a hospital in Tylissos that had been built and was free to the patrons.

"Only that it's a children's hospital for those parents who can't afford big medical expenses. Stella told me about it last year and wished the government would build one here in Heraklion."

Lys was stunned. "The government has nothing to do with it. I just found out tonight that Takis is the one who had it built and pays for everything."

A long silence ensued. "*Your* Takis?"

If only he were… She gripped the phone tighter. "Tonight Kyrie Simon, the minister of finance from Athens, checked into the hotel. He saw Takis. They appear to know each other well and it slipped out during their conversation."

"Your fiancé is a dark horse in many ways. What a lovely thing to find out about the man you're going to marry. If Nassos were still alive, he'd be bursting with pride."

"The man who should be overjoyed is his father, but I'm sure he doesn't know anything about all the great things his son has accomplished. It kills me that Takis lives with this terrible pain. I love him so much, Danae." They spoke a little longer before she hung up.

After another minute, Takis came back in her office. Her gaze fused with his. "I just got off the phone with Danae. Why haven't you told me about these hospitals?"

He stood in front of her with his legs slightly apart, so handsome, so masculine, she couldn't look away. "I would have gotten around to it."

"You told me your niece had to go to the hospital for an asthma attack. You had it built for *her*."

"For all children with medical problems whose parents struggle to make a decent living."

She shook her head. "But no one knows you were the one."

"I want it that way."

"Even your parents?"

"Especially them."

"But these hospitals aren't hotels. Your mother and father would be so thrilled and proud if they knew what you've done. And you're building another one?"

"I'd rather remain anonymous."

"Takis—they deserve to know more about your life!"

"They didn't deserve to be abandoned by their son."

Lys got to her feet, upset by his comment. "What can I say to convince you that they love you and never thought any such thing?"

His brows furrowed. "You can't. I'm sorry Elias let that information slip."

"I'm not. Don't you know how proud I am of you?"

"Thank you for that. But I know I can trust you not to say anything when we go to the family party tomorrow evening."

They weren't getting anywhere with this conversation. She took a deep breath. "Thank you for helping Magda out of a difficult situation. You've won her devotion." Takis had a rare potent male charm that had made mincemeat of Lys.

"It was my pleasure. Elias can be very intimidating. That's why he's in his particular position. Between us I think he makes the president of the country nervous."

Lys chuckled. "By tomorrow morning Magda will tell everyone that my fiancé is on first-name terms

with a top-level Greek government official. You'll
have elevated me to new heights in our staff's opinion."

His eyes narrowed on her mouth, sending darts
of awareness through her. "Didn't you know it's the
other way around? Elias insists on being invited to
our wedding. He has a worse case on you than Basil.
I didn't think that was possible."

She chuckled despite her out-of-control desire for
him. "Don't be silly."

"Do you still have work to do, or shall I walk you
to your hotel room?"

Lys wanted to be alone with him. She was bursting
with feelings she was dying to share. "I'd like that."
She grabbed her purse and left the room, turning out
the light. They nodded to Magda and walked down
the hall to the elevator. By the time they reached her
suite, her heart was jumping all over the place.

Lys unlocked the door. "Come in."

"I'm afraid I can't."

She swung around in surprise. "Do you have to
go right now?"

"Yes." Lines darkened his face.

"Why? Is something wrong at home?"

"No. The only problem is the way I feel about you.
If I come in now, I'll make you my wife tonight and
forget the ceremony. As it is, if I thought you'd say
yes, I'd ask the priest to marry us in three weeks instead of three months' time."

Those words brought her close to a faint.

"Think about it and give me your answer tomorrow when I come to get you." In the next breath, he

walked down the hall to the elevator, leaving her totally bereft.

She didn't want him to go. "Takis?"

He turned.

"Please don't leave yet."

"You'd better think hard about what you're asking. If I cross over your threshold, I won't leave till morning. Is that what you want after everything Nassos did to protect you from moments like this?"

For once in her life she was going to be honest and throw caution aside. "Yes."

"Why?"

"Because—because I need you and don't want to be alone tonight."

He moved closer, causing her heart to leap. "I need you too, but that's not a good enough reason to break all the rules."

"We've already broken several."

"But not the most important one."

"In my office earlier you said you wanted to be with me day and night."

"I do, once we're married."

His moral strength astonished her. "Nassos is no longer alive."

"Which leaves me to watch out for you. Weren't you the one who told me he probably gave me half ownership of the hotel to help keep you from making a mistake?"

"He didn't mean the kind of mistake we're talking about right now and you know it!" Her cheeks had grown warm. "You're going to make me say it, aren't you."

"Say what?" he murmured. "That you love me? That you can't live without me?"

The blood pounded in her ears. "You're a man who didn't plan to marry right away. I wonder what you'd do if I said those words to you."

His eyes gleamed an intense green. "Why don't we find out?"

He was toying with her, not helping her out. If he truly loved her, he wouldn't be so cruel. "To hear them would scare the living daylights out of you."

Takis cocked his head. "If you don't say them, we'll never know."

You're a fool, Lys. He was the most aggravating, incredible, beautiful man alive. "So you're really going to leave."

"It's your call. I dare you to sleep tonight, *agape mou*."

Two words that meant beloved. *Was* she his beloved?

"*Kalinikta*, Lys."

"Good night!" she snapped at him in English.

She heard his chuckle clear down the hall until he disappeared. He was driving her crazy.

Takis, feeling pure joy, headed for the garage to get his car.

After saying good-night to Elias, he'd waited another couple of minutes outside Lys's office until she'd hung up from her phone call. He hadn't meant to eavesdrop, but it had been clear she'd been talking to Danae. That's when he'd heard the truth come from her own lips.

I love him so much.

Tomorrow evening they'd be with family and the

answers to all questions would come straight from their hearts. There'd be no deception, no regrets.

Early Friday morning Lys's phone rang. Excited because she knew who it was, she reached for her cell on the bedside table. "Takis?"

"No, Lys. It's Danae."

She sat up in bed. "What's wrong? You sound worried."

"If you haven't seen a newspaper or turned on television, then don't."

Alarmed by her words, Lys slid off the bed and got to her feet. "Tell me."

"The paparazzi have taken pictures of you and Takis together. One of the write-ups reads: 'Lys Theron, heiress to the Rodino fortune, sets her sights on marrying billionaire New York hotelier Takis Manolis. Is there nothing this gold digger won't do for money?'"

Lys's thoughts reeled. Though she'd been used to this kind of coverage after Nassos's death, she hadn't imagined that it would continue. How had the press discovered their relationship? Could it have been that car she had seen following her a couple of times. It must have been! But what concerned her was the impact it would have on Takis's parents.

"Thank you for telling me. I love you and am indebted to you. Now I've got to phone Takis and warn him in case he hasn't seen the paper yet." She hung up and rang him. *Pick up. Please pick up.*

To her chagrin the call went to his voice messaging. She left the message for him to call her immediately. Without hesitation, Lys took a quick shower and got dressed in a black sweater and skirt. Once she was ready, she hurried to the garage for her car.

Maybe he was painting and had turned off his phone. All she knew was that she had to find him. If the paparazzi were still following her, she didn't care. What mattered was tonight's get-together with Takis's family.

They would have seen or read this new barrage of sensationalizing information linking the two of them. Her desire to protect him from any pain had her pressing hard on the accelerator all the way to Tylissos.

Lys spotted his car at the house before she pulled up behind it. After getting out she ran to the door and knocked. When there was no answer, she tried opening it, but he'd locked it.

"Takis?" she cried out and knocked harder.

Maybe he was over at his parents' hotel. If Danae had seen the news, there was no doubt he'd seen it too. Possibly his brother might have come over to the house to talk to him and they were out somewhere. Or maybe he'd driven Takis over to the hotel.

She simply didn't know, but she intended to find out and dashed to her car. It didn't take long to reach the hotel. She parked near the front entrance and hurried inside. An attractive dark-haired woman manned the front desk.

"May I help you?"

Lys took a deep breath. "My name is Lys Theron. I need to speak to Takis Manolis. Is he here by any chance?"

"You're Lys!"

"Yes."

"I'm Doris, Lukios's wife."

"Oh—I'm so happy to meet you."

"We're all very excited about tonight."

If Takis's sister-in-law had seen the news this morning, she was hiding her reaction to it well.

"So am I, but I need to find Takis. Do you have any idea where he might be? I went over to the house and his car is there, but he didn't answer the door."

"Let me check with Hestia. She'll know." Lys waited while she made a phone call. When Doris hung up she said, "After breakfast he went to the village with his father and hasn't come back yet. If you'll wait just a minute, she's going to phone him and find out when he'll be back."

Lys held back her groan. "Thank you." The poor darling was probably trying to defend her reputation the best way he could, but it didn't look good.

Doris's phone rang and she picked up. Their conversation didn't last long before she clicked off. "They may be gone for a while. Hestia would like you to come back to their apartment. She wants to talk to you. Their door is at the end of the left hall."

"I appreciate your help, Doris."

Shaking inside as well as out, she headed for the apartment where Takis had been born and grew up. Hestia met her at the door with a hug and asked her to come into the living room. Wonderful smells from the kitchen filled the room.

"I'm sorry to come by now when I know you're preparing for this evening, but I need to see Takis as soon as possible."

His mother eyed her with concern. "Something's wrong. What is it?"

She sat on the couch, folding her arms against her waist. "I wish I could tell you."

"If it's about the latest tabloid gossip, I pay no attention to it."

Lys let out a slight gasp. "Then you know what was in the paper this morning."

"Takis mentioned it at breakfast before he and his father left the hotel together."

"I went over to his house, but he's not there. I—I'm so afraid."

"What is it?" she asked in such a kind voice, Lys had to fight the tears that threatened. "He asked me to marry him, but I fear I'm not the right kind of woman for him. That's what I need to tell him so we can call off this engagement party."

"My son has never done anything he didn't want to do. He wants you for his wife."

"But gossip follows me wherever I go and it will rub off on him. I'd do anything to protect him and your family."

"Tell me something truthfully. Do you love him?"

Her question brought the tears rolling down her cheeks. "Desperately, but he loves you and your husband with all his heart. He's been so traumatized all these years for hurting you by leaving Crete, the last thing he needs now is to marry a woman who will bring more hurt to you."

His mother shook her head. "What hurt are you talking about?"

Lys wiped her eyes. "He carries this terrible guilt that he abandoned you when he left for New York. He can't forgive himself for it."

"Oh, my dear—" She came over to the couch and

put her arm around Lys. "By the time Takis was a year old, his father and I knew he was different than the other two. He insisted on exploring his world and needed more to make him happy. When his girlfriend died, we knew he had to find his life and were thrilled that Kyrie Rodino gave him that opportunity."

"You were?" Lys cried. "Honestly?"

"Of course. We're so proud of what he's done and accomplished."

Lys couldn't comprehend it. "Then he's the last person to know. He's been afraid that he's let you down and can never win your approval. And he's worried that there's—" She stopped herself before she said something she shouldn't.

"That there's what?" Hestia prodded.

"If I tell you, I'm afraid he'll never forgive me."

"Of course he will."

"H-He's afraid either you or your husband are seriously ill," her voice faltered. "He thinks that's why you asked him to come home for good."

His mother lifted her hands in the air. "We're in the best health we can be at our age."

"Oh, thank heaven!" Lys half sobbed.

"Where would he get an idea like that?"

"Because you asked him to come home. He thought there had to be a vital reason."

"There was. There is. We love him, and we miss him. We figured he'd made enough money on his hotels that he could come back and do something else amazing here in Crete."

"He has done that!" Lys jumped to her feet. "You know the children's hospital where your granddaughter had to go the other day?"

Hestia nodded.

"Takis had that hospital built and funds it completely." At this point tears spilled down his mother's cheeks. "He's building another one in Athens."

"Our dear son," she whispered.

"Please, Kyria Manolis. Let him know how you feel. Tell him you're both healthy. Reassure him you wanted him to find his way in the world. He needs to know how much you love him so he'll be whole. But he doesn't need a woman with my reputation ruining his life. Forgive me, but I don't dare marry him." She removed her ring and handed it to Hestia. "Please give this to him. Now I have to go."

Hestia called to her, but she dashed out of the apartment to her car. The tears continued to gush as she drove toward Heraklion. Her phone rang, but she didn't answer it. When she reached the hotel, she parked the car and rushed to her suite.

Once inside, she ran sobbing to her bedroom and buried her face in the pillow. When her phone rang again, she refused to answer it in case it was Takis. If he knew what she'd done by confiding in his mother, then he might never want to speak to her again.

Takis was surprised when his mother met him and his father at the back door of the apartment. "I'm so glad you're home! Your fiancée has been trying to reach you."

"I know. I tried to call her back, but she hasn't answered yet."

"I'm not sure she's going to."

He frowned and followed her inside to the kitchen. "What do you mean?"

She glanced at his father. "Both of you need to sit down so we can talk."

Takis lounged against the counter, unable to sit until he knew what was going on.

"Lys came by the hotel earlier looking for you."

Takis groaned aloud. "We went into the village to pick up the bedroom furniture you ordered and set it up at the house. I wanted it to be a surprise for her."

His mother nodded. "While you were busy, we had a very informative talk about many things including the children's hospitals you've been building. I'll tell you everything, but first I want you to know you're the luckiest man on earth to have found a woman who loves you so much."

"She admitted that to you?" Takis was stunned.

"You'd be shocked what she told me." In the next breath she related their whole conversation, leaving nothing out. After she'd finished, his father spoke first.

He stared at Takis through eyes that glistened with tears. "Your mother and I have loved you since the day you were born. We were so afraid for you after Gaia's death, we rejoiced when Kyrie Nassos opened a new door for you. We didn't want to say or do anything to discourage you from leaving, and we've never regretted that decision. You have no idea how proud we are of you."

Takis couldn't believe what he was hearing. Cesare had been right about everything. As for Lys...

"We're not ready for the grave yet, son. We expect to enjoy years of life with you and the wonderful woman who loves you enough to have confided in your mother."

Takis was so overcome with emotion, he could only hug them for a long time. After clearing his throat, he said, "Since Lys was so honest, I have something important to tell you too. You may not love me so much when you hear what I've done. It's about the reason we're engaged. Nassos left a will."

Once his whole confession was out, silence filled the room. His father walked over and clapped him on the shoulder.

"I only have one thing to say. The fact that Kyrie Nassos thought so much of you he would give you half his hotel tells me and your mother that you're the finest, most honorable Manolis we've ever known. I think all that's left to say now is that you go find your fiancée and thank her for making this family closer than ever."

His mother smiled. "I already love her." She reached in her apron pocket and pulled out the engagement ring. Takis was aghast Lys had taken it off. "Give it back to her with our love."

Takis's heart was running away with him. He looked at his father. "Will you drive me home so I can get my car? I need to go after her before she decides to do something crazy like leave the country."

"Where would she go?"

"To a friend of her mother's in New York. If that's her plan, I've got to stop her."

Takis broke all speed records driving into Heraklion. It was a miracle he wasn't pulled over. To his relief, her car was still in its space when he parked his Acura. But she could have called for a limo. There wasn't a moment to lose.

He hurried to her suite and knocked on the door. When she didn't answer, he phoned her. Still no response. Without a second to lose, he raced to the front office. Magda was on duty.

"Have you seen Lys this afternoon?"

"No."

"She hasn't left the hotel?"

"Not that I know of. Let me check with the manager." She came right back. "No one has heard from her."

"Then I need a card key to her room. I'm worried about her. We're due at our engagement party."

Magda seemed hesitant.

"Tell you what. Will you come with me and let me in?"

"Yes." She grabbed a card key. Then she turned to the other woman manning the desk and said she'd be right back. Together they hurried to the third floor.

Magda knocked on Lys's door and called out to her. After no response, she used the card key to let them inside.

"Lys?" Takis called her name. "It's Takis. Are you ill?"

"What are you doing inside my suite?" sounded a familiar voice in an unfamiliar tone. He could rule out sickness. Her voice sounded strong.

Relief flooded his system that she hadn't gone anywhere yet. He thanked Magda. "I'll take care of this now. I promise you're not in any trouble."

"I'll have to take your word for that."

After she left, he started down the hall. "I'm coming in the bedroom, so if you're not decent, you'd better hide under the covers."

"I'm dressed if that's what you mean."

He moved inside. She looked adorable sitting on the side of her bed in a pink robe and bare feet, her face splotchy from crying.

Her purple eyes stared accusingly at him. "How did you get in here?"

"I'm part owner of the hotel, remember?" He sat down on a side chair.

"Nobody knows that."

"Magda let me in."

"Of course she did once you used your charm on her. She should be fired!"

"On the contrary, she passed the most important test for me by functioning in a crisis."

"What crisis?"

"I couldn't find you anywhere. After the talk with my mother, I feared you might be in here too ill to respond. In my opinion we should make Magda general manager if Giorgos ever leaves."

Lys lowered her head. "Then your mother told you everything."

Takis loved this woman with every atom of his body. "Yes."

She got to her feet. "The headline in the paper has probably ruined everything you've tried to do where your father is concerned. For all I know it already has."

"You couldn't be more wrong."

Lys paced the floor, then turned to him. "Why didn't you answer your phone this morning?"

"I was out shopping for our bedroom furniture with my father and turned it off."

Lys blinked. "You went with your father to do that?"

"Yes. It's tradition for the parents. He insisted and we had a lot of fun."

"Then it means he didn't see the paper this morning."

"True, but *I* did, and I told my parents about it at breakfast."

He heard her take a quick breath. "Did your mother tell you I've broken our engagement?"

"Yes." He reached in his pocket and pulled out the ring. "Here's the proof. It would have been nice if you'd told me first."

"I did try, but you weren't anywhere around."

"We've got all the time in the world now."

"You don't need an explanation. We both know we can't go on with this lie any longer. It's not fair to your parents who love you."

"What lie is that?"

"The only reason two people should get married is because they love each other. Your parents have to know the real reason we got engaged. But since you don't want them to know about the will, I can't go on with this deception."

"You don't have to. They know about it."

He could see her swallowing hard. "When did they find out?"

"I told them this afternoon."

She sank down on the end of the bed. "I don't understand."

Takis got to his feet. "I finally had the talk with them you urged me to have. You were right about everything and I was wrong. When I explained about the will, they told me they were thrilled Nassos thought enough of me to give me such a gift."

"Oh, Takis—" she cried, sounding overjoyed. "Then there are no more shadows? You're happy at last?"

"No. I'm still waiting for you to tell me if you love me. The other night you wanted me to stay with you. An admission of love would have brought me running to you."

She looked away from him. "You're being very unkind, Takis. After talking to your mother, you *know* I do."

"You do *what*?"

"Love you."

"When did you know?"

"In your office in Italy. But none of it matters because a love like mine needs to be reciprocated, which it isn't, so I wish you'd leave now."

"I can't do that because I love you more than life."

A gasp escaped her lips. She turned to him. "I don't believe you," she whispered.

"Do you honestly think I would have asked you to marry me if you hadn't turned my world inside out? I knew at the funeral you were the woman for me. The moment was surreal to watch my destiny walk past me. The feeling I had for you transcended the physical. How can you doubt it?"

"Because I'm afraid to believe it."

He reached for her left hand and slid the ring back on her finger. Then he cupped her beautiful face in his hands. "I can understand that fear. You lost your parents and Nassos. But you're never going to lose me. We're going to get married and raise a family."

She wrapped her arms around his neck. The love-light in her eyes blinded him. "I love you so much I don't think I can contain it."

"I don't want you to try." Driven by desire, he picked up his bride-to-be and carried her over to the bed, following her down on the mattress. "If you had any idea how long I've been waiting to love you like this. Give me your mouth, my love."

Her passionate response was a revelation to Takis, but they'd no sooner started kissing each other than her cell rang, followed by a loud knock on the hotel room door.

He was slow to relinquish her luscious mouth. "I'll get the door while you answer the phone."

When he hurried down the hall and opened it, he discovered Danae standing in the hallway, the phone in her hand.

A smile broke out on her face. "I'm relieved you're the reason Lys hasn't answered her phone."

He reciprocated with a smile of his own. "I'm relieved it's you instead of the manager. Come in. She'll be thrilled to see you."

Danae kissed him on the cheek. "Liar," she whispered.

Lys came hurrying into the living room and gave Danae a hug. "I'm sorry I didn't answer the phone earlier."

"That's all right. I'm thinking you two need to move up the wedding date. How about three weeks from now? Check with your parents. We'll have the reception on Kasos."

Takis had never known this kind of happiness.

"You're a woman after my own heart, Danae. Since you're here, I'm going to leave."

Lys darted him a beseeching glance. "Do you have to go?"

This was like déjà vu. Luckily Danae had interrupted them, preventing him from breaking his vow not to make love to her before the wedding.

"Yes." She knew the reason why. "I'll be back later to take you and Danae to our engagement party." He gave her a brief kiss on the mouth before letting himself out.

CHAPTER TEN

Three weeks later

THE DAY BEFORE the wedding, Takis's close friends flew in from Milan. While the men met together, Gemma, Vincenzo's wife, and Filippa, Dimi's fiancée, came to Lys's hotel room to talk. Lys was delighted to get acquainted with the two women, who were best friends and so important in Takis's life.

It was clear to her they were all going to become close, especially when Gemma announced that she was pregnant.

"Does Vincenzo know?"

She smiled at Lys. "Oh, yes, and now he's so excited and worried over my morning sickness, he never leaves me alone. The doctor gave me an antiemetic and now it's under control, but Vincenzo has been driving me crazy. If he behaves like this until the baby is born, I might lose my mind."

"No, you won't," Filippa quipped. "He won't allow it."

Lys couldn't stop laughing. "Do you think your doctor will let you go on in your position as executive pastry chef?"

"I've already talked to my ob about that. He's monitoring me carefully and will tell me when it's time to quit. Vincenzo and I have already talked to Cesare, who is in the process of looking for a replacement."

"I don't know," Lys murmured. "Takis says you walk on water."

"She does," Dimi's fiancée concurred.

Gemma grinned. "Stop it, you two. There are plenty of great cooks out there and there's still plenty of time." She eyed Lys. "I'm so excited for you and Takis. He's the most gorgeous, wonderful man. He'll move mountains for you because it's the way he's made."

"I knew that about him before we even met and was halfway in love with him sight unseen."

"You really never met him when he was working in New York?" Filippa couldn't believe it.

"No. I was a sixteen-year-old high school student when he first started working for my father and I was hardly ever at the hotel. A year later my father died and Nassos brought me to Crete."

"Takis's story is an incredible one. So is yours," Gemma murmured. "I'm so glad you'll be spending some time at the *castello* after your honeymoon. Takis loves it there."

Gemma nodded. "We can't wait to all be together. The men have missed him more than you can imagine, Lys. You have to promise you'll fly to Milan often or life won't be the same around the place."

"It's true," Filippa said with a smile. "Dimi looks upon him as a brother. They're all so close."

"I think it's very touching," Lys murmured.

"In case you didn't know, that man can't wait to

marry you. Dimi says if he has to wait one more day, he's not going to make it."

"I feel the same way."

"We can tell." Gemma chuckled. "Since we've been given our specific instructions, we'd better hurry out to the limo to meet the men."

"They're taking us to lunch," Filippa informed Lys. "We don't dare be late or Vincenzo will come charging in here to find out what's wrong with Gemma."

Laughter broke out as they made their way down to the lobby. Lys hadn't known what it was like to have a sibling. Now she felt she'd acquired several for life.

The next day Lys stood before the black-robed priest dressed in floor-length white silk and lace. She carried a sheaf of purple roses that matched the genuine purple sapphire earrings Takis had given her as a prewedding gift.

During their midmorning wedding ceremony at the flower-decked church in Heraklion, surrounded by their families and a few close friends, Lys was in a complete daze.

The sight of Takis, her tall Cretan prince in his dark blue suit and wedding crown, pushed everything else out of her mind. That picture of him would be engraved in her thudding heart forever. He was now her husband, the most wonderful, gorgeous man in the entire world!

As they were led in the walk around the table three times where they drank from the cup, signifying their journey through life together, she prayed you couldn't die of happiness. By keeping his vow to her, he'd made this sacred moment meaningful in a way nothing else could have done. But now that she was his wife, she couldn't wait to show him what he meant to her.

They would be spending time on the yacht Danae had offered them, but where they were headed was a secret. Every time she thought about their wedding night and being alone with him, waves of desire swept through her. Once they left the church, she was scarcely cognizant of their helicopter flight to Kasos for the reception.

Danae had outdone herself to make Takis's family and friends comfortable. She'd arranged for every one of them to stay overnight where they could swim and eat and enjoy this wedding holiday.

What delighted Lys most were the three children who adored their uncle Takis and hung around the two of them. The girls touched her dress and veil and asked dozens of questions.

Deep inside Lys hoped she'd get pregnant soon. When she saw how happy he was teasing them, playing with them, that day couldn't come soon enough. The second bedroom upstairs would make the perfect nursery when the time came and she knew the color she wanted.

In the midst of the excitement, Takis's father stood to make a toast. "I'm the proudest of men to see my last remarkable child married to a lovely woman who I hope will do her Cretan duty and provide us with more grandchildren." He'd read Lys's mind.

Takis gripped her hand and clung to it.

After Nikanor's toast, Dimi stood up. "I couldn't love Takis more if he were my own brother. I'm thrilled he married a woman I already love. Lys has accomplished something no one else could ever do by putting the light in his eyes that was missing."

"It's true," Takis whispered against her ear.

Lukios followed with a toast. "Guess what, Dimi? I *am* blood and couldn't be prouder of my remarkable brother, whose greatest achievement is sitting next to him. Welcome to the family, Lys."

She teared up while other toasts followed. Eventually Cesare raised his glass of champagne. "Here's to the groom, a man who kept his head even while he lost his heart. I was there at the *castello* the day he lost it and witnessed the earthshaking event with my own eyes."

Everyone roared, especially Takis, whose laughter told Lys it was a private joke between the two of them. She'd have to ask him about it later.

Then Vincenzo gave the final toast and lifted his glass. "Here's to the newest Manolis couple on Crete. Like my beloved wife and me, may they remain lovers for all of life and the hereafter."

"You can plan on it!" Takis declared without shame, causing everyone to laugh and clap. Then he pressed a kiss to her cheek. "It's time for you to change. We're taking a helicopter ride to the yacht. Hurry. I can't wait to get you alone."

Those words said in his deep voice charged her body and she left for her bedroom to put on the stylish new cream-colored suit she and Danae had picked for her. She pinned a purple rose corsage to the shoulder. It was heaven to be out of mourning at last. The sorrow of the past was gone. With Takis waiting for her, there was nothing but joy ahead.

Twenty minutes later everyone followed them outside to the helicopter. Twilight had crept over them. Lys hugged Danae, both of them shedding happy tears. "I have no doubt your parents and Nassos were looking on today."

A sob caught in her throat. "I think so too. I love you. Thank you for everything and for making his family and friends so welcome. We'll be back soon."

"You've married a very exciting man, Lys. I envy you for what's in store."

Lys watched Takis hug his family before he helped her climb on board and told the pilot they were ready. Earlier in the day their luggage had already been flown out.

Lys was thankful they didn't have to fly a long distance. She'd anticipated this moment too long to wait any longer. Before she knew it, they'd put down on the landing pad of the yacht. She practically leaped out of her seat, anxious to be alone with Takis who helped her out.

"Am I dreaming, darling?"

He stopped to kiss her thoroughly. "If you are, I'm in it with you. *Forever.*"

Their wedding night was about to begin. Now if her heart would stop running away with her, she might be able to breathe.

When they reached the outer doors of the master cabin, he swept her in his arms and carried her over the threshold. "At last," came his fierce whisper.

"Takis—"

His friends had prepared the suite to his specifications. The flower-laden room was lighted solely with candles. Bless Danae for confiding in him about Lys's fascination with the prince in the fresco. Not only had she told him there was a strong resemblance to Takis, but Lys had once said that in a fairy-tale world, she would love to be married to the prince.

Upon hearing that, Takis had made up his mind that on their wedding night, he'd treat her like a princess. He couldn't re-create a Minoan palace, but he would convince her she was the most precious thing in his life. As he lowered her to the floor, adrenaline gushed through his veins in anticipation of what was to come.

Her heart kicked her ribs hard as she looked around, leaving him to freshen up in the bathroom. She'd been on this yacht many times before, but rarely came in this room and had never seen it looking like this. Takis had transformed it into a bridal chamber fit for a queen. The perfume from the flowers was intoxicating. She walked over to smell the ones next to the bed.

"Takis?"

"I'm right here."

She turned to him and almost fainted. He looked so beautiful in the simple white terry cloth robe, she couldn't think, let alone talk. His eyes gleamed like green gemstones in the soft light.

He handed her an identical robe. Her knees came close to buckling. With hands that were trembling, she went in the en suite bathroom. After removing her clothes, she put it on.

Lys had known he had a creative side to his nature, but to go to this kind of trouble to please her endeared him to her in a brand new way. With her heart beating out of control, she walked back into the bedroom.

He stood at the side of the massive bed. "Come closer so I can look at the most beautiful bride in all Crete."

"Takis—"

"You're not frightened of this surely? Not after all we've been through."

"I—I don't know what I am," her voice faltered.

"You're my desirable wife, the compassionate-hearted woman I've wanted from the moment I first laid eyes on you. I don't deserve you, but I swear an oath that I'll love you forever. Come here to me, *agape mou*."

She flew into his arms. He swung her around before lowering her to the bed. Their mouths met in frantic need and they began to feast on each other. One robe, then the other landed on the floor.

Their bodies came together in an explosion of love and desire. Lys hadn't known it could be like this. All night long they gave and received unimaginable rapture. "I love you so much, Takis. You just don't know…"

"Then you have some concept of how I feel. You're the light of my life, Lys. Love me, darling, and never stop."

They didn't stop. It wasn't till midmorning there was a loud knock on the cabin door.

Lys groaned and held him tighter. "Tell whoever it is to go away."

"If it wasn't for the fact that Cesare prepared our breakfast before leaving, I would. But he's sure to have given explicit instructions to make sure that we ate a perfect Cretan breakfast."

A chuckle escaped her lips. "And he knows how

hungry you are for every meal. I love him for that since I forgot all about feeding you."

He kissed a certain spot. "You've fed me the nectar of the gods, but it's true I still need mortal food and his creations are out of this world. In truth he should be the new cook for the restaurant after Gemma leaves."

"Have you told him that? Maybe he'd like to do it for a while."

"I'll have to run it by Vincenzo. Do you know Cesare had always said his mother was the best cook who ever lived?"

"That's a thought. We'll have to talk some more about it, but right now I know you're hungry. So am I." She kissed his hard jaw that needed a shave and let him go long enough to slide out of bed and put on her robe. "Stay there and I'll get it."

He lay back on the pillows, looking every inch the prince of her dreams. There wasn't enough she could do for him. "I love you desperately, Takis, and want to do everything I can to make you happy."

After kissing him passionately, she flew across the room. A staff member had left the tray with Cesare's breakfast beside the door. It was laden with every conceivable dish Takis would love. She carried it to their bed, where they could lounge and eat to their hearts' desire.

After eating as much as she could, she lay back. "You're right. I've never tasted better food in my life." She eyed her fabulous husband. "Would it hurt his feelings if you actually approached him with the idea of being the chef at the hotel in Milan?"

Takis put the tray on the floor, then pulled her back

in his arms. "Of course it wouldn't," he murmured against her throat. "After running his own chain of restaurants in New York, he's been begged by restaurants around the world to be their executive chef. All he has to do is name his price."

She covered his face with kisses. "But he wants to be with you and Vincenzo and Dimi. You four have an amazing relationship. I'd be jealous if I didn't understand how it all started, and why."

"We're very close, but you will always come first."

"Why did you laugh so hard when Cesare made his toast?"

"I was afraid you would ask." He kissed her again. "After you left my office, he witnessed my meltdown. I couldn't understand why Nassos had left me half a hotel.

"To make matters more complicated, I'd just met you after seeing you at the funeral. Since then you'd never been out of my thoughts and I knew in my soul *you* were the woman meant for me. But I didn't want to be in love. At the height of my frustration, I threw the deed across the room, but it landed on Cesare's chest."

She burrowed her face in his neck, chuckling quietly. "Thank you for telling me. You have no idea how much I love you." Her eyes filled. "It was the perfect wedding, wasn't it?"

"Almost as perfect as you. Thank God for Danae giving me her blessing. And thank God for Nassos for bringing us together. If I didn't know better, I could believe he had an inkling that he might not be on this earth long. Every time I think about his letter to you and the deed to me, I get a prickling down my spine."

"So do I," she said in a shaken voice. "I—I can't imagine life without you now."

"Don't try. I'm planning to love you all day and night for the rest of our lives, Kyria Manolis."

She smiled and kissed him with fervor. "That's right. I *am* Mrs. Manolis, and I want a baby with you as soon as possible. The next time we go to the paint store to pick out the color for the nursery, *I* plan to be the one that woman deals with, not you. I want blue."

"I was thinking pink."

They kissed again. "For once we disagree."

"No. We'll simply build another couple of rooms on the rear of the house. I'd like to call our first daughter Lysette, in honor of Nassos. He brought us together, my love."

"That's so sweet." She covered his face with kisses. "Spoken like my unmatchable husband. I think our first boy should be Nikos Takis Manolis, in honor of your father and *you*!"

Takis's low chuckle melted her bones before he rolled her over and began kissing her into oblivion.

Much later they were served another exquisite meal. After they were replete, Takis lay on his side so they could look into each other's eyes. "I have an idea what we should do with the hotel in Heraklion."

"So do I. We'll keep it and run it together."

"Yes, and whichever one of our children shows an interest in running it, we'll let them have at it."

She traced his lips with her finger. "What if one of them wants to change it in unorthodox ways? How will you feel about that?"

He took a deep breath. "One thing is for sure. All of us will talk everything out together so there can be no chance for misinterpretation that can lead to years of uncertainty."

"Oh, I'm so glad you said that!" she cried. "No woman was ever so lucky. Come here, my husband, and let me love you like you've never been loved before. I might not let you out of this room for days."

"I'm going to hold you to that promise, you beautiful creature."

By the first of June the weather was actually hot in Florence, Italy. Lys had felt sick before they'd flown here and had welcomed the cool of Dimi's villa.

Either her symptoms meant she was coming down with the flu, or... *Was it possible she was pregnant this soon?* Gemma had confided that she'd had similar symptoms when she realized she was carrying Vincenzo's baby.

Before leaving for the church the next morning, Lys did a home pregnancy test. To her joy, it showed she was pregnant with Takis's baby. But she didn't want to tell him the news until after Dimi's wedding.

The festivities leading up to the big day and exquisite marriage ceremony had worn her out and after they left for Dimi's villa following the reception, she noticed the temperature hadn't cooled down.

For the moment, she longed to lie down in their room until their flight home tomorrow. But once they were in the limo, Takis told the chauffeur to drive them to the airport. She turned to her husband in alarm. "I thought we weren't leaving until tomorrow."

He flashed her his mysterious smile. "Don't worry. I made arrangements for our luggage to be put on the plane. We're taking a little twenty-four-hour detour to Milan before we go home. After our honeymoon on the yacht several months ago, I wanted us to enjoy another one in Milan, but decided to save this surprise until after Dimi's wedding."

She hated to tell him she wasn't feeling well and spoil his plans. "I—I didn't realize you have work to do at the *castello* this trip," her voice faltered. All she wanted was to get back to the villa and go to sleep in a cold room, but he'd been so wonderful to her, she couldn't dampen his happiness right now. With Dimi's marriage, he was on a high.

Takis kissed her. "This isn't for work. Humor me, *agape mou*."

She loved him so much she would do it if it killed her.

Two hours later when they pulled up to the front entrance parking, he kissed her awake. "Come on, sleepyhead. We're here."

She tried her best to cooperate as they walked up the endless stairs leading to the main entrance. He hurried them inside and down the hall to the rear of the *castello,* where she had to face a winding stone staircase.

Her head began to swim as they ascended the medieval tower, and positive she wouldn't make it, she sagged against him.

"Are you all right? We're almost there."

"My darling husband—are you sure you don't hope I'll expire before we reach the top?"

The whole shadowy medieval stairway echoed with his laughter. "A few more minutes and all your fears will disappear."

When she reached the fortress-like door, he opened

it for her. "We've arrived where it will be my joy to wait upon my precious wife."

Her heart kicked her ribs hard as they walked over the threshold and he led her toward the bedroom. The tower suite was a vision of ducal elegance dating back several centuries. The light through the stained-glass windows covered the room in thousands of different colors and nearly took her breath away.

"Takis?"

"Go ahead and lie down on the bed. I'll be right back."

It was heaven to take off her suit and just sink onto the bed. She had no strength at this point. A minute later she heard him call to her and she opened her eyes.

Lys didn't know what to expect, but it wasn't to see the prince of her dreams come to life before her eyes. He looked so magnificent in the white tunic, and in the dimly lit room, Takis's eyes gleamed from his bronzed face.

In spite of how ill she felt, Lys's heart began to beat in time with the desire that thrummed through her veins and she tried to sit up, but he sank down on the massive bed next to her.

"Don't move. I want to look at my beautiful wife."

"Takis—"

"Since the moment you became my wife, since the moment I met you, I knew that you were the one person I needed, the one person I loved. I swore on our wedding night that I'd love you forever. And I intend to show you just how seriously I take that oath. Come here to me, darling."

But as he lowered his mouth to kiss her in frantic need, she had to turn away from him.

"Lys—are you all right?"

"I'm fine," she cried gently. "It's just that… I'm not feeling too good."

He smoothed his hand against her cheek. "I had no idea you felt ill. You should have told me."

"It's been coming on for a couple of days. I didn't want to say anything."

"I'm sending for the doctor." Anxiety had wiped the glow from his face and eyes. It reminded her of the way Vincenzo had looked at Gemma, who'd suffered serious morning sickness in the beginning of her pregnancy.

"No. It's all right. I don't need a doctor. I took a test."

"A test?" Takis looked at her expectantly.

"We're pregnant, darling, isn't it wonderful?"

For the second time in a minute the expression on his handsome face changed. This time to one of shock and joy. His hand slid to her belly. "Our baby…?" His voice of wonder reached the core of her being.

"I'll go to the doctor as soon as we get back to Tylissos. But as much as I want to make love to you right now, I can't."

Suddenly she rolled off the bed and hurried into the bathroom and was sick. He followed her in to help her.

"What can I do for you?"

She rinsed her mouth and face before turning to him with a faint smile. "I think you've already done it, big time." He helped her back to the bed. "But I do have one more favor."

"What is it? I'd do anything for you."

"Promise you won't make too much fuss."

"I promise I'll try to take this in my stride."

"Liar," she teased.

"I only want to take the best care of you and the baby," said Takis. "That's why I took you here."

"And it was a beautiful surprise to be brought here to the castello by my Cretan prince. I love you, Takis".

"And I love you too, Lys," said Takis, "I can't wait to spend the rest of my life with you, my love, my everlasting love."

* * * * *

*If you really enjoyed this story
then you won't want to miss
RETURN OF HER ITALIAN DUKE,
the first book in Rebecca Winters's*
THE BILLIONAIRE'S CLUB *trilogy.
Available now!*

*If you want to read about another gorgeous
billionaire hero then make sure to indulge in
THE BOSS'S FAKE FIANCÉE by Susan Meier.*

"Do you like bourbon? It's all I have right now. Bourbon or water. Or bourbon and water."

"It's fine," she said. When Zane picked up the bottle and poured them each about two fingers' worth of the amber liquid, she accepted the glass.

"I didn't know you were a bourbon drinker."

She wasn't. She didn't drink much, and the strong taste of bourbon wasn't her favorite, but tonight it would do.

"There's a lot you don't know about me."

This time his right brow arched. A challenge. He didn't quite smile, but his eyes lingered on hers long enough to be suggestive. He made a harrumph noise that seemed as if he was considering the possibility of them or sizing her up. It was thrilling and frightening, electric and grounding.

Flirting with Zane was like a wild roller-coaster ride that twisted her every which way. Sometimes it made her feel as if she was about to tumble out of herself, or shoot straight off the edge of the universe. But when the car that was his attention finally delivered her to the station with a buzzing rush, she was always well aware she'd never been in any real danger of falling. Scratch that—she'd fallen a long time ago…

* * *

Celebration, Tx:
Love is just a celebration away…

A BRIDE, A BARN,
AND A BABY

BY
NANCY ROBARDS THOMPSON

First Published in Great Britain 2017
By Mills & Boon, an imprint of HarperCollins*Publishers*
1 London Bridge Street, London, SE1 9GF

© 2017 Nancy Robards Thompson

ISBN: 978-0-263-92311-7

23-0717

National bestselling author **Nancy Robards Thompson** holds a degree in journalism. She worked as a newspaper reporter until she realized reporting "just the facts" bored her silly. Now that she has much more content to report to her muse, Nancy loves writing women's fiction and romance full-time. Critics have deemed her work "funny, smart and observant." She resides in Florida with her husband and daughter. You can reach her at www.nancyrobardsthompson.com and Facebook.com/nancyrobardsthompsonbooks.

This book is dedicated to Kathleen O'Brien
for your friendship and spot-on plotting advice.

Chapter One

May 2017

"I know I should've called first," Lucy Campbell said when Zane Phillips opened his front door, "but I come bearing gifts."

Standing in the doorway, looking cranky, his big frame taking up a lot of space, Zane silently eyed her offerings.

"I brought *The Breakfast Club*, *Pretty in Pink*, *St. Elmo's Fire* and *Say Anything*... and a few others." She handed the DVDs to him one by one as she read off each title. He frowned as he looked at them, and then he held up the one on top.

"This is a problem," he said, looking at the movie

as if he didn't know what to do with it. "I'm not in the mood to *say anything*."

"That's why I brought over a selection." Lucy reached into his personal space and tapped the DVD case. "If you're not in the mood for that movie, you can choose another one."

He shook his head. "No. Luce, you're not understanding me. I'm not in the mood for talking. Period. I don't feel like company tonight."

"I understand you better than you think I do. Hence the movies." And the reason she hadn't called before showing up. "You don't have to talk. All you have to do is watch. And eat Chinese food."

She held up a brown paper sack.

"Are you going to let me in? The kung pao beef is getting cold."

Storm clouds were rolling in and the fragrance of rain hung in the humid air.

"You brought kung pao?" His tone was lighter.

She nodded. "And General Tso's chicken, fried rice and egg rolls."

She'd known it wouldn't be easy getting past his front door. That was why she'd brought the food. She thrust the large brown sack at him, and he almost dropped the stack of movies. He shifted the DVDs into one hand and accepted the bag. Pushing past him, Lucy stepped onto the beige carpet into the living room of Zane's Bridgemont Farms house and squinted into the dim light. The curtains were drawn. The only light on was the one in the kitchen.

It cast enough of a golden glow to illuminate the mess in the front room. An empty pizza box, spent beer cans, a couple pairs of socks, some wadded-up jeans and a pair of mud-caked boots lying askew on the carpet. It all looked as if he had left it where he had dropped it, amid the stacks of cardboard boxes and piles of things he'd been sorting.

"Sorry about the mess," he mumbled as he grabbed up the jeans and socks and kicked the boots into a corner. A guy's way of cleaning. Her brother Ethan had similar tactics before Chelsea came into his life. Now, thanks to his future wife, Ethan was not only in love, but his house was also spotless.

"I'm still trying to figure out what to do with Mom's things. I've been bringing over a few boxes at a time. There's still so much stuff in her house— er, your family's house."

"You know there's no hurry to move her things out," Lucy said. "We don't have renters. You can take as long as you need. You don't have to bring everything over here to sort it if you don't have room for it. Just leave it at the house."

"Bossy." He scowled. "I've got a system. It's working fine."

For decades, his mom, Dorothy, had rented the small bungalow on the lower edge of the Campbells' property. Zane and his brother, Ian, had grown up there with their mother, who'd stayed in the house long after her boys had moved out and moved on with their lives. Lucy thought she and her brothers had made it clear that Zane could take all the time he needed to get Dorothy's things in order before he turned over the keys. That was how people treated each other in Celebration—they compromised and met each other halfway, especially in the wake of a family crisis. And Dorothy Phillips's surrender to an aggressive form of lymphoma that had ended her life nearly as fast as the disease had appeared hadn't been just a family crisis—it was a loss felt by the entire town. Many friends and neighbors, including Lucy, had reached out and offered to help Zane with the move out, but true to his lone-wolf ways, Zane had politely turned down the gestures of goodwill in favor of going it alone. He said he needed time to think, time to figure out what to do with the remnants of his mother's life. Everyone had respected his wishes and left him alone. Well, everyone except for Lucy. She knew him well enough to understand that sometimes Zane's pride kept him from asking for or accepting help. Sometimes Zane needed to be shown that his way wasn't always the best way. Tonight was a case in point.

"Why don't you take your *system* into the kitchen and get us some plates?" Lucy said. "I'll get the first DVD queued up and ready to play."

"The *first* one? You're not planning on watching all of them, are you?"

"Of course we are, that's why I brought them."

"You'll be here all night."

Lucy smiled and cocked a brow in the most suggestive way possible.

He shook his head. "Don't start with me, Campbell." He handed her the movies and grabbed a trio of beer cans off the coffee table to clear a spot for the sack of food. She watched him disappear around the corner into the kitchen, where he rattled around for a few minutes. It sounded like he was tidying up in there, too.

Lucy turned on a table lamp. In the light's golden glow, she could see that the place wasn't dirty as much as it was cluttered boxes of Dorothy's things. What with juggling the funeral arrangements, moving his mom's possessions to his house and his job as general manager of Bridgemont Farms, his living room looked rougher around the edges than usual. Then again, it didn't take much to make such a small house look messy.

A stack of boxes lined the far wall. Several small piles consisting of various household appliances and articles of clothing, shoes and accessories sat waiting on the floor. A couple of garbage bags sagged in the corner, probably filled with items that hadn't made the cut.

Ian had come back to Celebration for the funeral. He'd done what he could to help clear out the house while he was here, but Zane had mentioned that sifting through more than a quarter century's worth of their mother's life had proved too arduous a task in the days immediately after the funeral. They hadn't even made a dent before Ian had had to leave and get back to his job in Colorado. That left Zane to finish the job and tie up all the loose ends.

As Lucy picked up the empty pizza box and started to put it in one of the garbage bags, she spied Dorothy's sketchbook in the trash. She set aside the box and took out the book, running her hand over its tattered and faded no-frills cover before she leafed through the pages of hand-drawn fashion illustrations.

Lucy's heart clenched. In her mind's eye she could see Dorothy sitting on the house's back porch at the patio table with a cigarette and a cup of coffee, drawing in this book. Lucy used to love to watch her. Dorothy had patiently answered Lucy's never-ending stream of little-girl questions as the woman's deft hands brought to life the magical vignettes. After Dorothy had made Lucy's prom dress, Lucy had always thought of her as her very own fairy godmother.

Why would Zane throw this away? Lucy started to call to him in the kitchen, but it dawned on her that if he'd tossed such a personal item, it had to mean that in this moment it was too painful for him to keep it. She turned a few more pages, marveling at the delicate lines and brilliant color choices, at the fabric swatches Dorothy had pinned to the pages. It might be too painful for him to hang on to the sketchbook right now, but she was sure that someday, he would be sorry he'd thrown it away.

She'd slipped the book into her purse and had resumed her mission of tidying up the living room when Zane returned with a bottle of bourbon and two crystal highball glasses that looked out of place in his rugged bachelor digs. He balanced a ceramic cereal bowl full of ice atop the glasses. The makeshift ice bucket looked much more Zane-indigenous than the crystal barware.

"Those are fancy," she said, indicating the glasses.

"They were my mom's."

Even more than being her fairy godmother, Dorothy had been like a second mom to Lucy after her own mother passed when Lucy was just fourteen. Being here for Zane—looking in on him and making sure he ate something more than take-out pizza—was the least she could do to honor Dorothy's memory. Zane was big and strong and stoic. He wouldn't let on that he was hurting over his mom's passing, even though undoubtedly he was. That was why Lucy hadn't listened to him when he'd said he wasn't in the mood for company. That was why she'd shown up uninvited and pushed her way into his house.

"This wasn't hers." The ice clinked in the cereal bowl as he set it down on the table.

"Clearly. That ice bucket has *Zane Phillips* written all over it."

"Do you like bourbon? It's all I have right now. Bourbon or water. Or bourbon and water."

"Whatever you have is fine," she said. Zane picked up the bottle and poured them each about two fingers' worth of the amber liquid and she accepted the glass.

"I didn't know you were a bourbon drinker."

She wasn't. She didn't drink much and the strong taste of the liquor wasn't her favorite, but tonight it would do.

"There's a lot you don't know about me."

This time his right brow arched. A challenge. He didn't quite smile, but his eyes lingered on hers long enough to be suggestive. He made a *harrumphing* noise that seemed as if he was considering possibilities, or, at the very least, sizing her up. The thought of him thinking of her *like that* was thrilling and frightening, and she loved it.

Flirting with Zane was like a wild roller-coaster ride that twisted her every which way. Sometimes it made her feel as if she was about to tumble out of herself, or shoot straight off the edge of the universe. But when the car that was his attention finally delivered her to the station with a buzzing rush, she was always well aware she'd never been in any real danger of falling. Scratch that—she'd *fallen* a long time ago, but with Zane she knew she was never at risk of getting hurt. Because he didn't think of her *like that*.

"Want some ice?" he asked.

"Straight up is fine."

He touched his glass to hers. She followed his lead and tossed back the shot. It burned her throat as it went down. She fought the urge to cough. Finally, the fire settled into a gentle warmth that bloomed in her chest and then in her belly.

"Another?" Zane asked.

She nodded, even though she knew she needed to pace herself. She had no illusions of trying to hold her own with Zane, who had been drinking a bit too much since Dorothy died.

After he refilled her glass, she spooned three ice cubes into the bourbon. With ice, he wouldn't expect her to throw it back in one gulp again. Of course, she could've just told him she wanted to sip it straight up. For that matter, she could've just told him she'd had enough. He wasn't the kind of guy who would force her to do anything she didn't want to do. But she didn't want to make an issue out of it. Honestly, since Zane had been so closed-off lately, she wanted a little liquid courage—just enough to take the edge off and lubricate the hinges—so that she could open up and draw him out. Icing the bourbon would make it a sipping drink, a prop she could nurse for hours.

Obviously, Zane had no need for a prop. He tossed back another shot the same way he had the first one and went to pour one more.

"Whoa there, Bucky." She put her hand on his. "We don't have to polish off the entire bottle in the first five minutes. Why don't we eat something?"

"All I've done the past two weeks is eat," he said as he finished pouring himself a third drink. "People brought over so much food, I had to start freezing it."

"Ahh, which explains the pizza box," she said. "Makes sense. People bring food, you order pizza."

The right side of his mouth quirked. "Smart-ass."

Lucy shrugged.

The ladies of Celebration had seized the opportunity to cook for Zane. He was the most deliciously eligible bachelor in town. Every woman in town, young and old, loved Zane. Dorothy's passing, as sad as it was, was an excuse for them to bring him food and flirt. Lucy wondered if any of them had offered more personal means of comfort. Then she blinked away the thought. But not before pondering the possibility of him accepting said *comfort*.

No!

"I can only eat so much of Mrs. Radley's tuna-noodle surprise."

That's better. Let's talk about Mrs. Radley. She'd attended enough church potlucks and picnics to understand what he meant. Mrs. Radley's tuna-noodle surprise was infamous. The older the woman got, the more suspicious the congregation grew about the *surprise* mixed in with the tuna and noodles. Popular speculation wondered if she inadvertently used her cat's food in place of canned tuna. Only the bravest souls dared to try to figure it out.

"Did you actually eat it?"

"Of course. I appreciate her going to the trouble to make it for me."

Lucy winced. "And what was the verdict? Tuna for humans or fur babies?"

Zane thought about it for a moment as he added a few ice cubes to his drink, like Lucy had. "Hard to tell."

Lucy made a gagging sound and Zane laughed.

Maybe it was the bourbon that was lifting his mood, but she preferred to think it was her company.

"Chinese food sounds really good, Luce. Thanks for bringing it over."

The ice cubes clinked as he swirled his glass. He took a sip. As he watched her over the rim, she sensed something else in his demeanor shift. It made her senses tingle.

"I'm glad it sounds good. I know you've been showered with food gifts lately. I mean, I helped organize the deliveries."

Ugh. Stop talking. There's nothing wrong with a little silence.

She clamped her mouth shut so she wouldn't let it slip that she'd rescued Dorothy's sketchbook from the trash and ask him why he'd thrown it away. Or babble more inane thoughts about food gifts, like how when people died everyone wanted to feel useful. Help usually came in the form of neighbors dusting off recipes, firing up stoves and cooking way more food than anyone could reasonably consume.

Then after the funeral, life went on. People went back to the day-to-day grind and left the survivors hungry for more than a casserole, leaving them to make emotional decisions that resulted in tossing out beloved belongings that were too painful to look at now.

Tonight was all about showing Zane he wasn't alone. That he could lean on her. That she would keep him from making mistakes he'd regret later.

Really it sounded a lot more altruistic than it was because there was no place on earth she'd rather be right now than drinking bourbon, eating Chinese takeout and watching '80s movies with him.

And thank God she hadn't said *that* aloud, because it was definitely the bourbon talking.

Sort of.

Bourbon with a healthy chaser of truth.

"I'll get those plates." He set his drink on the coffee table and disappeared into the kitchen again. While he was gone, she moved several books about horse training and some industry-related magazines off the sofa, making room for them to sit.

Next, she pressed Play on the DVR remote. The opening scene of *Say Anything...* appeared on the screen. They didn't have to watch it now, but at least it would be background noise to fill any awkward silence so that she didn't feel the need to go on and on about everything that popped into her mind.

"If you don't want to keep these boxes here, I have room in the storage room in the barn," she said.

Earlier this year, Lucy had turned a dream into a reality when she'd converted the old abandoned barn on the property she'd inherited from her parents into a wedding venue called the Campbell Wedding Barn. During the first phase of renovations, she'd had the builder add on a good-sized, air-conditioned storage room.

"That way you can take it a box at a time and figure out what you want to do with everything."

He returned with the plates. "Thanks. But I'm good."

"Of course," Lucy said. "Zane, you're doing a great job. I know your mom is looking down on you from up there, appreciating all your hard work."

He frowned. "It is what it is. It has to be done. So I'm doing it."

"Be sure and let me know if you need any help sorting things out," Lucy said. "You know I'm here for you."

A small smile lifted the corners of Zane's mouth. He lifted his glass to her again. "Yes, you are. If I didn't say so before, I appreciate it."

"I know you do."

She thought about pointing out that sometimes she knew what he needed better than he knew himself, but she kept that bit to herself. Instead, she occupied herself taking the food out of the bag and opening the various containers. Better to show him than tell him. Her heartbeat kicked up a little bit. Yes, definitely better to show him.

Zane watched Lucy put her empty plate on the coffee table, kick off her flip-flops and pull her knees up to her chest. She looked small sitting there like that on his couch, with her long brown hair pulled back into a ponytail and her face virtually free of makeup. Since her attention was focused on the movie, Zane had free rein to watch her. It was a good thing, too, because tonight he couldn't keep his eyes off her. He loved her smile and her laugh and the way her eyes got big when the movie surprised her, even though she'd probably seen it dozens of times.

His reaction to her baffled him.

This was Lucy. *Lucy*. He had to be out of his damn mind to be looking at her like she was anything else than a little sister. Ethan Campbell's little sister. Ethan Campbell, his friend—a guy who was more like a brother to him than his own brother.

Lucy threw back her head and laughed at something in the movie that Zane hadn't heard. All that registered with him was the music of her laugh; it surrounded him, lifted him up, made him feel as if everything just might be okay. All he could see was the delicate curve of her neck and the way her upper lip was slightly fuller than her bottom lip. How had he never noticed that before?

Despite all his screwups, he must've done something right to have someone as good and pure as Lucy in his life.

"You doing all right?" She'd caught him watching her. He could see that her eyes were slightly misty from laughing.

"Fine," he said, even though he was feeling a weird kind of off-kilter right now.

He took a fortifying sip of his bourbon. The ice had melted and watered it down.

"Do you like the movie?" she asked.

"Not really." He smiled to make it clear that he was yanking her chain.

She shifted so that she was facing him, her tanned legs tucked underneath her. "We can switch to another one if you want."

He waved her off. "You're enjoying it enough for both of us. So no worries."

He took another sip and she mirrored him, picking up her glass and raising it to her lips. She closed her eyes she drank. He had the ridiculous urge to reach out and run a thumb over her cheek to see if her skin was as smooth and soft as it looked. He didn't know because he'd never touched her like that.

This is Lucy, man. Be cool.

The world really was upside down if he was suddenly wanting to touch Lucy Campbell in ways that were decidedly unbrotherly, but he had to be honest with himself—that was exactly what he wanted to do. Even if he hadn't realized it until now. Since she'd been back in Celebration, it had never been so clear to him that Lucy was a grown woman who was decidedly *not* his sister.

He picked up the bottle and refilled his glass. As he started to set it down, he realized Lucy was holding out hers even though most of the original pour was still in it.

"Are you going to be okay to drive home later?" he asked as he filled her glass.

She shrugged. "We have a lot of movies to watch. And if I'm not, I can just spend the night here." She patted the sofa.

"Or I can call you a cab," he added quickly, as

much to chase away the thought of her spending the night. "People might talk if they see your car parked here overnight."

She laughed. "Let them talk. I didn't realize you were so worried about your reputation."

She held his gaze as she reached over to set her glass on the table and missed the surface by a fraction of an inch. Bourbon sloshed over the edge and the *ting* of crystal hitting the wooden edge of the coffee table sounded just before the glass fell. She caught it a split second before it hit the carpet. Good reflexes. She must not be that drunk.

In an instant she was sitting up straight, both feet on the ground, simultaneously blotting the spilled liquor with the white paper napkins that came with the takeout and examining the glass for signs of damage.

"Oh, my God. Zane, I'm so sorry. I can't believe I did that. I'm such a klutz."

"Don't worry about it." His hand touched hers as he commandeered the napkins—not so much because he was worried that there might be a stain, but because he didn't want her to feel bad. "It won't hurt the carpet. The bourbon will probably be an improvement."

He laughed.

"No." She shook her head, tears glistening in her eyes. "This is your mom's good crystal. I would've never forgiven myself if I'd broken it."

He stopped blotting. "It's just a glass. It's nothing special."

"Of course it's special. It's beautiful. And it was hers."

He shook his head. "I gave her the set for Christmas a few years ago, but she never even used them. I just took them out of their original box when I was in the kitchen."

Lucy blinked. "But they're so pretty. I can't believe she didn't love them."

"She did. Or at least she said she did. But she never used them because she said she was afraid something would happen to them."

"Yeah, someone like me would break them."

Zane waved her off. "Said she was saving them for a special occasion. Or, I don't know, something ridiculous like that. She was never particularly comfortable with nice things. God knew her louse of an ex-husband didn't even help with child support, much less spoil her with personal gifts."

Yeah, that was the poor excuse of a man Zane and his brother, Ian, were loath to call father. He preferred to not even think about the jackass who maintained that Dorothy had gotten pregnant with Zane on purpose. That she'd trapped him. He was so busy carrying around the chip on his shoulder, he seemed to think he was exempt from supporting his family. Never mind he'd gotten her pregnant again after they'd been married for a couple of years. It was always her fault.

After he'd divorced Dorothy, he'd married again and had kids. Zane didn't know his half brothers.

There were three of them and they weren't too much younger than him and Ian. He could do the math. He knew what that meant—that while his father was *away*, he was probably with his other family.

The real kicker was that Nathaniel Phillips had had the audacity to show up at Dorothy's funeral. After the service, Zane had confronted him, asking him what kind of business he thought he had showing his face. Ian and Ethan Campbell had flanked him like two wingmen. Ethan had herded Zane away, while Ian had asked Nathaniel to leave. And he did. He'd slithered away just as silently as he'd appeared.

Zane sipped his bourbon, needing to wash away the bitter taste in his mouth.

"My mom scrimped and saved and worked her ass off. Thanks to her, we never went hungry. We were always clean and clothed and we always had a roof over our heads. Our clothes were always from the thrift shop and the meals she cooked were nourishing, but never anything fancy. Although, if the Redbird Diner had pie left over at the end of her shift, she'd bring it home to us. I didn't even realize how poor we were until I was a lot older."

When Dorothy discovered she was pregnant and she and Nathaniel had gotten married, they'd moved in with her parents at the family's ranch on Old Wickham Road. A couple of years later, she'd inherited the land after her folks passed. When Nathaniel divorced her, they'd sold the ranch. Nathaniel got half.

His mom had lost her family home—his and Ian's legacy—and after paying attorneys' fees and relocating her sons, she had to struggle to make ends meet.

Nathaniel never paid a lick of child support. Dorothy had always claimed it would cost more to take him back to court than she'd get. But Zane suspected the real reason was that she didn't want to deal with the hurt of having to acknowledge that her husband had chosen his new family over them.

Out of sight, out of mind. Or at least she could pretend it was that way.

Zane's earliest and happiest memories were of working the Old Wickham Road Ranch alongside his granddad. Someday, he'd love to buy back the ranch. It wasn't for sale right now, and even if it was, he didn't have the money, since he'd used almost every penny he had to help his mom pay for her medical expenses.

Someday… But he knew that someday might never come. Dorothy's death was proof of that.

"She was a good woman, Zane. She was like a second mother to me after my mom died. Did you know she taught me how to sew? She was so good at it. Remember how excited she was when the traveling production of *Guys and Dolls* bought that dress she'd designed?"

Zane nodded.

"They offered her that wardrobe position with the show," he said. "She should've taken it and gotten out of here. Ian and I were out of the house. She could've traveled all over the country. I don't understand why she didn't do it."

Zane shrugged. "I wanted her to do it. I think everyone in this town wanted her to. But she said she was too old to become a nomad and *gallivant*."

He slanted Lucy a glance. "*Gallivant*. Her word."

He and Lucy laughed, but then they fell silent.

His mom had been a good, strong woman. Salt of the earth. You could rely on her like you could count on the sun to rise in the morning. But for all of her strengths, she didn't take chances. She'd worked her way up from waitress to manager of the Redbird Diner in downtown Celebration and she did clothing alterations and freelance sewing jobs in her spare time for anyone who was willing to hire her. That didn't leave a lot of extra time for fun.

When Zane turned fourteen, he'd gotten a job at Henderson Farms and helped his mom with expenses. He'd hoped that the extra income might make things easier. But somewhere along the way the person Dorothy Phillips could've become faded away, her potential lost to the demands of life, her fondest hopes and wants and wishes set aside in a box for a *special occasion* that never happened.

Lucy was quiet and Zane knew he should stop talking, but it was like he'd broken the lock on the compartment where he'd stuffed all his emotions, and everything was pouring out.

"You think you have all the time in the world to do all the things you want to do, but you don't." He took another swig of bourbon. "I have to get out of this town, Luce. I don't know what I've been waiting for. I'm thirty years old and I still don't know who I am or what I want. I mean, I know what I want, but I'm not going to find it here, not in Celebration."

Ironically, most people thought he was doing well. In fact, one woman who dated him was surprised to discover he wasn't rich. He'd owned a small horse ranch but had ended up selling the property after his mom got sick. The crappy insurance policy she had didn't cover all of her medical bills and there was no way in hell Zane was going to stand down and let her worry when he was sitting on assets he could sell and use to help her out.

Again, it wasn't that he was so magnanimous. Bridgemont Farms, the property that abutted his, had been pushing him to sell his land. Zane had been restless and they'd made it worth his while. They offered him enough money to allow him to help his mom and put a little bit in the bank; and he got to stay in his house because Bridgemont had hired him on as their general manager. Housing was a perk of the job. It was a means to an end, but there was no chance for advancement and Bridgemont's owners weren't interested in breeding champions.

Even though it was his choice to sell, it chafed to be limited by someone else's vision when he'd once had such big plans. Once, he'd dreamed of using the proceeds of the sale of his farm to buy back the Old Wickham Road Ranch.

Fate had different plans.

Even so, he still had an ace up his sleeve.

"Leaving isn't always the answer." Lucy pulled him from his thoughts. "Remember how I couldn't wait to get out of here?" Her eyes sparkled with optimism, or maybe it was concern. Zane couldn't tell. "I went away to school, and then I went to California, but nothing fit. Isn't it funny how once I came home, I found exactly what I'd been looking for and who I wanted to be."

"But you have roots here," he said. "You have your brother and your business. Of course you belong here. I have nothing keeping me here."

"I'm just saying you don't always have to go away to find your heart's desire. Sometimes it's right in your backyard, Toto."

She laughed at her own joke. He knew she was trying to cajole him out of his funk, but he couldn't even muster a chuckle.

He was happy for Lucy, that everything was working out for her. Of all people, he'd never begrudge her success and belonging. But she was six years younger than him. He needed to get his act together.

"I just have to get out of here—"

Zane's voice cracked and he swallowed the wave of emotion that was trying to escape on the coattails of his words. He hadn't gotten emotional since his mom had died. Until now, he hadn't realized that for the past two weeks he'd been pushing through life—through everything that had to be done—on some kind of foggy autopilot. Tonight it felt like the autopilot had died and he'd fallen from his fog into this hard new reality.

And he would've been okay, but Lucy was looking at him with those huge brown eyes. The gold flecks in her eyes that sparkled a moment ago had darkened a few shades. Her expression suggested she didn't know what to do with him. Hell, he didn't know what to do with himself. How was she supposed to know what to do with him?

That was why he was better off being alone until he'd sorted out all this emotional crap.

But Lucy's full lips quivered as if she was trying to figure out what to say to him. For a split second, all he wanted to do was lean in and kiss her so they didn't have to talk anymore. He wanted to lose himself in the taste of her, bury his face in her silky brown hair and keep going until he forgot about everything else that was going on in his life.

He cursed under his breath and balled up the soggy napkins he'd been using to blot the spilled drink a few moments ago. He tossed it aside before pushing to his feet and walking over to the window, where he could give himself some space to get his head on straight and stuff this damn sentimentality back into the box where it belonged.

"Are you okay?" she asked from behind him. His awareness of her had his body responding.

He didn't turn around. "Yeah, I—"

He needed to forget he'd ever wanted to do the

things he was thinking about to Lucy. What the hell was wrong with him? "I need some space, Lucy. I think it might be best if you left."

Because putting physical space between them—moving away from her—wasn't helping him shake it off. No matter how far away he moved, he couldn't unsee those lips or the way she was looking at him with those eyes… Worst of all, he couldn't unfeel the way his body was reacting to her.

As he stood at the window, he listened to the DVD playing in the background, but it was just noise because he hadn't been paying attention to it before now. He tried to think of anything else besides Lucy: his job, the part he needed to buy for his truck, baseball.

Strike one had been the thought of his mom never getting to celebrate that elusive *special occasion* that would've allowed her to use those *f-ing* fancy glasses. Strike two was the realization that the first ping of the damn crystal was marking her passing. Strike three was even though the first two strikes hadn't made him lose it, the way Lucy was looking at him was going to finish the job. Or make him do something he knew they'd both regret later.

He was a mess.

And it wasn't her fault. That was why she needed to just leave him alone.

"Zane?"

A violent clap of thunder had the sullen clouds bursting open and spilling rain in angry splats.

"Lucy, you shouldn't be here."

"Why?"

Why? He couldn't answer her, because if he did, he knew she would see right through him.

Thunder sounded again, this time it was like a fist pounding something hard.

"Surely you're not going to send me out in this weather," she said. "Not after all that bourbon."

He turned to face her. She was standing so close to him now, much too close, and he could feel the heat of her—of them—radiating in waves. "You're right. I'll go."

"No." She put a flat hand on his shoulder as if to stop him, and their gazes locked. "It's okay, Zane."

He wanted to ask her how she could think this was *okay*. Nothing about this was *okay*. He turned back to the window. The rain was falling harder now, punishing everything it touched.

"I'm sorry Dorothy didn't get to use the glasses," she said.

Her words hung in the air between them. He didn't have words of his own.

"Life is too short to wait for special occasions, or until the time is right—" She paused as a shard of lightning ripped through the sky. It was punctuated by another explosive clap of thunder.

"Life is too short to put off doing the things you want to do," she continued. "Don't you think so, Zane?"

Yes.

No!

Ah, hell.

She gently caressed his shoulders. He knew he should stop her, but instead he sank into it, his body needing her touch. She slid her hands down his arms, past the sleeves of his T-shirt. Goose flesh prickled in the wake of her touch, at the feel of skin on skin— her hands on his bare skin.

As she slid her hands around his waist and pressed her body to his, he closed his eyes and leaned his head back, letting her warmth soothe him, allowing it to melt his better judgment.

He wasn't drunk, though he might have been lightly lubricated. He knew what he was doing by letting her touch him like this. But did she?

"Lucy—"

"Shhhh." She leaned in and the heat of her sweet breath on his neck made him forget what he was going to say.

"Zane, we can't wait for someday. All those things we've always wanted to do…" Those lips were kissing his neck now and every inch of his body was responding. "We need to do them. Right now."

Somehow, she'd smoothly maneuvered so that she was standing in front of him, her back to the window, her arms around his waist. Maybe it was wishful thinking, but her eyes looked as clear and alert as they had when she'd first arrived. She'd had only one shot of bourbon and had spilled most of the second one he'd poured for her.

"Zane, I won't break if you touch me."

When he hesitated, she whispered, "I want you to touch me."

He put his arms around her and she slid her hands down to his butt, pulling him in so that his body aligned with hers. There was no way she wasn't feeling how much he wanted her.

His lips were a fraction of an inch from hers. He rested his forehead on hers.

"Lucy, I don't want you to regret this. I don't want you to think I got you drunk and took advantage of you."

"You didn't. I know exactly what I'm doing, exactly what we're about to do. I've wanted this for so long. I think you want me, too, Zane. Don't you?"

If you only knew.

His mouth found hers and he showed her exactly how much he wanted her.

Chapter Two

Six weeks later

Peeing on a stick was not supposed to be this complicated, but Lucy had found nothing easy about the task—especially when it kept giving her the result she did not want to see.

Her hand shook as she tossed aside the seventh stick that showed a positive result.

No! No! No! This was not happening. This couldn't be right. She could *not* be pregnant. But a little voice inside her told her that the odds of seven wrong results were slim to none. Her hands shook even more as she pressed the pump on the top of the liquid soap and turned on the warm water to wash up.

She stared at herself in the mirror as she rubbed her hands together under the warm running water.

She was pregnant.

What was she going to do?

She and Zane had spent one night together. *One night.* Six weeks ago. While she was well aware that it took only *one time* to get pregnant, they had used a condom.

How could this happen?

What was she going to say to him?

Lucy turned off the tap and dried her hands on the fluffy pink towel hanging on the rack behind her. The color looked astonishingly bright in contrast to the bathroom's white tile walls. Then again, all of her senses seemed to be amplified right now. She'd finally bitten the bullet and taken a pregnancy test after living in denial, chalking up what she now knew was morning sickness to food poisoning and the flu—a very, very long bout of the flu. Never mind she was usually as regular as the Fourth of July falling on July 4 every year.

She was certain the only reason she was late was because she'd been under a lot of stress lately. The Campbell Wedding Barn had been booked solid since *Southern Living* had featured the venue as one of "The Most Beautiful Wedding Barns in the South." She couldn't have purchased better advertising. So she had to admit her work stress was good stress. Too bad she couldn't say the same about her relationship with Zane.

While the air between them since that night wasn't exactly bad—in fact, they were sickeningly polite to each other—they had agreed that it would never happen again. Zane had been racked with guilt. "It's not you, Luce, it's me," he'd said. "It was wonderful, but I care about you too much for it to happen again. I don't want sex to ruin our friendship."

Umm...okay.

Not quite the morning-after talk she'd been dreaming of writing in her diary all these years. It was confusing and hurtful. At first, Lucy wasn't sure if it was his polite way of giving her the brush-off, but then he'd told her he was seriously pursuing job opportunities outside of Celebration. Rumor had it that a once-in-a-lifetime opportunity at a ranch in Ocala, Florida, was about to become available soon—literally, people stayed in those positions for life. So they were rare. He'd already sent in his résumé. There and to several other ranches that weren't in Florida. Because of that, he'd decided it was in their best interests if they just remained friends.

After she had gotten past the first few stinging moments of him dropping the it's-not-you-it's-me bombshell, he had reverted to acting like his old self again. Lucy had too much pride to let him know that their one night together had been simultaneously the best and worst thing that had ever happened to her. Although, for one insane moment, she had seriously considered countering with a friends-with-benefits offer—because even though her sexual experience wasn't vast—*OMG*—she knew a good thing when she, *umm…experienced* it. And that night with Zane had been *that good*. Out-of-this-world good. Ruin-you-for-others *good*. Total justification for a friends-with-*bennies* relationship, because now that she'd had a taste of Zane, she was starving for more.

But then hard, cold reality set in. Lucy knew herself well enough to realize she'd never be content with something so casual when she was in love with him.

Yep. She loved him.

But he didn't love her.

It was hard to wrap her mind around his saying that he cared about her too much for it to happen again. He promised he had enjoyed it. He'd even gone so far as to say it was his *best ever* and that was why they needed to keep things platonic.

Umm… It sounded like an oxymoron if she'd ever heard one. *It was so good; I never want to sleep with you again.*

That did not make one bit of sense.

Of course, she'd been upset and that was when he'd told her that he was one-hundred-percent certain that he was leaving Celebration and he would never ask her to give up her business to follow him and there was something about long-distance relationships not making sense. So they needed to be friends.

Now it had gone from friends-with-benefits to friends-with-a-baby.

How in the world was she going to tell him she was pregnant?

She'd been in love with Zane Phillips for as long as she could remember. And, yes, she might have had a daydream or two about having his babies, but she never would've gotten pregnant on purpose.

She covered her face with her hands and hoped that he wouldn't think she'd tried to trap him. When her hands fell, she stared at her pale face in the mirror.

He was going to think it was history repeating itself. And not in a good way.

It was no secret that there was no love lost between Zane and his father. Everyone in the community knew that Nathaniel Phillips was a bad husband and an even worse father—that was, when he'd bothered to come home. Before he'd served Dorothy with divorce papers, he'd been gone more than he'd been at home, leaving Dorothy to basically single-parent their two boys. When Nathaniel Phillips got remarried, it came to light that he had children with another woman who lived in Dallas. The one he claimed was the love of his life. Once Zane had confided in her that his dad resented Dorothy and him because Nathaniel thought Dorothy got pregnant on purpose, to trap him. He never loved her, and that was why he divorced her and married the woman he did love.

As far as Lucy knew, he was still married to her.

Lucy swallowed the lump that was forming in her throat. She would give Zane credit for being more evolved than that. She knew without even a second's hesitation that he wouldn't blame her or accuse her of trying to manipulate him. Of course, she had to prepare herself for the fact that this news was going to blindside him. She also had to accept the very real fact that he loved her about as much as Nathaniel Phillips had loved Dorothy. Although she wouldn't insult him by comparing him to his father.

"Zane does not love me," she said to her reflection, thinking if she said it out loud her heart would hear it and wake up to reality.

She said it again and listened hard.

The words echoed off the bathroom tile as she said them again. Reinforcement. She needed to make sure the words sank in, that she fully understood the reality of the situation. He might care for her as a friend, and they might be darn good together in bed, but he did not love her.

But of course, he was an equal partner in this, too.

Even if she had started it, because she had been the one who had gotten the love train rolling, because she knew Zane well enough to be certain that if she hadn't spelled it out, if she hadn't made it clear that not only was it okay for him to cross that line but she'd wanted him to make love to her, he never would have touched her.

Once the train was out of the station, so to speak, they had both been equally willing participants. She put her hand on her flat belly.

This baby was nobody's fault. The pregnancy was

unplanned and not ideal, and Lucy was still reeling from the shock of it, but none of that changed the fact that next March, she was going to have Zane Phillips's baby.

In the meantime, she needed to figure out how to tell him.

Chapter Three

Even if Zane hadn't readily admitted it to himself, on some subconscious level he'd known from the moment he'd picked up the call from Lucy that she was upset. He'd known by the tone of her voice that something was off, but she said she was simply having *one of those days* and didn't want to talk about it over the phone. She'd insisted that she was fine, but she needed to talk to him today and asked him if she could come over. He should've told her about the interview and asked if it could wait until he got back, but he didn't. Instead, he'd told her to come over.

She'd promised she wouldn't stay long. He certainly wasn't bringing out any bourbon and he wouldn't let himself be seduced by kung pao beef.

He used the word *seduced* lightly, though. It wasn't as if he was blameless when it came to their night together. He'd been weak, and he'd given in to his basest urges. He was perfectly willing to take full responsibility for what had happened between them. And along with that, he was fully prepared to make sure it never happened again. The last thing he wanted to do was hurt Lucy, or toy with her emotions. Even though he hadn't been cognizant of that the night of the bourbon, he was well aware now and it wouldn't happen again.

He knew he couldn't change the past and beating himself up over things he couldn't change was pointless. However, he could help them move forward.

In the past, if Lucy had called saying she needed to talk, he'd always made time. Now was no different.

And when he heard her arrive, he thought he was being authentic to their friendship when he answered the door, got a good look at Lucy and said, "You look like hell."

He instantly regretted it when she glowered at him.

"Gee, thanks."

"I mean, you're always beautiful," he countered. "You just don't look like yourself. Are you okay?"

She made a sound that was somewhere between a squeak and a harrumph. When she didn't come back with one of her usual quick-witted responses, he knew something wasn't right. Then again, telling a woman, whether she was a friend or lover—

or both—that she looked like hell was a boneheaded thing to do. He never had been good with words. He should just shut up before he dug himself in deeper.

"Come in. It's hot out there." He stepped back and held open the door, letting her pass into the living room.

They hadn't been alone like this in weeks—since *that* night. It hadn't been a conscious decision not to be alone together, at least not something they'd discussed. It was as if they'd mutually decided to stay in safe territory.

They'd seen each other in the company of others and had gone on as if nothing had changed. And it hadn't…had it? Or had he been so damn determined to make things normal again that he hadn't let himself see it any other way?

As Lucy stepped inside and he closed the door behind her, memories of the last time they'd been alone flooded back and his body responded.

He was leaving within the half hour. His bags were packed and waiting by the door. He could exercise enough self-control to be alone with her. But judging from the look on her face, that wasn't going to be a problem. Though she'd said she was fine when she'd called and asked if she could come over and talk to him, it was clear as the summer sky now that something was very wrong.

"Are you going somewhere?" Her face had softened to a look of concern, but the characteristic sparkle was still absent from her brown eyes.

"I am." It was all he could manage to say before a look of dawning replaced her look of apprehension.

"Did you get the Ocala job?"

He shook his head.

"It's just an interview."

Over the past six weeks, he'd had several interviews at various ranches in the South—he'd even had a couple of offers that he'd turned down because they weren't exactly right. There was always something amiss—either the salary had been less than what he was making now or some aspect of the job wasn't right. Actually, he'd been holding out for the job at Hidden Rock in Ocala, Florida. It was the real deal. The one he'd been waiting for. A chance to work with champion horses; potential for great salary; opportunity to do the kind of work he'd been itching to do. While he'd mentioned the Ocala prospect to Lucy in passing—that the ranch was looking for a general manager—he hadn't told her that he'd finally gotten a call for an interview. The stakes seemed so high and he was enough of a realist to know he shouldn't get his hopes up. It was a coveted position. He hadn't wanted to say anything to anyone, especially not to Lucy, until he had something more substantial to report.

A first-round interview, especially since it had taken them nearly two months to respond to his résumé, was not substantial.

But in typical Lucy fashion, she seemed to zero in on what he wasn't saying as if she was reading his mind. The thought was simultaneously comforting and unnerving, since everywhere he looked in his small living room, he saw reminders of the night that they had made love.

The window across the room, where it had all started. The couch that was right in front of them, where they had made love the first time. The hallway to his right, where they had somehow managed to walk while staying tangled up in each other on their way to the bedroom, where they had spent the rest of the night.

Reflexively his gaze fell to Lucy's lips and his groin tightened as he remembered how sweet she had tasted and how it had felt to explore her body.

No. He wasn't going to fall down that rabbit hole again, despite the way he was dying to reach out and pull her into his arms. It wasn't because things between them hadn't been good. Hell, they'd been great. Off-the-effing-charts great. And he had spent the past six weeks cursing himself for being so weak that night. He hadn't been himself. He had been out of sorts and overwhelmed by the magnitude of everything that was happening around him that he'd taken comfort in her when she'd told him she wanted him.

It wasn't an excuse, but it was a reminder that Lucy Campbell was his kryptonite.

That was why he needed to have a will of steel when he was with her.

He did not want to hurt her and he knew damn good and well that was what would happen if he lost control again. She deserved better than he could offer. Besides, if he got the job in Ocala, he would be moving. He wasn't about to try a long-distance romance. She deserved someone who had his life together, someone who could take care of her the way she deserved to be cared for. As far as he was concerned, Lucy was a princess and he was about the furthest thing from a prince anyone could imagine.

The truth sobered him.

Plus, given the mood she was in, she would probably slap the crap out of him if he did try to touch her again, and he would deserve it.

Yeah, it was a good thing that the car that Hidden Rock had hired to take him to the airport would be here any minute. He glanced at his watch to remind himself of that.

"Why didn't you tell me about the interview?" Lucy demanded, sounding more like herself.

He shrugged. "It's just a first-round thing. I'll be back the day after tomorrow. You wouldn't even have missed me in that short time span. In fact, you wouldn't even have noticed I was gone."

She frowned again and said in a small voice, "I would've noticed."

Of course she would have. If anybody in this town would've noticed he was gone, it would've been Lucy. And that was the perfect example of just how deeply in denial he'd been since he'd done the morning-after, let's-be-friends walk back, when he'd tried to explain it wasn't that he didn't want her. His life was a hot mess right now and the uphill climb he was facing to get himself back on track required all of his focus. There were the job interviews, plus his itch to get out of Celebration and start over. All of that added up to the fact that she just deserved so much more than he could offer her right now.

Things were starting to happen for Lucy. She was having success with the wedding barn. The last thing she needed was dead weight to drag her away from what was important in her life.

"Depending on how things went," he said, "you were going to be the first person I told when I got back."

Her mouth tilted up into a Mona Lisa smile and she looked sad for a split second. But then she lifted her chin and gave her head a quick shake. Again, the Lucy he knew and adored came shining through.

"So, tell me what they said," she demanded.

"They haven't said anything yet. That's why I'm going. To get the scoop. We're going to talk about all the details when I'm there."

She rolled her eyes, clearly exasperated with his reluctance to share what he knew. "Well, surely they gave you some indication of what the job entails. Didn't they? I mean, if not, you could be walking into a situation where they are looking for someone to muck out the stables. It would be a shame to go all that way only to find out you're highly overqualified."

"I'll take my chances," he said. "Especially since

I'm certain mucking out stables isn't part of the general manager's job description."

"What? Are you too good to muck out stables?" She smiled.

"Of course not. I have vast experience with that. So, let's just say I've already paid my dues."

They were quiet for a moment, looking at each other, and for a few seconds it felt as if nothing had changed between them.

"So, this is the one, isn't it?" she asked. "The job you really want."

It was. At least he thought so, but he hated to say too much, because it was a long shot. Anyone who was anyone in the equestrian industry wanted this job.

But who was he kidding? Lucy knew him well enough that if he said no, she would see right through him to the truth.

"Yeah," he said. "I'd love this job."

She drew in a deep breath and nodded. "Well, good. Since you'd been turning down offers left and right, I was beginning to worry that you were being too picky." She shrugged. "Or that you had finally decided you didn't want to leave me after all. Hey, how are you getting to the airport?"

"They've hired a car to transport me to and from Dallas," he said. "But thanks for offering."

"Who said I was offering?" Her smile was a little bit too bright and the dullness that had stolen the shine from her eyes didn't match it.

He wanted to ask if they were okay. Instead, he said, "If they weren't transporting me, I would've asked you to take me."

"Yeah, well, good thing, then," she quipped, her smile still in place. "I would've probably been busy."

The sound of the air-conditioning kicking on filled the vortex of weirdness swirling between them. Okay, so he'd screwed up by sleeping with her. This was too complicated. He could tell she didn't believe him when he said he cared too much about her for it to happen again. But he didn't want to hurt her, and if things were this weird after only one time, it was bound to only get more difficult if they did it again.

"What brings you all the way over here?" he asked. "Surely you didn't come here just to see me off."

"Sorry, Charlie. Given the fact that I didn't know you were going anywhere, that's not why I came over. But since you are leaving, it can wait."

"That sounds ominous," he said. "The car's not here yet, so what's on your mind?"

She bit her bottom lip and looked at him as if she was forming her words, then she shook her head. "No, it can wait until you get back. We don't have enough time to get into it."

"Get into it? Are you mad at me? Is this about what happened? Because, Lucy, I really do care about you. I'm so mad at myself. I don't want you to feel like I took advantage of you—"

"No, Zane. Stop. It's not about that—"

"You are perfectly within your rights to be mad at me. And that's okay. You can punch me if you want to. You can be mad at me for as long as you need to. But I hope it won't be too long because what's not okay is for us not to be okay—"

The sound of a honking horn cut him off.

"Your car is here. You need to go."

Dammit.

"I don't want to leave you like this. Will you please just talk to me for a moment? Tell me what's on your mind."

She had that look on her face again. The look that made him uncertain whether she was upset or maybe she really wasn't feeling well. Only this time, she put her hand up to her mouth as she closed her eyes and drew in a deep breath. She really did look like she was going to be sick.

"Lucy? Are you okay?"

"I—I'm sorry. I'll be right back."

She dashed off down the hall. He saw her close the bathroom door behind her, heard her turn on the water.

For a moment he wasn't sure what to do. He wondered if he should ask her if she needed anything. But suddenly he had a sickening realization of what she'd wanted to talk to him about. He understood perfectly.

He stood there for a moment, seeing stars and cursing under his breath as reality sank in.

Someone knocked on his front door. Zane answered, knowing it would be the driver. He steeled himself before speaking. It wasn't the driver's fault that this day had become a huge cluster of bad timing.

"Hey, man, sorry to keep you waiting," Zane said, to the guy. "I'll be out in a minute. Just as soon as I take care of something."

"Not a problem," the driver said. "I just wanted to make sure you knew I was here. The name's Raymond. May I carry your bags out to the car?"

Zane cast a quick glance over his shoulder to see if Lucy had emerged from the bathroom yet. Then his gaze fell to the time, which was displayed in glowing green numbers on the front of his DVR. It was already after four o'clock. His plane was supposed to take off at just before seven o'clock and he still had a half-hour ride to the airport.

"Thanks, but no. I'll bring them when I come out."

A moment after Raymond left, Lucy emerged from the bathroom, clutching a wad of toilet paper. Tears trailed down her cheeks and she shudder-sobbed when she looked at Zane.

He finally gathered his senses enough to go to her and put an arm around her and walk her to the sofa.

"Lucy, did you come over here to tell me you're pregnant?"

"The bride wants to drape every single wall in the barn in gossamer tulle," said Juliette Lowell. "From floor to ceiling. The ceilings are so high. I don't know if that's even possible. Is it?"

Juliette was Lucy's friend and neighbor. Her family had owned the property to the south of the Campbell ranch for generations. Now she was the owner of a wedding-planning business called Weddings by Juliette and was sending a lot of brides and grooms to the Campbell Wedding Barn.

Lucy shrugged. "We haven't tried anything like that before, but I suppose anything is possible."

By the grace of God, she managed not to snort. Because, yeah, after the turn of events in her life, anything could happen. Proof of that was that she was pregnant with Zane Phillips's baby. So, yeah, *anything* was possible. Well, maybe not *anything*. Not the good things—not that this baby wasn't good. She just hadn't had a chance to wrap her mind around it yet. And she had to do that and find out if Zane had gotten the job in Ocala before she could find the good in anything these days.

After Zane guessed her news, he hadn't exactly fallen to one knee and professed his undying love. Not that she'd expected that. Well, okay, she wouldn't lie. It would've been nice if he'd declared that his eyes had been suddenly opened and he realized he couldn't live without her. But he hadn't. Zane had reacted like a man in shock, and then he had gone to Ocala to interview for his dream job.

In all fairness, he'd offered to skip the trip. She'd insisted he go. Basically, she'd pushed him into the hired car that had been waiting to take him to the airport. And how about that—a *hired car*. As if paying for overnight parking wasn't more than adequate, Hidden Rock Equestrian had actually sent a car and driver. This ranch was no rinky-dink outfit. No wonder Zane wanted the job so badly.

A wave of nausea crested. She inhaled and rode out the feeling. She wasn't sure if it was caused by the pregnancy or the reality that Zane might really be leaving. But she couldn't think about that now because Juliette was saying something to her.

"What?" Lucy asked, feeling dazed.

Juliette was staring up at the apex of the pitched ceiling.

"I asked you what the ceiling measures at its highest point."

Lucy followed Juliette's upward gaze. "Oh. Umm… I have no idea. I mean, I could take a guess, but I don't know exactly."

It was a long way up, that was for sure. Tall enough to accommodate a second story, which was planned in another phase of the renovations Lucy would do to the place once she had generated enough capital. She'd already implemented phase one, which turned the formerly ramshackle barn into a place suitable for fairy-tale weddings. It had cost a lot of money to make a place hospitable while keeping the rustic integrity that was so popular with brides these days. She was taking the renovations slowly, keeping an eye on her margin so that she didn't get in over her head. With the way things were going, the steady stream of bookings would allow her to pay cash for the next phase of renovations sooner rather than later.

But now that she was pregnant, she might have to rethink things. She might have to use some of the money she was allocating for renovations for hiring extra help.

She was pregnant.

The reality kept washing over her in waves. Each time it hit, the force of it threatened to knock her down.

Juliette was frowning at her. "Are you okay?"

Again, Lucy wanted to snort. Because she was so far from okay right now she didn't even know where she stood. But the only thing she could do was say she was fine, because she and Zane hadn't had a chance to discuss matters fully. There was no way she could confide in anyone else about it right now. Not that she didn't trust Juliette. In fact, Juliette was one of the most trustworthy people she'd ever met.

But talking to anyone about it before she and Zane came up with a plan just wouldn't be right.

"I'm fine."

"You just don't seem as if you're all here today."

Oh, she was all here—plus some. Literally.

Since none of life's usual rules seemed to apply anymore, they might as well try something they'd never attempted before and cover the barn's walls in shimmery gossamer. At least it would be pretty.

"Is your client supplying the tulle or are we?" Lucy asked.

"I'll have to confirm with her," said Juliette. "But judging from how hands-off this bride has been, I'd wager that she'll want us to provide it. That's been her MO so far. She wants a miracle and expects us to make it happen. You know, no biggie."

Juliette laughed and Lucy forced herself to laugh right along with her.

Lucy could've used a couple of miracles herself.

Zane had nearly missed his plane to Florida because after he had guessed what was going on—that she was pregnant—he had insisted he couldn't leave her. That was why she hadn't wanted to tell him after she saw his bags sitting by the door and learned that he had gotten the interview. The only way she had been able to convince him to go was by pointing out that nothing would change while he was gone, she would still be pregnant when he returned and they would talk about it then.

Reluctantly, he'd gotten in the car, and he'd texted her an hour later to let her know he was at the gate and his plane was boarding. At least he hadn't missed it. But Lucy would've been lying if she said she wasn't a little worried about this job interview. This was the big one. Nothing had fit until now, and at the rate he'd been refusing offers, she was beginning to hope that maybe he really didn't want to leave. But just looking at his face as he told her about the Hidden Rock job, she knew this one was different.

After he'd arrived in Ocala, he'd texted her pictures: the Hidden Rock grounds, with lush, rolling green hills surrounded by miles of white horse fencing; the quaint downtown with shops that looked like something out of a European village. The occasional palm tree in the background added a bit of whimsy. Ocala looked regal and horsey. It looked like everything he wanted.

She felt terrible because a selfish part of her didn't want him to go, didn't want him to move on to a new life in Ocala without her. But even as she let the thought take shape in her head, she regretted it. Another part of her only wanted him to be happy, wanted him to get everything he wanted.

It nearly broke her heart to think that she would never be the one to make him that happy.

"Earth to Lucy." The words shook Lucy out of her reverie. Juliette was staring at her as if she'd missed something.

"Sorry, what?" Lucy asked.

"How are we going to get gossamer tulle all the way up to the apex of the roof?"

As both women looked toward the barn's ceiling, it was uncomfortably quiet. Lucy could feel Juliette's irritation. She needed to give her full attention.

"I don't know how we can do it unless we bring in scaffolding," Juliette said. She felt her friend's eyes on her, studying her. "Are you okay? You just don't seem like yourself today."

"I'm fine. I just have a lot on my mind," Lucy said, crossing her arms.

Juliette's scrutiny made Lucy want to squirm and

after another too-long stretch of silence, Juliette said, "I know what's wrong with you. I mean, come on, honey, it's obvious."

Lucy froze. What was obvious? How was it obvious? She wasn't even three months pregnant. How could Juliette know?

"Luce, you can confide in me," Juliette said. "I'm one of your best friends."

That was true. In fact, many moons ago, Juliette was almost family. She had been nearly engaged to Lucy's brother Jude. But that was a lifetime ago. Jude and Juliette hadn't seen each other in ages. Still, Juliette was her friend and she was one of the most intuitive people she knew. But Lucy wasn't about to tip her hand without being darn sure they were talking about the same thing.

"What do you mean, *it's obvious*?" She made her best are-you-crazy? face.

"Look at you. You're exhausted. You're a wreck. I know you well enough to see the signs."

Okay, there was intuitive and then there was freaking mind reading. This was whacked.

Had she let something slip? She'd been careful to confine all of her pregnancy research to her home computer. Even then, she'd searched incognito. She'd written the obstetrician's name, number and the date of her appointment on a piece of paper and had tucked it inside her wallet. She'd written only the time on her calendar, without explanation, so as not to double-book. However, she knew she hadn't been herself. Maybe she'd let something perfectly obvious slip.

Lucy decided to test the water. "You can't tell anyone, Jules."

A look of compassion spread over Juliette's pretty face. "Of course not, but, Lucy, this is a huge commitment. You need to know there's no shame in asking for help. No one is going to judge you."

Lucy didn't know whether to run or stand there and let Juliette see her burst into tears. Her eyes were already beginning to sting. She wasn't sure if it was from relief that she would finally be able to talk to someone about it, or because she wasn't sure how she was going to tell Zane that Juliette had guessed their situation.

"I mean, if they do judge, let them. Who needs them?" Juliette said. "I don't see anyone else raising their hands to help you with Picnic in the Park. They want to make suggestions and leave all the work to you."

Wait. What? She's talking about Picnic in the Park?

It was the annual Fourth of July event in Celebration's Central Park. It was a big, labor-intensive deal.

"When you volunteered to chair, I was afraid it was going to be too much for you to handle on top of everything else. Not that you're not perfectly capable. I just know how all-consuming a new business can be, and even though getting involved can be good exposure for your business, chairing the event is another level altogether. Not to be smug, but when you raised your hand, I saw this coming."

Lucy saw stars. She had nearly spilled the beans to Juliette when Juliette had been talking about something totally different. She stood there unable to speak, unable to breathe, because of the close call.

But it didn't matter, because Juliette continued, "That's why, if you'll have me, I would love to be your cochair. I was going to talk to you about it later, but since you brought it up, there's no time like the present, right? So what do you think? Want some help? May I be your cochair?"

Cochair?

Cochair. Holy…

That was when Lucy realized she was shaking. Her head was spinning and before she could stop herself, she enfolded Juliette into a hug that was laced with equal parts gratitude and numb relief. Relief for obvious reasons; gratitude because she was right that she had bitten off a little more than she could chew. Throwing a pregnancy into the Picnic in the Park/ fledgling-business mix was going to add a whole new level to the challenge. But the event would be over in a few weeks and she'd cross that bridge when she came to it. For now, she would focus on how fortunate she was to have such a selfless friend in Jules. Her brother Jude had been an idiot to let her get away. But that was between Jude and Juliette.

When she and Zane did decide to share the news

of the baby, Juliette would be one of the first people she told.

As Juliette pulled free from the embrace, Lucy realized she had been holding on a little tighter than she should have.

Juliette frowned. "Are you sure you're okay?"

Lucy needed to get herself together—and fast.

"Yes. I'm fine. I'm great. I'm so happy that you offered to help me. It will make things so much better and it'll be so much more fun to work together."

"Luce, one of the first and most important rules of being in business for yourself is to know when to ask for help. You don't have to go this alone. Okay?"

The lump returned to Lucy's throat. She nodded, afraid that if she opened her mouth she might give herself away. She was already acting way too emotional for Picnic in the Park turmoil.

"Good, then," Juliette said. "I am going to get quotes on how much this gossamer-tulle endeavor is going to set back our client. I'll call John Rogers and see what he'll charge us to rent scaffolding. By the way, what are the dimensions of the barn?"

"About forty-eight by sixty feet," Lucy said, happy to ground herself in business talk.

Juliette pulled a notepad from her purse and scribbled down the information. "I'll call Maude's Fabrics and see if she can give us a deal on the tulle. I'm thinking wholesale. I'll let you know what I find out."

Lucy walked with her toward the doors.

"Let me know what I can do to help lighten your load with Picnic in the Park," Juliette said.

"Since you're offering, do you want to be in charge of herding Judy Roberts or Mary Irvine?" The women were longtime committee members who loved to make suggestions but never wanted to do the work.

Juliette's nose wrinkled. "Yikes, that's like choosing between bamboo shoots under the nails or eating an entire casserole of Mrs. Radley's tuna-noodle surprise. Let me ruminate on it and I'll get back to you. Maybe if I take long enough, you'll forget you asked me."

"Don't count on it."

After Juliette left, Lucy stood in the middle of the barn watching dust motes dance in a ray of sun streaming in from the skylight overhead. She put her hand on her flat stomach. This baby was going to change everything, but she was already attached to the tiny being growing inside her. They were going to be okay. No matter what Zane had to say, no matter where Zane ended up working and living, she and her baby would be fine.

During the two days that Zane was in Ocala, Lucy learned that she was much better off if she stayed busy. It gave her less time to dwell and obsess over the photos Zane had been texting her. She'd nearly driven herself crazy trying to decipher whether Hidden Rock was a good fit for him by looking at the photos and the level of his enthusiasm in his brief messages. It was like trying to read tea leaves. Since her to-do list was a mile-and-a-half long, she actually did need to stay busy so that she didn't fall behind.

The following night, she was in her office, a small nook toward the back of the barn, which she'd had built as part of the first phase of renovation, when her cell phone rang, startling her out of her zone. She glanced at the crystal clock on her desk. It was nearly eleven o'clock. She'd lost track of time. But who in the world would be calling at this hour on a weeknight?

She muted Harry Connick Jr. singing "It Had to Be You," which was streaming from her computer— her favorite music was old standards, and '60s and '80s retro tunes; tonight she was in a Harry mood— and fished her phone out of her purse.

A photo of Zane mugging for the camera, the default picture for his phone number, showed on the screen.

"Hey," she said. "What's going on?"

"Hey, yourself. I'm home from Ocala. Where are you?"

She leaned back in her chair and savored the butterflies incited by the sound of his voice. He must've just gotten in. And he was calling her.

She hadn't expected to hear from him tonight... tomorrow, maybe.

"I am in my office working. I didn't realize it was so late."

There was a pause on the other end of the line. "I didn't even think about the time. I'm glad I didn't wake you up. I'm actually outside the barn, can I come in and talk to you?"

Lucy sat up in her chair and looked around as if she might be able to see him, which was silly because the lone window in her office was covered by shutters. No one could see in or out.

"You're outside the barn?" she asked, smoothing her hair into place and licking her dry lips, then biting them to create some color.

"Well, I'm sort of in between your house and the barn. I'm in my truck. I knocked on the front door of your house and then I tried the barn door, but it's locked. I know it's late, but I really need to see you."

He *needed* to see her? *Needed to?*

An entire troop of butterflies swarmed in her stomach in formation.

Common sense warned her not to get carried away. It was doubtful that Zane had come to profess his love. But the hopeful side of her, the romantic in her who had been in love with Zane since she was old enough to know what love was, wanted to believe he had finally realized the love he needed—the love of his life—had been in front of him all these years.

Her old daydream suddenly played out in her head: Zane taking her hands, getting down on one knee and saying, "It's you, Lucy. It's always been you."

"Okay" was all she could muster and the word sounded more like a squeak than an invitation.

Okay? Ugh. Way to woo him with your quick wit and charm. No wonder it's never been you, Lucy.

She squeezed her eyes shut. The phone was still pressed to her ear.

"Meet me at the door," she said. "I'll be there in a sec."

She ended the call and gave herself a good mental shake before she got up and started toward the front door. This was Zane. *Zane.* The same guy who had always been so easy to talk to…before she'd slept with him. Now he seemed out of reach. Even though everything had changed, at heart they were both still the same people. Weren't they? Because of that, there was no need to get all goofy and moony and shy around him now.

After all, he'd seen her naked. She'd seen him, too, and *gawd*, he was beautiful.

The memory generated a slow heat that started at her breastbone and worked its way upward. She wished she could blame it on her pregnancy hormones, but she was experiencing a one-hundred-percent Zane-induced moment.

When she opened the door, he was standing an arm's length away from the threshold, a safe distance, in the outer reaches of the carriage lights' amber glow. The scent of jasmine from the bushes that grew in reckless abundance on the ranch loomed heavy in the humid air. Off in the inky distance a nocturnal creature hooted mournfully. She understood the feeling.

"Come in," she said.

He stayed rooted to the spot, looking stiff, with his hands folded one on top of the other in front of him.

Lucy shooed away a mosquito that buzzed between them. She was just opening her mouth to say "Come inside so the bugs don't get in," but Zane spoke first.

"I've decided we should get married."

Zane realized he could have *proposed* in a different way. Maybe he could've tried to make it more romantic, but this wasn't about romance and it wasn't really a proposal, in the traditional sense of the word. It was a partnership.

Didn't most marriages end up as partnerships anyway? The good ones did—the marriages that lasted involved two people who may have thought they were in love at one time, but they managed to hang on after the fireworks died and enter into something more permanent and lasting.

He'd never had that with anyone he'd dated. That was why he'd never considered getting married, but now that there was a child on the way, everything was different.

While he was in Ocala, he'd had a lot of time to think. He realized that he and Lucy were just skipping the doomed romance and diving straight into real life.

Too bad she didn't see it that way. She stood there in the doorway blinking at him, as if he had just suggested they put soap bubbles in Celebration's Central Park fountain. Or go swimming in the water tower on the outskirts of town. Both of which they had done when they were teenagers.

As they stood there in silence staring at each other, it dawned on him that his asking her to get married really was just as outlandish as soap bubbles in the fountain and water-tower swimming. Only, their situation deemed it necessary.

While he was away, he'd come to the conclusion that if pregnancy had to happen, he was glad it happened with Lucy. He liked her. He enjoyed spending time with her. Didn't it say something that not even sex could screw up their friendship? This could work.

Really, settling down wasn't such a bad thing. While he was away, he kept having a crazy thought that his past dating life had been like a big game of musical chairs: when the music stopped, you grabbed a chair. But it was almost a given that sometime in the course of things the song would end and you'd be without a chair. The pregnancy had left him without a chair. Or maybe another way to look at it was that he had been the one to claim the last chair.

Lucy was his prize. He cared about her more than anyone he'd dated. That was probably because they'd never dated.

"Just hear me out, Lucy. Please, can we talk about this?"

She stepped back, clearing his path, but still looked as if she smelled something bad.

"I know this isn't what either one of us wants, but it's logical," Zane said.

He heard her shut the door behind them. It echoed in the cavernous belly of the empty barn, which was empty of chairs and props because it wasn't set up for an event. He walked straight through to her office.

When she joined him in the office, he repeated the question. "Don't you think that's the logical thing to do?"

"I'm not going to marry you, Zane."

"What? Why not?"

He lowered himself onto one of the chairs across from her desk. She walked behind the desk and sat down.

"How was Ocala?" she asked.

"It was great. Pretty darn near perfect. Exactly what I've been looking for. But don't change the subject. You didn't answer my question. Why won't you marry me?"

She winced. She actually *winced* at the thought of marrying him. *Ouch.*

He knew he was no prize, but he was trying to do the right thing. He wasn't going to flake out on his child like his own father had. His dad had ignored his sons—at least the ones he'd had with Dorothy—and he'd treated her like crap. He never took responsibility, always blamed someone else, and had so many excuses for his shortcomings that Zane couldn't even keep track. Then the bastard had had the nerve to show up at his ex-wife's funeral.

Zane was going to be different. Different started by marrying the mother of his child and sticking around for the kid.

"Did they offer you the job?" Lucy asked.

"Not yet."

Lucy raised an eyebrow at him.

"I mean, it seemed to go well and I'm hopeful that they'll make me an offer. We talked money, I spent time with the staff, they showed me the cottage that comes with the job as a benefit."

She was still looking at him in that way that was so un-Lucy-like. The Lucy he knew and cared about would've cracked a joke by now. This Lucy was way too serious. But then again, he had just suggested they get married. It was a sobering thought. Obviously, she found the idea pretty unpalatable.

"So you're going to take the job if they offer it to you?" Lucy asked.

"Well, yeah. Especially now with circumstances being as they are." He put a hand on his stomach. "The money is good. A baby is expensive."

She nodded. "I've heard. Do you want something to drink? I have water and there's some soda in the refrigerator left over from an event we had last week."

He really could use a beer right about now, but she wasn't drinking alcohol and it just didn't seem right to drink in front of her. "No, thanks, I'm good."

Lucy stood up. "Well, I need some water."

She grabbed a glass off her desk and left the office. Zane followed her into the barn's kitchen. It was a functional space, a working kitchen with ovens and an industrial-size stainless-steel refrigerator that could accommodate food for wedding receptions and other catered events. He'd lent a hand with the construction to help save Lucy money. He got a boost of pride every time he entered the room.

He planned on helping her with phase two of the renovations—the second-story loft area she planned to build in the near future. Well, if he got the job in Ocala, he would help as much as he could whenever he was in Celebration. But they would cross that bridge when they came to it.

The humming of the fluorescent lights and the splash of Lucy pouring water into a glass from a pitcher she'd taken from the refrigerator were the only sounds in the room.

"I didn't expect you to do cartwheels at the suggestion of getting married, but I had hoped you'd be a little more enthusiastic."

She glared at him and he felt like an idiot. Of course—

"You probably need time to digest this," he said. "I've had a couple of days to think about this—about what we should do. I'm sure you've been thinking about it, too. But don't you think we owe it to our child to be a traditional family? That's the conclusion I keep coming back to."

"I think we owe it to our child to be the best parents we can be," she said.

"Exactly." He smiled at her. Now they were getting somewhere. "How do you feel about having the ceremony right here?"

She set down the glass on the counter with a thud. "You're either not hearing me or you're completely misunderstanding me. So let me make myself perfectly clear. I am not marrying you, Zane."

He really didn't think this would be so hard. When she stormed out of the kitchen, her rejection made him feel…empty. This wasn't a game, obviously. It didn't have anything to do with the thrill of the chase, but he had ended things with more women than he could count after they'd started pressing him for commitment. Now that he was willing to take the ultimate leap, Lucy couldn't get away from him fast enough. If he didn't know better, he'd think she hated him.

Maybe that was the problem. Maybe she did. He had let her down in a big way. They had both been weak that night. He should've been strong for both of them and stopped things.

That night came pushing back with a sensual punch that had his primal instincts warring with what he knew was right—what he knew he needed to do… Or not do.

Damn it all to hell.

He took a deep breath. Then he opened the cabinet, took down a glass and poured himself some water from the pitcher. He guzzled it down, the coldness of it giving him brain freeze.

There.

That was better.

He set the glass on the counter and walked back to her office.

She was sitting at her desk with her head in her hands and he hated himself for being the cause of her pain. "I know this is a lot to spring on you all at once. Why don't you take a few days to think about it—"

"I don't need time to think about it, Zane. I appreciate the sentiment of what you're trying to do. But I'm not going to marry you. It's not personal, but—"

"Of course it's personal. Everything about this is personal."

"Okay, so it *is* personal. What I meant was it's not *you*. I am not rejecting you."

"You just won't marry me. I see. No, I don't see. That makes absolutely no sense at all."

She swiveled in her chair to face him. "Yeah, that sort of has the same tones of your telling me our night together was the best sex you'd ever had, but it could never happen again." She clamped her mouth shut for a moment. "But that's beside the point. When I get married, it's going to be for love—mutual love—and it's going to last forever. It's not going to be a forced situation—like one of those fake Hollywood back-lot sets, where it's all show on the side, but really there's no heart or substance to it."

"I understand that you don't love me, but I can live with that, Lucy."

She laughed. She actually laughed out loud and he had no idea what the hell was so funny.

"You don't understand anything at all, Zane. At least not when it comes to you and me."

Now she was just talking in riddles. And even though this conversation was one-hundred-and-eighty-degrees different than any of the other conversations he'd had about marriage with anyone else, it did have one thing in common—it always seemed to come down to women speaking a different language, which was something he was obviously supposed to understand, but he didn't.

Another way that it was different was that this was the point when he usually exited. When it got too complicated or too heated or too heavy, he simply called it quits. It didn't take a genius to see the similarities between him and his old man, but now there was a baby in the mix and he wasn't going to take the easy way out like Nathaniel had.

"Obviously, I don't understand," he said, taking care to keep his voice calm and steady. "I asked you to marry me—you said no. I asked you to think about it—you said no."

"That's right." She looked so small sitting in her chair. She wasn't wearing any makeup and her hair hung loose around her shoulders. He could see shades of the girl he'd grown up with, but he couldn't sense in her the friend that she'd become. Right now she seemed like a stranger. And it was killing him.

"What I don't understand," he said, "is how you can just close your mind to the possibility. Lucy, we are good together, we've known each other forever. We would make such good partners. Most people get married because they think they're in love, when actually they're just hot for each other. That never lasts, and when it fades, some couples realize they don't even like each other very much. You and I, we like each other. We don't have to mess this up by complicating it with love and all that other emotional stuff. So think about it, okay? Would you do that for me?"

The look on her face was heartbreaking and for a few moments he thought he'd actually gotten through to her.

"Is that what you think of love? Is that all it is to you—just some hot-and-heavy sex, and when the sex isn't good anymore, it's all over?"

This was one of those trick questions. He knew it.

"I stand by what I said, Lucy. I believe the best foundation for marriage is friendship."

"So do I, Zane. But I also believe in love. You have obviously never been in love, have you?"

Okay. This was probably a good time to wind things down. It was late. They were probably both tired. She was getting into territory that he didn't want to touch.

"So let's back up here for a minute," she said. "You want us to get married. Let's say we did. Let's say you get the Ocala job. Of course you should take it. That means you'll be in Florida. My business that I've worked so hard for is here. Someone's going to lose and I have a sneaking suspicion you will expect me to pack up and go with you. So that we can live out our pretend marriage and be a pretend traditional family. Is that how your version of the story goes, Zane?"

He shoved his hands into his pockets. "Lucy, we should probably call it a night. My offer still stands. But let's discuss it when we're fresh. I probably shouldn't have come over here tonight. I just wanted you to know that you don't have to worry. That I plan on taking responsibility—for you and for our baby."

She stood up suddenly and slammed both of her palms on her desk. Her eyes glistened with tears. "You just don't get it, do you, Zane? Can't you see? All this baby and I are to you is a responsibility. I can't marry you simply to appease your sense of guilt."

Now she was full-on crying. He wanted to go to her, but he was frozen, rooted to the place he was standing.

"This isn't the way things were supposed to turn out." She was sobbing. "You really can't see it? You really have no idea?"

"Lucy?"

"Well, since we're laying it all out on the table, you might as well know. For as far back as I can remember I have dreamed of marrying you. Yes, Zane,

I have dreamed of being your wife and having your babies. But not like this. I am in love with you. I always have been and unfortunately I probably always will be. I thought going away, leaving Celebration, expanding my horizons and all that crap would help me get over you. That maybe I'd meet someone who would make me forget about you, but I didn't. I didn't quit loving you because that's the way I'm wired. And it really sucks that you don't love me. I get that, you can't just turn it on like a light switch. But what you need to understand is *that's* why I won't marry you. Because no matter how good of friends we are, a one-sided marriage, a marriage where I'm in love with you, but you're only there out of obligation, will never work.

"*That's* why I won't marry you, Zane."

Chapter Four

The next morning, Lucy opened her eyes and the magnitude of what had happened last night came rushing back like a punch to the gut. She bolted upright in bed and pressed her hands to her face.

Oh, my God, what did I do?

She had told Zane that she'd been in love with him her entire life. That was what she'd done.

Sure, Zane had provoked it by asking her to marry him, but— *Gaaah!*

She squeezed her eyes shut, as if she could obliterate the nightmare. Because that was what it was— the stuff that nightmares were made of. Only, this was real. It hadn't happened in a bad dream. It had played out in living color between her and the only man she had ever loved.

She ran her fingers through her mussed hair, tugging a little too hard. She couldn't blame her slipped filter on the pregnancy hormones because she knew it wasn't the truth. She wasn't going to use this pregnancy as a crutch, an excuse for saying and doing things she shouldn't have done.

Instead, she tried to convince herself it was no big deal, that given the present circumstances, it was something he needed to know. Didn't he need to know she loved him? But it didn't make her feel any better. Because *no*, he didn't need to know that.

Major *TMI*.

It wouldn't change anything. Well, the only thing it might do was make life more difficult. It was as if something had possessed her and ripped the confession right out of her heart.

No, enough blaming everything else. She had betrayed herself by not having better self-control.

Oh, God. Oh, God. Oh. God. No.

Again, she covered her face with her hands, pressing her fingers into her eyes. How could she ever face Zane again?

She wasn't sure which was worse—having to face him, or worrying her confession might have sent him packing. She wouldn't be one bit surprised if last night's episode of *True Confessions: Lucy Spills the Goods* had inspired him to hightail it back to the airport and hop on the next flight to Ocala.

But she knew him better than that. Of course that wouldn't be the case. He wouldn't run. Besides, they hadn't offered him the job yet. Still, they would soon enough, and if he needed one more good excuse to add to all the reasons he wanted to leave Celebration, surely her blurting the *L* word would be all the reason he'd need.

She took a deep breath and let her hands fall from her face. She tried to blink away the blurriness caused from pressing so hard. Once she could see straight again, she realized the world was still turning; the sun had risen and was shining in through the spaces between the white plantation shutters, casting light and shadows, just like it did every sunny morning.

Obviously, life would go on despite her deep mortification. She resisted the urge to lie back in her bed and pull the pink-and-white duvet over her head. There was no time to wallow. She had a Picnic in the Park meeting and she was going to be late if she didn't get up and get a move on.

The situation was what it was, she thought as she padded on bare feet across the hardwood floors, into the en suite bathroom. She braced her hands on the counter and forced herself to take a good, hard look at herself. There was no taking back the words. No changing what had already happened. So she might as well get over it. She would need to figure out what kind of damage control she should implement so that they could move on accordingly. She wasn't going to marry a man who didn't love her and Zane would have to come to terms with that.

But for now, she had a meeting she needed to prepare for. She turned on the cold water and splashed her face. Even the bracing tap couldn't wash away the memory of Zane standing there, one cool cowboy. After her confession, he'd stood there stoically for a moment, and then, without missing a beat, he'd acted as if he hadn't heard her. He'd simply repeated his original suggestion that she take some time to think about getting married and they'd talk about it later. Then he left.

That was it. On the surface, it seemed like it hadn't even fazed him. After he'd gone, she'd stood there for a few minutes wondering if he'd even heard what she'd said. But of course he had. She'd blurted it loud and clear and now he knew.

It was simmering underneath and that was what made it worse. It would've been better if he had acted shocked or repulsed—okay, maybe not repulsed. That would've been worse. But some kind of a reaction would have been better than none at all.

Did he think by not acknowledging what she said it would simply go away?

Maybe that wouldn't be such a bad idea.

Maybe she should borrow a page from his playbook and pretend like it hadn't happened. Pretend like she hadn't made a total fool of herself, that she hadn't said anything at all.

If only.

She grabbed her toothbrush and squeezed out a pearl of toothpaste.

No, the only way to handle this would be to face it head-on and…and then what? Dissect the fact that she loved him and he didn't return her feelings? What more was there to say? She understood. She didn't need to make it any more painful than it already was.

Loving someone wasn't a heinous act.

I love you.

Boo. Hiss. You terrible person. How dare you love me?

In fact, if he had a problem with it, wouldn't *he* be the jerk?

But Zane wasn't a jerk. He'd never been a jerk to her. Not even when he'd told her they needed to just be friends. Even then, he'd been warm, and tender, and concerned about her. And he had been the one to first reach out in friendship, proving that nothing had changed between them.

Even though *everything* had changed.

She continued the mental pep talk as she brushed her teeth.

Plus, he was the one who had suggested that they get married. Of course, he had basically acknowledged that it would be a loveless marriage—and in his eyes, that was the beauty of the arrangement.

Then she had to spoil it all by saying "I love you." Ugh. Great. Now the song "Somethin' Stupid" would be stuck in her head for the rest of her life.

She rinsed her mouth and toothbrush and returned

the brush to the rack. As she showered and got ready for the day, she decided the best plan was to do nothing. She'd give Zane some space. Maybe her great revelation would make him think twice about the proposition he'd presented last night.

As she sat at her dressing table, she pulled up her music streaming app on her phone and found the Frank and Nancy Sinatra version of "Somethin' Stupid," the song that had earwormed its way into her brain since she'd inadvertently quoted it earlier. She wallowed in how perfectly the lyrics fit her situation as she put on her makeup. For balance, next she played "I Told Ya I Love Ya, Now Get Out." It fortified her.

The reality that had been swimming in her subconscious, just below the surface, came up for air: it wasn't supposed to be like this. In the past, when the going got tough, she'd always fallen back on her daydreams. In those fantasies, Zane had loved her. He would look at her and say, "It's you, Lucy. It's always been you." And then he would kiss her, they'd get married and they would live happily ever after.

But the reality of the situation was that Zane didn't love her. He was willing to marry her out of obligation.

She supposed she could take a chance that he might grow to love her—maybe she had enough love for both of them. But what would happen if the right woman came along and he did fall in love with someone else? He would be saddled with her and their child. Given all that Zane had gone through growing up, she didn't think he would cheat—he probably wouldn't leave her, either. But what kind of life would that be, stuck in a loveless marriage? Stuck with someone who you liked a whole lot but just couldn't love? It wasn't his fault. The heart wanted what the heart wanted. It wasn't as if he could reprogram himself to feel different.

But at the same time, she was only human and she couldn't help but fear being the one who was in love...the vulnerable one. The thought of such a lopsided relationship made her feel sad and sick. She'd experienced morning sickness enough to know the difference—this was what it felt like to be heartsick in a hopeless situation. For a hopeless romantic to have her fears of being unlovable validated.

The best thing she could do would be to do nothing. She would let Zane come to her, and when he did, she would tell him she'd had a chance to think about things, but she hadn't changed her mind.

Surely, he wouldn't argue with that, would he?

The Picnic in the Park event committee met in Central Park in downtown Celebration for a walk-through. Lucy was a visual person and she wanted to see the area where the community picnic would take place to get a better idea of where the games, tents and stands would go. They needed to make sure they had plenty of parking for those who were driving in, but they still needed to reserve an adequate amount of space for the fireworks and the food-truck brigade that was gaining a popular following in Celebration.

"How many tables do you think we need for the hot-dog eating contest?" Mary Irvine asked. "Last year Pat Whittington complained for a good six months that he didn't have enough elbow room and that's why he didn't win."

"Pat Whittington is a sore loser," said Sandra Riggs. "His not winning had nothing to do with whether or not he had enough elbow room. Maybe he should stop complaining, and stuff more food down his gullet. If nothing else, it would shut him up."

Sandra and Mary laughed. Lucy could see that this could digress fast, so she quickly steered them back on task.

"That's the reason I've asked people to sign up for all of the contests by the end of the day on July 1," said Lucy. "That way we'll have a better idea how much space we need for each event and we won't have to push people together."

Judy Roberts frowned. "You know we've never done it that way before..." She slanted a knowing look at Mary, who pursed her lips and raised her brows. "Word on the street is people think preregistering for the games sucks all the fun out of it."

Judy shrugged. "There. I said it. It needed to be said. I've been on this committee for as long as Picnic in the Park has been around and that's just not the way we do it."

Carol Vedder put her hands on her slim hips. "If

you've been on the committee that long, Judy, how come you've never wanted to step up and chair the event?"

Carol looked smug. "There. I said it. It needed to be said. You always have such good ideas, but you never want to do the work to get them done."

Judy blanched, and even though Lucy could have hugged Carol's neck for saying exactly what she was thinking, she did her best not to appear as if she was taking sides.

"It's okay. I appreciate everyone's help and all opinions are welcome," said Lucy. "Even so, I'm going to try out preregistering this year. If it doesn't work, the committee can always do away with it next year."

"I think it's a good idea to ask people to preregister," Carol chimed in. "It will make things so much easier for the volunteers on the day of the event."

Carol beamed at Lucy and suddenly Lucy wondered what the woman was up to. Carol could be just as challenging as the rest of the long-standing committee members. Why was she being so nice? What was she up to?

She knows you're pregnant.

The thought sprang into her mind unbidden. It was ridiculous. There was no way Carol would know. Just like Juliette, who knew her much better than Carol, hadn't known. Lucy had gone all the way to Dallas to purchase the pregnancy tests and she'd taken care to dispose of them in a public Dumpster when she'd been out of town on business. Besides, if Carol knew, she would undoubtedly be too busy broadcasting the news to anyone who would listen to be this nice.

Bottom line: there was no way Carol could know. Lucy forced herself to shake off the ridiculous thought and wrap up the meeting. Sure enough, as soon as they were finished and heading toward their cars, Carol caught up with her.

"Lucy, darling," she chirped. "Do you have a moment?"

Lucy's blood ran cold. There was no way she could know. She stopped and smiled. "Sure. What's on your mind?"

"Are you seeing anyone these days?"

Lucy took a steadying breath. "Why do you ask?" She took special care to infuse sunshine into her voice so that she didn't sound defensive.

Carol smiled like a Cheshire cat. "Because if you are unattached, I have somebody special I would like you to meet."

Oh.

Ooh.

What in the world was she supposed to say to that? She was in no position to meet anybody. She was in no position for anything that would make her life more complicated than it already was.

"I am sort of…seeing someone."

"What do you mean *sort of*? Either you are or you aren't."

"It's complicated," Lucy said.

Boy, was that ever the truth. It couldn't get much more complicated than this—she loved Zane, but Zane didn't love her. Zane wanted to marry her, but she didn't want to marry Zane. And the cherry on top—she was pregnant. Nobody in his right mind would want to date a woman who was pregnant with another man's baby.

"Oh, honey, why do so many nice girls like you allow themselves to be in situations that are *complicated*? Isn't that just another way of saying a guy is afraid of commitment? I'd say if he's so *complicated* that he can't recognize a good catch like you when you're standing right in front of him, he doesn't deserve you. I want you to meet my nephew, Luke. He will treat you right and he's a good-looking guy. A veterinarian. Lives in Houston. A good catch. Just like you."

Carol wiggled her brows and fished a photo out of her wallet.

He was, indeed, a good-looking guy. Even so, Luke might be the catch of the century, but he wouldn't think much of her when he found out she was pregnant.

Talk about *complicated*.

That was when something clicked into place—it really didn't break her heart to know that other men would find her unappealing, or even damaged, after they found out she was having a baby on her own.

She didn't care. She really didn't care. And it was the most freeing feeling she'd had in ages.

Her baby would be family and as far as Lucy was concerned the love of her family was all she needed.

Her phone dinged, signaling an incoming text from Zane. Her heart leaped at the sound of his special text tone, but she left the phone in her purse. She'd look at it when she got in the car.

"Carol, I'm sure Luke is a wonderful man. And I appreciate you thinking of me, but I have too much on my plate right now with work and the picnic committee. I'm sure you understand."

"Honey, just meet him. That's all I'm asking. I'm not saying you have to marry him."

This time Lucy's phone rang. It was the ringtone she had assigned to Zane. Thank God nobody knew her assigned rings. "I have to take this, Carol. I'll talk to you later."

Lucy turned toward her car before the woman could say anything else.

She waited until she was a few feet away before she answered Zane's call.

"Hello?" Her heart was beating like mad. She took care to keep her voice low.

"Hey, it's me. I need to see you tonight. May I come over?"

Just like that. As if nothing had happened last night. She should've said no. She should've told him to leave her alone. The words to the song "I Told Ya I Love Ya, Now Get Out" played in her head. Because he wouldn't be popping in like this once he moved to Ocala. And even though the words and her empowerment song were in her head, she said, "Sure. I'll be home after six."

"Why have we never dated?" Zane asked as he stood in Lucy's kitchen helping her chop the vegetables he'd brought her from the crate that Mrs. Winters had brought him from her garden.

Lucy's head jerked up and she looked at him as if he had just started reciting the words to a Dr. Seuss book.

"Because you never asked me out." She sounded a little irritated, or maybe she was just perplexed. He seemed to have that effect on her these days.

When he'd handed the vegetables to her in the rumpled brown paper sack, they'd seemed like a very inadequate peace offering after the run-in he'd had with her last night.

He would've given anything for her not to hate him. Anything.

Anything except his love, which was the only thing she really wanted and the one thing he wasn't able to give her, because he was incapable of falling in love. He had no doubts now, because if anybody was worth loving, it was Lucy.

Even so, he couldn't lie to her. She deserved better than that.

But she'd seemed pleased with the vegetables and

maybe even glad to see him—or at least willing to see him. And she had invited him to stay for dinner.

"Why have you never asked me out?" she countered. "Oh, wait, I know. Because you were too busy putting the moves on Bambi and Bunny and Bimbo—sometimes all at the same time—to fit me in."

"I never dated anybody named Bambi or Bunny or Bimbo."

"Yes, you did, because that's what I called them."

"Remind me to not let you choose the name for our baby."

"I will choose a lovely name for our child."

"*We* will choose the name," he said. "Luce, we're in this together."

The joking fell silent and the only sounds in the kitchen were the hum of the refrigerator and the sound of the knife hitting the cutting board. She had put him to work chopping the tomatoes, carrots and a cucumber for a salad that would go with the spaghetti and turkey meatballs she was making for dinner.

Now was as good a time as any to finish saying what he had come to say. But damn if he wasn't nervous. What the hell? When was the last time a woman had made him nervous? But he was. Dry mouth. Racing heart. Overthinking.

Get over yourself, man.

He set down the knife and turned to face her. "Obviously, I've gone through periods of my life where

I was looking for a *different* kind of woman. Different than you, I mean."

Her right brow shot up in a way that made him a little crazy.

"You keep digging yourself in deeper, don't you?" She was goading him. "At this rate, by the end of the night you'll probably be pretty close to six feet under. So, how am I different from your usual cast of fluffy woodland pets, Zane?"

But it was a good kind of crazy, one that, if he hadn't been so dense, might have made him realize a long time ago they had something good. That she was a good kid...er, *woman*. A good *woman*. Lucy may be a few years younger than him, but she was most decidedly a woman now. He had to keep an iron grip on his willpower so as not to let his gaze fall to her oh, so womanly curves, which were making him more than a little crazy, too.

He cleared his throat. "I don't care about the past, Lucy. The past doesn't matter. I care about now and what I came here to say is that I think we should try dating."

She scrunched up her face as if it was the most distasteful suggestion she'd heard in a long time. It wasn't the way he thought she'd react. Why should he be surprised when she always kept him guessing?

Not even twenty-four hours ago she'd told him she was in love with him. He knew better than to bring that up, but damn it all to hell, she was more confusing than any woman he'd ever met. She was like a riddle he couldn't figure out. A challenge that both thrilled and scared him to death.

The last thing in the world he ever wanted to do was hurt her. And he'd done that already. He'd let her down by letting *this* happen. He'd wanted her in the worst way the night they'd hooked up. He should've been stronger. He should've been strong enough for the both of them. Strong enough to walk away. If he had, then they wouldn't be where they were right now.

A strange feeling washed over him, because the more time he had to get used to where they were right now, the more it didn't seem like such a bad place.

"What did you say?" she asked.

"I said I think we should try dating."

"Other people? I think you've already established that." Her face fell and she turned back to the stove and stirred the spaghetti sauce.

"Lucy, I'm talking about us. I think you and I should try dating. Each other. You and me."

She didn't turn around. She just kept stirring the sauce. One of those sassy, old-fashioned songs from the '60s that she liked so much played in the background. Something about windmills and the mind. Whatever that meant.

Finally, when he couldn't take her silence any longer, he said, "Will you say something? Please?"

He saw her shoulders rise and fall, but she still didn't turn around. So he walked over to her, bridging the distance. He wasn't sure if he should touch her. He wanted to, but that was for purely selfish reasons. No, it wasn't. He wanted to comfort her, but he was afraid that, again, his good intentions would lead them straight into hell.

"Lucy, look at me."

She raised her hand to her face before she turned around to face him. He could virtually see her stiffening resolve.

"You want to date me? Why?"

Now she did look truly irritated.

"Because you and I need to get to know each other on a different level. I mean, we know each other well. In some ways, you know me better than any of the past fuzzy woodland creatures, as you called them."

"Fluffy woodland pets," she amended. Then she shrugged. "Although if you think *creature* is a better word, then go for it."

She rolled her eyes and chuckled a little, but it was dry and humorless. Still, he could sense that she was softening. He understood her hesitation. In fact, all day long it was all he could think about. She was all he could think about. Her and her earnest declaration of love.

Lucy *loved* him. How could he have missed that? How could he have been so completely blind to something that now seemed so completely obvious? After he'd left her, he'd sat with the newness of it most of the night. Even when sleep had found him, and it had come in fits and starts, he would wake up with the echo of her words in his head. And every time he closed his eyes he would see her heartbroken face, as if it had been imprinted in his mind.

More than anything, he wished he could return her feelings. But even though he cared about her— more than he'd ever cared about any woman he'd dated—he couldn't ever recall a time when he had been in love.

He was a lot of things, but he wasn't a liar. And telling Lucy he was in love with her would have been a lie. But that didn't mean he couldn't try. That didn't mean he couldn't treat her like the woman he wanted to marry. Like someone he could…love.

"You and I have sort of been all over the place. We grew up together. We're friends. We made love—"

She cringed, closed her eyes and made a face, but he wasn't sorry he'd said it.

"Lucy, we did. There's no sense in trying to sugar-coat it or pretend like it didn't happen. We did and it was great. And now we're having a baby. But I think we need to back up a little bit. We need to start over and build our relationship from the ground up. Even if you won't marry me, we need to know each other on a deeper level so that we can successfully coparent. That's why I think we need to try dating each other and getting to know each other as a man and a woman. So what do you say, Lucy Campbell—will you let me take you out on a date?"

Chapter Five

Lucy agreed to a date on one condition: things didn't get weird. Or any weirder than they already were. No flowers. No dressing up. No fancy dinners. That wasn't them, it wasn't who they were. Things like that upped the odds that things between them would be strained and…get weird. Things like that screamed *expectations*! The last thing she needed right now was to get her hopes up about anything. Especially when it came to Zane Phillips.

It was logical to put one and one together and expect two. It would be too easy to think that his willingness to downsize a marriage proposal to a first date, rather than getting mad and not speaking to her, might mean that Zane hadn't ruled out the possibility that he could love her. At least he was trying. He hadn't given up on her.

There she was, getting her hopes up. In this case, her better judgment warned that one plus one was more likely to add up to expectations. She always had hated math.

They were going downtown to get ice cream and take a walk. It would be simple and informal. Unpretentious. They could be themselves and just be.

Freshly showered, Lucy had blown out her hair and brushed some Moroccan argan oil through her brown locks to make them glisten. She'd kept her makeup to a minimum, just enough to make her look polished and put together—like she'd made an effort. Making an effort didn't mean she was making more out of this than she should. Nope. Absolutely no expectations here, she thought as she returned the lip-gloss wand to the container and gave herself a once-over in the mirror. In fact, she was doing this for herself because it made her feel good and everyone knew feeling good was the best armor a woman could wear.

As she stood in front of her closet, surveying its contents, her phone dinged, alerting her to a text. It wasn't Zane's text tone, but she took a look anyway. It was from Chelsea, her sister-in-law-to-be.

If you don't have plans this afternoon, do you want to go look at wedding shoes with me?

Chelsea and Ethan were getting married in a couple of weeks. The ceremony and reception were going to be at the Campbell Wedding Barn. Chelsea, who had relocated to Celebration, Texas, from London, was a real-life British noblewoman who had gone to college—or *university*, as Chelsea would say—with Juliette. Aside from her accent, people would never guess that Chelsea came from such a highbrow background. She was about as down-to-earth as anyone could imagine—except when it came to shoes. She had a penchant for good shoes—expensive shoes. Hence the reason the wedding was two weeks away and she had not yet found the shoes she would wear with her dress.

Lucy racked her brain for a moment, trying to figure out what to tell Chelsea about why she wasn't available. She couldn't say she was working, because with her luck she'd run into her downtown, or Chelsea would swing by the barn—and it wouldn't be the truth. Why did she feel she had to lie? Why not just tell her the truth?

Lucy texted back. Next time? I told Zane I'd hang out with him this afternoon. I doubt he would enjoy shoe shopping.

Chelsea responded quickly. No prob. Tell Zane I said hello.

See, Chelsea hadn't thought it was weird that she and Zane were getting together.

So, stop making it weird.

She was trying, but the fact remained that it shouldn't be this hard. She knew it was fanciful, but she wanted Zane to fall in love with her—like when the prince looked at Cinderella and realized she was his one true love. Too bad she didn't have a fairy godmother to help her out. If Dorothy was still here…what would Dorothy think of their situation?

There was no time for daydreams. He would be there soon and she needed to finish getting ready.

Before she chose a dress, she streamed "Somethin' Stupid," because making fun of herself was the best way to stop taking herself so seriously. She reframed her focus and selected a feminine yellow print sundress from her closet and a pair of cute cowboy boots to go with it.

The dress was fun and flirty and made her feel girlie. She debated whether or not to curl her hair, and even went as far as firing up her curling iron, but in the end she opted for pulling it back into a ponytail. Curls would look as if she was trying too hard. She probably was, but Zane didn't need to know that. He just needed to be captivated by the finished look.

It ended up being a good thing that she'd opted for the ponytail, because a knock sounded at her front door. She glanced at her watch.

Right on time.

She pulled the boots on and made herself slow down and take her time getting to the door, when what she really wanted to do was rush. Once she was there, she paused and took a deep breath before she turned the knob.

Zane stood on her front porch holding a…baby cradle?

"What are you doing? Come inside, quickly." Lucy tugged his arm and nearly made him drop the cradle, which was heavier than it looked, because it was one of those solid-wood, sturdy old-fashioned pieces of furniture. The type they didn't make anymore.

What the hell?

"Careful," he said as he cleared the door, but not before grazing the doorjamb with one of the runners.

"Someone might see you," Lucy said as she closed the door behind her.

"Am I not supposed to be here?" Zane asked. "I thought we had a date."

Lucy frowned at him. "Of course *you're* supposed to be here. Just not with a baby bed. That's not exactly a typical substitution for first-date flowers."

He set down the cradle on the living-room area rug so that it didn't scratch her hardwood floors.

"I thought we agreed that you didn't want me to bring you flowers."

"I didn't want you to bring me flowers. But that doesn't mean I wanted a baby cradle instead. Zane, it's too soon. How am I supposed to explain why I have baby furniture in my house? I haven't even told my brother and Chelsea the news."

She looked beautiful. And she'd put on a dress.

For him? He was used to seeing Lucy dressed casually, in jeans or shorts. He couldn't remember the last time he'd seen her in a dress. But he liked it.

"You look nice," he said.

"Thank you. But don't change the subject, please. Where did this cradle come from?"

Zane's gaze fell to the little bed next to him. "It was mine, and then Ian used it when he was born. My mom couldn't bear to throw anything away. She was such a pack rat. I used to tease her about that all the time. She used to say, 'You never know when something will come in handy.' I found it in the attic yesterday when I was packing up her place. It's old, but it's in pretty good shape. Sturdy. But if you don't want it, I can give it to the shelter in Dallas. They can always use things like this."

Lucy's face softened. "I do want it. Thank you. It's just that I need to tell Ethan and Chelsea before I start setting up a nursery." Her shoulders rose, then fell. "I hadn't even thought about that until now."

She puffed out her cheeks and blew out her breath. She looked nervous and small, standing there contemplating the task. He hated that she was still thinking she had to go through this alone. What did he have to do to make her see she didn't?

"We'll tell them together," he said. "Whenever you're ready."

While Lucy appeared to be weighing the suggestion, he was formulating all the reasons she shouldn't do this alone.

"We need to set the tone. I'm a grown woman. It's my life, but if we act like this is something shameful, then Ethan will be upset. Really, it's not his call to be upset." She sounded like she was trying to convince herself. "If you want us to tell them together, maybe we can have them over for dinner one night soon. But it's your face Ethan will wreck when he finds out."

The thought had crossed Zane's mind more than once. He and Ethan had been good friends since they were kids. There was a strong possibility that Ethan might take issue with him sleeping with his little sister, but they were all adults now. He was standing by Lucy. She was right—it really wasn't Ethan's business to render an opinion on the situation.

Despite how Lucy might have idolized her big brother, Ethan wasn't perfect. He'd faced his own demons. He would probably understand better than they were anticipating. Maybe they should give the guy more credit.

For a moment Zane grappled with the feeling that he had let Lucy down. That he hadn't protected her. Maybe it would serve him right if Ethan messed up his face.

"I can handle Ethan," he said. "Don't worry about my face."

She reached out and cupped his face in her palm. "But it's such a nice face."

Their gazes locked and this time he found himself grappling with a feeling similar to the one that had done them in that night. The sound of a thunderclap off in the distance broke the spell.

"We'd better get downtown if we are going to beat the rain," he said.

Her hand fell and she took a step back. "I didn't realize it was supposed to rain."

"Just another summer shower. Are you ready to go?"

"Sure, just let me grab my purse."

Lucy returned a minute later with her handbag, but the rain was already starting to fall in fat drops, which were pinging on the front windows and splattering on the porch.

"It's really coming down out there," she said.

She set her small leather purse on the table in the hallway and opened the door. The rain was blowing so hard it was slanting sideways. She turned back to him. "Do you really want to go out in this?"

He shrugged. "Not particularly, but I will if you want to."

She shook her head.

"What's the matter, sugar?" he teased. "You afraid you'll melt?"

She raised her right brow at the comment. "Something like that, because you know I'm so sweet. But don't call me sugar, honey."

He laughed. He loved her sass and the way she could poke fun at herself. He loved the way they bantered. He'd never had that with anyone else. He just wished he could love her the way she deserved to be loved. He didn't need to get ice cream and walk around downtown to know that Lucy Campbell was a good catch for the right man.

"I have an idea," she said. "I have some Rocky Road in the freezer. Let's improvise and eat our ice cream on the porch and listen to the rain. We can sit on the swing. How does that sound?"

It sounded fabulous. Actually, given the choice, he would choose the sanctuary of the rain and the porch swing and Lucy over the curious glances they were bound to get as they ate ice cream as they strolled around downtown together.

Five minutes later, they were seated on the swing with bowls of Rocky Road. She'd taken off her boots and he noticed that her toenails were painted a pale shade of pink. The rain nipped at their feet as they gently swung back and forth and enjoyed the refreshing treat. It hit the spot and took the edge off the humidity, which had been elevated by the sudden summer storm. It was cozy sitting there with her. The white wicker swing, with its cushioned cover and decorative pillows, was just big enough for the two of them, forcing them to sit a little closer than they might have if they had more room. It was nice.

He liked the feel of their thighs touching. He could smell her perfume—something light and floral that tempted him to move in a little closer. So he distracted himself by focusing on the view of the barn about fifty yards away, the gravel road that led to the house where he'd grown up and the fenced-off pastureland beyond that.

Lucy hadn't grown up in this house—her grandparents had lived here. She'd spent a lot of time here and in the barn that was now her business, and she'd inherited the land after her parents' death several years ago. Ethan and their brother, Jude, had inherited equally valued parcels of land. Ethan's was smaller but had the stables from which he ran his horse-breeding business. Several decades ago, his family's ranch had been one of the most successful in the area, but they'd run into financial hardship when alcoholism had gotten the best of Donovan Campbell. For a while it appeared that Ethan might fall down the same slippery slope after his parents' death and the end of his first marriage, but after some soul searching, he had pulled himself up from rock bottom and had set the Triple C Ranch back on the road to profitability.

He was not only a friend but was also an inspiration to Zane, who understood the heartbreak of failed marriage and disappointment of broken dreams. Zane looked up to Ethan, who had managed to not just come out the other side but had emerged on top of life, with his pending marriage and his thriving business.

Lucy had done well for herself, too—after some initial time spent finding herself, she now had the world by the tail. Zane stole a glance at her sitting next to him, looking pretty in her yellow dress.

She loved him. She could have any man she wanted and certainly deserved better than him. But she loved him.

"I'm so happy you could come for dinner tonight," Lucy said to Ethan and Chelsea. "I know it was short notice, but we wanted to cook for you before you get swept away by the wedding. Chels, did you find your shoes yet?"

Chelsea and Ethan stood in Lucy's kitchen, enjoying cheese and crackers that Lucy had set out as an appetizer, as Lucy took the chicken marsala that they were having for dinner out of the oven.

"Actually, I found two pairs. When you have a moment, will you give me your expert opinion as to which you think will work best with the dress? I thought I'd bring both with me when I go in for my final fitting and try them on with the dress."

"Absolutely. I'm sorry I haven't been a very good bridesmaid lately and I know Juliette has been out of town a lot on business. I've been so busy with work lately, too," Lucy said. "I feel like we've left you to your own devices. I'll make it up to you. I promise."

"Don't worry about it," Chelsea said. Her British accent sounded crisp and made everything she said sound *posh*. "You've been fine. No, not just fine. You've been wonderful. Especially considering you've been under the weather so much lately, too. I hope you're not spreading yourself too thin."

Lucy's stomach lurched. She wouldn't allow her

gaze to slant to Zane, who was sitting at the table, having a beer and a completely different conversation with Ethan. Ethan, who'd been sober now for more than three years, was drinking iced tea.

If she looked at Zane, perceptive Chelsea would surely twig that something was up. In fact, she might see right through her and guess why she and Zane had asked her and Ethan to dinner before they'd even had the chance to tell them. Actually, she was surprised Chelsea and Ethan hadn't questioned the invitation in the first place. It wasn't as if she and Zane were in the habit of hosting dinner parties together.

However, if it came up before they were ready to share the news, they'd planned a plausible excuse: as attendants in their wedding, they wanted to spend some time with them before everything got too hectic.

And that was true. But it wasn't the only reason they'd invited them over.

The plan was that they would get through dinner and Zane would break out a bottle of champagne— and sparkling cider for Ethan and Lucy—to have with dessert. They'd toast the upcoming nuptials and their own *good news*. Lucy hoped Chelsea wouldn't pick up on Lucy not drinking wine with dinner.

They'd considered waiting until after Ethan and Chelsea had gotten back from their honeymoon to break the news, because they didn't want to upstage the wedding, but Lucy couldn't take a chance of something slipping. It was best to be direct and set the tone.

She knew that; and everything was going according to the plan, but she was still nervous.

"You're sweet to worry about me, Chelsea, but I'm fine."

Chelsea helped her transport the food to the table in the dining room and they enjoyed some laughs and good conversation over a lovely dinner. As everyone finished their entrées, Lucy grew nervous. But finally, it was time for dessert.

"Zane, will you help me in the kitchen?" Lucy asked.

Chelsea started to stand. "Why don't you stay here and talk to Ethan? I can help you, Lucy."

Chelsea came from a family with a lot of money, and in their posh English estates they probably had a fleet of servants the likes of one might see on *Downton Abbey*. While her offer to help was sincere, living like a commoner—clearing the table and waiting on Ethan hand and foot—was still a novelty to her. If Lucy hadn't been so nervous, she might have laughed silently to herself at the thought of how fast that novelty would wear off once Chelsea was married.

"Oh, Chels, I do appreciate your offer. However, Zane brought the dessert—it's one of Mrs. Anthony's Black Forest cakes. You know she can never resist the opportunity to bake for him. She brings him goodies at least once a month. This month's offering just happened to come at the perfect time for our dinner party. But I will let him do the honors of serving it."

Zane was already on his feet and standing beside Lucy before Chelsea could insist, and the two of them disappeared into the kitchen.

Once they were out of earshot, Lucy asked, "Are you ready for this?"

"I am," he said. "But you look like you're ready to swallow your tongue, you look so nervous."

Lucy shrugged and took four champagne flutes down from one of the kitchen cabinets. Zane's eyebrows arched. "Four? You're not imbibing, are you?"

Lucy shook her head. "I will pour Ethan and myself a glass of sparkling cider, since he won't be drinking, either. I figured it would look very fishy if I walked in with only two glasses."

Zane nodded. "Are you still sure you don't want me to do the talking?"

For a moment, Lucy actually considered it. She obviously looked as nervous as she felt. Maybe it would be a good idea to let Zane take the lead, but then again, she knew what she wanted to say. She would probably be the better of the two of them at keeping the announcement light but to the point.

She shook her head. "No—thanks, though. I've got this. But you can pour yourself and Chelsea a glass of champagne while I open the sparkling cider. And then would you please take the cake into the dining room. I set out some dessert plates on the buffet behind the table."

Zane did as she asked, and before he left the kitchen, he leaned in and gave her a quick peck on the lips. It startled her and a little gasp escaped before she could help herself.

"What was that for?" she asked.

"It was for good luck. Even though we won't need it. We got this. Remember what you kept saying to me—we set the tone. We are not two sixteen-year-olds who are in trouble."

She wanted to ask him why it felt like they were, but she could still feel his kiss—quick as it was—on her lips, and it had bolstered her. It calmed her nerves.

"Right," she said. "We set the tone."

He nodded, one resolute nod, then he flashed that charismatic smile of his that had always made her feel weak in the knees, before he and the cake disappeared from the kitchen. With that, and with the phantom feel of his kiss still on her lips, she knew everything was going to be okay. *Eventually.*

When all the glasses were full and resting on the tray, the cider appeared to be the same light amber color as the bubbly. Unless her brother or Chelsea took a drink from her flute, they would never be the wiser that she wasn't drinking champagne. Of course, they would know soon enough, but at least Lucy would be able to settle in and gather her wits before she broke the news.

"Okay, it's now or never," she whispered to herself. Actually, *never* wasn't an option. She picked up the tray and carried it into the dining room.

"What's this?" Chelsea asked.

"I thought the occasion called for a toast. I have sparkling apple juice for you, my dear brother. And champagne for you, my sweet sister-in-law-to-be." She set the respective flutes in front of each of them and placed one with champagne at Zane's place setting. He served the cake.

"This looks delicious," said Ethan.

"I'm sure Mrs. Anthony made it with an extra dose of love," Lucy teased. Zane waggled his brows as he set the last plate at his place and took a seat.

Lucy and Zane exchanged one last fortifying glance before they lifted their glasses and he said, "A toast to you and your upcoming wedding." They all leaned in and clinked glasses.

Then Lucy said, "And a toast to Zane and me and baby makes three."

Lucy flashed her most brilliant smile as she and Zane clinked champagne flutes, but Chelsea and Ethan sat there with raised glasses and confused looks on their faces.

"What did you just say?" Ethan asked.

Lucy laughed as if she had just shared the news that she had won the megaball lotto jackpot. "I said that we're having a baby. Isn't that wonderful? We are so excited."

Okay, maybe that was stretching it a little bit—

actually, they were petrified—but no one needed to know any different.

The silence was deafening, but finally Chelsea broke the ice.

"Really? Congratulations! I didn't even realize you two were dating. Then again, everyone knows you're crazy about each other. I mean, it's been obvious to me since the moment I first saw you together."

Chelsea shrugged and raised her champagne flute for another go at the toast. Lucy and Zane clinked their glasses to hers, but Ethan sat stock-still, staring at his hands.

"It was that obvious that we're crazy for each other?" Zane asked.

A bubble of nervous laughter escaped Lucy's throat like a hiccup. What was he doing, pretending to be besotted? Probably just trying to lighten the mood—and be convincing. Maybe he was still thinking about the quip she'd made about Ethan messing up his face.

Of course, there were different kinds of "crazy for each other." Their particular brand was that they couldn't keep their hands off each other. Or at least they couldn't help themselves that night. And she could've sworn the other night, when their date had been spontaneously moved to the front porch, that if she'd just leaned in the slightest way, Zane would've kissed her.

But maybe that was just a by-product of the good-

luck peck on the lips he'd given her in the kitchen…
Or wishful thinking.

She hadn't leaned and he hadn't kissed her the
other night. But he'd kissed her just a few minutes
ago.

"What are your plans?" Ethan finally spoke and
he didn't sound happy. "What does this mean?"

Zane lifted his chin and stared Ethan squarely in
the eyes. "What it means is that Lucy and I are going
to have a baby."

Chapter Six

The next morning, Lucy looked up from her desk at the sound of someone rapping at her office door.

"Got a few minutes?" Ethan stood in the threshold. Judging by the look on his face, he was trying extra hard not to look grim.

"I always have time for my big brother," Lucy said. "Come in and have a seat. Have you had breakfast? Would you like something to drink?"

Just as he was trying not to look upset, she could feel herself going overboard being cheery and nice.

His hands were clasped in front of him and he shifted from one foot to the other, but he hadn't budged from the door. "No, I'm fine, Lucy, thanks."

She bit the insides of her cheeks to keep herself

from rambling on any more, but after a good minute passed when all they'd done was stare at each other, and he was still rooted to the spot, she finally broke the silence.

"Are you going to come in or are you just going to stare at me from across the room?"

Ethan cleared his throat, then flattened his mouth into a tight line before he finally said, "Why don't we go for a walk?"

She didn't have any appointments until this afternoon. "Sure, that sounds great."

Actually, it sounded pretty serious, like she was being summoned to the principal's office. She knew him well enough to know he wasn't going to get into anything heavy in her office, where people could walk in right in the middle of everything. Hence, the walk.

Even if she hadn't admitted it to herself before now, on a deeper level she'd known they were due for this talk. Last night, Ethan had remained silent as he'd eaten his dessert. Of course, Chelsea had chatted enough for both of them, asking about due dates—Lucy's obstetrician had said the middle of next March—and about whether or not they were going to find out the baby's sex before the birth. Zane had said yes at the same time that Lucy said no. She'd explained that it was like opening a Christmas gift before Christmas. That had inspired a discussion about what color to paint the nursery—gender-neutral sunny yellow, of course.

All the while, Ethan had sat there silently eating his Black Forest cake. And when he was finished, he'd carried his plate to the kitchen and proclaimed it was time to leave, that he had to do his morning rounds of the ranch early and then he had an early meeting. It was the most he'd said since the toast.

It was a good thing that they were getting this talk over with now rather than letting the awkwardness stretch on. Her gratitude that he'd made the first move toward that end overrode her nervousness at his disapproval.

She locked up her office and the barn's front door. This was something new that she'd been forced to start doing since the feature in *Southern Living* magazine. Even though tours were supposed to be by appointment only, several times a week she entertained people who dropped in. One time she'd gone out for lunch and came back only to discover a large wedding party camped out in her office. They hadn't caused any harm, but it was alarming to find them packed into the room. Her office door had been shut, but not locked, and they'd let themselves in and made themselves at home. That was when it dawned on her that she had the petty-cash box, the business's checkbook and other financial information in her unlocked bottom desk drawer. Anyone could let themselves in and help themselves. It felt like the moment Dorothy discovered she wasn't in Kansas anymore. Since the Campbell Wedding Barn had been lifted up and whirled around by the *South-*

ern Living twister—not that she was complaining—
Lucy had decided it was better to be safe than sorry.

Outside, it was a beautiful summer day. It was a
rare mildly warm day with a clear robin's-egg-blue
sky and a gentle breeze that ruffled the live oaks
and tousled Lucy's hair. Luckily, she had slipped an
elastic band onto her wrist that morning, because it
had been one of the rare instances that her hair was
behaving. But as unpredictable as the weather had
been lately, if the day decided to take a turn toward
hot and humid, she wanted to be prepared to pull her
hair back so that it wasn't on her neck. Maybe it was
just her imagination, but since discovering she was
pregnant, her body temperature was already running
warmer than usual.

Since Ethan had been so good to initiate this talk,
Lucy decided she would be the one to get the ball
rolling by easing into the inevitable conversation.

"How was your meeting this morning?"

It wasn't what he'd come to talk about, she knew
that, but at least it would get the ball rolling.

"Fine. A guy from over at McKinney wanted
to talk about breeding his mare. We'll see where
it goes."

They walked in silence for a few minutes, until
they reached the white post-and-rail fence that ran
between the gravel road that snaked through the
Campbell property and the pastures where Lucy's
land ended and Ethan's began. It wasn't so much
that they needed to define whose land was whose,

as much as it was that Ethan's business dealt with horses and Lucy's dealt solely with people. It was the best way to keep the two separate.

Suddenly, Ethan stopped and turned toward his sister, which forced him to squint into the sun. "Do I need to get the shotgun and make an honest man out of Zane?"

Lucy's eyes grew wide. She shook her head vigorously. "No, Ethan. No shotgun needed." She knew he was speaking figuratively. She hoped. Of course he was.

"Zane asked me to marry him."

A look of relief passed over Ethan's face. "Why didn't you say so? When's the wedding?"

"The only wedding on the books is yours and Chelsea's. Zane and I are not getting married."

"Why not? He proposed and all."

"I said no because I don't want to get married."

Ethan's face screwed up like he didn't understand a word she was saying. "But you're pregnant. Why don't you want to get married? Don't you think you should?"

"When did you become so old-fashioned, Ethan? No, I don't think we should get married. Zane proposed—if you can even call it that. It really wasn't a proposal as much as a very unromantic declaration that he had decided we should get married. I told him I had decided we would do no such thing. It's not what I want."

Ethan put his hands on his hips. "Lucy, you are

going to have a baby. You and Zane are going to be parents. When you got pregnant, you forfeited your right to fanciful notions about princes and princesses and saying no to a marriage proposal because the proposal wasn't romantic enough. You need to grow up."

"I said no because Zane doesn't love me. Okay? Are you happy now?"

"Lucy, what the hell are you doing messing around with a guy who doesn't love you? You should have more self-respect than that."

Her mouth fell open and she saw red. "That is none of your business, Ethan. I'm sure you slept with plenty of women you didn't love after you and Molly broke up and before you met Chelsea. And I'm sure you wouldn't be having this conversation with Jude. I really thought you were more evolved than to perpetuate double standards. But the bottom line is, you are not my father and you have no business imposing your hang-ups on me."

"And what do you think our father would be saying to you if he was here right now?"

Lucy's mouth fell open. Tears stung her eyes. That was a low blow.

"That's not fair, Ethan. Daddy isn't here anymore and it's hurtful for you to throw that at me right now." She turned to walk back to her office, because right now she needed to be as far away from her brother as she could get.

"Lucy, stop. Come back. Please."

She stopped and whirled around to face him. "I appreciate your concern, but I am a grown woman with a thriving business that allows me to support myself. I'm not marrying Zane and I am not asking for your blessing. So, you can just get over it."

As her tears started to fall, she turned around and started toward the barn, keeping a brisk pace and not looking back. When she was safe inside, she latched the door, went into her office, buried her head in her hands and sobbed.

Having a baby on her own should mean that she was strong and self-sufficient, but it broke her heart that Ethan seemed to be looking at her as his flaky little sister, the one who always managed to mess things up. For a split second she worried that maybe he was right, that maybe she was getting in over her head. After all, this decision wasn't just about her. It involved a tiny little life that hadn't asked to be brought into this situation. This baby wasn't something she could try out and quit like she had so many times in the past when she got bored or dreamed up something shiny and new.

She lifted her head to pull a tissue from her desk drawer, and she caught a glimpse of the sunshine that was streaming in through the skylights along the barn's rooftop. Turning this old ramshackle barn into a place that had become one of the South's premier wedding venues had taken every ounce of everything that she possessed—money, energy, blood, sweat and more than a few tears. It had been her baby, and she hadn't quit on it. Not even when times had gotten tough. She didn't intend to quit on it anytime soon, either.

Even if her brother thought she was a flake, she knew she wasn't. She was having this baby and she didn't need to tie herself to a man who didn't love her in order to make it work, in order to be a good mother. Of course, it would be so much easier if she had her family's support, but if she didn't...

The sound of somebody unlocking the front door had her scrambling to wipe away her tears. She needed to pull herself together. She needed to remember that this was her decision, and if Ethan was going to judge her for it, it was his problem, not hers. But a moment later, her brother was standing in the doorway to her office just as he had when he'd first arrived, before their walk.

"Ethan, we're not having this discussion here. This is my place of business and— No, you know what? For that matter, were not having this discussion anywhere. The discussion's over. You can go back to the stables."

"I'm sorry," he said. That was when she noticed that her big, strong oldest brother actually had tears glistening in his own eyes. "You are absolutely right. That was a sexist, chauvinistic thing for me to say and I'm sorry. Lucy, I only want the best for you. And I guess in some ways I do feel like more of a father to you than a big brother."

In many ways, that was true. After their parents

died, Ethan had come back to Celebration, uprooting him and his ex-wife, Molly, from Chicago to come home and care for her. She'd been only fourteen years old. Their father died the night of the accident. Their mother, who had been left a paraplegic, died a few months later. Rather than relocate her to Chicago, Ethan had moved back so that she could finish high school in Celebration. In the end, his own marriage broke up over the move back to their small hometown. Never once did he blame her or make her feel as if it was her fault.

Maybe she needed to cut him some slack. She wasn't changing her position, but she didn't have to excommunicate him.

"Ethan, I appreciate you saying that." She drew in a deep breath, trying to buy herself some time so she could weigh her words. "It's so important to me to have you on my side because you're important to me."

He shook his head. "You need to know that I am on your side, Lucy. I only want what's best for you. I want you to be happy. I don't want life to be any harder on you than it has to be."

"Then please understand that's exactly why I'm choosing not to marry Zane. We are going to coparent, and we're going to be great at it. He even seems pretty psyched about it. That will work, but tying myself to someone who doesn't love me, to someone who didn't choose to be with me out of love, won't make me happy. In fact, in the end, it will make both of us pretty darn miserable."

She remembered the feeling of Zane's lips on hers last night, she remembered the way their bodies had felt together—how they'd worked so well together. A profound sadness washed over her and she shuddered. She was damned if she did, damned if she didn't. But the most damning part of it would be if she roped Zane into a marriage he didn't really want and the two of them ended up being a new-millennium replay of his parents.

The person who would suffer the most would be their sweet child. Zane, of all people, should understand that after what he'd gone through growing up.

After work, Zane dropped by the hardware store and purchased two gallons of yellow paint called soft banana. He'd spent some time on the internet researching the best shade of yellow for a baby's room and had learned that a yellow that was too bright could make the baby agitated, while a soft, pastel shade had warm, calming effects. When he'd looked through the various color chips in the paint section, soft banana seemed to fit the bill.

He was going to surprise Lucy with it. If she hated it, they could go together and choose another color, but for now, he wasn't sure how many clues she wanted to drop around town—even though shopping for yellow paint together didn't exactly scream "we're having a baby!" it might raise a few eyebrows.

Now that they'd shared the news with Ethan and Chelsea, there was no reason they couldn't get a jump on converting Lucy's spare room into the nursery. Last night when she'd said she wanted to paint the walls yellow, he'd decided to go for it. Get the paint and get to work. Actually, he hoped his proactive approach would prove to Lucy how much he cared about his child—their child. And he hoped Ethan would consider it a sign of his commitment, that he wasn't going to flake out on Lucy and their child. Ethan had been pretty stoic last night after they'd shared the news. Chelsea, God love her, had enough enthusiasm for everyone, but Zane knew that he and Ethan were due a heart-to-heart before too long.

First, he and Lucy needed to figure out what they were going to do. He wasn't pushing her, but he still hadn't given up on the possibility of convincing her to marry him.

He might not believe in love the way she wanted him to, but frankly, he believed some things were more important than a nebulous, fleeting, highly overrated emotion.

He hoped she realized actions spoke louder than words. In this case, he hoped his gesture spoke volumes, filling in the spaces where he simply didn't have the words.

Next, he went to the Campbell property and found Ethan at the Triple C offices.

"Got a minute?" he asked.

It was almost imperceptible, but Zane saw Ethan

stiffen when he looked up from the paperwork on his desk and saw Zane standing there.

They needed to talk this out. Based on what Lucy had told him about Ethan's suggestion of a shotgun wedding, he was taking the news of his sister's pregnancy about the way Zane thought he would.

"Sure. Come in. Shut the door."

The office was small and rustic. Zane sat in one of the empty chairs in front of Ethan's desk.

"Thanks for letting me take my time clearing my mom's stuff out of the bungalow," he said. "I am going to wrap things up this evening. I've dragged it out long enough. It's time."

"We don't have any plans for the house yet. There's no hurry if you need more time."

Ethan was making all the right noises, but Zane could tell that he wasn't himself.

"Thanks, I appreciate that. But that's not the reason I came by."

Ethan nodded, but he didn't say anything. He was staring at a spot over Zane's left shoulder.

"If you want to punch me, go ahead," Zane said.

He was serious.

Unsmiling, Ethan locked gazes with him.

"Yeah, I thought about doing that more than a couple of times."

He was serious, too.

"Okay, how do you want to handle it? Do you want to set up a time, like a duel? Or do you just want to take me out right now?"

Ethan still didn't smile.

"Are you making a joke out of this?"

Zane raked a hand through his hair and then composed his most serious face.

"This isn't a joke to me. It's one of the most serious things that's ever happened to me and that's exactly how I'm treating it. But that's between Lucy and me. I came by as a courtesy to you to let you know that I intend to stand by your sister. I would marry her if she would have me, but that's something she's not so sure about."

Ethan was doodling on the yellow legal pad on his desktop.

"Are you in love with my sister, Zane?"

He had known this was coming. It was a perfectly logical question that a big brother would ask the guy who'd gotten his little sister pregnant.

"With all due respect, that's between Lucy and me."

Ethan let the pen fall from his hand and his gaze nailed Zane to his chair.

"Since you can't give me a straight answer, I'll take that as a no."

Zane should have been prepared for that, but he wasn't. It wasn't that cut-and-dried. He couldn't say he *didn't* love her. He cared about her—

Ethan smirked. "We could fall down a big black hole talking about all the reasons you shouldn't have slept with Lucy if you don't love her. But I know my sister. I know how she feels about you, and I know, deep down, you are a decent guy. *Don't* hurt her, Zane." He spat the word *don't* through gritted teeth. "And don't expect her to tie herself to a guy who doesn't return her feelings."

"I'm not going to hurt her. At least not on purpose."

"Yeah. That's what I'm afraid of," Ethan said. "It usually happens when we don't intend it."

They sat quietly for a few beats as the truth of Ethan's words swirled around them.

Finally, Ethan said, "Thanks for coming to clear the air. I was wondering how long it would take for you to slink in here."

That was better. He sounded more like himself again.

"I don't *slink*," Zane said. "The only one who's going to *slink* anywhere is you when I beat your sorry ass at bowling. Only you would have your bachelor party at the bowling alley."

They talked for a while, about horses and houses, and about how one of the guests at Ethan and Chelsea's wedding was her brother, who would most likely be the next prime minister of the United Kingdom. The security was crazy, but that would be their new normal when it came to Chelsea's family.

Zane was happy things were back to normal with Ethan, but he had to get a move on. The final boxes weren't going to move themselves. He drove his truck away from the offices to the gravel frontage road that led to the bungalow. He hadn't realized it until he was parked in the driveway in front of the house, but by delaying the move out, it had been easier to ignore the fact that his mom was gone. But she was. Putting it off wasn't going to bring her back. So tonight he would wrap it up.

He let himself inside the house. All the blinds were drawn, making the place dark and dank. The cardboard boxes were starting to smell a little musty from being closed up in the humid house all these weeks that Zane couldn't deal. He cranked up the AC, let in some light and got to work. He made himself focus on the task and not think too hard about how the place looked empty and sad without most of his mom's things. It didn't even resemble the home that his mother had worked so hard to make for them. She'd done her best to provide for them. That was why she'd hung on to so much stuff. But in the end, all the *things* she'd accumulated, the stacks of fabric, piles of old patterns, half-finished projects and mounds of sewing supplies he couldn't even identify—the stuff that had made her feel safe, as if she owned a little bit of something in this world— didn't mean a damn thing. None of it had saved her when it mattered. The remnants of her life only served as a reminder to Zane that she'd gotten a raw deal when she trusted Nathaniel Phillips.

Zane was going to do better by his child.

A few hours later, he'd packed the last of her stuff. The boxes were ready to load into the bed of his truck. He'd separated things into four piles: keep, give away, trash and to be determined. The latter pile consisted of things he didn't know what to do with. He'd snapped photos of things Ian might want and sent them to him. He'd ask Lucy about the other stuff. She might want some of it. She and his mom had bonded over crafty things. She might want some of her sewing supplies.

He loaded the last box and went back inside for one more look around. He'd hire Virginia Kelly, who had a cleaning service, to come over and put the final shine on the place. But his work here was done. The only thing he had to contend with was the trash. He started to tie off one of the lone remaining industrial garbage bags, but his well-loved and time-ravaged stuffed bear peeked out of the opening. Zane pulled it out.

He'd loved that thing when he was a child. Rather than a blanket, the bear had been his comfort and best friend. He'd dragged it around everywhere. He'd tossed it because it was too old and threadbare to be of any use to anyone. It wasn't worth saving for the baby, but for some reason, instead of throwing it away, he wanted to share this connection to his past with Lucy.

Suddenly, he was grateful that his mom had kept things like the cradle and his bear. Zane realized that they were not only links to his past, but also links to his mom. She hadn't just managed to give Ian and him a good, loving upbringing, but, even after she was gone, through the things she'd chosen to keep, she'd helped him realize that maybe his past did hold some memories worth hanging on to. For a melancholy moment, he wished Dorothy could be there to hold her first grandchild the way she'd tenderly held him when he'd needed her, but she wasn't here. At least not in the flesh, but he felt her presence all around him like a hug—just when he needed it. Just like she'd always done.

Zane was filled with the overwhelming realization that the best way he could honor his mother was by being a good father to his own child. By being more like her and not like his own father.

As he stared down at the ugly stained bear in his hands, a quiet calm came over him. Maybe it was all in how he looked at life. From one angle, the bear, which had once been snowy white, but was now a funky tea-stained yellow brown, looked like trash. From another perspective, it represented the comfort of his past.

Maybe he could apply the same lens to love. He knew that was what his mom would tell him.

He closed his eyes, stood there still in the empty house and tried to imagine himself in love with Lucy.

While it didn't crash over him like a breaking wave or envelop him like the sticky Texas humidity, something was there—like a swell in the ocean or the feel of a warm spring breeze. But where he turned a corner was when he looked at it from the opposite perspective and tried to imagine his life without Lucy and their child. That was the biggest shift. He knew without a doubt he needed them in his life.

He tied up the trash, tucked the one-eyed teddy bear under his arm and let himself out. As he was locking up, he heard the crunch of tires on the gravel drive behind him. It was just getting dark. Through the inky twilight haze, he could see a big black pickup parking next to his own truck. The windows were tinted, and the way the headlights shone in his eyes, he couldn't readily recognize the driver. But soon enough the door opened and Nathaniel Phillips unfolded his lanky body as he exited the truck's cab.

Zane's ire prickled. His mouth flattened into a hard line. He cursed under his breath but kept his attention trained on the house door until he was sure it was locked. Then his fingers reflexively fisted into his palms.

What the hell does he want?

Zane was certain he'd made it perfectly clear where they stood when the bastard had the audacity to show up at Dorothy's funeral. The guy couldn't have been bothered to come around for the past twenty-five years. Now the jackass seemed to turn up around every corner.

Zane stood there stoically. He would let Nathaniel speak first. Or better yet he could turn around and get back in that fancy Ford F-150—Zane could see now that he wasn't blinded by the headlights—and drive off a cliff, for all he cared.

Those trucks didn't come cheap. The bastard must

be doing all right for himself. Of course, he could never spare a penny for them. He lived in Dallas now. Or at least that was the last address that Zane knew of. He hadn't cared to keep track of him over the years.

"Son." Nathaniel hesitated for a minute. "I saw your truck from the highway as I was passing by."

It was on the tip of Zane's tongue to tell him to never call him *son* again. He had three sons with Marianne Crawford—the three kids he'd bothered to take responsibility for and raise. Wasn't that enough? Why was he suddenly coming around now?

"What do you want, Nathaniel? I was just leaving." Zane took a step toward his own truck, but Nathaniel moved at the same time, blocking the way. It wasn't an aggressive move, but it put Zane on alert.

As a general rule, Zane wasn't a violent person. He didn't get in bar fights, he thought road rage was ridiculous—everyone had places to go—and he didn't believe beating someone's ass made him more of a man. Still, Nathaniel seemed to bring out the worst in him, because suddenly all he wanted to do was pound the sorry excuse for a man who was standing in his way.

"Move," Zane said through gritted teeth.

Nathaniel seemed to shrink, but he didn't budge. "I stopped here to ask you if you'd have dinner with me sometime."

Zane laughed in his face. "Why would I want to do that?"

Nathaniel closed his eyes for a moment, and Zane took the opportunity to scoot by him. But Nathaniel must've sensed the movement, because he opened his eyes and turned toward Zane.

"I know I've never been much of a father to you," he said. "And I'm sorry about that. If you would let me, I'd like to try to make it up to you."

The words pierced Zane like arrows. They stung on impact but left him numb. It made no sense. After all these years, now that Dorothy was gone…now that Nathaniel was ready, he thought he could come around and everything would be fine?

Zane didn't know whether he wanted to punch the guy or laugh in his face.

No, he didn't deserve his anger. It was too good for him. He didn't deserve any of Zane's energy. Anger took energy. Anger meant he cared. Zane wanted to give the bastard exactly what he deserved: absolutely nothing.

Even so, all kinds of thoughts—all of the frustration and hurt and things he'd wanted to say to Nathaniel over the decades that the man had turned his back on Dorothy, Ian and himself—got log-jammed in his throat. Zane knew if he didn't get in his truck right now and drive away, those words were going to organize themselves and he was going to unload them all over Nathaniel Phillips. He had never been a father to him. What the hell made him think he could come blundering back now?

"My mother worked herself into an early grave

because you wanted nothing to do with us when we needed you." His voice was calm and even, void of emotion. "You made her sell the ranch that had been in her family for generations when you decided you didn't want to hang around anymore. You thought you deserved half so you could take care of your other family with Marianne. We got by without you then. What makes you think that you can make it up to me now?"

Nathaniel opened his mouth to say something, but the words were lost when Zane got into the cab of his truck. He tossed the sorry-looking stuffed bear into the backseat and slammed the door. As he pulled away, he glanced in the rearview mirror only once and he saw Nathaniel's silhouette illuminated by the taillights of Zane's truck. His father looked like the sorry man he was.

Zane probably should've gone home, because he wasn't in a very good head space. In fact, he felt like he needed to punch a wall. But his instincts led him to Lucy. Suddenly, she felt like the only tangible thing of substance in his miserable life.

He didn't blame her for not wanting to marry him. She deserved so much more than his offering of soft-banana paint and a stained, threadbare stuffed animal.

After seeing Nathaniel and remembering all the years of heartbreak he'd put Dorothy through and all the broken promises he'd dished out to Ian and him, was it any wonder he had no idea what love was?

Nathaniel Phillips withheld a lot from him when he was growing up, but he'd be damned if he was going to let the bastard cost him his future. For the first time in a long time he knew the only future he wanted was with Lucy and his child.

He was tired of words and lame promises. No, he had to let his actions speak for themselves.

Lucy's red Toyota sat beside the house when he arrived. He parked next to it, then stomped up the front porch steps and pounded on the door.

When she answered, she looked surprised. "Zane—"

But he didn't give her the chance to say anything else, because he pulled her into his arms and covered her mouth with his. As her lips opened under his, passion consumed him. In that moment, he wanted to walk her backward right into the bedroom and make love to her. Instead, he deepened the kiss and pulled her even tighter against him.

He wasn't sure how long they stayed like that, but when they came up for air, Lucy looked dazed. Her hand flew up to her kiss-swollen lips.

"What was that for?" she asked. "I mean, I loved it, but… Zane? What's going on?"

He wasn't quite sure what to say, how to tell her about his epiphany at the house and that he'd just seen his father and the combination of the two encounters had caused his entire life to flash before his eyes. That he didn't want to be like Nathaniel Phillips. That if she would have him, he would never hurt her.

"I realized today that I don't want to lose you."

"You did?" She took his hand and pulled him inside, shutting the door behind them. She looked cute in the denim shorts and red blouse she was wearing. More than cute, actually. She looked sexy as hell. How had he been so blind all these years?

"And what exactly inspired this epiphany?" she asked.

He weighed his words and thought about what to say. Telling the truth was best, but it was messy. It contained too much baggage and he was tired of lugging it around. "It doesn't matter. I know I'm not any good at this love thing, but if you'll give me a chance, I can promise you that I will never let you down. What do you say, Lucy? Will you give me a chance?"

Chapter Seven

What was Lucy supposed to do? The love of her life had asked her to give him a chance.

After he'd kissed her senseless, every bit of resolve she had cobbled into place systematically unraveled, as if he had pulled a single thread and left her guard lying in a tangled heap at her feet.

Of course she'd give him a chance. As if she even had a choice in the matter. A girl could only be so strong.

However, *a chance* didn't necessarily mean she'd marry him. Not yet, anyway. Maybe not ever. She didn't know. She was still reeling from the force of that kiss. Her lips were still tingling.

All she knew right now was that Ethan and Chelsea needed to get married first. It wasn't a competition, of course, but if Lucy had learned one thing since opening the Campbell Wedding Barn, it was that every bride, no matter how humble, deserved to be a princess for a day. Lucy wasn't going to do anything to upstage Chelsea on her big day.

Lucy knew that the truth of the matter was if she and Zane ran off and got married—or even hinted that they were considering it—the focus of the entire town would turn to them and how little Lucy Campbell had run off and married Celebration's most eligible bachelor. People would speculate about the reason—and they'd be right.

So, no, Lucy wasn't going to even consider anything until after her brother and Chelsea had tied the knot.

That was fine. After *the kiss*, Zane had presented her with two gallons of paint—not just any paint, but the perfect shade of yellow for their baby's nursery. In some ways, this gesture made her even more inclined to entertain the thought of marrying him. It had made her really ponder—what exactly was the meaning of love? How was the best way to declare love? Anyone could say those three little words. He could've very well told her exactly what she wanted to hear and she would've fallen for it. Because she had already fallen for him.

But in the Zane fairy tale in her mind, his going to the trouble of finding the perfect shade of yellow was almost metaphorical to Prince Charming searching the kingdom for the woman whose foot fit the glass slipper.

Well, sort of… It had seemed a bit more romantic as it came to her in a rush. Practically speaking, she could use two gallons of the perfect shade of yellow much more than she could use a glass slipper.

Or had Cinderella ended up with a matching pair? If so, why did everything but the glass slippers revert to their original state at the stroke of midnight? And if only a single slipper remained… Oh, who cared? Hadn't fairy-tale standards caused her more trouble than they were worth? And who needed glass slippers anyway, when the man of her dreams gave her a whole heck of a lot more than lip service?

Zane had come through. He had been there for her. Shouldn't the little gestures like the cradle and the thought he'd put into the perfect shade of paint and that ragged, one-eyed teddy bear prove that he was in this? That he was committed? If this wasn't love, what was?

If only she could exorcise the demon that kept saying, "Everything is fine now, but what if, like Cinderella, everything does evaporate at the stroke of midnight?" In this case, midnight would happen if Zane met another woman who ended up being the love of his life and he fell head over heels in love.

It had happened to his own father with Marianne—though Lucy would never insult Zane by showing him that parallel.

That would be her midnight; it would be the darkest night of her soul.

And the earth would end someday and she might walk outside and get hit by a car smack-dab in the middle of the crosswalk. Nothing was guaranteed. Not even tomorrow. The angel on her shoulder began to override the demon: what if Zane never fell in love with anyone else and she had wasted her chance with him? What if this *was* Zane in love?

As they worked side-by-side, painting their baby's nursery soft banana, Lucy began to ignore her doubts. Not only did she let down her guard, but she also let herself hope and imagine what it would be like to become Mrs. Zane Phillips and have a family with the man she loved.

Lucy was in the middle of finalizing the seating configuration for Ethan and Chelsea's wedding ceremony when a text came through from Zane.

Are you up for a lunch break?

She wasn't, really, because she was already behind the eight ball with the seating plans. Two hours ago, Chelsea had asked if they had room to add twenty-five more people. Space was already tight, but Lucy told her she would get creative and see what she could do. She was supposed to meet with Lauren Walters, the assistant she hired on an as-needed basis to help with larger events. She'd planned on

working through lunch to have the seating arrangements ready for the meeting. But now she was suddenly famished. Funny how that always seemed to
happen when Zane called.

She replied to Zane. What did you have in mind?

Actually, I'm right outside. You keep this place
locked up like a prison. Will you let me in?

Are you equating my wedding venue to a prison?

A moment passed without a reply and Lucy
wished she'd included some kind of emoticon to in-
dicate she was kidding. Surely, he realized she was
kidding? Didn't he?

And then he texted back. I brought subs and
chips.

So much for trying to joke around through the
magical medium of texting. She should know better.
Sometimes humor got lost over the waves. She got
up from her desk and opened the barn's front door.
There stood Zane. Her first glimpse of him after
spending time apart always knocked the air out of
her for an instant—in the very best way—and this
was no exception.

"Hi," she said. "Are you here to turn yourself in?"

He laughed. Sort of. Had something in the double meaning of equating marriage to prison struck
a nerve? Because his sense of humor was notably
absent.

"Sure," he said.

"Good, because I deal in standard-issue ball and chains. But you can bond out of jail with the payment of one sub sandwich and a bag of chips."

He held up the white paper sack. "Sounds like a deal."

That was more like it.

Lucy motioned for Zane to follow her into the kitchen. He unwrapped the sandwiches and set them on the paper that they came in while she poured them each a glass of iced tea and put a lemon wedge on the rim of each glass.

"You look nice," he said, giving her an approving once-over.

She was wearing jeans and a simple white lace blouse. Casual and comfortable, but she had a jacket hanging on the back of her door to dress up her look if a potential client came by.

"Thanks, cowboy. You don't look so bad yourself."

Zane always looked sexy no matter what he was wearing. Today, his plain khaki green T-shirt brought out the hazel flecks in his brown eyes. She could lose herself in those eyes, she thought as she waited for him to look up and catch her staring. She wanted him to catch her, wanted to flirt with him and turn the flirting into kissing, but he was too busy contemplating his sandwich.

She resisted the urge to fill the silence by asking him if everything was all right. They ate without talking for a while. Something felt a little bit off. Lucy couldn't put her finger on it, but something was definitely weird. Then again, it was probably her. She was tired and short on time, which was probably making her a little anxious. She needed to cool her jets.

After all, he was the one who had surprised her by showing up with lunch, just when she needed it. She was hungrier than she'd realized. This was probably just a blood-sugar episode. Or simple overthinking.

If things were to work out between the two of them, she could not melt into a heap of self-doubt at his every quiet mood. He was human—he was allowed to have good days and bad days, vocal days and days when he just needed to turn inside. The best relationships were the ones where the couples could be equally happy interacting and spending quiet moments side by side in companionable silence. She was going to have to become best friends with her self-confidence. All her life, she'd never been short on self-confidence. Lately, she was needing to dig deep and get reacquainted with it. This off-kilter feeling, this sensation of spinning out of control and not knowing where she was going to land when she stopped, was so uncomfortable.

But she needed to get her bearings so she could land on her feet.

She pondered this as she ate her sandwich. Zane had already finished and was cleaning up his trash. He took his glass to the sink, washed and dried it.

"Thanks for bringing lunch," she said. "I needed a break more than I realized." She glanced at her watch. "Lauren should be here in a few minutes to go over the details of Ethan and Chelsea's wedding. I'm counting on her, since Juliette and I will both be part of the wedding party." She shook her head. "Maybe I should've brought someone else in to help Lauren, given all the added security."

"It's not like you won't be right here," he said over his shoulder. "Plus, as hard as you and Juliette have been working on this, it could probably run itself."

"If only. Events only look effortless when someone is doing a darn good job of steering the ship behind the scenes."

Zane walked back to the kitchen island and sat down. Resting his forearms on his thighs, he looked at her for a moment. She could virtually see the wheels turning in his head.

"What is it? Are you okay? You've been really quiet." The look on his face didn't do much to make her feel better.

"I have some news," he said, and she had a sinking feeling she wasn't going to love what he had to say. As she swallowed the last bite of her sandwich, it stuck in her throat. She had to wash it down with a gulp of iced tea.

"Good news, I hope."

He gave her a half smile and a one-shoulder shrug. "Depends on how you look at it."

Silence stretched between them until she couldn't stand it anymore.

"Are you going to tell me or do I have to guess?"

"I heard back from Hidden Rock in Ocala."

"Oh." She did her best to put a smile in her voice and on her face, one that reached her eyes, because she should be happy for him. She wanted to be happy for him.

But the truth was she was scared to death. What did this mean?

Things had just started going so well she'd actually forgotten about the Ocala possibility. Of course, it had lived somewhere in the corner of her subconscious. She had to admit that she'd hoped the job had lost its shine for him, and that maybe, just maybe, after all that had happened, he'd decided that he wanted to stay in Celebration.

"Did they offer you the job?" She held her breath as she waited for his answer.

"Not exactly," he said. "They want me to come out again. So they can show me the ropes. They want to introduce me to the rest of the staff and talk specifics—probably negotiate salary and such."

"So, basically, it's imminent? They're going to offer you the job, Zane. I mean, they wouldn't bring you all the way back out and introduce you around there if it wasn't a strong possibility, right?"

"I don't know. Maybe?"

She arched a brow at him and he shifted in his seat and ran a hand through his unruly hair.

"Probably," he said.

"I know how much you want this job." It hurt her heart to acknowledge that. But she had to.

"Of course." His eyes flashed and then in an instant a look of unfathomable realization commandeered his expression as his gaze dropped to Lucy's belly. "But things have changed. I can't leave. I probably should tell them I can't take the job."

Their lives flashed before Lucy's eyes. This was how the end would begin. He would turn down his dream job. For a while he would pretend it didn't matter. Maybe he'd even convince himself it didn't. He'd keep working at Bridgemont, and resentment would take root and grow inside him, until it spread like kudzu and strangled the life out of them and anything that might resemble a relationship.

"Why would you do that?" she asked, working so hard to keep her voice from breaking.

"Really?" His smile was a challenge.

"Zane, I'm serious. You are not turning down a job because of me. Don't put that on me."

"Did I say I blamed you? Because I don't remember mentioning your name."

He flashed that lopsided smile and she could tell he was trying not to let the conversation devolve into a fight, trying to pretend as if this was no big deal, but his eyes gave him away.

"I think we're getting a little bit ahead of ourselves here. They haven't officially offered me the job. You're trying to ship me off already." There was that teasing smile again. "I guess I never considered the fact that you might want to get rid of me."

"Then who would bring me lunch on those days when I didn't even realize I needed it?" she said.

He reached out and toyed with a strand of her hair. "I imagine there would be someone who would be eager to take my place."

Take my place.

His place.

"No one could ever take your place." She'd said the words before she could stop herself and immediately wished she could reel them back in. He reached out and took her hand, brought it to his lips and kissed it.

"Come with me, Luce."

She shook her head, a little dazed. "You know I can't do that." She gestured around her. "Zane, my life is here. I have my business. My family is here."

"You don't have to give it up. You could get Lauren to run it for you—at least for a while. I mean, when you're out on maternity leave."

His words swirled around her. The mere thought of leaving everything she'd worked so hard to build made her feel light-headed. She couldn't even respond.

"You've done a great job with the Campbell Wedding Barn. Maybe you could branch out and do something similar in Florida. Aren't you ready for a new challenge? A chance to try something new? Or here's a thought—you and Juliette have been working so closely together. Have you ever considered merging your businesses? If not Lauren, maybe Juliette could manage the Texas location while you expand the operation in Ocala. I mean, I'm just thinking out loud, but what do you think? You and Juliette are both entrepreneurs. You're great at things like that."

She shook her head. Her heart was pounding and she felt like she was on the verge of tears. "I think Juliette should be part of that conversation before we start making business decisions for her."

"I know, I said I'm just thinking out loud."

She tried to swallow her emotions and see it from his point of view. It was a good idea in theory. Taking a leap of faith and following him to Ocala. It could be an adventure…or a disaster.

Even so, a merger with Juliette was a tall order.

"If Juliette is here managing the barn, who will tend to her business? She travels a lot. I'm sure she wouldn't be too keen about the idea of giving up everything she's built just to accommodate us."

"Okay, I see your point, but that's where Lauren could come in. You're going to have to take some time off when the baby comes. You're going to need someone to cover for you while you're on maternity leave."

She blinked. Her head swam at the thought. She hadn't even thought that far ahead. She was still getting use to the idea of being pregnant. Still trying to figure out exactly how she and Zane fit into each other's lives. Because just when she thought she had it figured out, everything changed. His pending offer for the job in Ocala was case in point.

"I don't know, Zane. I haven't gotten there yet. All I know is I don't want you to turn down this job for me."

He inhaled sharply and then blew out the breath. It wasn't an impatient sound—it seemed more like a nervous gesture. "All I'm asking is for you to think about it. We don't have to make any decisions right now."

She brushed some sandwich crumbs into a small pile with her finger.

"Good, because right now I'm on overload with all the last-minute details for Ethan and Chelsea's wedding. My head is too full."

So was her heart.

He nodded and unfolded his tall body from the chrome bar stool. "I understand. I do. I get it. I know this is a lot to spring on you all at once. Are you finished with your lunch?"

She nodded and he gathered up her trash. He was good to her in little ways like that. Small, kind gestures that she was getting used to.

"I have to get back to work," he said. "You don't have to answer me now. Not until after your brother's wedding. Just promise me you'll give it some thought. Okay?"

"You're going after the wedding?"

"Yeah. Last time I checked, I was standing up with Ethan."

"When he and I talked, he asked if he needed to get out the shotgun."

"He mentioned that." He smiled. "Maybe that's not a bad idea. Would it convince you to marry me?"

With his job offer pending, getting married seemed like the easy part now. The difficult choice was whether or not to leave everything behind and relocate.

"Are you going to tell him about Ocala?" she asked.

He crossed his arms over his chest and she was distracted by the way his biceps bunched, testing the limit of his T-shirt sleeves. She wanted to touch him. What would he do if she did? They were still in that strange limbo land—together…sort of. Lovers… once. Parents…almost. In love…one of them was.

It hit her that *if* they got married, she had no idea what kind of a marriage they'd have. Would they be lovers? If not—if he'd made his original just-friends mandate because he didn't desire her but didn't want to hurt her feelings—what was the postmarriage plan?

The fact that she even had to wonder about these things reminded her of what an emotionally precarious situation this was. She wasn't going to have an open marriage, but she wasn't okay with the thought of living like a nun for the rest of her life, either.

That song from the '80s that talked about looking at the menu but not being able to eat came to mind. She'd add it to her Zane playlist.

"I'm not going to tell anyone yet," he said. "Not until we have a plan."

"Right now, the plan is that we're having a baby."

He nodded. "What if you visit Ocala with me when I go?"

Her heart wanted to go in the worst—and best—way. Her heart wanted to follow him to the ends of the earth. But the logical part of her warned that it was an impossible situation.

"You could see the town. Try it on for size and see if it fits. See what you think. Because maybe if we got away from Celebration, we could figure out if we could be happy there together."

And that was the crux of the matter. They had no idea if they could be happy together in the long run. In Ocala, here or anywhere.

Wasn't it a telltale sign that they still wanted such different things? He couldn't wait to get out of town, while her entire life was right here.

At least for now, she thought as he kissed her on the cheek and walked out the door.

Chapter Eight

The day of Ethan and Chelsea's wedding dawned bright and beautiful.

Chelsea's immediate family—her father, the Earl of Downing; her mother, the countess; two brothers, Thomas, the probable future UK prime minister, and Niles, a doctor; her sister, Victoria, a fashion designer, who had created Chelsea's gown—had all arrived from the United Kingdom with all of the security required by a family of nobility with political ties.

The entourage made the Campbell family look low maintenance by comparison.

Jude, Ethan and Lucy's brother, had managed to find his way back to Celebration, on a break from the Professional Bull Riders circuit.

Even though they could've invited the entire town, and everyone would've gladly attended, the bride and groom wanted to keep their special day intimate and elegant. They had limited the guest list to one hundred people. Actually, the vast amount of security dictated the cap.

Not long ago, Chelsea had been hounded by a particularly tenacious tabloid reporter whose antics had bordered on stalking. One of the objectives for the wedding was to make sure no rogue reporters got past the barriers. But that was security's task. They were trained professionals. So Lucy was banking on them doing their job so that Lauren could do hers.

That morning, Chelsea, Lucy and Juliette had prepared for the big day in Lucy's house, which was right next door to the barn. There was a brand-new bridal room inside the wedding barn, which Lucy had built during the renovation, but since Chelsea was family, they had opted to get ready at the house.

While Chelsea was having her hair, makeup and nails done, Lucy had been back and forth between the house and the barn, checking and double-checking that Lauren had everything in place.

"Everything will be fine," Lauren scolded when Lucy, in her long blue bridesmaid dress and black strappy sandals, her dark hair styled in an updo, had sneaked away from the bridal party for the umpteenth time to check on another detail. "I have my work order. All I have to do is follow it. Today, your job is to tend to Chelsea. You're not doing a very good job of that when you're over here checking up on me."

She was right. Lauren was good at this. She had common sense, good instincts and great people skills. It was why Lucy had hired her in the first place, and why she was trusting her to oversee this very important wedding. Plus, if something did go wrong, it wasn't as if Lauren wouldn't be able to find Lucy.

On the way back to the house, Lucy ran into Jude, who was looking tall and handsome, if not a little uncomfortable, in the traditional tuxedo Chelsea had picked out for Ethan's groomsmen—Jude and Zane—to wear during the wedding.

Jude had missed last night's rehearsal dinner because his schedule had forced him to take the red-eye and arrive this morning, but he was here now, and that was all that mattered.

She hadn't had a chance to talk to him. So she grabbed the opportunity now.

"Hey, stranger." She gave him a big hug, sighing at how good it was for all three of the Campbell siblings to be together again. Lucy adored her brothers. Jude was the middle sibling; Ethan was the oldest. Jude was just as free-spirited and lone-wolfish as Ethan was rooted and inclusive. Where Ethan had always been practical, Jude had marched to his own drum.

"We should have weddings more often if it will get you home," Lucy said, pulling back to take in his ruggedly handsome face. "Speaking of weddings, have you seen Juliette?"

Jude stiffened. "Not yet, but I hear she is part of the wedding party. So I'm bound to see her soon enough."

If the town of Celebration, Texas, had been taking wagers on which Campbell sibling would have been the first to marry, most people would have cast their vote for Jude. He and Juliette had been high-school sweethearts. Both of them had itchy feet and couldn't wait to see the world. Everyone thought they'd go off together. But they ran into trouble when Juliette won a scholarship to a college in England. The two of them had surprised everyone when they had broken up right before she went away to school. After she left, Jude had thrown his heart and soul into professional bull riding. It had been a bitter breakup. As far as Lucy knew, the two hadn't spoken since. Probably because about three months after the breakup, Jude had announced his engagement to a barrel racer he'd met at one of the competitions. The engagement hadn't lasted long, but the blow seemed to have killed any chance of reconciliation between him and Juliette. Still, weddings tended to cast magical spells over people. Lucy wasn't counting them out yet.

"Speaking of weddings," Jude said. "What's going on with you and Phillips?"

Lucy felt heat flame in the area of her décolletage and begin a slow creep up her face until it burned her cheeks, which she was sure were the color of the red rose pinned to her brother's lapel.

Just be cool.

"What do you mean?" she said, trying to be as nonchalant as possible.

Jude studied her for a moment before his gaze dropped to her belly. Instinctively, she crossed her hands in front of her. She wasn't showing yet, but she had a sinking feeling that her brother knew everything.

"I think you know what I mean," he said. "Ethan told me the good news. You should know that he can't keep a secret, and since I'm only here on a quick turnaround, I wanted to be sure I had a chance to say congratulations in private."

"Thanks," she said, her cheeks burning again. "But that really wasn't his news to tell. Is he broadcasting it to everyone?"

She hated to have to bring it up on Ethan's wedding day, but she needed to make sure the news didn't get out before she and Zane were ready. They still had a lot to figure out.

"Since I have to leave so soon and the wedding is going to be pretty all-consuming, I think he wanted to make sure I knew. Ethan might have a big mouth around family, but he can be pretty damn stoic around everyone else. He won't tell anyone else. I'm happy for you, sis. As long as you're happy."

For a moment she was afraid she would start weeping with relief and joy. That was precisely the reason she loved Jude so much. When she felt at odds with the rest of the world, he was always on her side. He never judged, and, in return, he expected the same nonjudgmental treatment. Actually, Jude did a good job of pretending like he didn't care what the rest of the world thought. But Lucy knew his cool act hid a tender heart.

"I am happy, Jude." She put her hand on her still flat belly. "I'm not gonna lie. This wasn't exactly planned, but it feels right. I'm home. I'm settled. This baby feels like a new infusion of life for the Campbell family."

She tried to ignore the twinge of conflict that twisted in her heart as she thought of Zane asking her to go with him to Ocala. She still hadn't decided what she was going to do. Why did everything have to be so difficult? Just when she thought everything was falling into place, everything... Well, at least she couldn't say everything *fell apart*. Because it hadn't. Leaving everything she'd worked so hard to build so that she could be with the only man she'd ever loved, who still couldn't say he loved her, too, was just *complicated*.

"It does feel like new life," Jude said. "I love the idea of being an uncle. Uncle Jude." He nodded his approval. "I like the sound of that. I'm going to be the cool uncle. Ethan will be the grouchy dude."

They laughed, because that pretty much summed up the situation. Although Ethan would never admit it.

"Does that mean you'll come home more often once the baby's born?"

"Every chance I get. I've got to run. I told Ethan I'd get him a Dr. Pepper. Apparently, Chelsea mandated that he not be outside roaming around and take the chance of them seeing each other before the ceremony. You know, all that bad-luck superstition. I didn't know they believed in that in England."

Lucy scrunched up her face. "Why wouldn't they believe that in England?"

Jude shrugged. "I'm a cowboy. Shows you what I know."

As he turned to leave, Lucy said, "Jude?"

He stopped and looked over his shoulder. "Yeah?"

"I've missed you."

He winked at her and pointed his finger in a quick gesture before he turned to complete his groomsmen mission.

She thought about asking him not to say anything to anyone else, but she knew he wouldn't. She knew Ethan wouldn't, either. It was important that both of her brothers knew and that both of them were happy for her. Ethan would probably be happier if she took the more traditional route and accepted Zane's proposal. But that was her decision and hers alone.

She stood there for a moment feeling safe and loved and secure… And more confused than she'd ever been in her entire life. Then she shook it off, because today wasn't about her. It was about Chelsea and Ethan. Two people who loved each other madly. Two people who wanted to be together, to spend the rest of their lives together because of *love*.

The barn had never looked more beautiful, with its string lights and candlelit lanterns. There were so many flowers that she couldn't turn her head without seeing blossom-pink and white peonies, scarlet-red roses and garlands of jasmine and ivy. All the flowers had been gathered from the Campbell ranch, and they perfumed the air. Lucy couldn't decide if it was like a scene from *The Secret Garden* or a page torn straight out of a story about a princess wedding.

Maybe both. Chelsea was almost a princess.

One thing was certain—love floated in the air from the hearts of all who were there to witness this joining of two lives. It mingled with the scent of all those flowers and the sound of the string quartet playing a slow, ethereal Celtic serenade. The beauty of the moment, its sheer, effortless perfection, made Lucy breathless and wistful.

She wanted *this*.

She was the first to walk down the aisle before maid-of-honor Juliette and then Chelsea. As Lucy made her way from the back of the room toward the dais, her gaze found Zane's and they held on to each other, an invisible thread of longing—or maybe it was *belonging*—binding them.

As Lucy took her place up front, Zane's gaze was still on her, even though Juliette was walking down the aisle. It brought to mind a saying—the best kiss is the one that has been exchanged a thousand times between the eyes before it reaches the lips. She didn't know who'd said it originally, but it was perfect. Almost as perfect as Pablo Neruda hearing the unsaid in a single kiss.

How could Zane look at her that way and not love her?

How would she ever know if he could love her if she didn't at least let him try?

Maybe if we got away from Celebration, we could figure out if we could be happy together.

After the officiant pronounced Ethan and Chelsea husband and wife, Lucy had never seen the pair of them look happier than they were in that moment. They had been through separate hells, but by the grace of all that was good, they had managed to find each other. It was Chelsea's first marriage and Ethan's second. Their path to each other hadn't been an easy road for either of them. They'd struggled, but they hadn't given up—or maybe they had, but once they'd found each other, they hadn't let fear and past failures keep them from what was good.

Lucy and Zane were the last of the bridal party to walk down the aisle during the recessional. He offered her his arm and it felt so natural to accept it. Just as natural as it felt to dance with him and be by his side all night long. Wasn't this how it always was between them?

She'd spent all these years wishing that Zane would fall in love with her, wondering why he was so blind. Maybe she was the one who'd been oblivious all these years.

At the end of the night, after everyone had eaten

and danced and celebrated Ethan and Chelsea, it was time for the bride to throw her bouquet. A group of eleven single women, including a reluctant Juliette, who had done her best to avoid Jude during the moments when they weren't forced together as part of the wedding party, gathered for the toss. Before she turned around, Chelsea pinned Lucy with her gaze and smiled. When she threw the bouquet of white peonies, roses, jasmine and lilies over her shoulder, it landed right in Lucy's hands.

Everyone cheered and chanted, "You're next! You're next!"

Lucy wasn't sure if it was an omen. Maybe she should've ducked out of the way.

"You did that on purpose," she said to Chelsea. "Did my brother put you up to it?"

"No, I did," said Zane. "Will you please come with me to Ocala to just see what you think?"

"You must be Zane's *fiancée.*" Rhett Sullivan, the owner of Hidden Rock Equestrian in Ocala, shook Lucy's hand.

"Nice to meet you, Mr. Sullivan, I'm Lucy Campbell."

Lucy slanted a glance at Zane and he smiled at her. There'd be hell to pay for fudging the fiancée bit, he knew it. But maybe the power of suggestion would help her make up her mind. At least he'd gotten her here.

"I'm pleased as punch that you could come out

and see the place with him. We think Zane will be a great addition to the Hidden Rock Equestrian family, but I know he's anxious to get your approval before he makes any decisions."

When Rhett turned his back to lead them toward the golf cart so that he could drive to the stables, Lucy shot Zane daggers.

"Your fiancée?" she said under her breath.

He shrugged. "I might have said something like that."

"Are y'all comfortable over at the house? That place is part of the compensation package. That's why we wanted y'all to get a chance to try it out tonight while you're here. My wife, Luann, just redecorated after the last GM and his family moved out. You just let her know if you need anything. Just holler and she'll see that you get it."

"Thank you, the place is lovely," Lucy said. "Please tell her I said so."

"Well, you'll get a chance to tell her yourself after the tour," Sullivan said as he climbed into the golf cart. "I'd planned on stealing our boy away to talk horse business. You and Lu can grab some lunch. It'll give you two gals a chance to get better acquainted. We're a tight-knit bunch around here and y'all will be spending plenty of time together while Zane and I are working."

Sullivan motioned for Lucy to sit in the golf cart's backseat and patted the seat next to him for Zane. He couldn't see Lucy's reaction because her hair fell in her face as she leaned forward to climb aboard the cart. Lucy was friendly and kind enough to not thumb her nose at Sullivan's hospitality, but he knew the guy dictating who Lucy would spend time with was probably a strike against his cause of making her fall in love with this place enough to move here.

Of course, it probably hadn't helped matters when she'd learned that he'd told Sullivan she was his fiancée. But it probably hadn't hurt. The reason he'd said it in the first place was because it was too complicated to try to explain their current situation to an older, more conservative Southern gentlemen like Rhett. And, yeah, Zane had been thinking positive at the time. At least Lucy was graciously playing along, but he was going to get it with both barrels once they were alone.

The Hidden Rock property was beautiful. Set in the verdant, rolling hills of Ocala, the farm went on forever and was surrounded by clusters of live oak trees dripping with Spanish moss. They'd even had to drive through a canopy of trees to get to the ranch.

Zane had heard a lot about Hidden Rock because its reputation spoke for itself. If he couldn't have his own farm, this place was everything he wanted. He could see himself getting up every morning and looking forward to going to work here.

"We built this place back in 1972," Sullivan said. "I know we went over the details when you visited before, but I'll give y'all the spiel again for your little lady's benefit."

Little lady? She was going to love that. Zane glanced over his shoulder at her.

"Did you hear that? All this is for you, dear."

She grimaced at him. Zane turned around before Sullivan could catch on. Then again, Rhett was a good ol' boy, who probably wouldn't even realize a *little lady* like Lucy would take issue with being called a little lady.

"Yeah, we're sitting on a little over eight hundred acres here. We have just about everything you could ever want when it comes to breeding and training Thoroughbreds. We've got a seven-eighths-mile dirt training track, a swimming pond for the horses. And if I remember right, at last count we had sixteen barns with four hundred and twenty-six stalls, one hundred and fifty paddocks and a hell of a lot of grazing fields. We've got hot walkers and round pens. You name it, we've got it. And if we don't have it, we can get it. But most importantly, we do everything with the horses' safety and development in mind. I don't mean to brag, but you're not going to find a better operation in north central Florida. Aw, heck, I'd even stick my neck out to say we are the best outfit in the entire southeast. We breed champions here, Zane. With your background, you'll fit right into our mission."

"Yes, sir," Zane said.

Sullivan drove around for a good half an hour talking about the various points of interest on the farm. Zane wondered if Lucy's eyes were glazing over, but then he realized he wasn't giving her enough credit. She'd grown up among the horse crowd in Celebration, but Hidden Rock was a completely different species from what they were used to. This place was magnificent. It was a chance to make a name for himself. A chance to carve out a future for his family.

As Rhett parked the cart in front of a gargantuan white antebellum house with columns like something from *Gone with the Wind*, their host turned around and placed a beefy arm along the seat back and trained his attention on Lucy.

"What did you think of that?" He didn't give her a chance to answer. "It's a real opportunity for this man of yours. Yeah, we got résumés from some people with more experience, but I go on attitude. Your boy here has great potential. This is what I'd call a win-win situation. That means we both have something to offer each other. A guy with talents like Zane's can do big things at a place like Hidden Rock. And Hidden Rock can certainly benefit from his talents. So, I'm counting on you to work your magic on him and tell him everything you love about this place. I sense that's what he's waiting for before he tells me he's joining the Hidden Rock family."

"Lucy, darling, it's lovely to finally meet you." Luann Sullivan leaned in and air-kissed Lucy's cheeks, Euro-style. The woman was nothing like what Lucy had imagined. Her husband had painted a picture of a demure woman whose sole purpose was servitude, the consummate *little lady* who lived to fetch and please.

Luann was tall, blonde and regal. The type of woman who seemed more at home in jodhpurs, riding boots and a diamond ring the size of a headlight than being at a guest's beck and call. One look at Luann Sullivan and Lucy understood that any *fetching* would be performed by the huge staff, some of whom served their luncheon by the pool on the terrace of the Sullivans' six-thousand-square-foot home.

How Luann and Rhett Sullivan fit together seemed a mystery. He was Budweiser and plaid button-down shirts; she was Veuve Clicquot and Cartier. No doubt, he was one of those Southern men who had so much money he didn't have to worry about looking like he had anything. So, it was probably the money and the horses that had brought them together.

Later, Lucy and her hostess enjoyed lobster salad and sparkling mineral water under the biggest and most silent outdoor ceiling fan Lucy had ever seen. It stirred up a gentle breeze, rendering the punishing Florida humidity powerless, as it provided a pleasant place for the women to enjoy the panoramic view of Hidden Rock.

Luann was a timeless beauty. Her ageless, effortless elegance was probably a by-product of good genes, faithful sunscreen use, fresh air and sunshine. And probably regular Botox.

"Are you a horse lover like your husband-to-be?" Luann asked.

Lucy blanched at the reference to Zane and hoped Luann didn't notice. "I was raised with horses. My family has a small breeding farm in Celebration, Texas. My brother is running the ranch now."

"Is that so?" Luann smiled and leaned in. "What's the name of the ranch? Perhaps I've heard of it."

"It's called the Triple C. My family's name is Campbell."

"*Ahh*, how nice."

Translation: *I've never heard of it.*

"Do you ride?" Luann asked. "If so, let's take the horses out before you leave."

It had been a long time since Lucy had ridden a horse, and even at her best, she'd never been much of an equestrian. Not to mention, riding probably wouldn't be the best thing for the baby. Her doctor had told her she could participate in mild exercise that her body was already used to, but now wasn't the time to try anything new. Or go riding after all these years.

But she couldn't share that with Luann.

"It's been a long time since I've ridden," Lucy said. "I work a lot these days. It doesn't allow me a lot of free time."

Luann smiled one of those gracious, practiced smiles that made it seem like she was genuinely interested in Lucy's workaholic ways, but Lucy suspected she was just being polite.

"What do you do, dear?"

"I run a wedding barn."

"A wedding barn? What is that?"

"It's a barn that has been spruced up to provide a rustic venue for weddings."

Luann laughed. "Of course! You'll have to excuse me. Rhett and I have been married for so long that I'm not up on the latest in wedding trends. We have a daughter who is in her twenties, but she's not the least bit interested in settling down. Your job sounds fascinating. Will you try to find similar work when you move here?"

"Oh, well, I'm not sure about that. Actually, I own the venue. It's an old barn on my family's property that we renovated."

Luann waved her hand. "There are a number of ramshackle barns around here that I'm sure you could work your magic on. Are you into the DIY craze? It's a great way to keep busy." Something in the tilt of the woman's head and the polite tone of her voice seemed dismissive.

"We were featured in *Southern Living* magazine and named one of 'The Most Beautiful Wedding Barns in the South.'"

As a general rule, Lucy hated to brag. She had framed the magazine cover and the portion of the article that featured the Campbell Wedding Barn. But generally, she let the venue speak for itself. She'd only mentioned it now because Luann Sullivan didn't seem to understand that it wasn't just any old barn. It was a tie to her family. It had history and sentimental value that she couldn't simply recreate in Ocala's plethora of *ramshackle barns*. But how did you explain that to someone who came from a completely different world and had an obvious vested interest in making her fall in love with Ocala so that Zane would take the job?

You didn't.

Instead, Lucy smiled and nodded, borrowing a page from her mama, who used to insist, if you can't say something nice, be quiet.

So she listened to Luann, who obviously had little interest in ramshackle barns. She had switched the subject to her glory days as an Olympic dressage champion and Ocala's horsey crowd. Curiously, though she called herself an Olympic *champion*, she didn't mention winning a medal. Lucy had to bite her tongue to keep from asking, but she managed to resist.

It went against every bone in her body to be so passive, but she was feeling prickly and impatient. If her discontent came through as attitude, it might make things difficult for Zane. No matter her own trepidations and irritations, she would never do that to him. This could be a very good opportunity for him. The boss man was obviously gaga over him, certain that Zane was the man for the job.

Lucy dug deep to try to pull herself out of the

funk. If she put her own wants and needs aside, she was truly happy for him. She wanted good things for Zane. She only wished those good things were located in Texas.

Later that evening, the Sullivans hosted a barbecue. It wasn't specifically in Zane's honor, but it bore a strong resemblance to a welcome party.

She hated to jump to snap conclusions, but this didn't seem like it was going to work for her. She hadn't even been in Florida for twelve hours and already she was homesick for Celebration. This coming from a girl who at one point in her life couldn't wait to get out and see the world. But all that time away had proved to her that home was where her heart lived. Try as she might, she couldn't muster the enthusiasm she would need to pack up everything and relocate with a man who was only in this relationship because she was carrying his child.

She wouldn't dream of asking him not to take the job. How could she? But by the same token, how could he ask her to give up everything she'd worked so hard to build?

All of that was driven home when a woman who bore a striking resemblance to Luann, only younger and sexier, walked in and turned every head in the room. Her outfit, a shimmery little white dress that accentuated her perfect long blond hair and showcased her perfectly tanned long sleek legs, probably cost more than Lucy's entire wardrobe.

Damn her.

Lucy watched as she picked Zane out of the crowd and floated over.

"Hey there, Zane Phillips," she said, flirting with her eyes. "I told Daddy you are the man for the job. I'm so glad he listened."

So, this was the daughter who had no interest in settling down. Lucy's heart sank. The woman was tall and perfect and model gorgeous. Now that Lucy saw her up close, she realized she bore a striking resemblance to Blake Lively, only prettier. If that was possible.

Funny, Zane hadn't mentioned *interviewing* with the daughter when he'd returned from his first trip to Florida. But she had taken enough of an interest to recommend him to *Daddy*.

Daddy had listened.

"Hi, Taylor," Zane said. "Taylor Sullivan, this is Lucy Campbell."

She noted that this time he didn't introduce her as his fiancée.

Taylor's cool gaze slid to Lucy, lighting on her as if she'd just noticed her standing there.

Taylor flashed a perfect smile. "Nice to meet you, Lucy Campbell."

She turned back to Zane. "When do you start?"

"I haven't accepted the position yet," Zane said.

"Yet." Taylor looked confident. "Let me know when you do."

Zane's chin was cocked. Lucy wondered if he was making an effort to not let his gaze drop to the bit of

Taylor's cleavage peeking out to greet him. It was tasteful, but it did beckon the eye. Taylor was exactly Zane's type. Lucy had been in this position too many times not to recognize it. She was definitely fluffy-woodland-pet material. Only, she seemed smarter and had a decent name. And she came from a family with so much money her *daddy* could buy both Ocala and Celebration with his pocket change.

Lucy had Googled Rhett Sullivan after a staff member had transported her by golf cart away from Luann and the big house to the beautiful three-bedroom ranch-style home that would be part of Zane's compensation package. She'd learned that Rhett was a fourth-generation Floridian whose family had made its money in the sugarcane industry. Rhett and Luann Sullivan were both on several lists of the nation's wealthiest individuals. It seemed Lu had brought quite a dowry to the marriage.

"See you," Taylor promised as she floated away.

Zane had a funny look on his face.

So it began. Well, that hadn't taken long.

"I see you already have a Florida fan club," Lucy said.

"I do? What do you mean?"

"Oh, come on," Lucy said. "Don't be coy. She digs you. And I'd say she's just your type."

"Seriously?"

Lucy nodded. "Seriously. But you know what? I am exhausted. I'm going to call it a night. But you feel free to stay and mingle with the natives."

It was burning her tongue to suggest that it would

be in bad taste to sleep with the boss's daughter before he'd formally accepted the job, but she swallowed the bitter words, because it would sound, well,
bitter and snarky.

Even if it was good advice.

"If you're not staying, I'm not staying," Zane said.
"Let's at least pay our respects to the Sullivans."

"Zane, you haven't even eaten yet. You need to
stay. This party is essentially for you. Really, I'll be
okay. I just have a headache. It's been a long day
after the flight and the tour."

"You need to eat," he said.

She was just about to say that there was plenty
of food in the well-stocked ranch house kitchen, but
Rhett Sullivan appeared in front of them. After some
cordial small talk, he said, "Little lady, I need to borrow your boy. Now, you mix and mingle and make
some friends. These are going to be your people and
they're all dying to meet you."

"I'll be right back," Zane said. Then he mouthed,
Don't go.

It was the first time in her life she'd experienced
the sensation of being simultaneously relieved and
heartbroken.

Relieved to be able to make such an easy exit.

Heartbroken because she knew she would never
fit in in Ocala.

Chapter Nine

Zane got back to the house about an hour and a half after he'd realized Lucy had left the party.

"I'm sorry," he said. "I would've been back sooner, but I had a hard time getting away from Rhett."

Sullivan had kept signaling the servers to refill their bourbon glasses and introducing him to people. Zane had quit sipping his drink, but short of being rude, he'd had little control over the introductions. Finally, when Rhett, who had been tossing back his drinks like shots and refreshing every time a server offered, was blotto and distracted by a sexy blonde who looked dangerously close to his daughter's age, Zane had slipped away.

Lucy shook her head. "Zane, you shouldn't have

left the party. Please don't cut the night short because of me. Go back." She shooed him away with the wave of her hand and turned her attention back to one of those celebrity magazines she loved so much. She was curled up on the couch with the magazine, reading and sipping a mug of something that smelled warm and minty. She'd changed into an oversize T-shirt, piled her dark hair on top of her head and scrubbed her face clean of makeup.

"You look like you're settled in for the night," he said.

She nodded but didn't look up from her magazine.

He sat down on a chair and started taking off his boots.

"What are you doing?" she asked. "It's only nine o'clock. I would imagine the party is just getting started. You can't just cut out."

"I can't? Really? I just did." He lined his boots up on the floor at the end of the expensive-looking coffee table. The place was so nice, he probably should've taken off his shoes outside or at least left them on the wood floor and not the white area rug that resembled a pelt of the world's largest sheepdog. He would've described it as shaggy, but something told him it probably cost a fortune.

He got up and moved his boots to the door, came back and sat down on the couch next to her.

"Zane, you need to go back." She nudged him with her bare foot.

"It's been a long day." He grabbed her foot and put it in his lap. "I'm peopled out."

What he really wanted to say was that he didn't want to go back without her. But that wouldn't be fair. He knew this wasn't fun for her. She'd been a good sport all day, playing the supportive, if not pretend, fiancée. It was late and he knew she was tired. Even at this stage, the baby sapped her energy.

"The master schmoozer is peopled out? The end of the world must be near."

She closed the magazine and tossed it onto the coffee table. There was a picture of one of those royal dudes on the cover. Henry or Hank or Harry or whatever his name was. Lucy would know. She knew them all. Even before meeting Chelsea she'd always been obsessed with royalty. She probably should've been born a princess—

He should treat her like one.

She stretched her legs and put the other foot in his lap, too. He started massaging both feet. She had nice feet. They were soft and her toenails were always painted some color. Tonight, they were a bright red.

"Did you talk to Taylor after I left?" She smiled and quirked a brow at him in a way that was so Lucy.

"No, I didn't talk to Taylor. Why, are you jealous?" he teased. "If you are, it means you care."

"I'm not jealous. I'm just realistic. She likes you. I can tell."

He moved his thumb in firm circles along the bottom of one foot. She seemed to melt into it.

"I noticed you didn't deny the fact that being jealous means you care," he retorted.

She shrugged, still not disputing it.

"Taylor was just being friendly," he said. "Hospitable."

"I'm sure she is. She could be *the one*, Zane. Don't write her off."

"You *are* jealous." He slid his hand along her silky leg as he moved from one foot to the other.

"Why would I be jealous? This is the story of our life. You're a serial monogamist. I've watched you in action for years. You've been on your own for a while now. It's about that time in your cycle when you settle down with another temporary distraction."

"We've both got our history, Lucy. Nothing we can do to change it. All that matters is where we go from here."

He reached out and tucked a strand of hair behind her ear that had fallen down from her bun. She tilted her head toward him until her cheek rested on his hand.

"They say the past is where you learn the lesson, the future is where you apply the lesson. I guess we've both experienced enough loss and lessons in our lives to make us how we are. Maybe it's too late for us to change. For me it's holding out for true love, for you it's not believing in it."

He stroked her cheek. "I guess we're polar opposites when it comes to that. It's kind of a miracle we've always gotten along so well."

"You know what they say, opposites attract. I guess that means you're the yin to my yang."

He laughed. "Whatever that means. If it's good, then yeah, I guess so."

"It's a very good thing."

She was quiet for a moment as they sat together on the couch. Somehow, over the course of the conversation, she'd scooted closer. Zane was determined to not fill the silence, to let her do the talking.

"When I lost my parents, I realized what it was like to have the bottom fall out of my world," Lucy said in a small voice. "But seeing how much my mom loved my dad just deepened my belief in the power of love. After their accident, when my dad died, my mom was never the same. She only lasted ten months after he left her. I've always believed she died of a broken heart."

Zane reached out and took Lucy's hand. He squeezed it and shut his eyes for a moment. "I remember how hard that was for you, Lucy. I am so sorry."

"I couldn't do anything to help her," she said. "Truth be told, I never thought she'd die. I was only fourteen. I thought she was invincible. You know, that she'd never *do that to me*. That she'd never leave me. Like it was all about me. But she did leave—she left Ethan, Jude and me. She loved our dad so much, she just lost her will to live and wasted away—" Her voice broke and he saw her throat work as she swallowed.

They were both silent for a moment.

"See, that's the thing about love," he said. "When you open yourself up like that, you risk getting hurt."

"But it can be so worth it. I wish you could see that."

He pulled her into his arms and held her, just held her, for a long time.

"You were too young to lose your mom," he whispered in her ear. "I'm so sorry for all the pain that caused you. But I'm not sorry for who you've become because of it. You are one of the strongest, most amazing people I have ever met in my entire life."

He moved his head so that his cheek was on hers. The next thing he knew, her mouth, soft, warm and inviting, had found his.

It vaguely registered that he shouldn't be doing this—again. She was vulnerable right now. But he was kissing her and she was kissing him back and the realization that they both knew what they were doing overrode the doubt.

The taste of her lips awakened his hunger more than it satisfied his craving for her. Need churned inside him, and for an endless moment he let himself be raw and vulnerable. Maybe loving her could fix everything that was broken inside him.

A moan, deep in his throat, escaped as desire coursed through him, a yearning only intensified by the feel of her lips on his, her body in his arms. His one lucid thought as Lucy melted into him was that she tasted familiar: smooth and sweet as home-made caramel and warm…like peppermint and fire.

It made him reel. He never wanted to breathe on his own again. He could be perfectly content right here with her in his arms for the rest of his life.

His hands slid down to her waist and held her firmly against him as his need for her grew and pulsed, taking on a life of its own.

He slowly released her, staying forehead to fore-head as if he was drawn to her magnetically. He reached out and ran the pad of his thumb over her bottom lip.

"We said we weren't going to do this again," he whispered. "If we don't stop now…you know what'll happen."

"I know," she said. "I don't care. I want you."

He claimed one more kiss. It took every bit of strength in him, but he knew this was as far as they should go.

"What about the baby?" he said, his lips brush-ing hers.

"As long as we don't do anything acrobatic," she said, "my doctor said we should be fine. In fact, she told me it would be a good way to relax."

She'd thought about this happening again. That was all he needed to know.

The nearness of her, the heat they generated, sent electricity ripping through him. Then, when she gently nipped at his bottom lip, he warred with the need to take her right there on that ridiculous shaggy rug. He wanted to make love to her in a way that would reach back through the years and right all the wrongs and erase all the hurt both of them had experienced.

Zane didn't know if this was love, but this thing between them felt deeper and more right than anything he'd ever felt in his entire life. Lucy's essence had imprinted on his senses. For the first time, his heart was no longer his own.

Lucy got to her feet and took Zane's hand. She led him to the first bedroom she came to.

She wasn't going to allow herself to dwell on the difference between love and lust, on where they were going versus where they'd been. For once, she was fully in the moment. All that mattered was how she needed him and the way his hands felt on her. He made her feel powerful and strong and desirable. No one had ever made her feel like this before. She had never felt like this for anyone. It had always been Zane.

Slowly, they undressed each other, their clothes falling away until they stood naked in front of each other in the dim light. The bedroom was lit only by light from the lamp they'd left on in the living room. It filtered in through the open door.

For a brief moment, his tender gaze searched hers, as if he was giving her one last chance to turn away.

"We don't need to worry about birth control," he

said. "But I wanted you to know that I haven't been with anyone else since we were together."

She answered him with a kiss so deep that it had him walking her backward to the bed and gently lowering her onto it. He straddled her, keeping his weight on his knees as he traced gentle circles on her belly. It gave her a chance to see him, to drink in all his hard, masculine beauty. Their only other night together had been such a rush and a blur; she hadn't been able to live in the moment. Tonight was different.

She wanted to photograph him with her mind, commit him to memory. Just in case this was the last time— No!

There was no "just in case." There was only right now. And it was exactly what she wanted. She wanted him. She needed him. He traced a path from her belly to her breasts and smoothed his palm over the sensitive skin, making her inhale sharply.

"You are so beautiful," he said.

She felt beautiful. He made her feel beautiful.

He bent down and closed the distance between them, possessing her lips. She opened her mouth to let him all the way in. She ran her hands down his arms, then up his back, learning the planes and edges of his body. He was at once brand-new and hauntingly familiar. Now his lips were trailing a path over her collarbone, then dipping down into the valley between her breasts.

All the nights she'd dreamed of being with him

like this seemed real now. As if those dreams had
come from an alternate reality, where the two of
them had always been in love. A land of alpha and
omega, or maybe it was a place where there was no
beginning or end. Just a place where their souls had
always lived, endlessly entwined.

He deftly shifted his body so that he was stretched
out beside her. She turned to face him so that they
lay stomach to stomach, bare chest to breasts. The
feel of his skin against hers almost put her into sen-
sory overload. She was so aware of him, of the two
of them fused so closely, that it seemed they were
joined body and soul. The entire world evaporated as
they touched and caressed and explored each other,
each taking turns bringing the other to the outer
edges of ecstasy.

The feel of him worshipping her body with his
mouth and hands brought out all the desire and longing that had been bottled up in her since the night
they'd first made love.

She'd never felt this way about anyone. She wasn't
sure what was going to happen after tonight, but she
wasn't going to think about that now. All she cared
about was the hot tender way he was touching her
and how she wanted to live inside the bubble of this
moment, suspended in time and space forever.

No Ocala. No Celebration. Just them. Together.
Now.

Tonight they existed in the here and now. Just
them. No one else. Tonight she intended to make love

to him like there would never be another moment like this one. Because there might not be—

He preempted the wayward thought with kisses that found their way to her abdomen and circled her belly button. Then, gently pushing her onto her back, he took a detour and kissed the insides of her thighs. She inhaled sharply and her eyes widened.

"Why did we decide it was a good idea to just be friends?" His voice was soft and breathless in the darkness.

"I don't know. It was a dumb idea. We are too good together."

He flashed a wicked smile at her as he climbed back toward her. With a commanding move he turned her onto her side. He spooned her, kissing her neck and pulling her body snugly against him. She could feel the hard length of him pressing against her, and she gave in to the temptation to slide her body down and take him inside of her.

He found his way so naturally, entering her with a tender, unhurried push, that the sensation made her cry out. He gently inched forward, going so very slowly and being so careful. As her body adjusted to welcome him, she joined him in a slow rocking rhythm.

Another groan bubbled up in her throat as she savored the heat that coursed between them. It seeped into her bones as she reveled in the feel of him inside her. She drew in a jagged breath, determined to not rush things. Determined to savor every last delicious second.

"Zane," she whispered.

Her sighs were lost in his kiss. He touched her with such care and seemed to instinctively know what her body wanted.

Pleasure began to rise and she angled her hips up to intensify the sensation. Their union seemed so very right that she cried out from the sheer perfection of it.

"Let yourself go," he said, his voice hoarse and husky. "Just let go, Lucy."

Maybe it was the heat of his voice in her ear, more likely it was the way he made her body sing, but the next thing she knew, she had fallen over the edge in a free fall of ecstasy.

Again, he wrapped his arms around her, holding her tightly, protectively, until she had ridden out the wave.

She turned her head so she could see him, so she could breathe in the scent of him, of their joining, needing to get as close to him as possible. Still inside of her, he held her tight. She lost herself again in the shelter of his broad shoulders and the warmth of his strong arms.

"How was that?" His voice was a raspy whisper. His eyes searched her face.

"It was great. I can hardly speak."

He smiled. "And we're not finished yet."

Zane buried his head in the curve of her neck

and started the rhythmic motion again, slow, at first, building to a delicious pace. Again, she felt the energy building inside her body, like a starburst glowing warm, hot, hotter—until they both arrived at the brink together. It didn't take long before their bond, coupled with the pulsing of their bodies, carried them over the edge together. They were both sweaty and spent, and he cradled her against him. They lay together for a long time, their bodies so close, it was hard to tell where she stopped and Zane began.

Later, when Lucy turned onto her other side to face him, Zane stared into her deep brown eyes and felt the mantle of his life shift. All of a sudden, without explanation, *everything* was different.

How could that happen now when it had never happened to him before? He hadn't thought he was capable of experiencing it, because he'd never had a feeling like this.

He was in love with Lucy's laugh, in love with her mind, in love with the way she was able to keep him in line without making him feel as if she was trying to change him. He was in love with the way she felt in his arms right now, the smell of her skin and the way she gazed up at him with a certain look in her eyes that was equal parts sassy confidence and vulnerability. In her eyes, he glimpsed everything he already knew about her and all the things he had yet to discover.

In a staggering instant, he had the overwhelming

need for her to be the first face he saw in the morning and the last face he saw before he closed his eyes and drifted off to sleep at night. He wanted to be the shelter where she sought refuge and the storm who swept her off her feet.

The question was, did he have it in him? Could he be that for her on any ordinary Tuesday night, when they were both tired and life wasn't romantic or even fun anymore?

She deserved someone who was crazy about her all the time, someone who adored her and loved her the way she'd always dreamed of being loved. He wanted to prove to her that he was a good man. But that added up to ripping open his heart and rendering it vulnerable, leaving it in her hands.

This was *Lucy*. If he could trust anyone, it was Lucy. Still, the magnitude of it—of this rush of feelings, the slow, gradual coming back down to earth—scared him to death. But it was too late now. He'd already passed the point of no return.

Now he needed to figure out what to do.

"Zane?" Lucy's eyes searched his face. "Are you... okay?"

"I am better than okay," he finally said.

He kissed her deeply, pulling her to him so tightly that every inch of their bodies merged. He hadn't particularly cared how close he'd felt to other women after they'd been intimate. But this was different. He needed the connection. Not just body to body, but eye to eye and soul to soul.

As they'd made love, three words had been building in his heart. Now they'd worked their way to the tip of his tongue.

He turned onto his back and threw an arm over his eyes, trying to catch his breath. *Come on, man... You're caught up in the moment. Don't say things you don't mean.*

The problem was, he *wanted* to mean it. With all of his heart and soul.

Even so, meaning "I love you" and living it the way Lucy expected were two very different orders.

He couldn't bring himself to say the words out loud.

The next morning, they didn't have time for things to get weird. Zane had an early breakfast with Rhett Sullivan. He was gone by the time Lucy woke up.

She was relieved, really.

Okay, so she would've liked to have had a chance to read the relationship barometer before he'd dashed out the door, but this time alone gave her a chance to do a little soul searching of her own. Time to sort out why the best night of her life left her with such a feeling of dread.

There had been no breakfast invitation from the Sullivans for Lucy. She hadn't wanted or expected one, but it did seem glaringly indicative of what she should expect if she was to move to Ocala with Zane. Despite Rhett Sullivan's insistence that the Hidden Rock crew was *family*, Lucy could already

tell it wouldn't be an easy task for her to infiltrate
the ranks. She just wasn't cut from that cloth. Maybe
in time she and Luann would grow to be friendly—
friendly-ish—but Lucy knew the truth. It would
never happen.

Luann Sullivan was a wonderful woman, Lucy
was sure, but the two of them had zero in common.
Not only that, but Ocala was also a different world
from everything Lucy wanted from life. Just like
Luann, it was lovely. There wasn't a thing wrong
with either Luann or this place. But neither of them
was for her.

Zane, though… Hidden Rock was the perfect
place for him.

Hence Lucy's dark cloud of sadness. She tried
with all her heart to be happy for him. She would
never stand in his way, but the only thing she'd managed to accomplish by accompanying him on this
trip was to know beyond a shadow of a doubt that
she could not move there with him.

Zane must've had an idea of what was coming,
because the two of them didn't discuss the possibility of her moving to Ocala until after their plane had
landed at Dallas/Fort Worth International Airport
and the car that Sullivan had hired to pick them up
had delivered them to Lucy's house.

"Okay," Zane said after he'd put his suitcase in his
truck. "I've given you time to mull it over without
bugging you about it. But I have to know. What do
you think? It's a pretty great place, isn't it?"

Zane had managed to slip out of Rhett Sullivan's grasp without giving him a solid answer. Sullivan had granted him twenty-four hours to mull over the employment package and give him an answer. The boss had even complimented his negotiation skills. Sullivan said while he'd have preferred to solidify the offer before Zane left, his needing to think it over was a feather in Zane's cap, but a guy like Sullivan had to have been pretty confident that he would get what he wanted in the end. Men like that always did.

"I'm glad I got to see Hidden Rock, because now I know without a doubt it is the perfect job for you."

It really was. The salary was twice the amount he was making at Bridgemont. And that didn't even count the house and the truck allowance. Plus, it went without saying, all the bourbon he could drink.

She braced herself for what she knew was coming next.

"Can you see us raising our child there?" Zane asked.

She wanted to tell him exactly how she felt, but she couldn't form the words.

She loved her life in Celebration. She loved her friends and family. She loved her wedding barn. Even though she'd jumped from one thing to another in the past, it was clear that every mistake and wrong turn she'd made had prepared her for the life she was living in Celebration. She was established here. Even though both of her parents were gone, her family was here. And she had friends, lots of friends, in Celebration. If she moved to Ocala, she would have Zane, but she wouldn't really *have* him.

As good as she and Zane were together, he still wasn't sure how he felt about her. Or at least he couldn't tell her how he felt. That was an answer in itself. She'd known Zane long enough to understand that he was moody, that he could blow hot and cold.

If she moved to Ocala, they would be pretending to be a family, and all the while Lucy would live in fear that the spell would wear off and he would grow discontent. If that happened, like Cinderella at the stroke of midnight, her coach would turn into a pumpkin and her dress would revert back to rags. All too soon, her Prince Charming would start feeling trapped, the same way his own daddy had felt.

That spelled disaster.

The only way she and Zane could make this co-parenting arrangement work was if she didn't hold on to him too tightly. And that was why she had to let him go.

As she tried to gather her thoughts, she busied herself cleaning nonexistent dust off the potted philodendron on her windowsill.

"Did I ever tell you about the recurring dream that I used to have?" she said.

He hesitated. She didn't have to turn around to know that he was scowling because he thought she'd changed the subject. And she hadn't. He'd see.

"No."

"Well, once upon a time, I had this crazy recurring dream." Her back was still to him because she couldn't look at him. It was all she could do not to cry. "I dreamed that one day you would look at me and suddenly realize you loved me and couldn't live without me. In that dream, you'd suddenly see me and say, 'It's you, Lucy. It's always been you.'"

He was silent for a long moment.

Finally, he said, "And then what happened?"

"We got married and lived happily ever after, of course. Though, it's only fair that you know there were no fluffy woodland pets in this fairy tale."

"I would've been surprised if there were."

She swiped at her tears and picked up the watering canister to give the plant some water and herself something else to focus on. She didn't know what she would do next—she was running out of busywork. Pretty soon, she would have to turn around and face him. She didn't want to, because once she did, the clock would strike midnight and everything would be over.

"You're not moving to Ocala with me, are you?"

She shook her head.

"I probably shouldn't even have visited," she said. "I have to be honest, I knew before we arrived that I couldn't move there."

"It really isn't what you want, is it?"

She shook her head again and set down the can.

"What about last night?" he asked.

"Last night was one of the most beautiful nights of my life—" She choked on her words. "But it doesn't change the fact that if I moved to Ocala with you, we would live together in a weird state of limbo that's not platonic, at least not for me, but definitely not love, at least not for you. Zane, I would give birth in a strange city, without a support system beyond you. You're a whole lot of good man, but you're going to be busy with your new job, which involves a fair amount of schmoozing at events like that barbecue. I'm truly happy that you've found your place. That's why you must take that job. But I can't go with you."

Thinking about how good this was for him helped her get ahold of herself. She turned to face him. He looked as miserable as she felt.

"What am I supposed to tell the Sullivans when they ask about you?" Zane said. "About why you're not moving with me?"

"Tell them the truth. That we were never really engaged. I'm sure Taylor will be thrilled to know you're not otherwise encumbered."

He winced.

"Zane, I'm not being snarky. I only want what's best for you. And for our child. Think about it— moving to Florida, where everything is fresh and shiny and brand-new, maybe you'll meet someone and realize you don't want it to be just a temporary fling. Maybe your soul mate is somewhere in Ocala and you'll finally know what it feels like to fall in love."

"Would you stop with the *love* talk already?" he said. "Love has nothing to do with this."

"Exactly. I know it doesn't, but it should. It should be all about love. And that's why we are where we are right now. Your we-don't-need-to-be-in-love theory will only work until you meet someone else and fall in love. Because just when you least expect it, the right woman is going to come along. You'll take one look at her and she will knock you off your feet. If you're tied to me, things will get messy. That's not a good way to coparent."

Zane didn't say anything. His walls were up. She wondered if he'd even heard her.

Lucy smiled through her hurt. She needed to find some way to salvage this. She didn't want him to go away mad.

"I have something for you," she said. "Stay here. I'll be right back."

A minute later, she returned with Dorothy's sketchbook. She handed it to him.

"What's this?"

"It was your mom's."

His brows knit together. "I know it was hers. Why do you have it?"

"Because I pulled it out of the garbage that night I came over with the movies."

Zane thumbed through it. "I don't remember throwing it away. Why would I throw this away? This was important. It's *her*."

"I wondered the same thing," Lucy said. "I think you had so much on you and you were so racked with grief that night, you didn't realize what you were doing."

The minute the words escaped her lips, she wished she hadn't said them, because that was the night they had made love, the night they had conceived a baby.

But it was true. That night Zane hadn't been in his right mind. She had seduced him in a vulnerable moment and… Well, the rest was history. As much as she had always dreamed of finding her happily-ever-after with him, she knew she wasn't going to find it like this. That was why, from this moment on, she needed to stop pretending like anything was going to change between them. She wasn't Cinderella. Zane was a good guy, but he wasn't a prince who was going to show up at her door with a glass slipper and suddenly declare his love.

"I hope you will take this with you as a reminder of what can happen if you don't follow your dreams." Zane did a double take, as if he was just realizing the parallels between his and Dorothy's situations. "Dorothy missed the *Guys and Dolls* ship. Her dream was in sight, but the ship sailed without her. Don't you miss out on your big opportunity. You'll still be a great father if you live in Ocala. Between the two of us, we will make sure you have a strong presence in our baby's life."

He didn't say anything. He was just staring at the sketchbook in his hands. Even though her heart was breaking, she was happy she'd saved it for him.

"You've already found your perfect job," she said.

"Maybe Ocala is the complete package. Taylor might not be a temporary fling. She likes you, Zane. Maybe someday all of Hidden Rock will be yours."

He glowered at her. "That's insulting. You're making me sound like a gold digger. Or like I'm not capable of making my own way."

He wasn't just surly. He was furious. But she was certain most of it stemmed from hurt pride.

"You're so smart and so very capable. If I made it sound like I thought otherwise, I'm sorry. If you weren't capable, a man like Rhett Sullivan wouldn't be willing to trust you with his empire. Now, you need to do the smart thing and take that job. Don't miss the boat."

Chapter Ten

Zane had been gone for a week, but it felt like a life-time. Even though Lucy was swamped, consumed with prep for the Picnic in the Park celebration on the Fourth of July, it was all she could do to keep her mind on her to-do list.

Blake Shelton's song "Go Ahead and Break My Heart" came up on her Zane playlist. She'd compiled a bunch of songs that either reminded her of Zane or the lyrics pertained to their situation. She'd grouped them together on a playlist, which she streamed through the music app on her phone. Depending on her mood, she could either feel self-righteous, sing-ing along to songs such as Nancy Sinatra's "These

Boots Are Made for Walkin'," or wallow in her own self-pity to tunes like "Desperado" by the Eagles.

Her favorite songs were a variety of singers and standards, with some fun '60s and '80s era music added for spice, but Zane loved country music and she'd added some country tunes that tugged at her heartstrings.

"Go Ahead and Break My Heart" was making her want to wallow, so she shuffled the mix and advanced to the next song. A Brett Eldredge song about going away for a while came up next. At least it was upbeat and not as sentimental as some on the list. She let it play.

When she got home tonight, maybe she should separate the songs into sub-playlists—self-righteous, empowering songs, and songs to wallow in self-pity and feel sorry for herself.

At least she wouldn't get emotional whiplash each time a new tune played.

She was just settling down and reviewing proposals for her business's website redesign when her phone rang.

"Campbell Wedding Barn, Lucy speaking."

"Is this Lucy Campbell?" a man asked.

"Yes, this is she. How may I help you?"

She really should consider hiring someone part-time to help with odds and ends and answering the phone. Every time it rang and she answered, she was pulled out of what she was doing and usually ended up going down some kind of rabbit hole that kept her from getting her work done. That was why her to-do list was so long.

"This is Nathaniel Phillips. I am Zane Phillips's dad. I'm hoping you can help me track down my son."

Lucy set down her pen. Oh, boy, she did not want to get in the middle of this. Zane had told her that his father had shown up at Dorothy's house the night he was moving out the last of her belongings. That was after Nathaniel had made an unwelcome appearance at Dorothy's funeral.

Now he was calling and asking her to put him in touch with Zane?

No way.

"Hi, Mr. Phillips. I'd be happy to take your number and pass it along to Zane the next time I talk to him."

The truth was, she and Zane hadn't spoken since he'd left for Ocala. She kept telling herself it was better that way. Clean break. That was why she hated the way her heart leaped at the thought of having an excuse to call him—even if it was to relay the news that his father was looking for him.

"I have something for him," Nathaniel said. "Are you sure you can't give me any information on how I can get in touch with him myself?"

Lucy swiveled in her desk chair so that she was facing the door that looked out into the cavernous belly of the barn. It was not as if the man was standing there in person. So she didn't need to run. But for some reason it made her feel better to focus on the way out.

"As I said, I'm happy to pass along your number to him. Would you like to give it to me?"

Reluctantly, Nathaniel rattled off some numbers. Lucy repeated them back to him.

"I'll make sure he gets the message," she said.

"Will you also tell him that I have something I know he wants. I'd like to give it to him."

"Absolutely. I'll let him know."

She hung up the phone. Nathaniel had something for Zane? What in the world could it be?

Before she could talk herself out of it, she retrieved her cell phone from her purse and dialed Zane's number. She knew it by heart. When it started ringing, her heart thudded like a staccato drumbeat.

This was crazy. They meant too much to each other to be in a standoff like this. Well, thanks to Nathaniel Phillips, she had a legitimate reason to break the ice. That was ironic.

But soon her optimism slipped a notch when she got Zane's voice mail. He used to always pick up when she called. In fact, she couldn't remember him ever not taking her call. In the span of time it took for his greeting to play out, she talked herself out of hanging up and decided to leave a message.

After all, she had promised his father she would let him know. She always tried to keep her promises. Plus, if she left a message, the ball would be in his court to call her back.

At the beep, she said, "Hey, you! It's me." That was how they used to greet each other on the phone when they called each other—back in the days when they called each other… When they were talking. She made an effort to infuse as much sunshine and sweetness in her voice as she could muster. "I hope everything is going well and that you're all settled in and liking your job. We miss you around here. Mrs. Radley is looking for a new benefactor for her tuna-noodle surprise." Okay, she needed to get to the point. It wasn't as if the longer she talked, the more likely it would be that he would pick up. That was not how cell-phone voice messages worked. "Also, I needed to let you know that your dad called me today asking for your phone number. Don't kill the messenger. I didn't give him your number. I asked for his and told him I would pass it along. So here it is."

She read the number twice. The second time, she said it slowly.

"Oh, and he asked me to tell you that he has something for you that he is certain you will want. So please call him. That's part of his message, not me being bossy. Just so you know. And you might give me a call if you can spare a few moments. That is me being bossy. I miss you."

She hung up before she could say anything else. She wished she could go back and erase that last part where she asked him to call her.

Ugh. That was embarrassing.

Oh, well. It was what it was. Now the ball was definitely in his court.

Peter Gabriel's "In Your Eyes" came up in the

shuffle. Lucy sighed and turned off the music because it wasn't helping matters. It was only making her sad. Even though some of the music was designed to let her wallow, the overriding effect wasn't supposed to be this.

She sat in silence for a few minutes, which was hardly better, but at least she didn't have to listen to Peter Gabriel going on about days passing and emptiness filling his heart.

There was wallowing and there was morose.

She'd made her choice to not move to Ocala with Zane. She needed to live with it.

Lucy had just wrangled herself back into work mode when there was a knock at the barn door.

"Oh, for God's sake. I am never going to get any work done."

She clicked over to her to-do list and typed in "hire part-time assistant."

The knock sounded again, and this time was more persistent. For a split second she worried that it might be Nathaniel Phillips. Then her heart went in a completely different direction—what if the reason Zane hadn't taken her call was because he was driving on his way back to see her?

She knew it was just wishful thinking, but it didn't stop the disappointment when she opened the door and saw Carol Vedder standing there with a handsome blond guy in tow.

"There you are, Lucy," Carol said. "We were just

about to leave. But I saw your car over there, so I knew you had to be around here somewhere."

Lucy had to blink away the stunning disappointment. First because it wasn't Zane at the door and second because she'd actually let herself hope that it was. She had gone from ridiculous to pathetic in less than sixty seconds. She needed to get ahold of herself.

"I am so sorry to keep you waiting," she said. "I was in the middle of something. I didn't realize you were coming by. Did I miss your call?"

She knew Carol hadn't called, and she should've been ashamed of herself for the little dig, but…

"No, I didn't call. I just picked up my nephew, Luke, from the airport. He lives in Houston, but he was flying in from a veterinarian conference in Los Angeles. Lucy, this is Luke Anderson. Luke, this is Lucy Campbell. The young woman I told you about."

"Nice to meet you, Lucy." He shook her hand. "Forgive us for barging in like this."

Lucy picked up on the note of embarrassment in Luke's apology and glimpsed the accompanying look in his eyes. He was humoring his aunt and was much too polite to roll his eyes the way Lucy sensed he wanted to.

"That is absolutely not a problem, Luke. It's nice to meet you. Would you like to come in?"

"If you're in the middle of something, I don't want to disturb you—"

"We will only be a minute," Carol said. "I brought

Luke by to help me carry a heavy box. For the Fourth of July picnic."

Lucy exchanged another commiserating look with Luke. He must've known that Carol's *moments* could last three weeks. That was when she realized Luke was *seriously* cute—like Ryan-Gosling-eat-your-heart-out cute. And he was a veterinarian. That meant he was good with animals.

And he wasn't Zane.

The father of her baby. The love of her life, who didn't return her feelings. The guy who was gone.

If she wasn't pregnant, she might've tried to be interested in this guy. He was from Houston. Far enough away that she could've had her space, but close enough to see occasionally—unlike the prohibitive fifteen-hour drive to Ocala.

But he wasn't Zane.

"Where is the box, Aunt Carol?" Luke asked.

"It's in the trunk, dear." She handed him her keys.

Both women watched him walk to the car. "He's a good catch, this one." Carol gestured in Luke's direction with her thumb.

He came back carrying a large package of paper towels. "This was the only thing that was in the trunk, besides my luggage."

Carol smiled. "Yes, that's it."

Something heavy, huh? Lucy was tempted to ask if she should get the hand truck, but that wouldn't be very nice. She knew Carol well enough to know she was immune to embarrassment. It would only make this awkward situation more awkward.

"I can take that," Lucy said.

"No, let Luke carry that for you. How about if he sets it in the kitchen?"

Lucy shrugged and motioned for them to come inside. As they walked toward the kitchen, Carol said, "Luke is going to be here for Picnic in the Park. He is also going to help me with a few handyman tasks around the house, because he's very handy. But I won't keep him too busy. He will have plenty of free time. Lucy, maybe you could show him around?"

Her mind raced. On one hand being nice to someone and showing him around wouldn't even necessarily have to be a date. But who was she kidding? It was obvious that Carol was trying to fix them up. What was she supposed to say? Sooner or later the entire town would know that she was expecting. It was her new reality and she had already accepted it. She'd also come to terms with the very real possibility that she probably wouldn't be dating for at least the next eighteen years or so.

That was fine. Her baby was all she needed.

What was the use of dating if her heart belonged to her child…and the baby's father?

Zane had picked up Lucy's message, but several days had gone by and he couldn't bring himself to call her back.

Not yet. The hurt was still too fresh. He got it. He totally understood Lucy's point of view and he wasn't going to be selfish. But that didn't mean he had to like the way things had turned out.

As far as his dad was concerned, there wasn't a chance in hell that he was calling him. He didn't want whatever scrapbook or memento the guy had dug up for him. He didn't need or want anything the jerk had to offer now—now that he and Ian were self-sufficient adults who needed nothing from others.

Nathaniel Phillips obviously thought that he was perfectly entitled to skip the messy parts of child rearing and jump into the hands-off easy part. Zane was having none of that.

He was too busy with his new job. He still hadn't adjusted to Ocala, to being there alone when he thought Lucy would be by his side. That was such a bastard way to think, that she should give up everything she'd worked for to follow him. One of the things he'd always loved most about her was her strength. She deserved only the best and she deserved the love she was so certain existed.

Hidden Rock was a great job, but it still didn't feel like his world. He knew he should give a new position a good six months— Hell, with an outfit like this, he'd be better off giving it more like a year.

He was drinking too much and working too hard, too many long hours. One night, when he'd gotten particularly shit-faced, he'd gone out with a bunch of the ranch hands and woken up the next morning with Lucy's name tattooed on his biceps. He'd never gotten a tattoo before. He didn't remember much about that night, but he did recall with dubious clarity telling the guy that Lucy was the love of his life. Uh… In his drunken stupor, he had used the *L* word. He had to laugh—even though it wasn't funny—because he could hear Lucy saying bourbon was his truth serum. The only other memory of that night that was vaguely clear was of the guy telling him if things didn't work out with her, he could always have the tattoo changed from *Lucy* to *Lucky*.

He was still contemplating whether he wanted to have it removed, though he'd heard that hurt like a son of a bitch. Because it would be more appropriate to have the word *UnLucky* tattooed on his arm to remind him of all he'd lost.

He was trying, but even though, in theory, Hidden Rock was supposed to be his dream job, he didn't love it here like he thought he would.

If he'd had this opportunity five years ago, things might have been different, but it didn't feel like it fit him now. This routine of getting up at dawn, working until sunset, drinking himself to sleep and then getting up and doing it all over again wasn't the stuff dreams were made of. Even though he was well aware of the theory that new jobs took a good half a year to break in, it didn't feel like the life he wanted to grow into. Not when another little life that had his blood—and hopefully Lucy's good looks, brains and charming personality—would be growing and changing every day in Texas without him. His dream job pinched. It just wasn't the same without Lucy. Instead of feeling fulfilled, he felt empty. And at the rate he was numbing himself, he'd end up working himself into an early grave. Of course, that was the only part of this equation that was under his control. He could stop drinking if he wanted to. Especially since his being healthy was key to him keeping his promise to be a good father to their child.

That was why when the boys asked him if he was going to join them at the bar after work on Thursday, he declined. It would do his liver some good to sit this one out. When he got back to the house, there was a man waiting for him on his front porch.

"Can I help you?" Zane asked. "This is a private residence. If you have business with Hidden Rock, the offices are about a mile up the way near the stables."

The guy had an envelope in his hand. "Are you Zane Phillips?"

Zane looked around warily. "I am."

"I have a certified letter for you. Please sign here."

What the hell—

Zane didn't owe anybody anything. He wasn't in trouble. Lucy wouldn't be sending him anything certified, would she? This wasn't about him not returning her call, was it? Her message hadn't sounded all that serious. If she needed anything, he definitely would've called her back.

"What's this about?" Zane asked.

"I have no idea. I'm just the messenger."

Since he had no reason to fear the envelope's contents and curiosity was getting the best of him, he signed, and the guy handed him the letter.

Zane took off his boots and left them on the porch, then let himself into the house.

The return address indicated the letter was from a Dallas-based law office. Zane picked up a letter opener on the kitchen cabinet and opened it.

The letterhead said the correspondence was from the law firm of Dorsey and Rogers. The content said that they had been retained by Nathaniel Phillips, who had been trying to locate him to bestow a gift upon him.

"A gift?" Zane said out loud.

His first inclination was to crumple up the letter without even reading it, but it dawned on him that if his father had gone to the trouble to hire an attorney to track him down so that he could give him a gift, maybe if he simply accepted whatever token he was trying to give him to appease his guilt, Nathaniel would go away and leave him alone. This might be the only reason that having fifteen hundred miles between him and Texas was a good thing.

But the next paragraph in the letter had Zane pulling out a kitchen chair and sitting down at the table to reread the letter to make sure he was understanding it right. Was his father actually trying to give him and Ian the property on Old Wickham Road?

That was what the letter said, even after Zane read

it five times to be sure. All he had to do was call the law firm to discuss the details.

The Fourth of July had always been one of Lucy's favorite holidays. Who didn't love an excuse to eat grilled hot dogs and potato salad and corn on the cob? And just when you thought you couldn't stuff another bite in your face, someone brought out the hot apple pie and homemade ice cream. Oh! And the fireworks. She had always adored the fireworks. Celebration's Fourth of July Picnic in the Park always culminated in a pyrotechnics display to rival Walt Disney World.

This year, however, she was hot and cranky. The smell of hot dogs made her want to toss her apple pie and she hadn't even had a bite of apple pie because it seemed even more unappealing than the hot dogs. She'd had to get downright testy with Pat Whittington, who had refused, on principle, to sign up early for the hot-dog eating contest.

"That's not how we do it," he insisted when he showed up and there wasn't a place for him at the competition table.

"Next year, Pat, why don't you chair the event and you can make the rules."

When he told her that she didn't have to be rude about it, she realized it really didn't matter whether anyone had preregistered or not. She didn't care.

That was when Juliette stepped in and they agreed to squeeze in Pat at the end of the table. Of course, he complained that he didn't have enough elbow room and that was why he lost last year… That was when Lucy walked away.

She bought herself a bottle of ice-cold water and took a seat on the rim of the huge fountain in the middle of the park and watched all of the flurry going on around her. The world wouldn't end if they squeezed one more person into the hot-dog eating contest. Though, for a fleeting second, she may or may not have wished that Pat Whittington choked on a wiener.

Then she chastised herself because that was not very nice.

"Nope, I wish him nothing but the best. May he get exactly what he deserves this year." She laughed to herself.

"Are you talking to me?" Luke Anderson was standing next to her smiling and looking just as handsome as he had the other day, when he and Carol had dropped by. Great, he'd caught her talking to herself. At this rate, maybe she should go home and crawl back in bed before she really embarrassed herself.

He was a good guy. He had obviously picked up on her trepidations as Carol had tried hard to push the two of them together, because she hadn't called or made any effort to "show him around," as Carol had put it. Then again, maybe he didn't find her as charming and alluring as Aunt Carol had thought he would.

Just as well.

"I wasn't," Lucy said. "But now that you mention it, I wish you nothing but the best, Luke."

He sat down next to her on the fountain. "Are you okay?"

She must've looked pretty stressed if he'd picked up on it.

She waved away his concern. "I'm fine. Just hot and thirsty. Just taking a break from all the fun."

"It's a great event. Do you organize it every year? I know Aunt Carol has been involved for a while."

"No, it's my first year on the committee."

And probably her last… Though she wasn't going to say that now. She likened organizing events to having accepted the challenge to eat an entire jar of peanut butter. At this point she was about three tablespoons away from finishing the whole jar. While she loved peanut butter, right now she never wanted to see it again.

She was too close to the situation and she was exhausted. And Zane wasn't here.

She fought the most ridiculous urge to cry. All she needed to do to prove to Luke that she was, indeed, crazy was to burst into tears right here in the middle of Central Park.

Thank goodness Lauren Walters chose that moment to walk over and say hello.

"Lucy, you have outdone yourself," she said. "It's the best Picnic in the Park ever. Everyone loves the food trucks. And the band you hired is fabulous. I'll help you next year if you'll stay on the committee. Oh, who's this?"

Lauren was eyeing Luke, who was still sitting next to Lucy on the edge of the fountain but was eyeing Lauren with a look that you didn't have to be a mind reader to know he liked what he saw.

Of course! They would be perfect for each other.

"Lauren, this is Luke Anderson. Luke is Carol Vedder's nephew. He's visiting from Houston. Luke, this is Lauren Walters. She's a good friend and she helps me out at the Campbell Wedding Barn occasionally."

"You're from Houston?" Lauren said. "I have family in Houston. I'm from there originally."

They started chatting, figuring out people they knew in common. "Lauren, if you have a few moments, would you show Luke around? Have you seen the food trucks, Luke?"

He hadn't. Lucy all but mentally brushed her hands together as she watched them walk away. She stood up feeling better than she had felt all day. Her work here was done.

She sighed. "I love a good romance. Especially when it's shiny and new."

Maybe her new role would be that she would be the fairy godmother—or the matchmaker. Either one would do.

With a renewed sense of spirit, Lucy made her rounds, ensuring that everything was running smoothly. It was good to stay busy. It gave her a purpose and blunted the empty feeling of being on the outside looking in as she watched families spending the day together, and lovers strolling hand in hand or feeding each other French fries from a food truck as they lounged on plaid picnic blankets spread over the park's green lawn.

Finally, as it was getting dark, Lucy prepared herself to make the address that the Picnic in the Park chairperson always delivered. She slipped into the bathroom at Café St. Germaine to freshen up. She splashed water on her face to cool off and reapplied her makeup, adding a little more than she had worn earlier because she felt like making an effort. She was proud of the work she had done. Proud of what she had accomplished with the event. She had raised money for the community, and, yes, she had even generated some good public relations for the Campbell Wedding Barn. Because there was hardly a better showcase of her event-planning skills than this important, sometimes unruly, community event. As she brushed her hair and secured it into a low ponytail, she realized it was also her debut as the new person she would become once she shared the news that she was expecting a baby.

She squared her shoulders and looked at herself in the mirror. Sure, she would've preferred the more traditional route—what she wouldn't have given for Zane to have been able to love her. But he was happy and that was everything.

She had a thriving business, a loving family, good

standing in a community that she loved. She had so many more blessings than some people. She put her hand on her stomach. Now was the time—a new phase—when she would start thinking less of herself and more of others.

A twinge of regret—of missing Zane, of loving Zane—was still there, but she would live with it. The two of them were happy in their separate lives. That would go a long way toward creating a happy life for their child. She realized she just needed to reframe the way she looked at her relationship with Zane. Because of the child, they would always be a part of each other's lives, just in a nontraditional way.

As she packed up her toiletries and stowed them in the restaurant's office, she made a mental note to include Café St. Germaine in the acknowledgments. They had served as a handy home base today, and a cool reprieve from the summer heat.

Water bottle in hand and feeling refreshed, Lucy was going over her speech in her head as she made her way to the stage. She was on in five minutes and the fireworks extravaganza was scheduled to begin immediately after she finished.

The band was playing a medley of Fourth of July classics that sounded a little funky played on electric guitars, but the crowd seemed to be eating it up. That was all that mattered. Things didn't always have to be perfect—or her mind's-eye version of perfect. Different could be the spice that made life interesting.

As she waited by the side of the stage for the band to finish, she took out her phone to write that thought down in her notepad for the times she needed a gentle reminder.

"Excuse me," said a deep voice that made her heart compress and nearly explode. "Have I missed the fireworks?"

Zane was standing in front of her. Without thinking about it or asking his permission, she threw herself into his arms.

"Oh, my gosh, you're home! Why didn't you tell me you were coming home?"

"You didn't ask."

And just like that all the weirdness that had been between them melted away. Lucy could finally breathe. She hadn't realized she hadn't been able to breathe the entire time he had been gone—the entire time they hadn't talked. But standing here breathing the same air that he was breathing, she felt alive again.

"I'm so glad to see you. When did you get in?"

"About five minutes ago. Parking around here is hell. Do you know the name of the person who organizes this event? I want to file a complaint."

The lopsided smile that overtook his face was the most beautiful sight she had seen in ages. It took everything she had, every ounce of restraint, to keep from throwing her arms around his neck and kissing him. She took a physical step back as she reminded herself that she couldn't do that.

Don't mess things up.

Things were going to be okay as long as she remembered the boundaries.

"So you drove back to Celebration from Ocala today?"

"I did."

It was a Tuesday. The Sullivans had probably given him the day off, but it was curious that he hadn't stayed at the ranch. Surely, with their penchant for parties, the Sullivans would have a Fourth of July celebration that would make this one look like a rinky-dink outfit.

"When do you have to go back?"

He studied her for a moment and she wished she could read his thoughts.

"That depends. I had some business to take care of here in town."

Oh. It stood to reason. He was probably preparing to move out of the Bridgemont house. He'd need to clear out to make way for the new general manager.

"Hey, I got your message about my dad calling you. Thanks for looking out for me and not giving him my number. But there's a funny story that goes along with that. He has actually purchased the Old Wickham Road property. You know, my mom's family's old ranch. He wants to sell it to Ian and me for one dollar."

Lucy's mouth dropped open. "Holy cow. Are you serious?"

Zane nodded, looking a little dazed.

"What are you going to do? Are you going to accept his offer?"

Zane shrugged. "I talked to my brother and he says he can cough up the fifty cents for his part. Nathaniel says it's no deal for any other price. He said it's the least he can do for us after being such a louse when we were growing up. I mean, it's our legacy—and I quit the job at Hidden Rock."

"What?"

He nodded. "It was a great opportunity—for someone. But it wasn't for me. I'm back, but we can talk about that later. I need to mull over Nathaniel's offer…"

It sounded like Zane wanted her opinion on whether he was doing the right thing or not.

Of course, he would never come right out and ask her for advice. That was the way they'd always done things; he'd never had to ask because she had always offered an opinion, with the understanding that he could take it or leave it.

"Do you want to know what I think?" she asked.

He nodded, which was more than he used to do in the past. She was half expecting a snarky quip. But the band was finishing up and she was due to go up on stage—and Zane was here. He was *here and everything was going to be okay*. Her heart was so full she knew she needed to get herself together before she got up on stage in front of the entire town.

Her favorite song, "Somethin' Stupid," started

playing in her head. She looked at Zane and pushed the internal mute button on the soundtrack to her life.

She was just starting to ascend the stairs to the bandstand as the lead singer started introducing her. Or she thought he was introducing her. He was supposed to be introducing her. But instead he said, "If I could have everybody's attention, we have a special treat for you all tonight before we unleash the fireworks."

Special treat? She'd always wanted to be somebody's *special treat*, but not in this context. Her speech wasn't exactly a special treat, either. The guy had sort of oversold it.

Before she could take the microphone, Zane had slipped in behind her and took it in hand.

"Happy Fourth of July, everyone! It's good to be back in town. I'm Zane Phillips, for those of you who don't know me."

What in the—

Lucy looked around like she might find the answer to what was going on somewhere behind her, but, of course, she didn't. So she just let Zane do whatever it was that he was doing.

"Sometimes it takes getting exactly what you *think* you want to help you realize what's really important in life," he said.

He was looking right at Lucy.

Oh, my—

Was she hearing him right?

"Having your family around you is important. So

is the love of a good woman. Lucy, will you please come here?"

She hadn't realized it until now, but she had been backing up, small step by small step, until she was hiding safely in the shadows. Zane turned around and took her hand. "Come here, please? I have something important to say."

Most of her body was numb. The only thing she could feel was her pounding heart and her hopes rising ever so slightly with every step she took toward Zane.

"I have put you through hell the last couple of months. It's taken me a while to figure out what was in my heart, but while I've been away the only thing that I think of every morning when I wake up is you. You're the first thing on my mind in the morning and the last thing on my mind before I go to sleep. *It's you, Lucy. It's always been you. I love you.*"

Zane pulled something from the front pocket of his jeans and dropped to one knee. That was when she realized he was holding a small black box. "It took almost losing you to realize that I've always loved you. Will you make me the happiest man in the world and be my wife?"

Everyone in Central Park cheered. Through her tears, Lucy managed to choke out, "Yes."

As Zane pulled her into his arms and kissed her as if he was making up for all the hours they had been apart, the fireworks started behind them.

Zane grabbed her hand and led her off the bandstand to a picnic blanket, where he had a real ice bucket holding a bottle of champagne and Dorothy's crystal glasses waiting.

"I know they're not champagne glasses," he said. "I hope that's okay."

"They couldn't be more perfect."

As they toasted their love, the tears in her eyes made the crystal glasses gleam. Or maybe it was the sparkle of the diamond ring that Zane had put on her finger.

Zane loved her. He loved her.

Cinderella and Prince Charming had nothing on the two of them.

But the one thing she and Cinderella did have in common was that they both had found there happily-ever-after. Only, Lucy had Zane, who in real life was so much better than the Prince Charming in her mind that she had tried to turn him into.

Zane was the only man she'd ever loved. The only man she ever would love. His realizing that he loved her, too, was so worth the wait.

* * * * *

*And don't miss Jude and Juliette's
second chance at love in*
THE COWBOY WHO GOT AWAY
the next book in the CELEBRATION, TX
series, available October 2017!

And catch up with Ethan and Chelsea in
THE COWBOY'S RUNAWAY BRIDE
available now wherever Mills & Boon Cherish
books and ebooks are sold!

MILLS & BOON®

Cherish™

EXPERIENCE THE ULTIMATE RUSH OF FALLING IN LOVE

A sneak peek at next month's titles...

In stores from 13th July 2017:

- **The Boss's Fake Fiancée** – Susan Meier *and* **Mummy and the Maverick (Mommy and the Maverick)** – Meg Maxwell
- **The Runaway Bride and the Billionaire** – Kate Hardy *and* **Vegas Wedding, Weaver Bride** – Allison Leigh

In stores from 27th July 2017:

- **The Millionaire's Redemption** – Therese Beharrie *and* **Do You Take This Cowboy?** – Vicki Lewis Thompson
- **Captivated by the Enigmatic Tycoon** – Bella Bucannon *and* **AWOL Bride** – Victoria Pade

Just can't wait?
Buy our books online before they hit the shops!
www.millsandboon.co.uk

Also available as eBooks.

MILLS & BOON®

Why shop at millsandboon.co.uk?

Each year, thousands of romance readers find their perfect read at millsandboon.co.uk. That's because we're passionate about bringing you the very best romantic fiction. Here are some of the advantages of shopping at www.millsandboon.co.uk:

* **Get new books first**—you'll be able to buy your favourite books one month before they hit the shops

* **Get exclusive discounts**—you'll also be able to buy our specially created monthly collections, with up to 50% off the RRP

* **Find your favourite authors**—latest news, interviews and new releases for all your favourite authors and series on our website, plus ideas for what to try next

* **Join in**—once you've bought your favourite books, don't forget to register with us to rate, review and join in the discussions

Visit **www.millsandboon.co.uk** for all this and more today!